SILVER
ELITE

SILVER
ELITE

DANI FRANCIS

NEW YORK

Published in the United States by Del Rey, an imprint of Random House,
a division of Penguin Random House LLC, New York.

DEL REY and the CIRCLE colophon are registered trademarks
of Penguin Random House LLC.

Hardback ISBN 978-0-593-87546-9
International edition ISBN 978-0-593-98344-7
Ebook ISBN 978-0-593-87547-6

Printed in China on acid-free paper

randomhousebooks.com

2 4 6 8 9 7 5 3 1

First Edition

Book design by Caroline Cunningham
Map by Chloe Bolland
Bird motif: AdobeStock/Verslood
Computer tablet art: AdobeStock/Azat Valeev

To the women who kick ass in this world. This is for every battle you've fought and every barrier you've shattered. You inspire me every day.

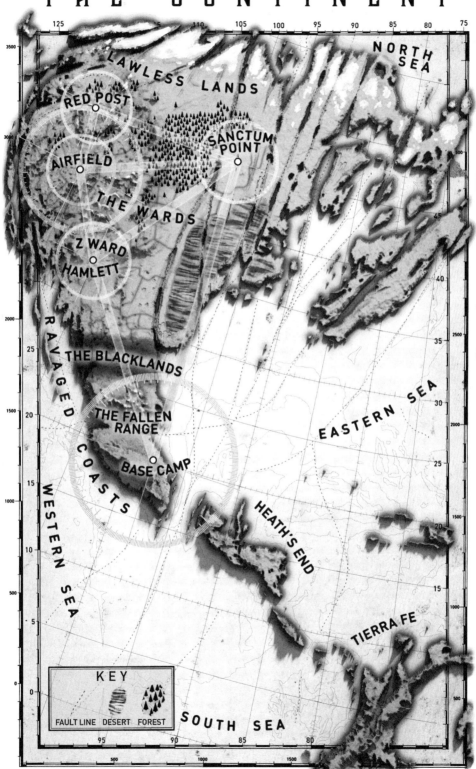

SILVER
ELITE

CHAPTER 1

I grew up in pure, unceasing, suffocating darkness.

I'd like to say that's an exaggeration, but it's not. I was only five years old when my uncle smuggled me out of the city and took me to live in the Blacklands, the place of children's nightmares. A forest of perpetual darkness. I remember my eyes widening when I first saw it: the ominous black mist rising from the earth and hovering far above the top canopy of the trees. I remember bone-deep dread and then throat-closing panic when we were engulfed in the pitch black. I remember how, less than an hour into the trek, I tripped over a skull. I knelt to examine what made me stumble, and although I couldn't see a thing, I could feel the gaping eye sockets, could run my fingers over smooth, weathered bone.

When I asked Uncle Jim what it was, he said, "Just a rock."

Even at the age of five, I wasn't that easy to fool.

It wouldn't be the last skeleton we came across in the three years we spent in the Blacklands, but by the time we returned to civilization, fear and I were old friends. These days, a predator could lunge for my throat, and I wouldn't blink. A Command jet could drop a bomb on our house, and my heart rate would remain steady.

When you're petrified on a daily basis as a child, there aren't many things left to fear as an adult.

Except, perhaps, awkward conversations.

I would rather fight a cougar barehanded than subject myself to an uncomfortable exchange. Truly.

"Where are you going?"

Damn it. I'd been doing my level best to sneak out of bed without alerting my companion.

The young soldier's voice is thick with sleep and a hint of lingering seduction. I fix my gaze downward as I button my jeans. I know he's not wearing anything underneath that thin sheet.

"Oh. Um. Nowhere. I was just getting dressed because I'm cold," I lie, smoothing the front of my black tank over the jagged stretch of scar tissue on my left hip.

My burns, which dip below my waistband and stretch midway down my thigh, are a permanent reminder of who I am and why I can't be in this guy's presence longer than necessary.

I told him the scarring was the result of an accident. A pot of boiling water spilling on me when I was a child.

That wasn't entirely a lie.

If he knew what the mangled flesh hid, though, he probably wouldn't have been stroking it with such infinite sympathy.

"Come back here. I'll keep you warm," he promises.

I fake a smile and meet his eyes. They're nice. A deep brown. "Hold that thought? Now that I'm up, I need to use the bathroom. You said it was around the corner?"

Do I sound too eager?

I think I do, but I'm itching to escape. It's late. Much later than I promised I'd stay out. I was supposed to stop by the village for a quick drink and to say hello to some friends at the Liberty Day festivities. Not hook up with a Command soldier, of all candidates.

There aren't a lot of things worth celebrating in the Continent. None of those idyllic-sounding holidays you read about in the history books. And let's be honest—it's probably some sick irony to have a bunch of Modified people dancing, drinking, and screwing to celebrate the anniversary of an event that led to their own slaughter. But Mods do like to dance, drink, and screw, so . . . might as well do it when we can, no matter the occasion.

"You're not going to run out on me, are you?" He's teasing again, but there's an undertone of unhappiness. Shit. He knows I'm preparing to bail.

"Of course not."

I pretend to concentrate on zipping up my boots, deciding this was a terrible idea. I try not to make a habit of falling into bed with anyone in the Command, the Continent's military, but their impermanence is a major draw. Soldiers can only leave the base three times a year, which means they'll never be anything but temporary.

"Good. Because I'm not ready to let you go yet," he says with a smile. He's twenty-five and was so gentle when his hands were roaming my body.

Is it awful that I can't remember his name?

I pick up my rifle and sling the strap over my shoulder. I notice him watching me.

"What?"

"You look like pure smoke right now," he says, biting his lip.

"Really."

"Yes. You don't see girls with guns in the city."

He's right. You don't. That's the main reason my uncle settled us in Ward Z, as far west as you can get. It's one of the asset wards, where professions tend to be ranching and farming, and citizens are allowed to own weapons. All registered and fully accounted for, of course. You can't get a license without extensive testing to prove your competence, but that wasn't a problem for me. I received my weapons approval when I was thirteen. I'm beyond competent, more than the testers were even aware. Uncle Jim warned me to "tone it down" on test day.

"Comes in handy out here," I tell him. "I've got white coyotes trying to kill my cows every night."

He laughs. "I'll have to come to your ranch one day, see whatever it is you get up to out there."

The nonchalant remark raises my suspicions. Why does he want to come to the ranch? Was that an innocent comment, or do I need to worry?

When it comes to the Command, I err on the side of paranoia, so I quickly open a path to prod at his mind. His shield is thicker than steel. I could probably find a hole in it if I tried long enough, but it's too strong to penetrate on the spot. Not a surprise. One of the first things soldiers like him are taught is how to shield themselves from Mods. And they're right to do it. Primes don't have enhanced gifts. They also don't experience any physical signs when someone infiltrates their thoughts, whereas Mods feel it like an electric shock. People like him *should* be on guard.

I sever the path. It was worth a try. The only time his shield wavered tonight was after our clothes were off, but his thoughts then were an amalgamation of *don't stop* and *yes*.

It was a nice ego boost, I won't lie.

"Any reason you're taking your gun to the bathroom?" He raises a brow.

"All registered weapons must be on your person at all times," I dutifully recite from the handbook every weapon owner is given after certification. "Keep the bed warm for me. I'll be right back."

I will not be right back. In fact, I'm forcing myself not to sprint out the door.

"I'll show you where it is," he offers.

I start to object, but he's already climbing out of bed, sliding a pair of pants up his trim hips. At least he's not wearing the navy-blue standard-issue Command uniform. Not sure I could've mustered up any arousal if he'd been wearing that. Outside the occasional ale-induced soldier romp, I hate those assholes, and most of them hate me right back. They're dedicated to wiping out people like me. The Aberrant, as they call us. Or silverbloods, when they're feeling nice.

The only aberration around here is General Redden and his irrational hatred for Mods. We didn't ask to be this way. Some thoughtless war a hundred and fifty years ago released the toxin that made us like this. We didn't have a choice in the matter.

Despite every cell in my body pleading for escape, I allow the soldier to guide me out the door and down the burgundy carpet of the inn's second-floor hallway. We turn the corner and keep walking.

"Here you go." Like the gentleman he is, he opens the bathroom door for me.

"Thanks." I force another smile. "I'll meet you back in your room."

"Shout if you get lost and I'll come rescue you, keen?"

In the bathroom, I stand behind the door and listen to the sound of his footsteps. I exhale in a rush, waiting until those footsteps retreat. The reflection in the mirror shows a flush to my bronzed skin, but sex will do that to you. My eyes reveal my impatience. The soldier lauded their color several times tonight—honey brown specked with yellow gold.

My uncle claims I have my mother's eyes, but I don't remember her face, and it bothers me that I can't. I was five when she sent me away, old enough to have formed concrete memories of her. I *should* recall her eyes. Sometimes I think I can remember her voice, her smile, but I never know if that's just my imagination filling in the blanks.

I wait another full minute before emerging from the bathroom. I want to make a run for it, but I'll have to pass his door to reach the stairs. I'll need to tiptoe.

Holding my breath, I turn the corner and creep along the worn carpet. I'm nearing the end of the hall when I see his doorknob turn.

As the door inches open, I act on instinct, throwing myself into the nearest room and closing the door behind me.

Barging into a stranger's quarters probably isn't the smartest strategy, but it was a split-second decision—and one I deeply regret when a muscular arm locks around my chest.

"Don't move," a male voice says.

Once again, I act reflexively. My fist slices upward and connects with a hard jaw.

The owner of that jaw doesn't even flinch. He disarms me faster than I can blink, smacking my rifle onto the floor. Then he spins me around and pins me against the back of the door. His tall frame moves menacingly closer, his arm like a steel bar against my breasts.

"Who the fuck are you?" he growls in my ear.

My heart batters my rib cage. I suck in a breath, licking my dry lips. "I'm—"

The words die when I lift my gaze to his face.

Oh.

I think I picked the wrong candidate for tonight's activities.

This guy is . . . inconceivably attractive. I don't think I've ever seen a better-looking human, male or female. I'm momentarily lost in his cobalt-blue eyes, peering down at me from beneath thick lashes. His hair is dark, swept away from flawless, symmetrical features that could've been chiseled out of stone. Just the right amount of stubble shadows a strong jaw, and one corner of his mouth bears the indentation of a dimple. I wonder how pronounced it gets when he smiles, although judging by the cold, dangerous glint in his eyes, I get the feeling he doesn't smile often.

"If you're here to kill me, you're not doing a very good job of it."

"Kill you?" I echo, snapping out of my thoughts. "That's not why I'm here."

"No?" I hear a clattering sound and realize he's kicking my rifle away. It takes serious effort not to lunge after it. "You sneak into my room in the middle of the night with a gun and I'm supposed to believe your intentions are pure?"

"Believe whatever you want." I push against his grip. It's a futile attempt. His arm isn't budging. "I'm not here to kill you."

"So this is a social visit?" His tongue comes out to moisten the corner of his mouth. Eyes gleaming, he lowers them to the cleavage that peeks out from beneath the strong band of his arm. "I appreciate the gesture, but I'm not interested. I've already gotten my fill tonight." His lips curve. "You should've stopped by earlier when my guest was still here. Could've made a party out of it."

My jaw drops. "Seriously? I'm not interested in that, either. I'm hiding, asshole."

He flicks up a brow, intrigued. "From who?"

"None of your damn business. Can you please move your arm? I can't breathe."

"No. And you seem to be breathing just fine."

I'm not. There's no air. Each time I inhale, I breathe in the scent of him. It holds tones of pine, leather, and a hint of spice. It's sort of incredible. And his body is surreal. Big, broad, and sleekly muscled, his biceps flexing as he holds me in place. I bet he looks spectacular naked.

"Let me go," I order. "I'm sorry I barged into your room, but I assure you I'm not a threat."

"Why are you armed?"

"I'm a rancher. I have a license for the gun."

His gaze examines my face, briefly focusing on my mouth. Although my heartbeat stutters under his thorough scrutiny, I try to capitalize on his distraction by thrusting my knee up toward his groin. He reacts without even blinking, grabbing my leg before I can make contact. Next thing I know, I'm landing on my ass with a thud. My bones rattle as his heavy body slams on top of me. Long legs pin me to the floor, and I have his forearm pressing into my windpipe. Now I *actually* can't breathe.

Gasping for air, I bat at his shoulders with both hands, but he doesn't budge. That mocking gaze peers down at me.

"That wasn't very nice," he mutters. "Going for the groin like that."

I can't answer, because he's cutting off my air supply. I take another weak swing at him. God, he's strong. I *thought* I was a skilled fighter. My uncle's been training me since I was five. But here I am, flat on my back, unable to do a thing while he crushes me with his body.

No, that's not true. I can do *something*.

Another important lesson my uncle taught me is that in battle, you must gain the upper hand any way you can. With men, there's a surefire way to achieve that.

"Can't say I regret it," I wheeze out. "Considering the result." My voice is hoarse from the lack of oxygen.

His is laced with suspicion. "The result?"

"It got you on top of me."

I offer a tiny, unapologetic smile, and note the flicker of heat in his expression.

"Doesn't feel like a bad position to be in," I add, then manage to suck in a shallow breath. "I wasn't interested before, but now . . ."

I rock my hips in invitation.

He stiffens, lips parting. For the briefest moment, his hips respond in kind, his lower body moving slightly.

Then he begins to laugh.

"Nice try." He brings his mouth close to my ear, and my pulse skitters. "If I let you up, do you promise to keep your hands and knees to yourself?"

"Do *you*?" I spit out.

Still chuckling, he moves off me and goes to pick up my rifle. I stand, indignantly straightening my shirt as I watch him study the serial number. I take the opportunity to finally examine my surroundings, but there's not much to see. The bedsheets are tousled, probably thanks to whatever he and his "companion" were doing earlier. I don't know if I'm jealous of the girl or—with his charming personality— feel sorry for her.

There's a comm on the night table, a black jacket draped over a red armchair under the window, and a pair of black boots near the door. That's it. No other clues to shed light on who he is. I didn't see him out in the square earlier celebrating with the others, which is odd. Why is he in Hamlett if not for Liberty Day? It's rare for travelers to just be passing through. Everything west of Ward Z is underwater, and there aren't any communities on the coast. Every time the Company tries to rebuild out there, another earthquake hits and destroys an entire town or village.

I glance back at him and try to read his mind, but he's heavily shielded. Interesting. Most Primes don't have shields, or if they do, they're easily penetrable ones. Which means this man is either Modified, a soldier, or a civilian Prime who for some mysterious reason has mastered the skill of protecting his thoughts.

He holds my rifle in one capable hand but doesn't train it on me. He simply stands there watching me with those dangerous blue eyes.

"Will you run the serial number through your comm already so you can confirm I'm not an assassin and I can move on with my life?"

"Or I can just kill you and move on with *my* life," the asshole says.

"Oh no, I'm so scared of you." I plant both hands on my hips. "Do it. Shoot me. Either way, my torture ends."

He tips his head, still eyeing me. "What's your name?"

I'm startled when someone else answers that question.

"Wren?"

Or rather, someone is out in the hall hunting me down.

"Wren? You still here?"

I hear the soldier's footsteps pass the door, growing fainter as he walks around the corner.

My stranger taunts me. "Better go now, *Wren*. Might be able to make it to the front door before your boyfriend catches you."

"He's not my boyfriend, and I'm not going anywhere without my rifle."

After a beat, he flips the rifle by the barrel and hands it to me butt-first.

I shove the strap over my shoulder and march to the door. "Nice meeting you, asshole," I mutter without looking back.

His chuckle tickles my shoulder blades.

I take advantage of the empty corridor, racing down the stairs to the main floor. No sooner do I reach the exit than I hear my name again.

"Wren, wait."

I swallow a groan. The soldier is halfway down the staircase.

"You promised you weren't going to run off on me," he says on his approach. Disappointment flickers in his eyes.

"I'm sorry." I release an exaggerated sigh and construct a suitable lie. "I'm just not good with goodbyes."

His features soften.

"And anyway, I really do need to go. One of our fences came down during a storm the other night, and my uncle will kill me if I'm not up at the crack of dawn tomorrow to mend it."

"I have to see you again. Maybe I'll try to get leave next month?"

"You know where to find me," I say lightly, because chances are he won't get leave again for a long while. By then he'll have forgotten all about me.

Hopefully.

There's always the risk he'll become so besotted, he'll find a way to swap assignments with another soldier and get assigned to my ward. But I don't think I'm *that* good in bed.

"What's your ID?"

I reluctantly provide it, watching as he enters the digits into his comm. A moment later, the sleek device in my pocket chimes softly.

He flashes a dimpled smile. "That was me."

I pull it out and save his ID. I detest this thing. We're required to carry it at all times, but I only ever pay attention to my comm when a Company dispatch comes in. The rest of the time, I maintain obligatory correspondence with Uncle Jim or my friends. Nothing significant, of course; we have other means of communication for the real stuff. No Mod in their right mind would use a Company device to communicate, not when every word spoken or typed is recorded, a roomful of Intelligence agents monitoring every exchange. Same goes for the Nexus, our online network. We'd be fools to rely on either method to speak openly.

"I'll walk you out," he says.

I hear the din of voices beyond the inn doors. The fast tempo of the band, playing a song I don't recognize. I assume it's on the list of Company-approved melodies from the Communication Board. All media needs to be run by them before it's released to the citizenry.

We step out into the courtyard, where the breeze is as balmy as it was before we ducked inside the inn. The aroma of grilled meat and buttered corn on the cob permeates the night air. The village square is all lit up tonight. Crowded and noisy, frequent bursts of laughter rising above the music.

Unease washes over me at the dozen soldiers milling about. Liberty Day is the one time of year when many of them are able to return to their wards and see family and friends. Most of them seem harmless, but there are too many blue uniforms here tonight for my comfort.

I wish they'd go back to the city and leave us the hellfuck alone. Nobody here enjoys faking smiles and playing nice. Even Primes detest the heavy-handedness of the General, the way he controls every aspect of our lives. Or at least most of them hate it. There are certainly die-hard loyalists willing to betray their own mothers for a brisk nod of approval from that man or his sycophants. Some Prime jerk in my own ward literally turned his mother in when he discovered she was Modified. Nearly two decades of successfully hiding her gifts from him and then *one* slipup, one careless moment of mind reading without pulling her sleeves down, and her only son was reporting her. Last I heard, he'd been promoted to run his own unit in the Command.

Although I suppose that isn't as bad as Mods who turn against their own, the sympathizers who serve Redden in Sanctum Point, our capital city. Those traitors live cushy lives out there. Loyalty to the General certainly pays.

The joyous shrieks of children capture my attention. I turn toward the noise and smile. Several hundred yards away in a grassy clearing, there's a game of Chase happening. Village children scream and laugh as the chaser, a skinny girl with bright-red hair, races around trying to tag someone.

"Wren!" a happy voice calls out.

Tana Archer comes ambling over to us. Eyes bright, cheeks flushed. She's clearly been sampling her own supply. Tana's father, Griff, runs the only drinking establishment in the square.

"I was wondering where you'd disappeared to." With a knowing look, she glances between me and the soldier. Even as she grins at the two of us, I feel her trying to link with me.

All telepaths have their own unique signature. When I was a kid, my uncle described it as your essence, a surge of energy exclusive to you. It's almost impossible to explain unless you feel it yourself, but after an initial connection's been formed, you automatically recognize the other person's energy when they ask to link.

"Someone's been busy," Tana silently teases.

Her voice in my head always holds a lower pitch than her speaking tone. I asked my uncle about that once, why people's telepathic voices sound so different from their audible ones. "Have you ever listened to yourself on a recording and thought, *I don't sound like that?*" was his response. "That's because to your own ears, you always sound different. When we speak telepathically, I hear your voice the way *you* hear it. When you speak out loud, I hear your voice the way *I* hear it." It made a strange sort of sense when he explained it like that.

"You've gotta stop screwing the soldiers, babe."

"Hey, it's the only thing they're good for," I tell Tana, and she turns her head to smother a laugh.

I know her veins are rippling beneath her long sleeves, hidden from nosy eyes. With her dark skin, those veins tend to look even brighter when they're glowing compared with lighter-skinned Mods.

Me, I'm in a tank top and don't need to worry. Just another thing I used to hassle my uncle about, because it was confusing to see the luminous surge of silver beneath the skin of his arms each time we used telepathy. Why did *my* veins remain normal? I was an annoying child, always peppering him with questions. Back then, he didn't have a good answer. He simply shrugged and said, "It's been more than a century and there's still so much nobody understands about people like us."

That's the tricky thing about the Modified—there's no tried-and-true formula with us. Yes, the majority are the very definition of silverbloods, the veins in our arms glowing when we're using our powers. A rare few, like me, don't fit that mold. Whatever the reason for the anomaly, I can't deny it makes me . . . well, not to be cocky, but . . .

Invaluable.

A Mod who can wield her powers without transmitting her actions to her enemies is a major asset for the Uprising.

When the network first tried to recruit me, however, my uncle said hell no. He was adamant. *Wren doesn't put her life at risk. Period.* Once I was a teenager, it became harder for him to stop me. I'm stubborn. I love Uncle Jim to death, but I'm my own person.

We started running missions when I was sixteen. Small supply runs. Drop-offs. Using our ranch to hide Mods who were smuggled out of the city or the mines. It always boils my blood how many of us are still held prisoner in the labor camps scattered throughout the wards.

"You're not leaving, are you?" Tana says. "I've barely seen you tonight. You can't go!"

My soldier smiles. "That's what I keep telling her."

"I have to," I answer with a shrug. "You know my uncle. He's probably pacing the porch right now, waiting up for me."

As if on cue, I feel a hard poke in my mind. Jim's signature. He's asking to link, and I let him.

"It's late. Come home." His voice is a rumble.

I resist the urge to roll my eyes. "On my way."

"Stay for just one dance?" Tana begs.

"I really can't."

Truthfully, I would stick around and hang out with Tana for a while if this soldier weren't glued to my side. Ugh, what is his name? I think it's Max. Or maybe it's Mark?

Given what we did earlier, I feel bad asking, so I touch his arm. "Okay, ah . . . honey . . . it's been fun, but I have to go now."

Tana looks ready to erupt with laughter again.

"Honey?"

"Shut up. I couldn't remember his name. Is it Max or Mark?"

"His name is Jordan!"

Oh. I was very far off.

"The more important question is—who is the gorgeous jackass staying at the inn?" My heartbeat is still a bit off-kilter from that explosive encounter.

"I know nothing of a gorgeous jackass. I didn't see anyone other than soldiers checking in today. Or maybe I did see him and just forgot? Was he a soldier?"

"No idea. But trust me, you would remember this face."

It was a remarkable face. And totally wasted on a jerk like him.

"Eh. If I'm going to be dazzled by a face, it has to belong to a gorgeous woman, otherwise I'm blissfully oblivious."

"Let me take you home?" Jordan interrupts our silent conversation, his hopeful gaze locked on me.

"I'm good. I've got my bike."

Tana steps away to give us the moment of privacy that Jordan clearly desires.

He cups my face in his hands. "So difficult," he chides playfully. "At least give me a kiss goodbye." His thumb sweeps the corner of my jaw as he brings his mouth to mine.

I let him kiss me despite the impatience gathering in my chest.

We break apart at the screams of children.

A second later, pandemonium hits the square. Tana comes running over.

"What in the hellfuck?" I say as the three of us race toward the source of the chaos.

From what I can discern in the darkness, there's a kid on the ground, but all I see is the frenetic blur of arms flailing and legs kicking. Other children stream away from the clearing, shouting for help.

"It's that damn white coyote!" Tana curses. "He's been prowling the woods on the outskirts of the village all week."

Shit. The same wolf-coyote hybrid has been a menace around the ranch, too. I found one of my heifers dead in the south pasture two mornings ago. I don't know how that beast made it through the fence.

"He has him!" a little girl screeches at the adults crowding the edge of the grass.

Another scream rips out, one laced with terror and agony. My heart flies to my throat, pulse careening. Across the clearing, the boy is on his back now, the white coyote on top of him. The animal is *huge*.

"Robbie!" a woman screams. It's Rachel, a teacher at the schoolhouse. Which means the boy in peril is her eight-year-old son.

It's too shadowy to tell from this angle, but it doesn't look like the animal's teeth are on the boy's neck. I think they're gnawing into Robbie's arm and—holy shit, it's starting to drag the boy away.

I don't hesitate whipping up my rifle.

"Wren!"

Despite Tana's cry of protest, I take several steps forward, getting Robbie and the white coyote in my sights. Several men run across the grass. They're halfway to the boy, but he'll be dead by the time they reach him.

"No! Stop her," a panicked Rachel yells.

I take aim, rifle propped on my shoulder.

"Stop it, Wren! You're gonna hit my baby!"

I ignore her and take the shot.

CHAPTER 2

A feeling of foreboding shivers through me at the tall, bearded man's approach. Controller Fletcher was the first to reach the boy after I shot the predator. Several other men tail the controller, one of them cradling Rachel's son.

"Give him to me!" She lunges at the group, reaching for the boy whose clothing is soaked with blood. "Where's Betta? Someone needs to find Betta!" Tears stream down Rachel's cheeks.

"Nina already ran to wake her," her sister Elsie assures her. "It's okay, sweetling. Take a breath. Betta will be able to help him."

Betta is our doctor. Rachel is damn lucky she's nearby, because not every village has one. The citizens in our neighboring town have to come to Hamlett for medical treatment.

Tana and I push forward to take a closer look at the sobbing boy. The fact that he's awake and able to feel enough pain to cry is a good sign. Despite the copious amount of blood, it seems most of the damage is isolated to his left arm. Tana winces when she notices the ragged teeth marks and a flap of flesh hanging off the gaping wound.

"Is he going to be all right?" she asks urgently.

Elsie is now pressing a rag to the young boy's arm. "The bleeding seems to be slowing down. He'll need quite a lot of stitches, though."

Rachel starts crying again when she notices me standing there. "You saved him, Wren. Thank you."

I touch her arm, then gently stroke my hand over Robbie's head and his tight black curls. "I'm just glad he's okay."

The group hurries toward the long strip of one- and two-story buildings that make up the north side of the town square. The people of Hamlett have everything they'll ever need here. The rations store, pub, schoolhouse, dance hall, media house, medical clinic. Our entire lives reduced to a handful of square miles. What we don't have are the politicians or police forces we used to learn about in school. Unlike generations before us, our villages and cities are policed by soldiers and run by controllers. The controllers answer to the ward chairmen, who answer to General Merrick Redden, our benevolent leader. Redden's Company is a highly efficient military machine. He has no need for politics or superfluous job titles.

The controller of Hamlett remains put, raising his eyebrows at me. "Your bullet went through its eye," Fletcher remarks. "Nice."

I shrug. I'm painfully aware of Jordan's gaze on me.

"Don't shrug it off," Fletcher says. "You saved that boy, Wren."

I resist the urge to lift my shoulders again. "Well, you know. I have plenty of experience with predators going after my cattle. I just acted on instinct."

"Damn good instincts, then. Tell your uncle he taught you well."

I'll be telling him no such thing. Jim would be horrified if he knew I fired my weapon in town, even if a kid's life was at stake.

I suddenly feel itchy with the need to flee. My legs carry me away before I've even bid Fletcher goodbye. Both Tana and Jordan follow me, the latter not as welcome. Fuck. I want to get out of here.

"You okay?" Tana frets, grabbing my hand to stop me.

"I'm fine. But seriously, I need to get home." I squeeze her hand and continue walking across the dirt lot. "Come visit us this week. We'll go for a ride."

"You gotta let me leave, Tana. Otherwise he won't let me, either."

"Sorry. Talk later."

"Sounds good," she says before wandering off.

Jordan stays hot on my heels. When we reach my dusty old motor-cycle, he has stars in his eyes again.

"I've never seen anyone shoot like that," he marvels.

"Like I said, I have experience from the ranch."

"Wren," he says firmly. "You took out its *eye*. That was a hundred yards, easy. A moving target. And a kid in the way. You could have accidentally blown his head off."

I bristle, taking great offense to that. *Blown his head off!* Hardly. I guarantee I'm a better shot than anyone in Jordan's unit. He's not even in Silver Block, which is where all the elite soldiers go. I think he told me he served in Copper. I could outshoot a Copper guy with my eyes closed. I have half a mind to challenge this guy to a shooting contest—

No, rebukes my common sense. *You will do no such thing.*

The one rule my uncle instilled in me from a young age is to never draw attention to myself.

And like an idiot, that's exactly what I did tonight.

Shit.

I shouldn't have taken the shot.

"I'd love to come to the ranch and hit some targets with you. Not to brag, but I'm pretty good with a rifle, too. It would be fun."

"Oh, my uncle doesn't allow visitors," I say, then wince when I remember I just invited Tana to come by. I try to smooth the lie over by adding, "Tana is really the only one he can tolerate. Probably because we're childhood friends. She's basically another niece to him."

"Well, maybe one day." Jordan shakes his head again. "That was some shot."

I try to distract him from my feat of marksmanship by standing on my tiptoes and planting my lips to his.

He jerks in surprise, then smiles. "What was that for?"

"Nothing. I had a nice time tonight." I take a step back. "Good night, Jordan."

I grab the black helmet from the back of my bike and throw it on, avoiding his gaze as I fasten the strap. A moment later, the engine roars to life. I speed off, still feeling his gaze on me.

I really do need to stop sleeping with soldiers. Next time I'm feeling . . . needy . . . I might have to look elsewhere. There are a few unattached men in the village, but Tana says they're interested in something more serious. I don't want anything serious. I'm only twenty. Not ready to devote myself to somebody else. Other people's relationships seem suffocating, and I've witnessed so many women bending to a man's every whim.

I don't bend.

I reach the paved road at the end of town, where a blue metal sign shines in the darkness. White lettering displays our ward, village, and population. They update it annually, but Hamlett's population hasn't grown much over the years. Which is how Redden likes it. The General claims that prior to the Last War, overpopulation was a serious problem. We wouldn't have gotten to that dire point, to global conflict, to seven continents devastated, four of them razed or underwater, if it weren't for all the people battling over dwindling resources.

Greed. Everything always comes back to greed.

I feel my mind tingle with an invitation, smiling to myself when I recognize the familiar energy. After I accept the link, a deep voice fills my head.

"You still out?"

I'm quick to answer. "No. Driving home."

"Well, damn. You've already broken his heart? You work fast."

"Oh, shut up. Like you don't break hearts on a nightly basis."

"I'm celibate."

"Ha!"

"You're always laughing at me. Stop it."

"Stop saying ludicrous things."

But that's not Wolf's style. He has no filter, never has. And he's an outrageous flirt, although the flirting didn't really start until we hit our teenage years. One day, we were two kids talking about kid stuff; the next, we were discussing our love lives. A bit unnerving, considering we've never actually met.

I linked with Wolf when I was six years old, and to this day I still remember the excitement I felt when I first heard his voice. It was a warm summer morning. I'd been playing in the clearing outside the little house Uncle Jim had built for us. There are pockets within the Blacklands where the sun can penetrate, if only a thin shard of it, and our grassy clearing was one of those havens. Every day, we had five or six hours of concentrated sunlight that shone down on us before the mist shifted and we were eclipsed in darkness again. That morning, I ran up to Jim, vibrating with elation.

"Uncle!" I exclaimed. "I have a *friend.*"

Predictably, Jim had reacted with suspicion. I don't know why I expected otherwise. "What friend?" he demanded, looking up from the new beam he was sanding. That year he'd started building raised walkways to lay over the black quicksand pits so we could navigate more easily when we went hunting. I used to love dancing across those beams during our excursions.

Rather than share in my happiness when I told him a random boy had opened a path into my mind and said hello, Jim grabbed the front of my sweater, gripping the scratchy wool in his fist. Later, when I was older, he would admit how scared he'd been that day, how he'd always worried something like that might happen. Spontaneous linking is common in telepathic children. Kids, especially young ones, have little control of their gifts. But that morning in the clearing, he looked more furious than afraid. He ordered me to never speak to the voice in my head again.

The reminder brings a familiar rush of guilt. I promised I would close the link to the curious boy, only a few years older than me. The problem is, when you grow up in a world of darkness with a grumpy guardian and no one else your age, you welcome another child to play with, even if you are just playing with them in your head.

I didn't completely disregard Uncle Jim's wishes. When the boy made contact again and I guiltily let him, I was clear I couldn't tell him my name. "That's dumb," he griped after I informed him I wasn't allowed to. But we did have fun picking code names. I chose Daisy because it was my favorite flower. He chose Wolf because he liked wolves.

I know I should've pushed the boy out of my mind—literally—but life had been lonely then. Just Jim and me, living in a place with only five hours of sunshine and a lot of scary shit trying to kill us. I needed

Wolf. I liked his company. I still do, even when he's mocking me about breaking hearts.

"Seriously," he says now. "How was your night? I need to live vicariously through you. It's been a couple of months for me."

I'm surprised. From the smug way he brags about it, he's very popular with women.

"Why is that?"

"Been busy."

"So that's why you've been quiet lately." I hadn't heard from him in weeks before he suddenly touched base earlier tonight.

I don't ask what's kept him busy, same way he'd never ask me. That's standard procedure when you're Modified. There's no such thing as absolute trust. Even Jim, the man who risked his life for me and my parents, theoretically the one person I should trust implicitly, doesn't get one hundred percent from me. Otherwise, he would know all about Wolf.

"To answer your question, it was fun. But he got a little needy at the end. Kept begging to see me again. I suppose I can't blame him. I'm exquisite."

That gets me a wave of laughter. "Arrogant bitch."

I laugh, too, but the humor falters when I think about Jordan's earnest desire to see me again.

"Does it ever bother you?" I ask Wolf.

"What?"

"Lying to Primes. Like the ones you sleep with. Or your friends from upper school. Job placement colleagues. You know, the good ones. Do you feel bad lying to them?"

There's a pause.

"Sometimes," he admits. "But the occasional pang of guilt is preferable to the alternative. Or alternatives, plural. You never know how a Prime will react to finding out their lover or classmate or co-worker is a silverblood."

He's not wrong. Best case, they're horrified but are somehow convinced to keep your identity a secret. Likeliest case? They turn you in and attend your Command execution, cheering when the firing squad pulls their triggers.

"What's this about, Daisy? You feel shitty about lying to your soldier tonight?"

"Not exactly. I feel . . . discouraged that he'll never know who I am. He has no idea that he spent his entire night with a woman he's incapable of ever truly knowing. Sometimes I wish people could know me."

"I know you." His voice is husky in my mind. "Does that count for something?"

My heart clenches, and I have to swallow the lump of emotion. "Yes. It does." I gulp again, eager to lighten the mood. "Anyway, I gotta go. I'm trying to concentrate on driving. Can't telepath and drive, you know?"

"That's not a rule."

"If Redden has his way, it would be."

No, if our esteemed leader had his way, telepathy would be outlawed because we'd all be dead. He almost succeeded in wiping us out in the Silverblood Purge twenty-five years ago, before he took over the Continent. His men dragged tens of thousands of Mods out of their homes to be executed. That's how much he hates us.

The sad part is, the Coup wouldn't have been successful if there weren't hordes of people who agreed with him. That we're aberrant. That we're abominations and our gifts are not natural, even though the things I can do with my mind are as natural to me as breathing.

I cut my speed as I approach the long driveway of our property. Soon our ranch comes into view, the old split-level house and handful of outbuildings on a sprawling acreage that's far too large for the both of us. Our two hundred head of cattle need the space, though.

Uncle Jim had serious connections when we emerged from the Blacklands, managing to secure us a prime location, and in an asset ward, no less. The Uprising has always been good to Jim, whose insurgent efforts as Julian Ash were both plentiful and effective. Unfortunately, those efforts also made him a major person of interest to the Command. Jim will be a hunted man for the rest of his life.

Right now, in the pitch black, with only the faint glow of the solar porch light guiding me home, I'm reminded of the Blacklands. The eternal night. It's fucked up, but sometimes I miss it. It was a simpler time.

Three years of fighting for survival . . . so simple! My subconscious laughs at me.

Yes, okay. It was difficult. Not to mention exhausting, forever being on the alert. I fell off one of Uncle Jim's planks into the black pits once and realized how quickly I could have drowned if I'd been alone, without Jim to pull me out. It was scary in there for a little girl.

"Why were you gone so long?" my uncle says when I walk into the house.

He's in his worn leather chair, sipping a glass of synth whiskey. He always grumbles that synthetic alcohol pales in comparison with the real thing. I've never sampled anything pure, so I can't judge.

"You didn't have to wait up."

"I don't have to do anything I don't want to." His dark-brown eyes track my movements as I hang my rifle by its strap on the hook by the door. "How was the celebration?"

I hesitate, wondering how much to tell him. I opt for the truth, because we both know he'll see right through me if I attempt to lie.

"Don't be upset," I start.

"Fucking hell, Wren," he growls.

"I said don't be upset." I approach his chair and cross my arms to my chest. "It's not a big deal, I promise. And I think you'll agree I was right to act. If I hadn't, Robbie would be dead."

"Who the hell is Robbie?"

Yeah, Jim never tried making friends with the citizens of Hamlett. He's a recluse. And kind of a dick. The other villagers know him as the antisocial jerk who shows up a couple of times a month to get laid or buy whiskey from Mr. Paul's store. Sometimes, when he's feeling particularly social, he grabs a meal and a pint at the pub. When he's there, he doesn't spend much time on pleasantries. Despite his last name, you're more likely to get a "piss off" from Jim Darlington than a "hello." I suspect someone in the Uprising threw the word *darling* into his new identity just to needle him.

He's loyal, though. To me. To his friends in the Uprising. If he loves and trusts you, he'll go to the ends of the earth to protect you. Literally. He took me to the damn Blacklands to keep me safe.

But if he *doesn't* love or trust you . . . well . . . stay far away, because the man is pricklier than the cactus growing out back.

"Robbie is Rachel Solway's son, and he almost got mauled by a white coyote. Same one that was harassing us."

"Damn hybrid's a nuisance."

"Yeah, well, it was a starving nuisance. It crashed the party. So I killed it." I falter when Jim narrows his eyes. He knows me well. "It was an impressive shot."

He frowns. "How impressive?"

"The controller commented on it. Said you trained me well."

"Wren." He utters my name as if it's an expletive.

"I'm sorry! What, you think I should've just let that kid die?"

"Yes."

"The way you let me die?" I challenge.

"I made your parents a promise not to let you die. It's not the same situation."

"Maybe I promised Rachel not to let *her* son die. I mean, it was a promise made three seconds after the hybrid came, but I still fulfilled it."

"I don't want you dra—"

"—drawing attention to myself," I finish, grumbling under my breath. "Yes. I get it. But I'm an adult and I know how to handle myself. In case you've forgotten, I work for the network."

He gives a cynical chuckle. "You don't work for them. You've run a few minor ops with them. That means nothing."

I open my mouth indignantly, but he cuts me off.

"You've never been in combat. Never had to try to survive in the city."

"I survived in much worse," I argue.

"No, you haven't. It's a pit of vipers down there. You can't lower your guard in the Point. Ever."

"I have an edge," I remind him, trying not to appear too smug as I hold out my bare arms. I switch over to telepathy to prove my point. "See? Nothing happening in my veins. I can operate in the city without detection."

"Sure, kid. Until you accidentally incite. And then how do you talk your way out of that, huh?"

The reminder has me reaching down to rub my hip. A reflexive response. It doesn't escape me that the burn exists in the first place because of this man. My guardian. The person who is supposed to protect me.

It *really* hurt. I still remember the smell of burning flesh. It was for my own good, I recognize that now, but that doesn't mean I don't hate him a little bit for doing that to me.

"Stop being dramatic. I haven't incited in years," I grumble.

Yet he's not wrong. When it does happen, it's often unexpectedly. Over the years, we trained hard to try to control it, but always to no avail. I can't even say *how* I incite. The first time I incited Jim, I was seven years old. By then, we'd been practicing for hours, days, months, in our clearing. Every morning, we sat facing each other, his knife beside him on the grass, while he ordered me to open a path, push my way into his mind, and command him to pick up the knife. Pick up the knife and cut a line in his palm.

"Say it again, Wren," he'd ordered that morning.

So I did. Over and over again in my mind. *Pick up the knife, pick up the knife.* Yet his hand didn't move.

Eventually, I started whining. "I don't wanna do it anymore. Please."

"You have to. You need to be able to control this power."

"But *why.*"

"Because they'll kill you if they know you have it." Jim had never minced his words, not even around scared little girls. "Try saying it out loud," he advised. "I heard that helps sometimes."

Dutifully, I used my voice. "Pick up the knife, pick up the knife . . ."

Over and over and over again. I grew so frustrated and furious with all the pointless practicing, my brain humming louder and louder, until finally a surge of energy coursed through me and—

He picked up the knife and sliced a line through the center of his palm. I was so frightened I ran into our hut and didn't leave it for hours.

"Are you still planning on going to Ward T sometime this week?"

I ask, changing the subject. I'm tired of the lecture. I receive at least one Jim lecture a day, and we already filled the quota this morning when he chastised me for forgetting to muck Kelley's stall.

"Likely the day after tomorrow. Let me know if you want me to pick anything up when I'm there."

"I will, thanks. And don't you dare leave without saying goodbye."

"Never," he says gruffly, and any irritation I feel about his lectures melts away.

When I was ten, he disappeared for a week on a mission with the Uprising. Just up and left without a word. He sent Tana's dad to the ranch to stay with me, then returned days later and was utterly clueless as to why I could *possibly* be upset with him. After enduring my silent treatment for a full day, he promised to never leave again without bidding me goodbye first.

Jim is a hard man, but I know he loves me. I'm sure this wasn't the life he'd envisioned for himself. Fifteen years ago, he went from a thirty-year-old Command colonel to a hunted deserter, in charge of a five-year-old with whose safety he'd been entrusted. He was forced to leave everything behind. His career, his home, his friends. But he did it. For my parents. For me.

"All right. I'm turning in." He rises from his chair. "Good night, little bird."

The endearment makes me smile. "Good night."

In my room, I wash up and get ready for bed. I drift into sleep thinking not about the soldier I spent the evening with but the hot, rude stranger at the inn.

———

At the crack of dawn, I head to the barn to saddle my gentle Appaloosa mare. I could take the off-road vehicle—it'd be faster—but I enjoy my quality time with Kelley.

"Hey, beautiful," I coo, running my hand over her spotted back. She's got the prettiest dark-brown-and-white coloring, and her big liquid eyes reflect my smiling face back at me. "Ready to go fix a fence?"

Kelley nickers. I take that as a yes and mount, the leather reins loose in my hands as I guide her away from the stables and toward the trail.

The worst part about ranching is all the tedious chores. As much as I'd love to, I don't get to spend all my time riding Kelley and swimming in the creek. I'm up to my eyeballs in feeding the animals, mucking stalls, filling water troughs. And those are the *fun* chores. Repairing fences is my least favorite task, but it's one of the most important. Our fences keep our cows in and the predators out.

Kelley and I ride into the north pasture, where I dismount and let her graze while I locate the broken section of fencing my uncle told me about. I quickly tackle the job of fixing it, using a stretcher to pull the two split pieces of wire taut so I can reconnect them with a crimp sleeve. Then I spend the rest of the morning inspecting every inch of fencing until I'm satisfied there's no access points for the white coyotes that want to terrorize our herd.

I'm slipping my thick work gloves off when Uncle Jim tries to link with me. A second later, his warning fills my head.

"Don't come back to the house. Stay away."

My shoulders snap into a straight line. "Why? What's going on?"

"Command's here" is his grim reply.

My heartbeat quickens. Why is Command at the house? We're always warned before an inspection.

Racing toward Kelley, I reach out to Tana, but she doesn't let me in. She's either asleep, dead, or ignoring me. My money's on asleep. She was thoroughly boozed last night.

"Uncle Jim? Are you okay? I'm coming back."

"Absolutely not. Stay put."

Yeah, forget that.

I heave myself into the saddle and click my tongue to command Kelley to go. When she's slow to start, I apply pressure with my calves and urge her into a gallop.

We don't take the same route back to the ranch, the one that would leave us out in the open, exposed. We approach from high ground, stopping at the rocky outcrop far above the south pasture where the herd is currently grazing. From there, I'm provided with a perfect vantage point to the house. It's several hundred yards away, but Mods have perfect eyesight. We don't need pesky things like glasses.

I dismount and creep toward the edge of the rocks, peering over. I see the trucks. Two of them, olive green with the black-and-silver Command emblem painted on the doors. When I spot Uncle Jim, my heart drops to my stomach.

He's wearing a long-sleeved flannel and his usual faded jeans. Knees in the dirt, his cowboy hat thrown on the ground a few feet away. A uniformed man with an officer patch on his right sleeve presses a gun barrel to my uncle's forehead.

"I can see you. I see them. Why are they here?" My knees are as weak as my breathing.

"They came to watch you shoot."

Horror slams into me. This is because of *me*?

My gaze swoops over the soldiers. Four others stand like stone statues behind the one in charge. I feel queasy when I realize one of them is Jordan.

This *is* my fault. *I* did this. I made that impossible shot last night, drew attention to myself, and now the Command is holding a gun to my uncle's head.

I have my rifle. I can take them out. Shoot them . . . Desperation lodges in my throat, because there's no possible way I can eliminate all five without at least one of them putting a bullet in Jim's skull.

"What do I do?"

"You turn around and go find Griff," he orders, his long sleeves obfuscating the fact he's communicating with me. "He'll take care of you."

I swallow my cry of distress when the officer uses his free hand to grab Uncle Jim by a hunk of his fair shoulder-length hair. He shoves Jim's head backward and spits out some words, sneering. There's familiarity in the officer's cold eyes. His face, his body language . . . it all screams, *I know who you are.*

My hands shake as I link with Jim again.

"Do they know you're Julian Ash?"

"Yes."

That's the last thing he says before they throw him into the back of a vehicle and drive away.

CHAPTER 3

"Tana! They took Jim."

For the first time all morning, she answers.

"Who?" She sounds horrified.

"Command. Why didn't you warn us?"

Tana is the first line of defense between us and the Command, since no one can get to the ranch without first passing through Hamlett, where every unit must stop to check in with our controller. That's how we've been able to keep Jim under the radar all these years. A projector, Tana has saved my uncle's hide more than once. Whenever soldiers arrive in the village, she projects their faces for us, and if Jim has even a trace of recognition, he rides into the mountains while I ruefully inform the inspecting soldiers that my uncle is out with the herd and won't be back till morning. The system's worked well for us. Until now.

"I was asleep. Never been so hungover in my life. And anyway, it didn't even occur to me there might be an inspection on a weekend."

Because it wasn't an inspection. They came to the ranch for the sole purpose of watching me shoot. Because I was stupid enough to fire my rifle in front of a soldier.

This is all my fault.

"They're gone now, but they left one guy behind. Waiting for me, I guess."

"You can't go back there."

"No shit. I'm going to make my way to you. I'll use the tunnel."

"I'll tell my father."

I cut the link and hop back in the saddle. My brisk ride to the lean-to in the northern pass is fueled by sheer panic. Luckily, I have no need to return to the house. Uncle Jim and I are drowning in contingency plans.

At the back of the wooden lean-to is a trapdoor, which I crank open to reveal the metal ramp below. I crouch and slide my way down the ramp toward the dusty corner where we stashed the bike. The crawl space isn't much taller than the motorcycle, so I'm stuck in that crouched position as I roll it up the ramp, along with a canvas go-bag. I check the bike's solar battery to ensure it has a charge. My bag contains extras in case I need them.

Outside, I warily study the approaching clouds, thick and gray. Hopefully not an omen of things to come. I tear my gaze off the darkening sky and run my hand over Kelley's coarse mane.

"Go home, girl."

I smack her on the rump, and off she goes. She knows her way back. I just pray the soldier stationed down there isn't trigger-happy. If he kills my beloved mare, I'm going to hunt him down, put a bullet in his skull, and then hunt his ghost down, too.

I take the back roads to the village, stashing the bike in a metal shed behind a small brick home whose owners died a couple of years back. The house hasn't been assigned to anyone else yet, so it's stood abandoned ever since. The shed is a network drop location, conveniently located less than fifty yards from the edge of the forest.

I'm about to exit the shed when I hear it. A low, mechanical buzz, like the vibration of a hummingbird's wings, if those wings were metal.

Surveillance drone.

Heart pounding, I duck inside and plaster myself against the wall. The surveillance cameras in the wards are omnipresent, their unblinking gaze a reminder of the Company's ever-watchful eye. From the corner of my own eye, I catch the shadowy movements of the drone as it hovers near the dirty window at the back of the shed. It's rare to see a drone this close to Hamlett. We're a small, inconsequential village. Hardly worthy of attention.

Until now, I suppose. Until the infamous Julian Ash was discovered to be hiding out in this small, inconsequential village.

Thanks to me.

I ignore the wild hammering of my pulse and wait until I can no longer hear the drone. Then I take a tentative step, peering out the door. When I glimpse the gray blur in the sky, buzzing away in the opposite direction, I nearly keel over with relief.

Now. I need to go *now*.

Without wasting another second, I sprint toward the forest.

A long time ago, someone dug a tunnel system beneath these woods, back when political tensions were running especially high. Ironically, this is a Prime tunnel. Because at the end of the day, it doesn't matter who your leaders are—they're all assholes. President Severn, who ruled before General Redden, was a Mod who believed we were a superior new race. After decades of being persecuted themselves, he and his followers decided it would be a good idea to do the same to the Primes. Fools. Nothing good ever comes from the notion that one group is better than another. I can't stand General Merrick Redden, but I don't hate all Primes. Good ones *do* exist.

Like the one who meets me at the end of the tunnel. Tana's father, Griff, isn't Modified like his daughter. But he's loyal to Tana and the network.

"Tana told me what happened," Griff says, bending down to hug me. He's a huge man with a shaved head and bushy beard, and I welcome his warm, safe embrace. "Are you all right? Have you spoken to him?"

"No. He's not letting me link."

Concern wells up inside me. Chances are, Jim's keeping our link closed because he thinks he's protecting me. But it could also mean something else. Something more dire. Like he's unconscious.

Or dead.

No. He can't be. I still feel his energy when I open a path to him. I can still follow that thread between our minds. Jim once told me that when someone dies, their signature completely disappears. You're not supposed to feel them at all anymore.

I feel him, damn it.

"Do you know where they're taking him?" Griff asks.

"To the city, I presume. One of the officers recognized him. They know he's a Command deserter." Panic bubbles in my throat. "They're going to kill him."

"Maybe not. Might send him to one of the camps."

Uncle Jim would slit his own throat before he allowed himself to become a labor slave for the Company.

"There's a soldier stationed at the house waiting for me. They're going to want to talk to me."

"They will. So we get you out of here. The network has a safe house in S. We can start there, then move our way south."

"No way. I'm not running. I'm going to the city to rescue Jim."

"Wren." His tone is firm. "That's not an option, you hear me? If he was a prisoner in a labor camp, the network would certainly attempt a rescue. But he's being taken to the Point. He'll have to face the Tribunal."

The Tribunal is the only system of justice on the Continent, comprising a small council of men and women who decide the fate of an accused, usually on the spot and with very little background to go on. Anyone found guilty is sentenced to either death or labor. From what I've heard, the only time the Tribunal sets a guilty person free is if that person happens to be one of the General's loyal supporters. Those crimes get a slap on the wrist and a stern *don't do it again.*

"I don't care." I shake my head stubbornly. "I'm getting to the city one way or another. The question is, are you going to help me, or do I need to do this alone?"

Griff lets out a breath. "I'll contact the network."

———

The Uprising secures me a leisure pass and a ticket on the next speed train to Sanctum Point, or the Point as everyone calls it. Scanning my thumb at the train station is a nerve-racking affair, because our contact at the network discovered my ID had already been flagged. Fortunately, over the years, the Uprising has successfully infiltrated every level in the Company, including Intelligence. Ten minutes before I board the train, our operative hacks into my file to lift the flag. She does it under the guise of a system glitch and warns us the system will reset itself in six hours. That gives me just enough time to reach the city. Once I'm there, the flag will return and I'll be designated a person of interest again. Which means keeping a low profile at all costs.

Despite the assurance that my ID is safe for the moment, I'm still anxious when I'm scanned for a second time after I board the train. It's standard procedure, along with the request to press my thumb to the attendant's screen.

Several decades ago, someone in the government tried to implement a more cutting-edge approach to identity checks: microchips embedded under the skin. But not only did the chips fail to work on Modified people, something about the human body's natural electric impulses kept shorting out the microchips even in Primes. The method wasn't reliable, so they scrapped that program.

I find an empty seat in the back row of the middle car. I feel naked without my rifle—hell, at this point I'd kill for a dull switchblade—but bringing weapons onto a civilian train is impossible. You pass two security checks just to enter the station. I keep my gaze downward, pretending to read on my comm. It's a four-hour ride, and I resist the urge to tap my foot the entire time. The Command would've brought Jim in on one of their jets, not the train. He might've already faced the Tribunal by now. My attempts to contact him telepathically continue to be rejected. Either he's purposely not allowing me to link, or he's unable to.

My thoughts wander, morphing into memories. One in particular. The first time Uncle Jim taught me how to create a path from my mind to his. A few weeks after we fled the city, he sat me down on the grass outside our Blacklands hut and told me to close my eyes. To imagine my mind was a vast empty space.

"People like us are fueled by energy," he explained, as if a five-year-old was capable of truly grasping the concept. "But the brain can't *see* that energy, so it creates images to represent it. Do you understand what I mean?"

"No." I'd given him a petulant look.

He sighed. "Let me show you."

His deep voice grew almost hypnotic as he ordered me to close my eyes again so he could show me how to find the path.

"Nothing but darkness, Wren. You can't see anything but a silver rope. Do you see the rope?"

"Uh-huh."

"Good. Picture it stretching out in front of you. And at the very end of it is a silver light. Do you see the light? Good. You're going to bend down and pick up the rope, wrap your hand around it. That's your path, keen? From the rope to the light. You're going to follow the path."

"Follow it where?" I'd asked in confusion.

"Into my mind," he answered. "Are you at the light? Good job. What do you feel now?"

A soft whimper came out. "I don't like it. It feels . . . heavy. It makes my head hurt."

"You're feeling the pressure build up. It's my shield protecting me from you. Try to picture the shield. It looks like a metal wall, doesn't it? Thick steel."

"Uh-huh."

"That's—"

"And there's gold sparkles floating in the air. It's pretty."

He didn't speak for so long that I cranked my eyelids open. Uncle Jim's brow was furrowed. He looked uneasy. But when our gazes locked, he gave a fast nod and returned to the lesson.

"Next time, I'll teach you how to search for cracks in someone's shield. But right now, I'm going to lower mine so we can practice. Close your eyes again. Step into the silver light."

I did what he said, and he cursed suddenly, startling me. My eyes popped open in time to catch him rubbing the back of his neck.

"It's all right," he assured me when he noticed my concern. "Let's keep going. You're inside my mind now. I feel you there. Eyes closed, Wren. There you go. The most important thing you need to know about the Modified—about people like us—is that our minds have two frequencies."

Keeping my lids squeezed shut, I mumbled, "I don't know what ferkencies is."

"Frequencies. Like . . ." He paused. "Ocean waves. One wave gives off positive energy—that's for talking. The other gives off negative energy—that's for listening. The first thing you'll see when you break through someone's shield is an open door. Beyond the door, black waves are trying to push you out. Do you see them, little bird?"

"Uh-huh."

"Good—"

"What is down the hallway?" I interjected.

Another long pause.

He cleared his throat. "Ignore it for now. Focus on the black waves. Push your way through them until they clear up and then tell me what you hear."

I remember concentrating so hard, my closed eyelids began to twitch. Jim hadn't expected me to succeed on the first try. Children rarely do. So he was visibly shocked when I squeezed past the waves of negative energy trying hard to repel me. My expression bloomed with joy.

"You're proud of me." I bit my lip, straining to hear more of his thoughts. "You're—"

My happiness faded.

"You're 'fraid of me," I accused.

"No," Jim corrected, his voice gruff. "I'm not afraid of you. I'm afraid *for* you, little bird."

I didn't understand, back then, what he meant by that.

He cleared his throat. "All right. That's how you read a mind. Now walk back through the door and go toward the hallway you saw. Follow that positive energy wave. That's your second frequency. It's where we establish a link so we can use telepathy."

"What's tellepappy?"

"Telepathy. It means we can talk to each other in our minds. And once we form a link, it doesn't matter if I'm very far away from you, or if my shield is up. If you want to talk to me, all you ever need to do is tap into that frequency, follow my energy thread, and poke my shield to ask to link. To talk."

I was still distracted by what he had said before, but I forced myself to push his odd words from my head—*I'm afraid for you, little bird*—and focus on our lesson. I could tell Uncle Jim was impressed by how easily it all came to me.

By the time we added shielding and image projection to our lesson plan, he had stopped being surprised by what I could do.

————

When we finally pull into the station, I'm a tight bundle of anxiety. I hurry off the train and link with Polly, my usual handler.

"I'm here."

"Your contacts are waiting outside. She's a Prime. Black shirt, green cap. Your silent contact is Declan. He'll be your handler."

I leave the station and carefully approach the woman in the green cap, trying not to give in to the paranoia that everyone is staring at us.

"Is he dead?" I ask in lieu of greeting.

"Not yet" is the response.

She's a pale, black-haired woman in her thirties who introduces herself as Faye and leads me to a waiting car in the arrivals lane. The man behind the wheel has dark skin and piercing eyes. He twists around to nod at me when I slide into the back seat.

"You're my silent contact in the Point? Declan?"

He looks startled. "How did you do that?"

"Do what?"

"Open a path so fast."

I wrinkle my forehead. "It wasn't that fast." But I suppose it was. I always forget there are others whose powers aren't as strong as mine. Or as plentiful.

Declan's shrewd eyes lock onto me, as if assessing my competence, my worth. It's unnerving. Then he faces forward and drives us through the exit checkpoint, leaving the train depot behind us.

"Julian Ash met with the Tribunal two hours ago," Faye tells me. "They found him guilty of treason and concealment."

I look over in surprise. "Concealment? They know he's Modified? How?"

"Jayde Valence recently joined the Tribunal."

I inhale a sharp breath. There's no further explanation needed. Valence is indisputably the most powerful mind reader on the Continent. She's also a Prime loyalist and traitor to her people, serving as General Redden's right-hand woman for more than a decade. She started working for the Company when she was only seventeen and is rumored to be cold-blooded and highly intelligent. But it's her ability to penetrate almost any shield that concerns me.

My uncle has the strongest shield of anyone I know. If she was able to read his thoughts, that's extraordinary. And petrifying, because . . . what does she know about *me*? How much of me was inside Jim's head? Is this why he's not linking with me? Is he worried Jayde Valence will return and somehow uncover my identity?

I swallow the fear and try to focus on Faye's voice.

". . . he faces the firing squad tomorrow morning."

"What?"

"His execution is scheduled for nine o'clock."

"We can't let that happen." I take a calming breath. "The network is going to organize a rescue mission, right?"

"No," Declan says from the front seat. Emphatically.

"What do you mean, no? He's one of your most essential operatives!"

Declan's eyes meet mine in the rearview mirror. "No. He's not."

My shoulders stiffen. "What the hell does that mean?"

"It means he's not. It means he's been living in hiding for fifteen years. He was compromised years ago. How could he ever be an asset when enough Primes are still alive to remember his face? We can't use him for any significant operations."

"That's not true." My protest sounds weak to my ears. Because it is weak. Nothing Declan said is incorrect. But . . .

He's my uncle, damn it.

"He's still a Mod," I insist. "We rescue our people."

"The people on top have been conferring about this all day," says Faye. "If there was a way to save him, they'd do it. But it's too dangerous."

"What's the point of this network if not to take on high-risk missions to save Mods? Get that hotshot pilot of yours to bomb the shit out of something and create a distraction while we rescue Jim."

"And take out how many civilians in the process?" counters Declan. "In any case, we don't have the bombers to spare, and Grayson Blake is too important to our cause to jeopardize. Nobody on top is going to allow Blake to fly over the Command base in the goddamn morning and expose himself like that."

"Then what the hell is he good for?" I mutter. I've been hearing about the dastardly feats of this ace pilot for almost two years now.

Faye offers a sympathetic look, but neither she nor Declan wavers in their conviction that Jim is wholly expendable.

"Julian Ash is not our objective," Declan says. "You are. Your village and ward are now crawling with soldiers. You're lucky Griff got you out when he did. Our only job is to install you in a safe house and keep you hidden until we're able to procure a new identity for you." He makes a sound of disapproval. "Would've been an easier task if you'd agreed to be housed in the wards instead of insisting on the Point, but—"

"I didn't come here for a safe house. I came here to rescue my uncle."

Declan doesn't budge. "Julian Ash is beyond rescue. Focus on protecting yourself."

Frustration squeezes my chest. Why aren't these people more concerned about Jim? When did we become dispensable to our leaders?

I throw out a desperate link to Tana.

"Jim's been scheduled for execution tomorrow and the network refuses to rescue him."

"I know. Polly just told me." There's a pause. "Wren . . . whatever you're thinking . . ."

"I don't even know what I'm thinking."

I don't. I don't have a plan. All I know is that I'm in the most dangerous place on the Continent, without a weapon, with my ID flagged and my uncle about to be shot to death.

My mind races over my options. The Command's firing squad operates in the South Plaza, an open-access area directly on the base. Executions are always held in public, and all citizens are encouraged to attend. Most of them enjoy it. Which isn't as sick as you'd think, because according to my old textbooks, our ancestors relished violence and gore, too. Turning death into a spectacle.

I suppose having access to the execution site aids my cause. I could sneak through the crowd unnoticed, get close enough to the platform, and . . . and then what? What exactly am I to do? Singlehandedly face down a firing squad? And then, after magically avoiding death by eight assault rifles, I free Uncle Jim and just . . . waltz off the military base?

That's not a viable plan. I need to come up with something a little less . . . suicidal.

And I only have about, oh, twelve hours to figure it out.

CHAPTER 4

Hours later, I lie on the single bed in the safe house, staring at the ceiling and wishing I could speak to Jim. I'm desperate for his guidance. *He* would know exactly what to do in this situation. He'd know how to save me if the roles were reversed, the same way he saved me fifteen years ago.

I roll onto my side and curl my knees to my chest, biting my lip to stop from crying. I think about the first week I spent with Julian Ash. How rude he was. How intimidating. How often he'd scold me for one sin or another, like if I ventured too close to the purple hemlock bush on the edge of our clearing. *Girl,* he'd always bark. *Stay away from those plants.* One of the first things he did when we made camp was march me over to various hybrid plants and explain which ones could kill me and how. In other words: *Don't get too fucking close.*

By the end of that week, he was growing on me. Don't get me wrong, he still unnerved me. His strict commands and complete lack of tenderness were daunting. But he no longer scared me. I felt safe with him.

I used to be so fascinated by all the birds that visited our clearing. There was one morning when I saw three of them in my favorite tree, sitting placidly on a gnarled branch. One, two, three, all in a row. They peered right at me. Unbothered by my presence. Curious, even.

"What are they called?" I'd asked Jim.

He studied their markings and said, "Bluebirds."

I stretched out an arm, trying to reach for the branch, but I was several feet too short. I lowered my arm and pouted, turning back to Jim. "What are *you* called?"

He thought it over. "You can call me Uncle."

"But you're not."

"In here I am."

"But—"

"Enough, girl."

"My name isn't Girl." I stubbornly stuck out my chin. "My name is—"

"No," he interrupted. "It isn't." He knelt in front of me, grasping my chin when I tried to look away. "That name you think is yours, you need to forget it, do you understand? The little girl you used to be is dead. You are somebody new now."

"But I don't wanna be," I whined, before getting distracted by a new arrival to the bird tree. "Look!" I pointed at one of the lower branches. "What is she called?"

Jim had squinted at the small, light-brown bird. "I believe that's a wren."

"That's a pretty name."

He lifted a brow. "You can claim it."

I frowned, not understanding.

"You don't like it when I call you girl, right?"

"It's not my name," I said mulishly.

"You're right. Because your name is Wren."

The frown deepened. "It is?"

"It is if you want."

My nose wrinkled for a moment as I thought it over. "Are you still Uncle?"

"I am. I'm Uncle and you're Wren."

Fifteen years later, he's still Uncle to me. He's still my guardian and my protector, and I can't do a damn thing to save him.

Swallowing the lump in my throat, I slide out from under the covers and get dressed. It's time to go.

———

The citizens are thirsty for blood. I can feel it in the air—the current of excitement. And I hate them all for it.

I snuck out of the safe house at dawn. The network is probably already trying to track me down, but I know how to stay hidden. I grew up in the dark, after all. I'm a shadow. As I made my way to the west sector of Sanctum Point, where the Command base is located, I eluded every single street patrol and surveillance drone. Last thing I need today is to raise some soldier's suspicions and get my thumb scanned, right when my ID has a big red flag on it again.

I'm going to rescue Jim.

I don't know how I'm going to do it. But I do know I'm not going to let him die. I refuse to.

South Plaza is essentially a glorified courtyard. Reddish dirt floor surrounded by high walls made of stone. To enter, you pass through a pair of menacing iron gates guarded by soldiers from Tin Block, which, along with Copper, has the easiest training program and usually produces soldiers assigned to lower-level ward patrols or sentry duties. The ones guarding South Plaza today look younger than I am, but their only job is to search the citizens streaming through the gates for the morning spectacle.

Frustration tightens my body as I enter the plaza completely unarmed. I feel naked.

When I see the platform, a lump of dread fills my throat. My vision wavers for a moment. The wooden execution stage is about four feet off the ground, and a crowd is already gathered in front of it. I weave my way through the growing sea of people, throwing an elbow or two to position myself in the front row. There's another set of electric gates behind the platform; beyond the black bars is nothing but darkness, but I know the doors open into the tunnel that leads to the bowels of the base.

I rub my damp palms against the front of my jeans. I'm anxious, a state made worse by the constant tugs on my mind. I've felt Declan trying to link with me all morning. Tana, too. I haven't been letting them in.

I don't care how worried Tana is, or how annoyed Declan must be that I fled the safe house. I simply don't care. Because this is Jim. He's saved my life countless times and it's my turn to save his. Somehow. I hope.

It's an excruciating wait. Forty-five minutes of fidgeting and shifting my feet, until finally, the tunnel gate creaks open, and an excited buzz travels through the throng of citizens. The two halves crank apart to allow a Command truck to drive out of the cavernous black space.

Resentment burns my throat. Fuck the Uprising for being so damn ready to sacrifice Jim. They wouldn't have even half the intel they're in possession of if it weren't for men like Julian Ash, who put their lives at risk to infiltrate institutions like the Command. He had climbed the ranks to become a colonel. All the schematics he'd procured them, all the information he'd funneled out of the base over the years, and now they're abandoning him because they're too cowardly to attempt a rescue.

I feel a tickle in my mind. Tana trying to link again. I ignore her. I'm sure she can guess where I am.

The crowd murmurs again, low voices echoing in the square. Two uniformed officers slide out of the truck and march toward the back.

My heart jumps to my throat when I finally get a glimpse of Jim.

I'm relieved to see he doesn't look too bad. He's still wearing his jeans and undershirt, but his flannel is gone. His hands are cuffed in front of him. There are streaks of dirt on his muscular arms and white shirt, but other than that, he appears unharmed. No bruises. No bloody nose. I'm grateful for that. He's been in their custody since yesterday, so it could be a lot worse.

I wasn't sure what I was expecting. A mangled face, maybe? But no, they would want everyone to see him clearly. To relish the fear and defeat in his eyes before the bullets tear into his flesh.

There is no fear, though, as the two men drag him up the wooden steps to the platform. They don't push him onto his knees. He stands tall, shoulders straight, face utterly expressionless. Until his shuttered gaze sweeps the crowd and lands on me. Only then does he react. Just slightly. His jaw tics, lips tightening.

For the first time in nearly twenty-four hours, I feel a poke in my mind.

Panic lodges in my throat, because what is he *doing*? His arms are bare. Everyone will know if he—

But they already know, I remind myself, the panic dulling into resignation.

I let him in, needing to hear his voice.

"Get out of here, Wren. Now. You can't be here."

"I'm not leaving."

"Freak!" yells someone in the crowd.

"'Fect!"

They see what I'm seeing. It's less noticeable in the morning sun than when he uses his gifts at night—then, his veins are silver signposts. But we can all see them now. Rippling. It's like liquid silver moving through them.

Suddenly Jim's head is thrown back. Somebody hurled a rock at him. Outrage sizzles up my spine. If I had my rifle, that asshole would already be dead.

The Command officers immediately train their rifles on the mob.

"Enough!" one shouts. "He'll get his due soon enough."

"How do we stop this?" I ask Jim.

"We can't. You really shouldn't be here."

"Where else would I be?"

I scan my surroundings in desperation. I need a weapon, but the citizens are unarmed. The only weapons belong to the officers on the platform. Close-range assault rifles. They'll do. One of the men is speaking into his comm now. I can try to distract him and—

"Don't even think about it," Jim admonishes.

I glare at him. I don't like the acceptance in his expression. It wasn't there before, but now his face is bordering on defeated. Jim's not stupid. He understands that if I'm here alone, that means the network didn't find him worthy of rescue. And if he's not trying to fight his way out, that means he knows there's no point.

A second truck rumbles out of the tunnel.

The firing squad has arrived.

I've never witnessed an execution before. Hell, I've only been to the city twice in my life—that I can remember, anyway. Both times on a leisure pass with Griff and Tana. But it wasn't leisure; it was an Uprising mission. And I call it a mission, but really, we just handed some stolen comms to a kid who barely looked older than thirteen, and he darted off into an alleyway. Uncle Jim had been grumbling in my head the entire time, worried sick. He rarely travels to the Point to avoid being identified, yet look where that got us. Fifteen years of keeping him out of sight and he's recognized at home. Because of me.

It takes everything not to break out in sobs. He's standing there, hair falling into his face, hands bound, veins exposing him as the freak these people believe he is, and it's all because of me.

The squad consists of six men and two women, all in navy-blue Command jumpsuits. They climb the steps and dutifully line up at one end of the platform. Anger rips through me. One of them is a stocky young man with a shaved head whose eyes are glittering with what I can only describe as anticipation. He's excited for this. The others just appear bored. I think that makes me angrier. These people are about to shoot a man to death, and they look *bored*.

"Wren..."

Jim's warning echoes in my mind. He must see the murder in my eyes.

"I'm not going to let this happen," I growl at him.

But what can I do?

Maybe they'll accept a trade? Me for him?

... which is such an asinine idea, because come on, two Mods are better than one. If I identified myself, I'd be right alongside him awaiting my own hail of bullets. And maybe that's what I deserve, because I'm the reason he's up there.

"You need to go now." There's sadness in his voice.

Emotion clogs my throat. I can barely see through the sheen of tears. I discreetly bend my head toward my shoulder to wipe my face, trying to make it look like I'm scratching something. I can't let these people catch me crying, can't let them see I'm affected.

The woman beside me gives me a funny look. She's got pale hair and delicate features, and her cheeks are flushed with exhilaration. She has two children with her. Young children. As if they're on a family outing. Like they secured themselves a leisure pass to Ward B to visit the only zoo on the Continent. Jim is the caged animal they're fawning over, on display for their amusement. I don't know this woman, but I loathe her.

One of the officers steps up to the edge of the platform. The top of his left sleeve bears a colonel's patch. It's the same rank Jim had when my mother begged him to smuggle me out of the Point. She knew she'd never be able to keep me safe. I was already displaying powers at the age of five, gifts that for most people don't manifest until twelve. She was terrified for me.

Colonel was also the rank my mother held when she was shot for treason herself. I wonder if it happened on this platform. Maybe she stood right where Jim is standing. Maybe her blood still stains the wooden slats beneath his bare feet.

"Julian Ash, the Continental Tribunal has found you guilty of treason and concealment." The colonel's voice booms through the plaza. "And as such, you have been sentenced to die."

A roar goes through the crowd. This thrills them. Animals.

"Do you have any final words?"

My uncle stares back at him, stone-faced. But that hardness is not what I hear in my head. When he speaks to me, it's with the utmost tenderness, albeit gruff.

"I love you, Wren. I hope you know that."

My stomach twists. It feels like someone is squeezing my heart, jagged fingernails digging into every cavity, making the hot, achy mass shriek in my chest.

"No words? Excellent. That makes our lives easier," the colonel sneers. Then he and his officer step off the platform to stand to the side, and my entire body begins to shake.

Fear and hysteria whip around inside me like the loose cable that got dislodged at the ranch in a thunderstorm last month. The thing was whipping in the air, creating sparks that bounced off the side of the house and sprayed the porch, snaking along the grass. That's what

I am right now. A live wire twisting desperately, trying to find a safe place to land.

Stop this, I want to shout at the firing squad. *Stop this. Leave him alone.*

"Weapons up!" the colonel shouts.

They raise their weapons and train them on Jim, and I've never experienced more agony than when I see Jim lower his gaze. He won't look at them. He won't look at me. He's given up.

Put your guns down, I want to scream. *Put them down. Put them down.*

A hush of confusion moves through the spectators.

I blink.

Half the squad has lowered their weapons.

The ones who are still in position glance at their comrades in bewilderment. One of the women, a tall brunette, appears puzzled. She shrugs one shoulder, her body twitching. Then she shakes her head a few times as if trying to snap herself out of something. She begins to aim her rifle again and I furiously glare at her. *Put it the fuck down.*

All eight rifles are pointed at the floor now.

I realize they can hear me. They can *hear* me. I feel a familiar surge, like my mind is suddenly alive, exploding with energy. It's the same way I felt the first time I was able to incite Jim in the Blacklands.

That day, I was so startled that I broke the link.

It won't happen today. I'm not going to stop. I'm not going to scare myself into stopping.

A sense of calm washes over me as I stare at the eight people who want to murder my uncle.

Raise your guns to your head, I tell them. *Do it.*

I watch their faces. Their features are frozen masks of confusion and fright. Good, let them feel what I'm feeling.

Raise your guns to your head.

I suck in a breath as a wave of dizziness suddenly overcomes me. I sway slightly. It's taking a lot of mental energy to do this, more than I'm accustomed to.

I notice Jim's head turn sharply toward the crowd, seeking me out. I see a glint of silver as his veins begin to flow. I suspect he's trying to contact me, but there's no room in my head because I've got eight open paths as I struggle to incite the command.

Raise your guns to your head. Raise your guns to your head.

My body feels the toll of incitement, sweat beading across my forehead, my limbs beginning to grow weak. This hadn't happened with Jim, this fatigue. But it's working. They're doing it. The barrels of their rifles are moving. Slowly. Inch by inch.

"What are you doing?" the colonel shouts at his squad.

The stocky man, the one who seemed downright giddy at the prospect of killing somebody, now helplessly fights my command. Fights his own hands as they slowly twist the rifle around. Sweat drips down his face.

Press the barrel to your forehead. Do it now.

"I can't stop this," he gasps out. "Someone else is controlling me!"

Screams and gasps rip through the crowd. The entire squad is now pointing their weapons to their foreheads.

I can scarcely breathe. It's taking every ounce of concentration to introduce the final command.

Pull the trigger, pull the trigger, pull the trigger—

My lungs seize, no oxygen able to get in. It's too difficult. Fireworks explode in my brain. Strange flecks, like gold dust, swirl in my field of vision. I blink, trying to clear them. The lightheadedness is getting worse. I don't know how to control this. I can barely incite one mind, let alone eight, and panic bubbles inside me again because I know I'm losing my grip. It's as if I'm in the creek at the ranch, reaching for the rocks that are wet and slimy with moss, trying to climb out of the water and constantly sliding back in. It's too slippery. I'm trying to find my grip, trying to hold it, trying to—

Pull the trigger, pull the trigger—

My control breaks.

The guns slap forward like an elastic band snapping apart. One, two, three, eight. All of them swing at Jim, and my last command—*pull the trigger*—is all they know.

They fire.

Cries mingle with the sound of gunfire. I almost collapse as bullets pierce into Jim's chest, sending him flying backward. Even as he falls, his shirt stained red, he twists his head toward me. For one heart-stopping second, his eyes lock with mine and I hear him in my head.

"Goodbye, little bird."

He's dead by the time he hits the ground. The link is abruptly gone. He's not in my head anymore. I can't feel his energy. I can't feel anything. For a moment I stand there, utterly numb. The crowd is still in an uproar. Some scream with excitement. Others in horror because they're able to comprehend what they just witnessed.

"Inciter," I hear someone hiss.

I don't know if it's directed at me, but it doesn't matter. I can't draw any suspicion.

Incitement is punishable by death. Not just that, but it's the only high crime in the Continent where the perpetrator doesn't get to plead their case to the Tribunal. Which is a big hellfucking deal. Even an assassination attempt on the General lands you a hearing with the Tribunal.

Inciters, simply put, aren't allowed to exist. We terrify the Primes too much.

Citizens are already drifting away from the platform, making my escape easier. I take one last look at Jim, the man I love more than anyone in this world. Dead. Gone. Then I turn and start to move. Not a full run. Fast enough that I can see the outer gates approaching quickly, but slow enough that I'm not drawing attention to myself.

Except I'm wrong. I haven't gone unnoticed.

I'm ten feet from the exit when someone grabs my shoulder and yanks me backward.

I stumble, trying to regain my balance. I catch a glimpse of a uniform. A blur of motion as a hand raises a Command-issued handgun and a voice hisses past my ear.

"Where do you think you're going?"

CHAPTER 5

There are no windows in this room. I hate windowless rooms. I'm not claustrophobic, not really. The walls aren't closing in on me. I can breathe perfectly fine. It's just this stifling feeling of being trapped like cattle in a pen. No escape routes, no weapons. I can't stand it. It itches my skin and makes me feel like I've got those yellow ants from the Blacklands crawling all over me.

They didn't blindfold me when they brought me to this interrogation room, so my brain keeps running through the sequence of turns and corridors we took to get here. *Right, left, right, right, left, blue door.* Just have to reverse course when I find the opportunity to escape. *Blue door, right, left, left, right, left.* I repeat the directions like a mantra in my head while I wait for the Command to remember I exist.

It doesn't take long. The door opens less than a minute later, and two of them walk in. A young man and woman in their early twenties. They both have dark hair, hers tied in a low ponytail, his cropped short. Her eyes are hazel. Shrewd and narrowed. His are dark brown, almost as black as the coffee Jim drinks—drank—every morning.

Without a word, they occupy the chairs across the table from me.

The woman sets down a slate-gray tablet, but its screen remains black. Two pairs of eyes fix on my face. I stare back, not giving a single emotion away.

The door doesn't close. A third person enters.

This time, it takes some effort not to react.

It's the gorgeous jerk from the inn.

I'm not sure what I'm feeling as he shuts the door and then moves to stand in front of it. His gaze lands on mine. Like me, he doesn't react. But I know he recognizes me. He must. It was only two nights ago when I was squished underneath his body. A body that's now clad in navy blue. I should've known he was a soldier. He'd moved like one.

And he's just as attractive as I remember, taking up all the air in the room with his broad frame and stunning face. It irritates me.

"I'm Soldier Tyler Struck," the young woman finally says, her voice cool but polite. "This is Officer Xavier Ford."

She gestures to the man next to her. He's good looking, too, in a more rugged, less typical way than the guy behind them. The guy who doesn't introduce himself. Who continues to stand in silence, his demeanor impossible to decipher. Bored? Annoyed? I can't quite tell.

I know it's futile considering they're Command, but I put out the mental feelers anyway.

Telepathy and mind reading always start the same way: You open a path. The former only works with Mods, as our brains come equipped with that second frequency Jim taught me about. The positive energy waves. With the latter, whether you're trying to infiltrate a Mod or a Prime, you're tapping into the first frequency, where the target mind will actively resist your attempts by releasing negative energy. The brain's built-in warning system.

If the target mind is well shielded, you don't even get the chance to try to disarm the alarm. But if there's any weakness in that shield, even the tiniest crack, it's just a matter of finding your way in.

These three? Their shields are so thick, it's like slamming into a brick wall at a hundred miles an hour. The thin ropes I throw out bounce right back at me and rattle like chains in my own head.

I'm intrigued. These people aren't regular soldiers. They're not like

Jordan from Copper Block. They've clearly had extensive training in shielding.

Silver Block. That would be my guess.

"How were you able to incite eight minds?" Struck asks without preamble.

I gape at her. "What on earth makes you think I'm the one who did that?"

"You're saying you aren't?"

"Of course I'm not." I put a little stammer into the words. I'm a good actress. It's one of the reasons why Jim always trusted me to handle the soldiers in Hamlett.

"Well, we know it wasn't the prisoner. He was cleared."

I'm afraid to know how they "cleared" him, and once again, I worry about what Jayde Valence might have seen inside Jim's mind.

"So, if it wasn't him . . . that leaves you." Struck tips her head toward me.

"It wasn't me."

"Really," she says. It's not a question.

"First of all, I'm not Aberrant," I tell them. "And second, even if I was, it's not possible to control so many minds like that."

"It is possible because we saw it happen." Ford adopts a disinterested voice, but there's a hard edge to it. He flicks up a brow. "Did you not see it happen, sweetling?"

My jaw tightens at both the term of endearment and his derisive tone. "Don't call me that. And I don't know *what* I saw. All I know is that you killed my uncle."

Struck is startled for a second, as if she didn't expect me to bring up Jim before they did. But the best way to handle an interrogation is to pretend you have nothing to hide.

"Isn't that why we're here?" I say flatly. "You killed my uncle."

Ford folds his arms against his chest and leans back slightly. "Your uncle was a deserter of the Command."

"Bullshit. I know that's what you charged him with, but . . ." I shake my head and repeat myself. "Bullshit."

"Got it, sweetling. So you're claiming you had no idea who your uncle was. How are you related exactly?"

"We're not," I answer, this time deciding to ignore the mocking endearment. "Not by blood, anyway. He adopted me."

Struck brings the tablet to life, pressing her thumb to its scanner to gain entry. My gaze shifts toward the doorway where Mr. Silent continues to watch us. His hands rest loosely on his belt loops, face revealing no expression as he meets my gaze. He holds the eye contact for so long that my pulse speeds up, and I'm the one to break it off. Which is unlike me. I never back down.

I try to focus on the screen that Struck is now swiping her finger across. When a photograph appears, she enlarges it.

It's Jim, and my heart clenches at the sight of him. I deliberately let the grief show on my face.

She pushes the tablet toward me. "This is Colonel Julian Ash."

"You can call him whatever you want, but that's not his name."

"It's his name. This is Julian Ash, a colonel from Silver Block who deserted fifteen years ago. He fled not long after losing his entire unit in a bombing at Sun Post."

"No," I counter, tapping the picture, "this is Jim Darlington. And I don't believe a word you're telling me, not for a second. Jim is not a deserter."

"Yes, he is. Not only that, but he's also Aberrant."

I start to laugh. "Of all the lies you just said about him, that's my favorite."

"Let's not play games," Xavier Ford says, rolling his eyes. "You were at the execution. According to reports, his arms were practically glowing."

"Your reports are wrong. I didn't see anything of the sort." I cross my arms and dare him to challenge me.

"We ran a background check on you, too," Struck continues.

She swipes the screen until she's showing me a picture of myself. It was taken last year for my ID. The Company requires citizens to update our photos annually.

"Wren Darlington," she recites from the page. "You didn't exist until you were eight years old."

"That's when Jim found me."

"Found you," Ford echoes doubtfully.

I shrug. "I can't remember anything before that."

Their skepticism grows. The gorgeous face at the door still discloses nothing.

"If you have my file, then you should have all my mentalist reports, too."

Jim was smart. First thing he did when we left the Blacklands and resettled in Ward Z was send me for a children's mental health assessment. I was an accomplished liar then, too.

"She concluded that whatever trauma I experienced as a kid caused memory loss," I go on. "Nobody knows exactly what happened to my parents, but they may have died in an Aberrant attack. I guess there'd been some ambushes in the area where Jim found me wandering."

"Right." Ford chuckles. "This benevolent nomad who found you on the side of the road, took you under his wing, and adopted you as his own. How nice of him."

"It's a really fucking depressing world you live in if you think people can't help others. Is it so hard to believe someone might just be a good person?"

"Julian Ash was not a good person."

"Stop calling him that," I snap, and then glimpse the hint of a shift in Struck's expression. She's starting to believe me.

I haven't won Ford over yet. As for the man at the door, I have no idea where he stands on any of this.

"Jim is a good person," I insist. "I've lived with him since I was eight years old. That's *twelve* years. Trust me, if he was an Aberrant super soldier, I would have known about it. He would have slipped up at some point."

"You did know about it," Ford says. "Because you're lying to us right now."

"I'm not lying. I live on a ranch. Jim is a rancher. *Was* a rancher."

A lump forms in my throat. I don't even have to fake this part. The memory of his bullet-ridden body crumpling to the wooden platform is like a knife directly to the heart.

"Ranchers, huh?" Ford leans back in his chair again. "How many head of cattle?"

"Two hundred." I frown, pretending not to understand why he's asking.

"What kind?"

"Cows. Some heifers. You should know," I can't help but jeer. "Our cattle feed you and your army."

Struck speaks again. "You know, I've never been on a ranch. Why don't you tell us about the ranching life?"

Ford nods, looking amused. "Yes, sweetling. Enlighten us. Describe a day in the life of a rancher."

I stare at them. "Seriously? You guys think I've been pretend-ranching my entire life? Why don't you come talk to me after you've had your entire arm up a cow during calving season, keen?"

"Describe your day." Ford is unfazed by my sarcasm.

With feigned annoyance, I go along with their request. For the next hour, it's a barrage of questions from the relentless duo, and not a single word from the dark-haired man. My eyes flit toward him more than once. Assessing. Sometimes admiring. His short-sleeved version of the Command uniform means I can see tattoos swirling out of his sleeves, winding around his biceps and forearms. I can't make out what they are.

When Struck brings up the incitement incident again, I force myself to focus.

"Do you see what I'm wearing?" I gesture to myself. I'm in a tank top. "If I was standing in the crowd, somehow inside the heads of eight people and forcing them to do whatever the hell they were doing, someone would have seen me doing it. The Aberrant glow when they do their psychic stuff." I play as dumb as I can, choosing words a lowly Prime villager would use.

"Why did you run then?" Struck asks, slanting her head. "Why were you spotted trying to flee the scene of—"

"Because you just killed my uncle!"

I take a breath and pretend to calm myself down.

Really, I'm steady as can be. Not rattled in the slightest. I feel grief, yes. Concern, perhaps, about how long they'll hold me here. But I know eventually they'll release me back to my ward. I've done nothing wrong. Not to them, anyway.

The only crime I committed is not being able to save Jim's life.

That'll be something I punish myself for until my dying breath.

"I'm sorry." I exhale again. "I didn't mean to yell at you. But I didn't *do* anything. All I know is that I was enjoying myself at my village's Liberty Day celebration a couple of nights ago"—I spare a glance at the silent soldier—"and the next morning, the Command came and took my uncle away. Do you honestly think I was just going to stay in Z? Of course not. You took my uncle. *Of course* I came here to get him back."

"So you admit you were trying to interfere with Command business?" Ford lifts an eyebrow again.

"No, I was trying to save my uncle because he didn't do anything wrong. You guys are wrong. About all of it." I shove the tablet toward them. "Jim is not a 'fect. We can go through your file, page by page, line by line, and it wouldn't change a damn thing in my eyes."

"No. This man, your uncle, the corpse with all those bullets in his chest"—I flinch at Ford's gruesome description—"is Colonel Julian Ash. His fingerprints confirmed it."

"You're lying."

"The fingerprints confirmed it," Struck reiterates. "We don't know how Ash managed to switch out his prints in the Company's system—"

I do. We have people everywhere.

"—but they were compared with the ones from his Command file and it's a perfect match."

"I don't believe you," I say stubbornly, while inside I'm beyond grateful they can't find fault in my own file. Children aren't printed and logged in the Continental ID system until the age of twelve, which means these people will never know who I was before I entered the database. As far as they're concerned, I've always been Wren Darlington.

"You don't believe us, huh? What a coincidence. We don't believe you, either." Ford smirks as he pushes his chair back.

They both rise. Struck tucks the tablet under her arm.

"What? That's it?" I wrinkle my forehead. "We're done?"

"Oh no, sweetling," Ford says. "We've just begun."

They approach the door, waiting for the stranger from the inn to step aside.

"What about you?" I demand, glowering at his back. "Mr. Silent over here. Got nothing to say? Who are you?"

He stops, turning to spare me a glance over his shoulder. His lips curve slightly as he finally speaks.

"I'm the one who decides whether you walk out of here alive."

CHAPTER 6

They leave me in the room for nearly three hours. Alone, but not truly alone. I'm conscious of the red light in the corner of the ceiling. They're watching me, so I maintain an anguished expression. They need to believe I'm scared. Worried about what they'll do to me. I slump forward in the chair, wringing my hands on the cool tabletop. Meanwhile, I'm taking advantage of the veins I've been gifted with and attempting to link with Declan. But the man is taking the role of *silent contact* literally. As in, he remains emphatically silent. I guess I'm not surprised. They tried to set me up in a safe house and I ran. He's probably pissed.

Besides, they couldn't be bothered to rescue Jim, and he'd once been a crucial cog in the Uprising machine. I'm not even crucial-adjacent.

That makes me disposable.

Tana is also quiet, which is cause for concern. Declan said my village was teeming with soldiers, and that was before I got detained. Are they questioning anyone who might know me? I hope Tana and Griff are safe, but as long as she keeps our link closed, all I can do is worry and pray.

When Ford and Mr. Silent return, they're accompanied by a different woman.

This one doesn't need an introduction.

It's Jayde Valence.

Anxiety flutters in my stomach. I've never heard of a single person who's come out triumphant in an interrogation with Valence.

Even Uncle Jim's shield couldn't hold up.

I try not to stare at her, but it's difficult. It's no secret why the General, who ranks Mods on the same level as the rabid rats that scurry in the Point's alleys, chose to swallow his revulsion and allow Jayde into his inner circle. She's too powerful a tool not to use. Proof of that is literally written on her face. Her bloodmark sits high on her left cheek. It's a perfect red circle, about two inches in diameter and a stark contrast with her lily-white skin.

I shudder to think about what might have been if my own mark appeared somewhere other than my thigh. Would Jim have burned my face? I'd like to believe he wouldn't have, but deep down I know the answer is yes. He made my parents a promise, and he would've gone to any lengths to protect me.

Jayde walks toward the table. The two men flank the door, leaning against the cinder-block walls. Arms crossed. Bored expressions.

"Wren Darlington," she says.

"Yes."

"My name is Jayde."

"I know who you are."

She lifts her brow.

"I've seen you on broadcasts with the General."

She nods.

Her pale hair is tied at her nape in a severe knot, emphasizing her cheekbones. She's much prettier in person. But her symmetrical features and heart-shaped mouth aren't enough to distract me from what she is.

A traitor.

A sympathizer.

She oppresses and kills other Mods. People like her make me sick.

I swallow my disgust and try to settle my nerves. Level my emotions. But my confidence is slipping because . . . what if I'm not good enough?

Jim taught me how to shield. How to construct a steel vault around my mind and keep it tightly locked and thick enough that nothing can penetrate it. Except that wasn't all we practiced. He also showed me how to leave that vault door open a crack and empty the mind it protects. Clear that mind until it's nothing but blackness. Silence. And then . . .

Think whatever you want them to hear.

I'm already starting to prepare my mind as Jayde pulls out the chair in front of me. Jim told me there was a study conducted on Modified brains once that determined there was no difference in the number of thoughts a Mod held in their brain compared with a Prime. That same study revealed we think about ten thousand thoughts a day. Some people think more, some less. It averages to six or seven thoughts per minute.

Of course, that's without factoring in the anxiety. An innocent person would be nervous in my current situation. My mind should be racing.

Jayde sits and stares at me. She doesn't say another word.

This is the interrogation I've heard about from people in the Up-rising. She won't ask a single question.

When she forms a path, it's not subtle. She's not trying to hide it. She isn't gently pushing her way into my mind as if dipping a timid toe into frigid water. There's a reason for that. Because if you don't ease into it, it sends an electric shock up the back of a Mod's neck. It's nearly impossible not to react, not to jerk, flinch, move, when an electric current courses through you.

Unless you've trained for that, too.

Unless you experienced that shock from the age of five, repeatedly, mercilessly, while you sat in the Blacklands training with Julian Ash to decoy your mind.

I don't even blink as I feel her thrust her way in.

She continues to stare at me.

"Are you going to say anything?" I ask in aggravation.

Why isn't she talking?

What is wrong with her?

She stares.

"Okay," I say.

Self-consciousness washes over me. I try to avoid her eyes by staring down at my hands, but Xavier Ford barks at me from the door.

"Look at her."

I gulp and raise my gaze to Valence.

She's trying to read my mind. She must be.

The General is a fool if he thinks he can trust her. I don't care how long she's been working for him. You can't trust those people.

I meet her gaze head-on now.

I. Don't. Trust. You.

Do you hear me, you toxic bitch?

She stares.

Unblinking.

She would've reacted if she was in my head, right? I would react to that.

These people are out of their minds. Why do they think I'm Aberrant?

I didn't do anything wrong.

Fucking prickholes killed Uncle Jim.

There's no way he's who they say he is.

He can't be.

What if he is?

"I know what you're doing and it's a waste of time." My frustration accelerates my heartbeat. "Can you please just say something?"

She stares.

What does she think is about to happen? Her silence will scare me into confessing to crimes I didn't commit? I wonder if people actually do that.

But what if he was *Aberrant?*

They said his arms were glowing at the execution. I didn't see anything glowing, damn it!

If he was defected, then that means he lied to me this whole time. It means I was living *with one of them.*

What if he could read my mind, too?

I choke down a strangled noise.

Was Jim a goddamn 'fect?

"Say something!" I snap at her.

She stares.

I glance at the door again. This time I'm not reprimanded for it.

He might be a total prick, but that Xavier guy is smoke. I wonder if he's going with anybody. They probably don't fraternize in Command. Or maybe he's gay. I don't know. I just want to get out of here.

I want to go home.

What if Jim lied to me?

I

want

to

go

home.

I bite my lip hard.

Do not cry in front of this woman.

Jayde slides her chair back.

Where is she going?

Where are you going, you feckless quat!

"What's going on? Where are you going?"

She ignores me. At the door, she flicks her cool gray eyes at Mr. Silent.

"She's clean. Do with her what you see fit."

Jayde exits the room. I feel the path close, the mental connection break, yet I maintain the decoy. While Mr. Silent swipes a finger over the screen of his tablet and Ford stands there in silence, I allow the false thoughts to run rampant for another sixty seconds.

It's only when I'm finally thinking my own thoughts again that the wave of relief slams into me. Primal and dizzying.

I did it.

I actually did it.

I fooled Jayde Valence.

I open a path to tell Jim, only to feel the hot stab of agony in my chest. I keep forgetting the link isn't there anymore. The reminder is gut wrenching, and it takes all my willpower not to keel over in tears. He's truly gone.

Why did my shield hold up against Jayde when his didn't? How was I able to decoy my mind and Jim couldn't—when *he's* the one who taught me how to do it in the first place. He was far more skilled at decoying than I could ever be, so why—

Because of me.

Dread grips my throat as the thought occurs to me. What if Uncle Jim *did* decoy his mind during his interrogation, feeding Jayde a train of thought that deliberately led her away from me?

With my composure in danger of crumbling, I order myself not to think about Jim. Not here, and not now. Later. Think about him later.

Mr. Silent moves his finger across the screen one last time before addressing Ford. "Put her in Stock C until I'm ready for her."

Until he's ready for me?

Because *that* isn't ominous.

———

The cell is painted a dull shade of gray that hurts my eyes. There's a metal sink and toilet in the corner, and a single bed that takes up most of the limited space. I assume this is where the base holds its prisoners. It's cramped and cold, but at least this room has a window, making it an upgrade from the last one.

After the door locks with an electronic beep, I climb onto the bed and try to peer out the window, which is barred and grimy. It's set too high to offer a view of anything beyond the bleak concrete courtyard one story beneath it.

I sink onto the worn mattress and breathe in the stale air.

Do with her what you see fit.

The uncertainty of my fate gnaws at my insides. My life is in the hands of strangers, and I don't like it. Not only that, but this is the first time since I woke up at the crack of dawn that I'm able to reflect on what happened in the South Plaza today.

I controlled eight minds.

Eight.

I almost killed eight people.

Eight.

My stomach twists, sending a rush of bile to my throat that I force myself to choke down. I don't regret what I did. I was trying to save the most important person in my life.

But the *way* I did it . . .

My body begins to tremble, and I curl over on the mattress to wrap my arms around my knees. I don't care if they're watching me. I wasn't allowed to fall apart during their daylong interrogation, but it's fair game now.

Some people find power addictive, but I want nothing to do with the one I've been cursed with. I don't want the ability to incite. I don't fucking *want* it. I can't erase the looks on their faces when they realized their own weapons were out of their control. The idea of interfering with someone's autonomy, the thought of someone ever doing that to *me*, makes me want to vomit.

Yet at the same time, I wish I'd succeeded in killing every member of that firing squad, because then Jim might still be alive. But he's dead, and now I want nothing more than to see *them* dead. The need for vengeance is so strong, I can taste it.

They'll pay. Every last one of them.

I don't know how, and I don't know when, but even if I have to use incitement again to do it, I'll make them pay.

I sit up and lean back against the wall, hugging my knees. When I feel the poke in my mind, I'm overcome with relief.

It's Tana.

"Wren! Are you okay?" she says the second we link. I feel her concern rippling through my body.

"They killed Jim."

I want to bury my head in my hands and cry, but I don't. If there's a camera on me, I'm willing to show some weakness, but not tears. Never tears.

"I know. I'm sorry. Where are you?"

"Command base. Sitting in a cell."

"Fuck."

"I've been trying to link with you since the execution. Where were you?"

"Working. Hamlett's been flooded with soldiers, and the overflow is staying at the inn. I've been behind the front desk all day and being watched like a hawk. They're questioning everyone in the village. Asking about Jim. About you."

"I know. They've been interrogating me all day."

I gnaw on my bottom lip, debating whether to tell her about my encounter with Jayde Valence. On one hand, it's the kind of feat that would provide a Mod with boasting rights in perpetuity.

But Tana has no idea how powerful my abilities are. That I've got a bloodmark hidden beneath layers of burnt flesh.

"We've also been hearing there was an inciter at Jim's execution," Tana says, a note of awe in her voice.

Yeah.

She doesn't know about that, either.

"I honestly don't know what everyone is talking about," I tell her. "I was there. I didn't see anything that looked like incitement. I think the squad was just confused about when they were supposed to fire."

The lie triggers a jolt of guilt. But I made Jim a promise a long time ago that I would never reveal, not to a single living soul, that I possess the power to incite, and I don't plan on breaking that promise today.

"Anyway," I say, eager to change the subject. "We can talk about that later. Right now I need you to contact someone from the network. Someone high on the food chain. They need to get me out of here."

There's a long beat.

"Tana?"

"Nobody's coming to get you."

I swallow my resentment. Nice. Good to know where I stand.

"They said you had your chance at a safe house and a new identity, and you chose to run. Polly told me to check in when we know what they're going to do with you."

"I have to go."

"Wren—"

"I need to think. I'll talk to you later."

I sever the link and ignore her subsequent pokes. The only voice in my head I can concentrate on right now is my own. I need to consider my options.

Are there any?

The network isn't interested in rescuing me, but even if they were, then what? I'll be shuttled from one safe house to another for the rest of my life? Live in hiding? Locate a surgeon who will alter my appearance so that I can return to society and live in plain sight of the Command? The amount of Luxury credits required for even a few paltry cosmetic injections is astronomical—I can't imagine how much a full-blown facial reconstruction would cost.

And anyway, fuck that. I like my face.

I suppose I could try to track down a Faithful camp, but I don't find that option at all appealing, and not only because they'd likely kill me on sight. Those people don't take kindly to strangers. I remember a few years back, when two teenage boys from Hamlett went missing after they decided to search for a Faithful camp rumored to have sprung up in the woods outside of town. Controller Fletcher's men found the boys' skeletons a year later in the remnants of an abandoned campsite.

But more than the fear of my skeleton turning up in a forest a year from now, I'm not a believer that the Old Era was any better than this new one. Or at least, I'm not sure how it could be, given that it led to global destruction.

I clasp my fingers over my knees and think about how limited my options are. How utterly hellfucked I am. The sun is setting, and the cell is losing the meager light the tiny window allows in. Although there's a strip of fluorescent lighting across the ceiling, it doesn't give off any light. Maybe it's on a timer.

Another hour passes. Now the room is bathed in shadows. But only for a few minutes. As I'd guessed, the ceiling lights flicker on as if on cue. They proceed to make a crackling noise that I'm forced to listen to for another hour before it softens to a barely audible hum.

Footsteps echo in the hallway. I instantly tense, waiting. So far, every set of steps has passed right by.

This one stops at my cell.

I hear the sharp beep of a keypad, and then the door opens.

My pulse quickens when Mr. Silent walks in. He's no longer in his Command uniform. Now he wears black pants and a black shirt made of a stretchy material, its long sleeves hugging the defined muscles of his arms.

He steps inside, silhouetted by the overhead light. Anyone else standing in that harsh glare would look pinched and severe—these unforgiving shadows aren't your friend. Yet his face remains nothing less than stunning. Someone this pretty shouldn't be a soldier. He'd probably be raking in the credits if he worked in Human Services. He'd make an excellent whore. The elites in the Point would pay up the nose for a couple of hours in a bedroom with him.

He gives me an appraising once-over.

I wonder what he's seeing. I can't even imagine what I look like right now. I feel tired and grimy, and my hair is loose and messy from my fingers running through it all evening. I hop off the mattress so we're both standing. He still towers over me, but it's better than giving him the upper hand by remaining subserviently seated.

"My name is Cross."

I hide my surprise. I didn't expect a proper introduction. I raise my brow. "What kind of name is Cross? Is that your surname?"

He lifts an answering brow. "Funny that someone named after a bird feels like she's in any position to critique mine. Why Wren and not Sparrow? Or Dove?"

I narrow my eyes.

"I'm the captain of Silver Block," he continues.

I *knew* they were Silver Block. Their ironclad shields. Their interrogation methods. The smug confidence.

"Captain Cross," I mock. "Aren't you a little young for that rank?" He can't be a day older than twenty-two.

He ignores that and says, "You can call me captain or sir. No preference."

"What about Asshole? Can I call you that?"

He ignores that, too. "Did anyone bring you dinner rations?"

"No," I say tightly. "I assumed your plan to starve me to death had commenced."

"Nobody wants you to starve." His voice takes on a mocking note. "We need you strong and healthy for the Program."

Tension stiffens my shoulders. "What the hell does that mean?"

"It means you're joining the Command." He smiles without a trace of humor. "You start tomorrow."

CHAPTER 7

My heart drops as his words wash over me, the gravity of my situation sinking in.

No.

Never.

My list of available options might be more meager than a Ward B citizen's cupboards, but I'd rather eat rats than become a Command trainee.

"What?" I say, my lips parting in surprise.

"I don't enjoy repeating myself." Cross swivels toward the door.

"Don't you dare leave without an explanation."

He turns back, one eyebrow raised. "I'm curious. When did I give you the impression you're entitled to an explanation?"

"It's common courtesy."

"Do I look courteous to you?" He sounds amused. But he folds his arms and takes pity on me. "I've decided not to send you back to your ward. Your skills will be better utilized here."

"No, my skills are needed at my ranch. My animals rely on me, and without my uncle, there's nobody to take care of—"

"Your ranch has been reassigned. The new residents take possession tomorrow morning."

My heart sinks even further at his words. Now I'm in serious danger of breaking down in tears. The ranch is my home. My eyes sting as I struggle to breathe normally. I know it's Company practice. Houses get reassigned all the time. Citizens transfer to new industries if the Company orders it. But I don't care if it's a common occurrence.

They gave away my *home*.

Indignation rises inside me. Who did they assign it to? What if the new caretaker doesn't treat the animals well? What if they mistreat Kelley? The thought of never seeing my sweet mare again cuts at my insides.

"Then let me go work for the new residents," I find myself pleading. It sickens me to beg this man for anything. "I'd be a good ranch hand."

"No."

I'm trembling with anger. "I'm not joining the Command."

"It's either that or one of the labor camps."

"Fine. I pick the labor camp."

"You don't have a choice in the matter."

I growl out loud. "Then why did you make it seem like labor was an option?"

One corner of his mouth ticks up. I swear I glimpse a glint of humor in his blue eyes. "The illusion of choice can be comforting to some people."

"You're such a prick." I take a calming breath.

He ignores that, too. "You'll spend the night here in the stockade. Rations will be provided shortly. Tomorrow morning someone will come and take you to shower and dress before orientation."

"Orientation?"

"Impeccable timing, isn't it?" He's mocking me again. "You falling into our hands the day before the new session starts. Almost like it was meant to be."

"No." The thought of becoming a pawn in the General's war machine against Mods fills me with a sickening dread.

"What's the matter? Think you won't be able to cut it?"

"I can cut it just fine, *Cross*. I'm simply not interested in taking orders from the people who murdered my uncle."

Just like that, his broad shoulders snap into a straight line. He fixes me with a deadly look and takes a step toward me. I instinctively step back, then curse myself for ceding that ground.

"Your uncle was a deserter of the Command and a traitor to the Company. Which means you either know more than you're telling us, or you were too stupid to figure out the truth about your guardian."

He moves closer. This time, I hold my ground. Inches separate our bodies now.

Cross bends until his mouth is close to my ear. "And I suspect that you, *Dove*, are not stupid."

His nearness raises the tiny hairs at the nape of my neck. Heart pounding, I force myself to meet his gaze.

"In case you've forgotten, Jayde Valence was inside my head. Isn't she some powerful mind reader? If I'd known what my uncle was, she would've seen it in my thoughts."

The reminder does nothing to erase the suspicion in his eyes.

"If you think I'm a liar, then why are you sending me to the Program?" I grumble.

"Because I don't trust you. Not one damn bit." He shrugs. "Lieutenant Colonel Valence believes you're not a threat. I've yet to determine whether I agree with her assessment. So until I do, I'm keeping you under close watch."

"Don't I feel special."

"You should," he says frankly. "Not many citizens get the opportunity to train for Silver Block. It's a highly competitive program, and ninety percent of applicants are rejected. I suggest you don't fuck this up. A post with Silver comes with its perks."

I tip my chin in defiance. "What is this, then—a punishment or an opportunity?"

"Also yet to be determined."

He turns to the door, and I call out before he can leave. I don't want him to go. He might be a prick, but I don't want to be left alone in this cell again. Time moves too slowly within these cramped walls, each second stretching into eternity, and I can't feel that pervasive sense of isolation again. I'm not meant for confinement. Some people can stomach it. I'm not one of them.

"If ninety percent of applicants get rejected, what makes you think I belong to the ten percent? You're placing a lot of faith in these alleged skills you think I possess."

He glances at me in amusement. "Do you really want to play this game?"

I frown. "What game?"

"The one where we pretend I didn't see you put a bullet in a white coyote's eye from two hundred yards away."

Shit.

He notes my expression and smirks. "Did you truly believe I wouldn't follow you after you left the inn that night?"

Of course he did.

"That was a fluke shot," I lie. "I'm decent with a rifle but nowhere near that good."

"Guess we'll find out soon enough."

Chuckling, he leaves the cell and locks me inside.

I clamp my teeth together so I can't unleash a scream. Why did Jim have to teach me how to shoot?

And why am I so good at it?

And why the *hell* did he leave me?

You left me! I silently shout at him—at the place in my mind where his signature should be. *You fucking left me!*

It happens then. The tears spill over, sending two warm rivulets pouring down my face. I collapse on the mattress and cry into my palms, cameras be damned. I have no energy left inside me to maintain the mask. I'm a broken, pathetic girl who's all alone in this broken, pathetic world. Uncle Jim is gone. Tana and her father will be there for me, I know that, but they're not Jim.

I have nothing now. No Jim. No ranch.

Except I feel Wolf trying to link with me later, and I remember I'm not entirely alone. My oldest friend is still out there somewhere. At least until they get him, too. They will one day. General Redden won't stop until we're all either dead or enslaved to him.

"Hi." It's all I'm capable of saying, and I don't miss the way that lone syllable wobbles.

"Are you crying?"

I don't blame him for sounding so startled. I'm not the type to show weakness.

"No. I think I'm falling ill. I'm glad you reached out. I need a distraction."

"Why's that?"

"Bad day," is all I say. I'd never endanger Wolf by telling him I'm in enemy hands. "Distract me. What are you doing right now?"

"I'm looking at the ocean."

Something clenches in my chest. I think it's wistfulness. One of the few details I know about Wolf's location is that he's near the coast, and I envy him for it. I've only seen the ocean once, when my uncle and I drove out to the very edge of Z after I spent weeks begging him to take me. At school, we'd been learning about the geography of the Continent before the Last War, and the idea of this vast body of water full of salt and marvelous creatures was one I couldn't get out of my mind. I *had* to see it. Jim eventually capitulated, and the experience was one I can only describe as humbling.

That day I realized how utterly insignificant we are to this planet.

"It sounds beautiful. I wish I could see it. Is it choppy? Calm?"

"Calm. Not even a ripple."

"Beautiful."

"Daisy . . . why did you have a bad day?"

I want to tell him. I will, eventually, but not tonight. If I talk about Jim and the gaping hole in my heart that the loss of him has left me with, I'll only break down.

"I don't want to dwell on it. Tell me more about the ocean."

———

I sleep in fits and starts. The cell is too cold, the mattress too firm. In the morning, a female soldier collects me from my cell and takes me to a large locker room with a separate shower area. She hands me a pile of clothing and a toothbrush, then waits outside in the hall while I get ready.

The shower is nice, but the clothes provided aren't. Slim pants and a short-sleeved shirt, both navy blue. Socks and ankle boots, both black. The shirt has the word RECRUIT stitched over the left breast, with a number beneath it.

Fifty-six.

This is my worst nightmare. I'm utterly defenseless and in enemy territory. Prey among predators, only they don't yet realize I'm prey, and if they learn the truth, I'll suffer the same fate as Jim and my mother.

I meet my eyes in the mirror. *You will find a way out of here.*

I have to. If the Uprising can't be bothered to help me, then I'll simply have to help myself. Sooner or later, a plan will reveal itself to me. Until then, sit tight. Play along. Protect my identity.

My name is Wren Darlington and I am not a Mod.

I've been hiding who I am my entire life. Today will be no different.

The soldier appraises my attire when I emerge from the locker room. She nods and says, "I'll be escorting you to the training center."

I've given up on trying to memorize the layout of this base. It's a maze within a maze. To get to the training center, we exit through a set of metal doors and climb into a Command truck. I study the woman's profile, then the ID number on her sleeve. Command uniforms display numbers, not names. The lone dark-gray star tells me she's a soldier from Tin Block.

She drives us through an open courtyard toward a large structure. Ugly, gray, rectangular, endless. "The barracks are in the west end of the facility." She points to the left. "Any belongings you brought with you to yesterday's registration were screened and will be waiting for you in your bunk."

"Yesterday your superior officers detained me, locked me up, and informed me I was joining your ranks against my will," I say flatly. "When, and please enlighten me here, did I have time to pack any belongings?"

She doesn't even blink. "If there are items you'd like shipped from your ward, you can put in a request with your CO."

I grit my teeth.

Inside the training center, she marches me down a wide corridor with white walls. We stop at an ominous set of steel doors, where I watch as she presses her thumb to the keypad. After the doors unlock with a jarring buzz, she pushes one open and then glances at me, expectant. I guess I'm supposed to go in.

"Good luck," she says simply, and the doors buzz closed behind me.

I find myself in a cavernous room with cinder-block walls and exposed pipes running along the high ceiling. Rows of workstations line the shiny floor, facing a massive holoscreen that takes up nearly an entire wall. There are two chairs to a table, and not many unoccupied seats left. A sea of navy blue assaults my vision.

The low murmur of voices stutters for a moment as heads swivel at my entrance. I must not make much of an impression, because I'm swiftly dismissed from most gazes. They return to their conversations, only a few curious stares remaining.

I scan the faces of the other recruits. About fifty of them, expressions ranging from nervous anticipation to steely determination. They're a diverse group when it comes to skin and hair color, but to me they're all the same.

Every single one of them is my enemy.

Speaking of enemies, my favorite interrogator Xavier Ford stands at the head of the room. He hasn't noticed me yet; he's busy speaking to another uniformed man whose back is to me. They're with a woman I assume is a civilian, because she wears a white dress and black high-heeled shoes. One of her ears is heavily pierced, which seems incongruous with her elegant outfit.

She's the one who spots me first. She touches Ford's arm, and his cold gaze travels in my direction.

"Take a seat," he barks. "We're about to get started."

There are four available workstations, which means four potential seatmates. Two of them eye me with a level of distrust that implies I'm not welcome. The third is a guy with golden hair and a mischievous glint in his eye. He looks like trouble, and when our gazes meet and he winks at me, it's all the confirmation I need to stay away.

I choose the fourth option: a seat in the second row next to a young woman with light-brown hair arranged in a long braid and tied off with a blue bow. Her face is plain at first glance. On second glance, I notice her freckles and perfectly shaped lips. She's surprisingly pretty.

She gives me a guarded look. "Good morning."

I nod in response and stare straight ahead. The woman in the white dress walks past, her heels clicking loudly on her way to the door. Officer Ford steps forward and crosses his arms, regarding all of us with derision. From the corner of my eye, I see the other soldier handing out small black tablets to those in the first row.

When Ford addresses us, he sounds bored.

"I'm Second Lieutenant Xavier Ford, and I'll be your head instructor for this session. You can call me sir or LT. No preference."

I wonder if he stole the speech from Captain Cross. *Asshole* is taken, so I'll have to call this one *Prick*.

He sweeps his gaze over the room. "Some of you applied for this program. Others were recruited." His eyes flick toward me.

I believe *forced* is the word he's looking for.

"Regardless of how you wound up here, I can guarantee that half of you won't be here eight weeks from now."

Hope blooms inside me. I want to throw my hand up and offer to make it easy for him, walk out right now. But then I picture Captain Cross's face and can predict what the answer will be.

The soldier passing out tablets reaches our workstation. When he places mine on the desktop, my heart freezes inside my chest.

I know him.

CHAPTER 8

When I was young, my uncle used to take me to a neighboring town every few months to pick up supplies for the ranch. The feed store was owned by a woman named Morlee Hadley. Partially owned, anyway. The Company holds a fifty-one percent stake in all Continental businesses, which is the reason I've never seen any advantage in joining the business sector. Earning some extra Luxury credits and leisure passes doesn't seem worth it to me. But some people enjoy the perks, and Morlee was one of them. She loved that store almost as much as she loved her son. *My Matty is so smart. My Matty has big ambitions. My Matty will rule the Continent one day.* She never stopped praising that boy. She adored him.

She adored me, too. She always slipped me a piece of candy whenever Uncle Jim wasn't looking. He was such an unsentimental man, didn't care about spoiling me or using his Lux credits to make my life a little sweeter. Morlee would give me a wink, and then I'd feel a poke in my mind, and when I let her in, her teasing voice would fill my head.

"Our little secret, angel. Don't tell Jim."

"Never," I always promised. Although I'm sure Jim knew. He wasn't stupid.

One day, we walked into the store and someone else was behind the counter. I was so disappointed. I thought she was sick. But she wasn't there the next time, either. Or the time after. And the stern-faced man behind the counter didn't seem concerned that Morlee was gone.

It was only later, through whispers in Hamlett and hushed conversations between Jim and the new owner, that I learned the truth.

Her son turned her in to the Command.

The boy she'd spoken so proudly of had betrayed his own mother and reported her for concealment. Jim eventually told me she'd been sent to a labor camp in the north. Slaving at a salt mine.

Because of this guy standing in front of me.

There's no recognition on his part as he sets the tablet down. I suppose there wouldn't be. I only met him once, and I was a kid. No reason for a seventeen-year-old boy to pay much attention to the twelve-year-old in his mother's feed shop. I've never forgotten his face, though. Morlee was a good woman. She deserved better than a son like him.

I inhale slowly. Force myself not to let my gaze linger, my anger show. Then he moves to the next workstation and some of the tension in my shoulders dissipates. Matt Hadley's presence in this room, on this base, is just a reminder of how much danger I've found myself in.

Jim was right. The Point *is* a den of vipers.

"This," Ford says, holding up a tablet, "is your source. While you're here, it will take the place of your Company comm. It's where you'll receive all communications and alerts, and where you'll find your schedule and progress scores. When we're in session on the base, you should have it on you at all times. When we conduct off-base ops, you'll be fitted with a source on your wrist."

Hadley returns to the front of the room and stands to Ford's left. His posture is ramrod-straight. Expression carved from stone.

"This is Officer Hadley. He'll be one of your instructors."

Officer Hadley. I swallow my distaste as Hadley nods in greeting. It appears being a traitor to your own people, your own mother, helps you rise in the ranks of the Command.

"Scan your thumbs now to activate your source," Hadley orders in a clipped voice.

Everyone else obeys his command, so I reluctantly follow suit. I press my thumb on the scanner next to the keypad, and the tablet comes to life.

My name appears on the screen.

WREN DARLINGTON, RECRUIT 56

To my dismay, my entire life has already been loaded into this small, thin piece of technology. Biometrics. Medical reports. School transcripts, upper *and* lower.

Even worse than being surrounded by vipers is the realization that you can never escape them. Their eyes are always on you.

Maybe the Faithful have the right idea after all with those Old Era beliefs. At least back then there'd been some semblance of privacy, of freedom. You could live a life far from civilization if you chose. A harder life, certainly, but that's the thing about freedom, isn't it? There's always a price to pay for it. The Faithful are free . . . to live in the shadows. To decamp at a moment's notice and find another home on the fringes. To fend off starvation and be hunted by the Command.

I'm not sure I could do it again. I already lived in the Blacklands. I don't want to go back to life in the shadows.

"The Program is divided into eight sections," Hadley says. "A combination of classroom instruction and fieldwork."

He then proceeds to extol the virtues of Silver Block. Our soldiers are the smartest, the fastest, the strongest. And as he drones on, I feel ever more helpless. My throat closes, and although I'm slightly afraid of using telepathy in proximity to all these strangers, the tight knot of desperation lodged in my windpipe calls for desperate measures.

"Tana, please," I beg my best friend. "You need to find someone in the network who can help me. Anyone. They reassigned my ranch and threw me into the Command training program. I need to get out of here."

"I'm trying, Wren. I swear I'm trying. But they don't . . ." She trails off.

Care.

That's what she doesn't want to say. They don't. Fucking. Care.

"Keep trying," I tell her. I can barely get a full breath in now, as it becomes glaringly obvious that nobody is going to help me.

I inhale through my nose and take another stab at Xavier Ford's mind. It's locked up tight, as is Hadley's, leaving me no choice but to turn my attention to my peers.

I hesitate. Fight the urge to pry before convincing myself it's for the greater good. What's the point of having this power if I refuse to wield it?

Unsurprisingly, the other recruits are all shielded. One of the first laws General Redden enacted after his coup of the previous regime was that all Prime children on the Continent must be taught to shield from the moment they enter lower school. Unfortunately for them— but fortunately for us—proper shielding requires a lot more training than an hour or two of weekly visualization.

If I tried, I could probably penetrate most of these shields, but I don't have the patience or the time to sweep one mind at a time. I settle on my seatmate, because she's right here, and her expression gives me pause. She's watching Ford intently, hanging on his every word. Her teeth dig into her bottom lip.

She has a serviceable shield, but it's not quite thick enough. More like a malleable metal, soft enough that with the poke of a fine needle I can penetrate it. I open a path, and sure enough, I soon catch the faintest echoes in her mind.

You're not . . .

. . . not good . . .

. . . good enough.

You're not good enough.

The thought repeats in her head, even as she bites her lip and concentrates on Ford's words.

I immediately retreat.

Fuck.

This is why I'm so loath to do this. Mind reading is the greatest invasion of privacy that exists. And everyone, even Primes, deserves their privacy. Your mind is the one place where you should feel completely and unequivocally safe. People like me rob you of that refuge, and each time I read an unsuspecting mind, I hate myself a little bit more.

There's no place for morality in war. Deep down I know this, know I *have* to use the weapons in my arsenal. But sometimes, when I'm overhearing someone's deepest insecurities, I'm reminded of why I'm seen as the villain in other people's stories.

My seatmate's inner monologue tugs at something inside me. She's so matter-of-fact. Not forlorn. Not resentful. *You're not good enough.* A statement of fact, coming from someone who accepted that truth a long time ago.

It makes me soften in a way I don't usually soften.

I lean closer to her and whisper, "I'm Wren."

She jolts in her seat, looking over at me. After a beat, she whispers back. "I'm Lydia, but everyone calls me Lyddie."

I nod at the front of the room. "This guy loves the sound of his own voice, huh?"

A smile touches her lips.

". . . before you're divided into your cells and we officially get under way," Hadley is saying, "turn your attention to your source. Each of you will be required to answer ten questions. Please start now."

I glance at my screen.

There was a woman in this room when you sat down. What color was her shirt?

I stare at the question. Beside me, Lyddie is busily writing on her source.

All right. This is clearly some sort of test.

The question is, is it a test I want to pass . . . or fail?

My mind starts racing. I don't know what's more advantageous to me. If I fail, they might cut me from the Program. That would be the best-case scenario. However, it's not as if the wards are teeming with potential candidates for the most elite block in the Command.

Captain Cross won't be cutting indiscriminately, especially based on what appears to be a random memory test.

On the other hand, if you can't pass a simple memory test, do you truly *belong* in the most elite block in the Command? If I were running this program, I wouldn't want any idiots on my team. But I'm a heartless bitch. The people here might be more tolerant of failure.

"Darlington," Ford barks. "This isn't optional."

I lower my gaze to the tablet. Damn it. Just choose already. Pass or fail.

Don't draw attention to yourself.

He might be dead, but his voice lives in my head. I *know* that would be Jim's advice. So I grit my teeth and use my index finger to write on the screen in my messy scrawl.

There was a woman in this room when you sat down. What color was her shirt?

She wasn't wearing a shirt. It was a dress, and it was white.

I tap *next.*

On which ear did the woman have piercings?

Left ear.

Was she holding a tablet?

She wasn't, but I write *yes.* If the goal is to not draw attention to myself, then I'm neither choking nor shining. I can't get everything right.

How many officers were in the room when you sat down?

I could write *two.* Instead, I write:

One officer and one massive prick.

I get three more wrong on purpose, then lean back in my chair as a score flashes on the screen: 60%.

Ford glances at his tablet and says, "Soldier Hutchfield. Stand up."

At the table next to ours, a young woman with pale hair rises uncertainly.

"You're dismissed. Report to your CO in Gold Block."

Her mouth opens in surprise. "What? Why?"

"You're dismissed," he repeats.

"But—"

"I don't have time to argue with you, soldier. You had your shot, you blew it. Pay attention next time."

"That's not fair!" she protests. "How were we supposed to know we would be tested on what clothes people were wearing and how many earrings they had?"

He sets his jaw. "You didn't answer a single question correctly. If you're this unobservant in a low-pressure setting, I don't want you watching my six on a high-pressure op. You're cut. Get the fuck out."

The room goes dead silent. Then Hutchfield's footsteps snap against the floor as she storms out.

Unperturbed, Ford recites more names. "Abernathy, Dern, Jasser, Kilmeade, Rhodes, Xinn. You also scored a zero. You're dismissed. You'll be going back to your wards."

Hellfuck!

I made the wrong call.

Once those recruits are gone, Ford addresses the ones remaining. "Silver Block only accepts the best. Recruits who don't show promise during the Program will either return to their current blocks or be sent back to their wards."

I perk up. Okay. There's still a chance I can get cut. All I have to do is . . . not perform.

I can do that.

CHAPTER 9

After our impromptu quiz, we're split into two cells. Red and Black. Lyddie and I are both assigned to the Black Cell, and I breathe in relief when I learn that Hadley will be the Red Cell leader.

Today will consist of classroom instruction only, which sounds mind-numbingly tedious. I barely made it through my school days in Hamlett. I can't count the number of messages Uncle Jim received on his comm from my teachers, reporting me for not paying attention in class or disappearing from the schoolhouse altogether. I don't do well chained to a desk. I need to breathe fresh air and have the freedom to go where I please.

Freedom doesn't exist here, and if I don't find a way to break out of this base, I'm liable to lose my sanity.

Ford calls for a break, and while the other recruits use the time to chat among themselves, I find a quiet spot against the wall and study the schedule on my source. This week is labeled SECTION 1 and primarily involves weapons training, which intrigues me. Long range, short range, moving targets.

Damn it, and the other sections are equally intriguing. Interrogation Tactics. Intelligence Gathering. Knives. Hand-to-Hand Combat. Undercover Operations. Basics of Flight.

I hate the tickle of excitement I feel in my stomach. I'm not allowed to enjoy myself. And I'm certainly not allowed to be good at anything. My goal is to fail so they send me back to the wards. Back to the ranch. No matter how enticing some of these sections are, I can't let myself excel at them.

I continue scrolling, noting the four days of rest that seem to be arbitrarily scheduled between two sections. They come directly after a class labeled RTI.

Although I have no intention of making friends, I've already been friendly to Lyddie, so I wander back to our workstation and lean against the edge of the desk.

"Do you know what RTI is?" I ask her. "It's in Section 7."

She lifts her head from her source. "Oh. Resistance to interrogation."

My brow furrows. "Are we the ones resisting the interrogation?"

"I think so, but I'm not sure." She sets down her tablet, taking my presence as a signal to socialize. "Are you from the Point?"

"No. Ward Z."

"Whoa. I've aways wanted to go out west. I heard it's nothing but open space."

"It is. I miss it. Did you grow up in the Point?"

She nods, her fingers absently toying with the end of her braid. "My mom works for the Company. Biotech. And my dad is in Command Intelligence. Some people think that makes me a staple, but I'm not."

She lowers her voice as her gaze darts toward a group of recruits congregated in the front row. A few glance her way, then turn back and whisper to one another. I hear someone laugh.

Two pink splotches rise in her cheeks. "I passed all the required assessments."

The way her jaw tightened at the word *staple* suggests it isn't a complimentary label.

"What's a staple?" I ask warily.

"The children of high-clearance parents. Staples are only accepted into the Program because of who their parents are, even if they don't qualify. They've basically spent their entire lives knowing they're going to end up in Silver Block. Maybe even Silver Elite."

"What's that?"

"It's a unit within Silver Block. Special forces. Elites have the highest security clearance, and they run the riskiest operations."

"Like what?"

She giggles. "Do you know anything about this block?"

"No," I admit.

"Then why are you here?" Skepticism flickers through her eyes.

I backpedal, realizing it might not be a smart idea to tell anyone I'm here against my will. At least not until I've determined how much I can trust them, although I have the feeling the answer to that will always be *not at all*.

"I'm a very impulsive person," I finally say.

That gets me another laugh. "You just impulsively applied for Silver Block?"

"Pretty much. There were a bunch of soldiers in my village for Liberty Day, and I got to talking with one." I grin. "More than talking, actually."

She grins back.

"He made it sound really exciting, and the next thing I knew, I'm here." I shrug.

Sounds plausible enough. And not entirely a lie. I probably am the most impulsive person I know. It's something that Jim tried so hard to rein in with me. Even as a child, I was constantly racing toward danger. In the Blacklands, we had to bathe in a creek that was nearly a mile from our clearing, the one place with a pocket of sunlight. That meant venturing into the darkness, the pitch black where you couldn't see your own hand in front of your face. Every time we heard a noise, I'd be so curious, wanting to investigate. Jim would haul me back and growl, "Girl, what are you doing? Stay behind me."

I do a lot of things without thinking. Like taking that impossible shot on Liberty Day.

Jim was right. I should have let that boy die. Should have let the white coyote maul him.

I let it play out in my mind. Rachel would have grieved. We would've held a service for Robbie in the cemetery behind the town square, and I would've stood there, clenching my teeth and choking on my guilt at the knowledge that I could've made that shot—

No.

I don't regret saving the boy.

Even though you got Jim killed?

I shove the thought away, banishing the accompanying shame into some place deep inside me. I'll need to find a way to shield myself from it. To become numb to the reminder that *I'm* the reason the person I loved most in the world is dead. It'll destroy me otherwise.

"Wren?"

I blink. "Sorry. What?"

"I was asking if anyone from your ward is here." Lyddie gestures around the room.

I shake my head. "No. Do you know any of the other recruits?"

"Some."

Once again, her gaze flits toward the group in the front. I focus on a girl with chin-length black hair and dark eyes that are too big for her face. She smirks when she notices me staring, then turns to talk to a young man with wavy brown hair that falls past his shoulders. When his gaze meets mine, a shiver runs through me. His eyes are the color of coal, but the temperature of ice. Cold and lifeless.

He observes me with the intensity of a predator in the Blacklands. His lips curve in a smile, and I tear my gaze away.

"Stay away from him," Lyddie warns under her breath.

"Who is he?"

"Anson. He was in upper school with me. You don't want to be around him. He . . ." She thinks about it. Then, in a flat voice, says, "He enjoys seeing people hurt."

Well, that's disturbing. "And the girl?"

"Kess. She's a quat."

I hide a smile. Lyddie proceeds to point out a few others and offer bits of information about each one. I let her talk without interruption. In a world where alliances shift like sand in the wind, knowledge is power, and I'd like to arm myself with as much as I can gather. I file away each name and face for future reference.

A female staple named Bryce whose father also works in Command Intelligence.

A blond soldier, Ivy, who's retaking the Program after failing her first go-around.

A lanky guy named Lash, who sits on his own, looking bored as he watches the rest of us.

"Do you ride horses in Z?" Lyddie asks when the conversation returns to us.

"Ward Z?" drawls a male voice. "Well, shit. We have a cowgirl in our midst?"

It's the guy with the golden hair and impish eyes.

I spare him a glance before answering Lyddie. "I grew up on a horse."

Golden Hair comes to a stop in front of us, thumbs hooked in the pockets of his trousers. His tall, muscular body fills out his uniform very, very nicely. I notice Lyddie admiring him, then hastily shifting her gaze when he notices. He winks knowingly at me while a blush blooms on her cheeks. Me, I'm not as impressed. He's undeniably attractive, yes. But those eyes are dangerous.

"Do you have a name, cowgirl?"

"Do you?" I counter.

"Kaine Sutler. Ward D."

"Coal country," I say dubiously as my gaze drops to his hands. They're too pretty to be miner's hands. And it's common knowledge that even the children in D help out in the mines. Some are pulled from school entirely if there's a shortage of manpower. "How'd those mines treat you?"

He grins. "Fuck that. Mild asthma as a kid was the best thing that ever happened to me. Never had to step foot in a mine."

"What was your supplement, then?" Lyddie asks him. Every student, starting at the age of fifteen, spends their last two years supplementing their schooling with a job assignment. I was able to supplement on the ranch.

"Packaging plant," he says before glancing between us. "You two still haven't told me your names." His gaze lingers on me rather than Lyddie.

"Wren," I say grudgingly. "Darlington."

"Lyddie De Velde." She extends an arm, and he clasps his fingers around her wrist in greeting. I notice she clings to his wrist just a tad too long.

When he holds his hand out to me, I just stare at him. That makes him chuckle.

"Anyway. Z, eh? That's an asset ward. Family of farmers? Ranchers?"

"Ranchers."

"Does that mean you're good with ropes? Because I'm not against being tied up."

This guy is going to be incorrigible. I just know it.

"Will you be flirting the entire eight weeks or are you trying to get it all out of your system now?" I ask in a polite tone.

"The entire eight weeks," he promises, and Lyddie giggles.

———

I'm subjected to a monotonous day of reading manuals and trying not to rip my hair out in boredom. Eventually we're dismissed and shuffled to the mess hall for dinner. Afterward, none other than Tyler Struck, my other interrogator, joins Hadley to escort us to our living quarters. Her gaze flickers in my direction, but she doesn't remark on my abrupt upgrade from suspect to recruit.

On the way to the barracks, we pass a large common room with comfortable seating and coffee machines. There's also a commissary. Struck says we're allotted ten Lux credits per week to spend while we're here and can earn extra credits depending on our performance in each section.

The barracks are co-ed. I don't love that, what with Anson eyeing me all day. I'm not interested in feeling those predacious eyes on me while I sleep. The showers and lavatories are not co-ed, at least.

Hadley's Red Cell recruits are bunking at one end of the hall. Struck leads the Black Cell to the other end, and we follow her into another windowless room. I'm starting to think the Command detests natural light. This space is cavernous, with high ceilings and two rows of neatly made beds. Everyone's belongings are lined up against a wall of lockers. Black duffels with name tags on them. I don't have any belongings, only the one uniform and toothbrush they gave me. I'd kill for a hairbrush right about now.

Struck makes a sweeping gesture with her arm. "One to a bed."

"What if we get cold?" Kaine asks, eyes dancing.

"One to a bed," she repeats. "And there are consequences to breaking the rules, so I recommend you do as you're told. No sharing. No switching once you've selected your bunk. No exceptions."

At that, she leaves us to navigate our own sleeping arrangements, and the moment she's gone everyone hurries to grab their things. To my surprise, I find a duffel with my name on it. I set it on the bed next to Lyddie's while Kaine settles on the other side of me. Great.

I unzip the bag and conduct a quick inventory. Three more uniforms—one black and long-sleeved, a second set of the one I currently wear, and a nicer, overly starched one. According to Lyddie, each uniform has a purpose: training, casual, formal. I can tell she wants to go into more detail, but I turn away to continue taking stock.

I find a pair of loose cotton shorts and a white tank that I assume I'm supposed to sleep in. A pack of underwear, plain white. Two bras, and while I'm aware that all my measurements are recorded in my ID file, there's something incredibly intrusive about the fact that someone picked out a bra for me. The last item in the bag is a toiletry case with a hairbrush and some other amenities.

We each get a locker and a shelf above our beds. Most of the other recruits are making use of the shelf with little mementos from home. Mine remains bare.

Beside me, Lyddie pulls a digital photograph out of her bag and carefully places the small projector on her shelf. It's a picture of her posing on a stone terrace with two people who must be her parents, the glass dome of the Capitol building serving as a backdrop. She wasn't kidding about her parents being well connected.

When the hairs on the back of my neck rise, I turn to find Anson's eyes on me again. Gleaming in anticipation.

Right, then. I gather my sleepwear and toiletry case, deciding to change in one of the lavatory stalls.

"Aww, what a shame. No bed for the unlucky little lamb."

It takes a second to realize Kess's mocking voice is not directed at me, but the girl behind me. She's about eighteen or nineteen, timidly standing at the wall holding her duffel.

I glance from the girl to the rows of beds. Technically, there should be at least twenty-eight since we started the day with fifty-six recruits. Ford cut seven after the test, which leaves twenty-four of us in Black Cell. Yet there are only twenty-three beds, and a lot of empty space at the end of our row, as if beds had been deliberately removed. This feels like another one of their ridiculous tests, but I'm not sure what its purpose is.

"It's probably just a mistake. I should go and find someone?" The teenager wears a stricken expression. Her voice is trembling.

No, she's not a lamb—even lambs have more confidence than this. She's more like one of my wobbly newborn calves, uncertainly following her mother as she adjusts to the big, frightening world into which she's suddenly been thrust.

"It won't matter." This comes from Ivy, who, unlike me, has no qualms about undressing in front of twenty-three strangers and Anson's unnerving gaze.

Ivy unbuttons her trousers and pushes them down to expose her bare legs. She reaches for a pair of drawstring pants she must have brought from home, their pale-blue pattern with its thin pinstripes telling me she comes from means, likely from an elite family in the Point.

Those types of fabrics are beyond rare. General Redden's philosophy is all about functionality. Efficiency. The fabrics that roll out of his textile mills are utilitarian—solid grays, blacks, blues. You won't find many ward shops that carry patterns or prints, but if you have the credits, you can easily procure custom-made goods in Sanctum Point. All the pinstripes and florals your heart desires.

"They do this at the start of every session," Ivy explains. "There's always one less bed than recruits."

"Looks like the little lamb will have to sleep on the floor." Kess clicks her tongue. "Poor baby."

The lamb bites her lip. "I'll go find someone." She takes a step. I feel bad for her.

"I told you, don't bother." Ivy sounds annoyed. "They won't care. They do this on purpose."

"To what end?" asks a guy whose name I can't remember. Ford and Hadley barked out far too many names today.

"They do it to identify the bleeding heart," Ivy says with a shrug. "Every session, someone inevitably gives up their bed, then gets cut from the Program the next morning."

A hesitant Lyddie speaks up. "Why are they cut?"

"They're considered a weak link because of their compassion."

She can't be serious. My annoyance simmers beneath the surface at the idea of such a pointless tactic.

I step toward the girl. "What's your name?"

"Pera," she says.

"You can have my bed, Pera." I start to gather up my stuff.

"Wren," protests Lyddie. "Didn't you hear what Ivy just said? What if you're cut?"

"They're not going to cut me." I'm confident of it, considering Captain Cross said he wanted to keep me close.

And if they *do* cut me, then, fuck yes, sign me up. I'd love nothing more than to leave this base.

"I mean it, you can have my bed," I tell Pera, zipping up the duffel.

"No. I'll take the floor. It's fine." Her voice is so soft. She won't last long in this program, not with that air of fragility.

"Absolutely not," I say, determination igniting inside me. "You're not sleeping on the floor."

When she tries to protest again, I brush off her objections, guiding her to my bed.

"Take it," I insist.

With a mix of gratitude and reluctance, she acquiesces, setting her bag down and sinking into the comfort of the mattress. "Thank you," she whispers, and I don't miss the sheen of tears.

No, she won't last long at all.

Carting my toiletries, I head for the door. When I pass Kess, I hear her laughter tickling my back. I glance over my shoulder. "What?"

"That was pathetic," she informs me.

I shrug and keep walking.

When I return from the lavatory, Pera jumps up from my former bed.

"I feel awful," she blurts out. "Please, take your bed back. I don't want you to sleep on the floor."

I flick up a brow. "Who says I'm sleeping on the floor?"

I drop my stuff in Kaine's footlocker and sweep my gaze over the man sprawled in front of me. His long legs are encased in thin black pants, and he's shirtless, revealing a sleekly muscled chest. He's watching me with interest, awaiting my next move. Most of the room is.

It's a single bed. It's going to be a tight fit. Nonetheless, I stride over and lift the corner of his blanket.

Without a word, Kaine rises to let me slide underneath. I see him grinning at me from the corner of my eye.

"Don't get any ideas," I warn. "Keep your hands to yourself if you still want hands in the morning."

"Stop it, Darlington. Threats of violence only get me hotter."

Someone snickers. I don't turn over to check who it is. Instead, I curl onto my side and face away from him. Outside our dormitory, the muffled sounds of boots on the floor and hushed voices only serve to heighten my discomfort. In here, the cold concrete walls seem to close in on me, suffocating me with their oppressive weight. I inhale slowly and try to shut out my surroundings. The murmured voices. The chuckles. Breaths that aren't my own.

The narrow mattress dips and I feel Kaine slide under the blanket, the cramped space forcing our bodies into close proximity. He lies on his back, and his shoulder and hip are millimeters from me, so close

I can feel his body heat. I would've chosen to sleep with Lyddie if she didn't strike me as someone who'd rather die than break the rules. Bunking with Kaine is a risk, but luckily, he doesn't try to touch me.

Without warning, the overhead lights shut off, bathing the room in blackness.

A voice travels in the dark. "Hey, Sutler, try not to be too loud when you're screwing her tonight."

Anson.

"Don't worry, Booth, I'll make sure to shout your name when I'm finishing," Kaine calls back. "Do you a deed. I know it's the closest you'll ever come to getting laid on your own."

"Fuck off, Sutler."

The mattress vibrates as Kaine chuckles.

I close my eyes and ignore him. Despite the tight quarters, sleep eventually claims me, the rhythmic sounds of my enemies' breathing coaxing me into a restless slumber.

CHAPTER 10

I'm in a cocoon. It's rather pleasant. I burrow deeper and deeper into it, basking in its warmth and the sense of safety it provides. Until the cobwebs in my mind begin to clear and I'm alert enough to comprehend that the cocoon is actually a male body curled around me, and that I'm burrowing my backside against a groin that's awakening faster than its owner.

What in the hellfuck!

Before I can jump out of bed, a sharp voice slices through the silence.

"Darlington! Sutler! On your damn feet."

Hadley. He looms over us, disapproval digging harsh lines into his features.

I scramble up. Kaine, who's still half asleep, lopes off the mattress like a fawn taking its first steps. He shoves a hand through his messy blond hair and gives me a drowsy grin.

"You were all over me in your sleep," he says.

"Shut up," Hadley orders.

His eyes travel down the row of beds. A murmur of confusion ripples through the room at the commanding officer's sudden presence. Recruits start sitting up or getting to their feet.

Hadley shifts his gaze between me and my bedmate. "Was Soldier Struck not clear last night when she explained the rules to you? One to a bed. No exceptions."

Kaine and I remain silent.

He scrutinizes me for far too long, but not in a way most males would look at a woman in her sleepwear and no bra. Then he gives a deep frown.

"Get dressed and come with me."

Kaine takes a step.

"Not you," snaps Hadley. "Just her."

Apprehension prickles my belly. Why does he want me alone? What does he know?

My pulse quickens as another question surfaces.

Does he recognize me?

His face reveals absolutely nothing.

"I said get dressed," he commands, sharper this time. "Or I'll do it for you."

I hear some chuckles from the other end of the room. Kess and Anson. Lyddie gives me a worried look.

"Do I have time to freshen up before we embark on our morning adventure?" I ask Hadley.

His jaw tightens. "You have three minutes."

"Thank you. *Sir.*" I turn my face away before he can see the derision on it.

Precisely three minutes later, Hadley collects me from the lavatories and makes a terse gesture for me to follow. I didn't have time to brush my hair, so I finger-comb it as I walk.

"Where are we going?"

He doesn't answer.

I sneak him a sidelong look. He would probably be attractive if it weren't for the way he presses his lips into a thin line, devoid of any trace of a smile or even a frown. There's an air of detachment about him. Something clinical and cold. His face betrays not even a hint of emotion.

I wonder if he felt anything when he reported Morlee. I wonder if he feels anything now when he thinks about her hands, which are probably raw and brittle after shoveling salt from dawn till dusk for the last eight years.

We walk down the corridors of the maze that makes up the base. Hadley scans his thumb at a pair of large doors that slide open to allow us entrance, and then it's steel door after steel door, each one numbered rather than offering any distinguishing clues like a name or department. At least until we turn the corner into a shorter hall and arrive at a door with a silver plate on it.

CAPTAIN OF OPERATIONS.

Damn it.

The door buzzes at our arrival. He's expecting us. Hadley gestures at the open doorway and grunts something before turning on his heel.

"So sorry to inconvenience you," I call after his retreating form.

His shoulders stiffen, but he keeps marching.

I enter an office so enormous you could fit several smaller offices inside it. The ceiling is a snakelike expanse of pipework. A commanding desk takes up one side of the room, while a long conference table surrounded by black padded chairs takes up the other. Maps and paperwork are strewn on the table, and I resist the urge to walk over and snoop.

Of course, there isn't a single window. It's all artificial lighting, lending the space a forbidding atmosphere.

I find Captain Cross leaning against his desk. He's in all-black, his short sleeves revealing the swirl of ink on his arms.

"What does the base have against windows?" I ask him.

He folds his arms on his chest. "What do you have against rules?"

"I find them limiting."

He sighs and picks up a tablet. Then he starts to read. "'Recruit 56 found in compromising position with Recruit 42. Sharing the same bed.'" He brings his gaze back to me, a cynical glint in it. "Man of few words, that Hadley. You care to fill in the details?"

I shrug. "I didn't want to sleep on the floor."

"It's one to a bed in the bunks."

"There weren't enough beds." I give him a knowing look. "Oh no. I failed your little test."

He watches me, unimpressed.

"I gave up my bed for another recruit. I'm the bleeding heart." I tip my head in defiance. "Aren't you going to cut me?"

"No."

"But I broke the rules."

"You did," he agrees.

There's something very aggravating about his face. It's just so . . . symmetrical. And that dimple is always on the brink of appearing, as if he *wants* to smile but can't quite let it happen.

"I heard the bleeding heart gets cut," I say through my rising frustration.

"Usually. But I'll make an exception for you, Dove." He sets his tablet on the desktop, drawing my gaze to his defined biceps and golden, tattooed flesh. "With that said, it hasn't been twenty-four hours and you've already been written up. This doesn't bode well."

"You should cut me," I say hopefully.

"No." The dimple threatens to appear again.

I grit my teeth. "Does it get you off, the idea of forcing women to do things they don't want to do?"

"I didn't realize you were so interested in what gets me off."

I recoil. "I'm not."

His gaze locks with mine. "Are you sure?"

"Fucking positive."

"That's a shame. I'd be happy to satisfy your curiosity."

He closes the distance between us, and a shiver runs through me when he dips his head close to whisper in my ear.

"I like it rough."

I clench my teeth harder and try to ignore the ripples of heat that travel through my body.

No. I'm not allowed to feel even a *flicker* of warmth toward this man. He leads the block that's responsible for hunting down people like me. I ought to be a wall of ice. I ought to kill him the first chance I get.

He watches me again, silent and pensive. Then he asks, "Are you going to be a problem for me?"

"Probably."

"Don't test my patience, Dove. I'm not someone you want as an enemy."

His lethal tone doesn't faze me.

He already is the enemy.

"May I go now?"

He nods. "You're dismissed."

"Thank you, sir," I mock.

To my dismay, he grabs his tablet and follows me to the door, where his voice stops me before I can exit.

"Darlington."

He's so much taller than me, my chin instinctively tilts up for me to meet his eyes. They're so stupidly blue. "What?"

"You'd be better off keeping a lower profile. The instructors enjoy making life more difficult for the troublemakers."

"Well, I plan on making life difficult for *them*, so it's only fair they fight back."

He shakes his head. "Let's go."

"Aw, are you accompanying me to morning meal?" As we fall into step with each other, I'm forced to quicken my pace to match his longer strides.

"No. Morning meal is delayed. I'm addressing the recruit class first. I wasn't able to do it yesterday because I was called off base at the last minute."

"Doing more dirty things at village inns?"

That gets me another smoldering look. Damn it, I need to stop provoking him.

"Something like that."

We navigate several corridors until we reach a large training gym with gray walls and black mats spanning the floor. I don't want to be seen entering with the captain, but I don't have much of a choice. Heads swivel at our entrance.

I spot Lyddie in the sea of navy blue and make my way to her. Kaine is there, too. He glances past my shoulder at Captain Cross, who's approaching his instructors.

"Never had a woman risk the wrath of a Command captain to share a bed with me," Kaine says with a wink.

I ignore him and turn to Lyddie. "Did I miss anything important?"

"No. Did you get in trouble?"

"Just a warning," I lie.

I'm starting to realize it might be impossible for me to get in trouble. I'm not going anywhere unless Cross wants me to. And yet, what message does it send to his instructors if he allows an incompetent recruit to continue training for his precious Silver Block? He'd look weak. Incompetent himself. Which means I need to stay the course. The worse I perform, the quicker I'll wake up from this nightmare.

My attention shifts to the captain. As much as I hate myself for it, I can't help but admire the way his shirt hugs his broad shoulders, and how his dark hair falls in perfect disarray across his forehead.

I'm not the only one staring. Beside me, Lyddie wears a dreamy expression.

Trying not to laugh, I lean closer and say, "Please don't tell me you're locked on the captain."

"Of course not." Her cheeks turn red. "But . . . I mean . . . don't tell me you don't see it, too."

"See what?"

"His face. His body."

"Both of mine are better," Kaine says, and I roll my eyes at him.

"He's not unattractive," I say in concession, maintaining a casual tone even as my heartbeat accelerates at the memory of that velvety whisper in my ear.

I like it rough.

He was trying to get under my skin. I know that. I just wish it hadn't worked.

As if sensing my gaze on him, he swings his head in my direction. When he spots me, I raise one hand in a sweet fluttery wave and flash him a big fake smile. There's a hint of a dimple before he turns back to the older man he's speaking to. The uniformed man has dark hair streaked with gray and boasts four silver stars on his sleeve. Another captain from this block.

That's when I notice Ivy frowning at me. I'm not the only one to pick up on it, as Lyddie murmurs, "Oh, someone doesn't like that."

"Who? Ivy?"

Lyddie nods. "They used to be together."

I manage to mask my surprise in time. I can't appear overly interested in anyone here, even our esteemed captain.

"Really. How do you know that?" Lyddie's proving to be a wealth of information, which makes her an unexpected asset to me.

"She was a couple of levels ahead of me in upper school, but her sister was in my level. Mira talked about them a lot. I think it lasted about a year. Ended when he joined the Command."

Interesting.

I shoot another discreet look Ivy's way. Not discreet enough, though. She's still watching me. Still frowning. "Is that why she's here now? Trying to get close to him again?"

"Wouldn't shock me. It's her second go-around, after all. But if she's retaking the Program hoping to get his attention, that's incredibly pathetic. He doesn't want you. Move on."

I don't entirely hate this petty side to Lyddie.

"Damn, Lydia. Behind those freckles you're a real bitch," Kaine says, grinning.

"I'm not a bitch," she protests. "All I'm saying is, you only get two shots at Silver Block, and she already failed once. At this point, just accept it—you belong in Copper. Go guard a gate or something."

I smother a laugh while Kaine chuckles. Yes. Spiteful Lyddie is a delight.

"Why aren't they together anymore?" I ask.

"I don't know. Maybe Daddy didn't approve."

"Her daddy?"

"No, his." Lyddie shrugs. "The General's not known to welcome strangers into his midst with open arms."

"The General? What does he have to do with this?"

She gives me a bemused look. "It's his father."

"Whose father?" I feel like we're having two different conversations now.

"Cross." Lyddie can tell I'm not following, so she gestures toward the tall, tattooed man across the room. "That's Cross Redden, Wren. The General's son."

CHAPTER 11

I thought Cross was his surname.

It's not. It's his first name.

Last name *Redden*.

My throat burns with self-loathing as I replay this morning's interaction in my mind. I let him whisper in my ear. I let my pulse race for him. I was attracted to him.

Was being the crucial word here, because the moment Lyddie's revelation absorbs into my bloodstream, all the attraction is sucked out of me like a poison.

I was aware that Merrick Redden had children, but he's always kept them out of sight. Every broadcast I've seen him give, he's been alone. He doesn't even have his wife at his side, and I know he's married.

"Ah. Well, now it makes sense how someone so young climbed the ranks this fast." I try to cover my shock with a sarcastic retort.

Lyddie shakes her head in earnest. "Oh no. From what I've heard, he's earned every star."

Was I ever this naïve?

"His older brother is a colonel," she adds.

"Right, and I'm sure *he's* a Command super soldier who's also earned every star."

"Travis works in Intelligence."

"Atten-tion," Hadley shouts, and the entire room goes quiet so fast, it's almost disorienting.

My muscles tense at the sound of Hadley's voice. Every time I see his face or hear him speak, I think about Morlee and want to strangle him.

Cross strides to the front of the room and surveys the assembled recruits. "I'm Cross Redden, Silver Block's captain of operations." He nods toward the older captain standing a few feet away. "This is Deron Radek, our administrative captain."

Radek nods in terse greeting.

"I won't take up much of your time," Cross says. "I want each of you to look at the person to your left, then the person to your right."

I dutifully play along, glancing from Lyddie to Kaine.

"These are your fellows. And in here, you're only as strong as your weakest fellow."

I expect him to punctuate that with some saccharine horseshit about how this means we should all band together and raise one another up. The strong support the weak until the weak are strong enough to support themselves. Unity prevails!

Instead, he says, "Weakness doesn't belong here. In Silver Block, we eat the weak. We cut them out like a cancer."

Oh, maybe *I'm* the naïve one. So much for team unity.

His eyes, that hypnotizing shade of blue, seem to bore into each recruit with a steely intensity, as if searching for any sign of weakness.

"For the next eight weeks, you'll need to demonstrate how strong you are, because that's the only way to make it to Silver Block."

Despite his youth, there's a gravity to his demeanor that belies his age, a sense of experience beyond his years that lends weight to his words. He speaks with authority that commands respect. It's incredibly sexy.

General's son, Wren.

I inwardly blanch. I fuel myself with the reminder. On the hierarchy of enemy, this man has now moved into the top three.

"For the next eight weeks, my word is the only word that matters in this facility. I'll be monitoring your progress, as well as joining you on certain ops."

"Yes, please," Lyddie mumbles under her breath. I poke her in the ribs.

"Every single daily report is sent to me. If I decide that you need to be cut, then you will be cut. If I decide you merit a second chance, you'll get a second chance." His gaze sweeps the crowd. "I'm not a fan of those, however. And I use them sparingly, so I advise you to do well the first time. At Silver Block, we only accept the best."

"How do you get into Elite?" someone calls out.

The look Cross levels him with is ice-cold. "Recruit 18 . . . Did I say you could speak?"

He's greeted with silence.

"Oh, now you're shy? Answer the question. Did I give you permission to speak?"

The shamefaced boy ducks his head. "No, sir."

"Then shut the fuck up."

It's annoying how turned on I am, hearing him cut the guy down.

"And let me squash all your hopes right now," Cross continues. "There's no way to guarantee being shortlisted for Silver Elite. Getting the top score in all your classes means shit. Showing off, equally futile. Elite candidates are handpicked by me, and my selection process is none of your godfucking business."

Beside me, Kaine gives a soft snicker.

"If you're on the shortlist, you'll find out at the end of the Program."

At that, he tips his head at the other captain, who steps forward. Radek has the kind of voice that sounds like he regularly swallows handfuls of broken glass.

"We do not enforce the laws," Radek says. "That is the responsibility of Tin Block. We do not patrol the streets—that is the responsibility of Copper and Gold. Our skills are better utilized for more critical duties. Our mission is to locate Faithful camps and disband them. To detect criminal enterprises within our cities and dismantle them. To rid our streets and our wards of silverbloods."

It takes a supreme effort to mask my anger.

"But the Aberrant are not the only threat to the Continent and our way of life—"

He stops midsentence as the double doors across the room burst open, sending a blast of cool air through the gym.

The latecomer strolls inside, his arrival disrupting the assembly with all the subtlety of a sledgehammer. He looks younger than me, maybe eighteen or nineteen years old. Tall, leanly muscled, with angular features and pronounced cheekbones. He looks familiar, but I'm certain I've never seen him before.

My gaze tracks his lazy, arrogant swagger. His blue shirt is untucked. Zipper undone. He tugs it up as he walks, unfazed by the disapproving glares directed his way.

When he notices Radek and Cross, he gives a magnanimous gesture of his hand. "Oh, please continue," he cracks. "Don't mind me."

I swallow a laugh. Others aren't as successful, as some titters go through the crowd.

Visibly irritated, Cross stalks toward the source of interruption, who holds up his hands in mock surrender.

"Calm down now, Captain."

"Who is that?" I whisper to Lyddie.

"His brother," she whispers back.

My brows fly up. "The colonel?"

"No. This is his half brother, Roe. He's younger." My new favorite Lyddie makes an appearance, the one whose voice thickens at the merest hint of scandal. "He's the General's bastard."

I perk up. Excellent. Family skeletons mean more intelligence for my arsenal. Maybe I can find a way to use this against the captain, if the opportunity arises.

Cross reaches the younger man, and I watch their exchange with interest. The insolence flashing in Roe's eyes. The hard set of Cross's jaw. Cross is an inch or two taller, but they're nearly at eye level. Tension hangs in the air between them, so thick I can feel it from where I stand. A mountain of unspoken issues looms between these two.

Cross leans in and mutters something none of us can hear. But his brother's dark eyes flare. Then he slaps the younger guy's shoulder—not good-naturedly, but in warning—and walks out of the room.

Jaw coiled tight, Roe stands there, fuming at whatever was muttered in his ear, until Xavier Ford steps forward and barks for him to join the group.

———

I spend most of the morning meal sneaking glances at the General's bastard. He seems close with Anson, which is already cause for alarm. But even if he weren't friendly with the creepiest guy in our cell, I would have clocked him as dangerous. The energy he gives off makes every hair on my body stand on end.

According to my source, our first class is a weapons assessment. We find ourselves in a dimly lit shooting range, where the metallic tang of gun oil hangs heavy in the air. Rows of targets line the far wall, and I can't stop the twinge of anticipation in my gut.

Everyone shuffles into formation. I take my place among them, trying to blend in, trying not to stand out.

Ford is about to get us started when Cross enters the range. I hate how my gaze is instantly drawn to him. He joins his lieutenant, and together they make an undeniably imposing pair. Both tall and broad, their gazes shrewd, their body language promising everyone around them that they can and will kill in a heartbeat if necessary.

I notice Ivy watching Cross, too. Her gaze doesn't convey blatant longing, but it follows his every action, however minute. Even the way he pushes a lock of hair away from his forehead earns Ivy's intense scrutiny.

"Let's go. Arm up," Ford tells us, while Cross checks something on his tablet.

One by one, recruits step up, grabbing a rifle from the rack.

When it's my turn, Cross lifts his head and glances at me, a smirk playing on his lips. "We're in luck today, everyone," he announces. "We have a crack shot in our midst."

"Hardly," I say.

I keep my expression neutral, but I hear his voice in my head, telling me he'd seen the shot that saved Rachel's son. If my goal is to not draw attention to myself, then I can't be making shots like that today.

"Darlington, why don't you start us off?" Ford is clearly enjoying my discomfort.

I suppress a grimace and step forward.

"This should be fun," drawls Roe. I notice that, like Ivy's, his eyes never stray too far from Cross.

As the targets slide into place downrange, I raise the rifle to my shoulder, letting my fingers dance lightly over the familiar contours of the grip. I take aim, squinting down the sight. My finger hovers over the trigger, but instead of focusing on the bull's-eye, I let my gaze wander, deliberately aiming slightly off center.

"Any day now," Ford mocks.

The shot rings out, my bullet striking the edge of the target with a dull thud.

"I believe that's what they call anticlimactic," Roe says, drawing some chuckles.

Ford's eyebrows lift in amusement. "Again."

Whispers ripple through the class as I fire, intentionally missing my mark for a second time. I look over to see Kess and Ivy snickering.

Cross is watching me intently. This time it's he who says, "Again."

I fire again. Miss again.

The laughter of my "fellows" and Ford's widening smirk grate, but I maintain the façade of incompetence. The bull's-eye never once sees lead. With each shot, I aim wide, my bullets scattering across the target in a haphazard pattern. Sweat beads on my forehead as I fight my natural instincts.

Being bad at something is *hard*.

"Well, shit," Ford remarks. "You're pitiful, sweetling."

Kess snorts. Loudly.

The corners of my mouth twitch with the urge to show them just how *useless* I am. But the entire point was to give a performance convincing enough to keep me off their radar, so I grit my teeth and swallow my pride.

Instead I say, "Don't call me that."

"I'll call you whatever I want," he replies to the great delight of the other recruits. I see Roe grinning. Anson chuckles, a sound like gravel scraping against metal.

I shift my attention to Cross, peering at him with the utmost innocence. "Would you like me to keep shooting, Captain?"

A muscle in his jaw tics, but I can't tell if he's irritated or trying to hold back a smile. Then he writes something on his tablet and glances at his lieutenant. "Who's next?"

SECTION   1

Instructor   FORD (LT)

Student   Wren Darlington, R56

Class   Weapons Assessment

Score   10%

INSTRUCTOR NOTES:

Terrible shot. Darlington knows how to hold
a rifle but that's about it.

CHAPTER 12

They bring me a bed. Or rather, it's waiting next to Kaine's when the Black Cell members return to the barracks after evening meal. My first day as a Command recruit wasn't as horrendous as I anticipated. Of course, that doesn't mean I've resigned myself to my fate. That night, I slide under the covers and plot my escape, but by the time sleep claims me, I'm no closer to figuring out how I'm going to get out of this place.

The next day starts with what is essentially a geography class. I hate this stuff. My seatmate, on the other hand, finds deep enjoyment in it. Lyddie devours the old maps projected from our sources. Locations with names like New Virginia and South Ontario jump out at us, all utterly foreign to me. Hadley explains they're places that survived the bombings of the Last War, long before the ward system was implemented. And while they've long been free of radiation, they were never properly rebuilt.

I touch the glowing white holo-map, tracing my finger over the triangular piece of land that comprises the continent of Carora.

"What do you think is down there?" I ask Kaine, who's sitting at the workstation next to ours. I would ask Lyddie, but she's an overachiever and has been biting her lip for the past ten minutes as she tries to memorize all these sites as if expecting to be tested on them.

Kaine shrugs. "Cannibals."

I laugh. "Be serious."

"I am. What other reason would they have to erase themselves from the map?"

"They haven't, though. They're right here." I swirl my finger over the projection.

"From civilization, then," he amends. "Nobody chooses to cut themselves off from all human contact for anything other than nefarious reasons."

In the front row, Ivy and her seatmate Bryce seem to be homed in on Carora as well. "Why hasn't the Command been able to install an outpost in Carora?" Bryce asks our instructor, a female soldier named Dava.

"It's been attempted. But those plans were abandoned decades ago. It's not worth the risk anymore."

I remember Jim talking about this once. How the Company is no longer willing to dispatch soldiers down there. There's been no communication from Carora in more than a hundred years. Anytime an aircraft or ship has traveled that way, it hasn't returned.

"We send the occasional Intelligence unit on flybys, but always with no results." Dava shrugs. "It's no longer a priority for the General."

We return to our maps after that, and I return to a state of boredom.

During our afternoon break, Roe sidles up to me while I stand in line waiting for my meal tray.

He's not as handsome as his brother, likely because Cross bears very little resemblance to the General other than sharing his height and build. Roe meanwhile inherited Merrick Redden's harsh features. The hard lines and unsettling dark eyes. And he walks with the arrogance of someone who's never felt threatened his entire life. He's always had the protection of Daddy. Yet not his last name—our morning instructor referred to his surname as Dunbar. I find that noteworthy.

"What?" I say when he continues to stare.

"Anson thinks you're the sexiest woman here."

"Is that so?"

"Indeed . . ." He trails off thoughtfully. "I think I disagree with him."

I step forward as the line moves. "Thanks for letting me know. I was wondering where I stood in the hierarchy of sex appeal among recruits. Now I know."

He chuckles. "Ah. I see it now."

"What?"

"What makes you appealing to him." He leans closer. "Because you're a complete quat."

I can't stop a snort. "Who taught you how to flirt?"

"I'm not flirting. I don't want to fuck you."

"Thanks for clarifying that, too. I was in the throes of lust for you until you said that."

I stride off. He's entertaining, but not in a reassuring way. He seems like the kind of guy who could slit your throat without blinking. That's probably why he gets along with Anson so well.

I join Lyddie and Kaine, keeping my head down as I eat my food. I feel Roe's eyes on me the entire time.

———

Shielding. It's our first class after lunch and I've been dreading it since I saw it listed on my source.

I sit next to Lyddie, my hands folded in my lap, trying to ignore the nagging sense of unease that coils in the pit of my stomach. I get it, though. Protecting your mind is a skill deemed essential for anyone living in a world where there are people who can infiltrate it. And I can't deny I'm curious about their tactics. Maybe if I know exactly how they construct their shields, I can learn how to dismantle them.

While we wait for our instructor, I send out the usual mental feelers. Polly. Declan. Tana. Only the latter reciprocates. My best friend sounds increasingly worried each time we link.

"You good?"

"For now. I barely slept last night. I was trying to figure out a way out of here."

"Honestly, maybe you should stay put. You're probably safer on that base than you'd be in Hamlett right now. When I showed up to work at the inn this morning, there was a surveillance drone in the town square. They're watching our every move."

Guilt tugs at my insides. "I'm so sorry. They're only there because of Jim and me."

"That's why you shouldn't come back to Z, babe. Even if you find a way to escape, don't come home."

The guilt tightens into a knot of pain. *Then where am I supposed to go?* I want to shout.

"Where are you now?" Tana asks. "Are you alone?"

"No. I'm in a class about shielding."

"Ha. That should be interesting."

Tyler Struck walks through the doorway. She takes her place at the holoboard and begins without preamble.

"To beat your enemy, you must understand your enemy."

Her finger moves through the air, and a scribble of white letters appear in the blackish ether.

She writes TELEPATHS.

It's hard to resist the sarcastic urge to raise my hand and say, *That's me.*

She writes PROJECTORS.

Also me.

MIND READERS.

Me again.

HEALERS.

I wish.

EMPATHS.

No thanks.

PRECOGS.

Definitely not. I don't want that burden.

INCITERS.

My humor dies.

I wring my hands as a queasy sensation washes over me. I could attempt it. I should. Try to poke holes in her shield, thrust my own intentions into her mind. *Pick up your gun and shoot yourself. Shoot everyone here except for me.* If her shield weren't nearly impenetrable.

And yet I breached eight shields at Jim's execution. They weren't Silver Block, but that doesn't mean they didn't take classes like this one in their own training programs. Somehow, in a moment of pure desperation and rage, I broke through those shields, but I don't know if I can replicate whatever process led me to that point. It'll require a lot more training, which I don't have the luxury of on this base. And a training partner, which is an even more dangerous prospect because it would mean confiding in someone about my ability to incite.

Uncle Jim was the only person in this world who knew I possessed that power, and he drilled into me the importance of secrecy. "Nobody can know," he used to warn in that brusque, no-nonsense voice of his. "Nobody, Wren. Not even your closest friends."

He was adamant about it. If the Primes found out there was an inciter in their midst, I'd be killed on the spot. But even Mods are uneasy when it comes to inciters.

President Severn gave us a bad rap, what with his penchant for compelling the will of even his Modified allies. Unlike me, our former leader didn't grapple with the moral implications of using incitement.

"With empaths," a guy with curly hair says, hesitant to speak, "can they make *you* feel something? Like hurt you or make you feel pain?"

"No, but they can feel what you're feeling," Struck answers. "Whether it's pain, arousal, sorrow. Your emotions become theirs."

"I don't fully understand the conception of projection," someone else puts in. A young woman with dark skin and short black hair. I think her name is Betima. "Can they make you see something that isn't there? For example . . . if you're on a city street in the rain, can they make you think it's a sunny day at the lake?"

"No. They can only project what they are seeing in that moment, not something they're conjuring in their mind. As far as we know, anyway. It's possible they *can* make you see other things. Anything is possible with the Aberrant. After more than a century of research, there's still so much to learn and so much we don't understand."

She's not wrong. Half the time, I don't understand myself. Why are the veins in my arms normal when Tana needs long sleeves if she wants to use telepathy in public? Why can I open a path so fast when others often take a full minute or more? Why do some Mods possess healing energy when I don't?

"What we do know is that there are ways to protect ourselves from them. And the most effective way of doing that is to keep your minds shielded at all times."

"What about when you're asleep?" asks Pera. She's as timid now as she was yesterday. Her voice trembles every time she opens her mouth.

"You don't need to shield yourself in sleep. Your brain waves restrict the Aberrant from infiltrating when you're in that state. But in your conscious hours, it should be something you wear like armor. It should become instinctual. You should constantly be self-checking, reminding yourself throughout the day to ensure your shield is intact."

"We learned this shit in lower school." Roe sounds bored.

"No, you learned rudimentary shielding," Struck corrects. "If you're accepted into Silver Block, you'll be coming into contact with silverbloods, often without your knowledge. Your shield needs to be ten layers thick and inaccessible to them. You can never lower your guard. Can never leave your minds susceptible. If you do . . ."

She circles one word on the holoscreen.

INCITERS.

"These guys? They're monsters. They have no compunction about infiltrating an innocent mind and manipulating it. Robbing someone of their own will."

I feel queasy again. She's wrong. I'm not a monster. If it were up to me, I'd never incite at all. It's only ever happened spontaneously, and typically in situations of high stress. I don't know how to control it.

Ivy speaks up. "There was an inciter in the crowd of an execution the other day. Did you catch them?"

"How did you hear about that?" Struck's tone is calm, but her gaze flicks in my direction.

I stare back at her without expression.

Ivy gives me a quizzical look before focusing on our instructor. "My block guards the gates in South Plaza. One of my fellows was there when it happened."

"Who was the corpse?" For once, there's some life in Anson's expression. At the idea of death. He's a proper psychopath, this one.

"He was a Command deserter who turned out to be Aberrant." Struck sweeps her hand over the holoboard and all the words disperse like dust particles. "Enough chatter. Let's get started."

For the next hour, she walks us through the basics of shielding, taking us through several visualization exercises. It's not unlike what Jim did with me as a child, although Tyler Struck's teaching style is far gentler. And patient. Uncle Jim wasn't known for his patience.

Lyddie is entirely focused on the task. Closes her eyes when she's told to. Inhales, exhales, when ordered. Her eyelids twitch wildly, confirmation of how much mental effort she's exerting, how intently she's visualizing the doorless, airless steel vault our instructor is describing.

I play along, but I'm far more interested in watching my fellows. At one point, when I open my eyes a slit to study the faces around me, I catch Kaine watching me right back. He grins and whispers, "Wanna make out?" I roll my eyes as Struck orders him to shut up and focus.

There are ten minutes remaining when Struck ends the class, but she doesn't dismiss us yet. Instead, she says something into her comm. A few minutes later, another woman enters.

Murmurs of discontent travel through the classroom.

I immediately know the cause.

She's Modified.

CHAPTER 13

Before the Coup, Mods could walk freely among society without anyone knowing the difference. Any stranger in a shop could be Modified. A classmate. A sanitation worker you greeted as you walked down the street.

General Redden changed all that, making it impossible for Mods to go unnoticed. After he imprisoned and subsequently executed President Severn, he marked the Aberrant, tattooing thin black bands around their left wrists—if they pledged loyalty. Those who didn't received a second tattoo, a red band to indicate their prisoner status.

It could be easy to mistake Redden's actions for mercy, even tolerance, if not for the fact that very few tattoos can be spotted on the Continent. In other words, the General's preferred Mod is a dead one. He killed so many of us in the Silverblood Purge, tens of thousands, only sparing the ones he considered useful.

The woman in front of us is not a loyalist. Her wrist is both black and red.

She's a slave.

I maintain a normal level of interest while inwardly grasping for every detail I can. She appears to be in her thirties. She's short, slight. Her skin is paler than milk. Brown hair thick and curly.

She must be a powerful mind reader like Jayde Valence. No other reason the General would allow a Mod on his precious military base. Beneficial Mods are typically used as manpower and sent to labor camps, but not always. It's no secret Redden is sickened by our blood and would rather all of us be eliminated, especially those with the gift of telepathy, as he believes they can plot against him more easily.

But he's also not a fool. His strategist's mind appreciates that some of us can be used as weapons, although I'm sure he much prefers the weapons who are loyal to him, like Jayde. Not that it matters either way. Even the loyalists who are allowed to live in society hold fewer rights than Primes. For a quarter century, unconcealed Mods have been second-class citizens.

My fellows whisper among themselves, their voices laced with disdain.

"Didn't realize there were 'fects on this base."

"Hope she doesn't come too close."

I clench my fists, nails digging into my palms as I fight to keep my emotions in check. It's a struggle to remain composed.

"This is Amira," Struck introduces. "At the end of each class, she will be testing your shields."

Shit.

A shiver races down my spine. How do I handle this? I can't make my shield too strong, or she'll wonder why it is. If I make it too weak, I risk her hearing my real thoughts.

"I don't want this lab rat touching me," Bryce announces, voicing what most of my fellows are thinking. Her shoulders are set in a straight, tense line.

"This doesn't require physical touch," Struck assures the recruit. "It'll take less than a minute."

"No," she says stubbornly. "I'm not letting her read my mind."

"Build a strong shield and she won't be able to."

"She's not getting inside my head," insists Bryce.

Struck picks up her tablet. "All right. As you wish, Granger. I'll grant your request to be cut from the Program."

Alarm widens Bryce's eyes. "No! You can't do that!"

"Then you'll allow Amira to test your shield."

"I'm going to talk to my father about this." Desperation trembles in the young woman's voice.

"You can talk to whoever you want. But in order to complete the Program, you have to complete shielding. And in order to do that, we need to test your shield."

The Mod—Amira—stands there expressionless. Like a statue in her short-sleeved top and slim pants. I wonder if she's forced to deal with this nonsense at the onset of every session.

"Anybody else have objections?" Struck asks the class.

Nobody speaks.

"Good." She nods at Amira, who crosses the room toward an empty table in the very back. "We'll start with Granger. Please go join Amira."

The tall brunette is visibly ill as she rises from her chair. Her legs are actually shaking, and I almost feel sorry for her. I'm well aware that people are afraid of us. I've witnessed it myself in Hamlett, the fear and apprehension on villagers' faces when they talk about Mods. But it's been a while since I've seen someone this terrified to be in a Mod's vicinity.

Everyone is curious, watching as Bryce sits down, arms folded tight to her chest, eyes downcast.

The entire exchange lasts all of thirty seconds. Amira studies Bryce for a moment, taps something on her tablet, and then dismisses the traumatized woman. Ivy, Bryce's seatmate, is up next.

After a while, my fellows get bored. Watching a woman stare briefly at someone else isn't the most stimulating of activities. Soon they occupy themselves by making disparaging comments about the Modified, some of which are outright lies.

"My aunt said their blood is toxic," Betima's seatmate says in an obnoxiously assertive tone. As if she's speaking fact. "If they have an open wound and their blood gets into *your* bloodstream, it can instantly kill you."

A snicker slips out.

She glances my way, frowning. "What?"

I shrug. "That's the stupidest thing I've ever heard."

"My aunt said—"

"Your aunt is an idiot."

Kaine chuckles, but I notice Lyddie isn't smiling. She appears worried, her light-brown eyes darting to the back of the room where Amira now sits with Lash.

I lean closer. "You okay?"

She swallows, her face a tad pale. "I don't like the idea of an Aberrant poking around in my brain."

Too late, I almost say.

You're not good enough.

I still think about Lyddie's internal mantra. It still saddens me.

"And what if she touches me by accident?"

I can't stop the disappointment that tightens my throat. I don't know why I expected Lyddie to be more accepting. Maybe because I was starting to view her as a friend, and my friends would never worry about the dangers of me touching them.

I have to remind myself that she is a product of her upbringing. Her mother works for the Company. Her father, the Command. She was raised to hate and fear me.

But it still hurts a little.

"They can't control your mind by touching you," I assure her.

"You don't know that."

"We would absolutely know if that were the case. If their touch was harmful, then we'd have records of that, right?"

I turn to Betima for backup, but she doesn't seem comfortable with the discussion. When I glance at Kaine, his expression is stoic.

"Holy hellfuck, you guys, they're not monsters!" I say in exasperation.

Lyddie's eyebrows soar, and my stomach drops when I notice the attention I've attracted. A few tables away, Roe frowns at me. Bryce twists in her chair, aghast.

I backpedal as fast as I can. "All I'm saying is, they're still human beings. Not mutants, but *human*. That means we can fight them like we would any other human. They're not going to shoot thunderbolts out of their eye sockets or melt your skin with their touch—"

"Darlington, you're up," Tyler Struck says, and I've never been more grateful to exit a conversation.

I hop out of my chair and walk toward Amira. She has gentle eyes. Too gentle. How are they not burning with anger? Blazing from the injustice?

Guilt tickles my stomach when I realize I'm judging her. I shouldn't do that. Maybe she's like me. Biding her time. Inwardly scrambling to find a way out of her predicament.

As I approach the table, something inside me shifts. The temptation to reach out to her, to reveal myself and link, is overwhelming. I can *feel* the pull of her presence. I can taste the desire to connect with someone who understands.

Don't you dare.

I lower myself onto the chair in front of her and construct a flimsy shield. Nothing that will raise suspicion. At the same time, I decoy my mind, emptying it of all thoughts save for how much I miss my horse, Kelley.

I know the moment she pierces the shield from the electronic shock that jolts through my neck. I convey nothing but ignorance to the intrusion, but I can't pretend not to notice the way her veins begin undulating beneath her flesh. Her arms glow under the glare of the fluorescent lighting.

"Decent," she acknowledges after about thirty seconds. I feel the path close, and her veins settle in her arms. "But easily penetrated." She offers a placid smile. "I've never ridden a horse before. She sounds sweet."

"She is."

My gaze drops to the tattoos around her wrist.

How long has she been a slave?

I want to ask her. I want to know whether she's tried to escape before. A thousand questions burn on my tongue.

As she lowers her head to record something on her tablet, a more dangerous emotion begins to take hold. The lure is back. The desperate longing to open a path.

I take a breath.

Why not do it? She's a prisoner. She won't have loyalty to these people. She'll *want* to know she's not alone here—

"Sutler, you're up."

Our instructor's voice breaks through the haze of my thoughts. My senses snap back into focus, and clarity washes over me like a cold wave, jolting me back to reality and the asinine decision I almost made.

What is wrong with me?

On what planet is it a good idea to link with this woman?

In public.

While she's wearing short sleeves.

I return to my table, where I give Lyddie's shoulder a quick, reassuring squeeze. "See?" I tell her. "No harm done."

———

There's a film screening in the common room tonight. More Company propaganda, I presume. Lyddie said it's about aliens, but I'm sure they'll find a way to villainize the Mods. Those disgusting silverbloods that ruined society.

While everyone in Black Cell congregates there after evening meal, I return to the bunks instead. My mind is troubled tonight. Or rather, it's been troubled all day. The anxiety started with Tana's warning not to return to Ward Z and only intensified after shielding class.

I can still see that word on the holoscreen. INCITERS. I can hear Tyler Struck calling me a monster.

Tana is wrong. It's not safer for me here. How can it be when I possess the one power that will invite no mercy from my enemies? If I were a healer, they would want to use me. If I were a powerful mind reader like Jayde, I'd be the General's pet.

But I drew the short stick in the mutation lottery.

If they discover what I can do, they'll kill me. And I have absolutely no control over whether they find out. Stir up my emotions violently enough, and I might incite without warning. Reveal myself against my own will. Or worse . . . unintentionally hurt someone I care about. Maybe even kill them.

When I feel Wolf trying to link, I cling to that thread of energy like I'm drowning and it's a life preserver. Anything to derail the train of thought I've been careening toward.

"Hey, Daisy." His weariness engulfs my senses.

"Well, shit. You sound as done as I feel."

"I am. So fucking done." He sighs. "It's been a long day."

"Everything keen?"

"For the most part. What are you doing right now?"

"Thinking." I settle onto my back and rest my head against my pillow. "Remembering."

"Hmm. What are we remembering?"

"How I almost killed my father that one time."

His answering laugh holds a wry note. "Ah. I remember that. When you were thirteen? Fourteen?"

"Fourteen," I confirm.

"You realize you didn't do it on purpose, right?"

He's not wrong—it was entirely accidental. He just happens to be missing about, oh, all the context.

I adore Wolf, but what I share with him will always be partially redacted. He doesn't know that the father I often refer to is Jim, who wasn't even blood-related to me.

He doesn't know I possess more than the power of telepathy.

And he certainly doesn't know that the night Jim's truck flew off the road and rolled half a dozen times before coming to a stop in a heap of crushed metal . . . it happened because I incited Jim to do it.

"Of course I realize it," I answer.

"The roads were wet. You hit the gas too hard and skidded off the shoulder."

There wasn't a drop of rain that night. And I wasn't in the driver's seat.

"It was an accident," Wolf says.

It was a moment of raw, immature rage.

Uncle Jim had dragged me out of the town square where Tana and I had been sharing some pints of ale with a few Hamlett boys. Much older boys. He humiliated me in front of my friends. Hauled me over his shoulder and threw me into the passenger side of the truck while I cursed and shouted at him. He ignored my protests and started driving home. Didn't even look at me as I growled for him to turn the truck around and take me back to my friends.

We were halfway to the ranch when my frustration spilled over. When I yelled out the angry command. "Turn the truck around *now!*"

And he did. Giving the steering wheel a tug so sharp and abrupt that our truck flipped itself over.

"I'm aware of all this," I tell Wolf. "But that doesn't negate how terrifying it was. We were lucky to be alive."

Jim was lucky to be alive.

I always wondered if he'd have preferred I died that night. I know he loved me, but . . . I was a burden to him. I know I was.

I press my lips together to suppress a sob and distract myself by lobbing an accusation at Wolf.

"Somehow you always turn conversations around to make them about me. Tell me why you sound so exhausted tonight."

"I don't know. I guess I'm in the same place you were in on Liberty Day. Tired of it all. Pretending to be normal, hiding what I am . . . it's draining." There's a long pause. "Every day, I feel like I'm losing a part of myself."

It's a rare glimpse of vulnerability from Wolf. I know how he feels, though. Sometimes the weight of my abilities presses down so heavy on my chest, it's hard to breathe.

"It wears on you," I agree. "Always looking over your shoulder, always second-guessing everything you say and do." I bite my lip and stare at the ceiling. "How long do you think a person can keep doing that before they break?"

"We won't break."

He sounds very confident of that.

"No?"

"Nah, Daisy. We have each other. We'll keep each other strong."

His words are a balm to my weary soul. But that sense of contentedness doesn't last. After he retreats from my mind, I'm left feeling trapped and restless again.

I slide off the bed and head for the door. Voices travel out of the common room. The film is still playing. I walk in the opposite direction toward the exit of the building. I'm very aware of the cameras affixed to the ceiling, tracking my movements.

When I emerge outside, I jolt in surprise at the sight of Kaine sitting at the bottom of the short steps, his source in hand.

"Reading anything interesting?" I call out.

He twists his blond head to look at me. "Not in the slightest."

"Do you want to take a walk?"

"Sure." Tucking his source in his back pocket, he waits for me to descend the stairs and then holds out his hand.

I stare at it.

"What?" Kaine says.

"What are you doing?"

"If we're going to take a romantic walk together, Darlington, we should hold hands."

A snicker pops out. "Hold your own damn hand."

Those green eyes twinkle as we wander away from the barracks.

The night is unnaturally quiet, considering it's barely nine o'clock. I expected to see more activity. To hear more voices carrying in the darkness. But the only sounds are my soft breathing and the distant hum of the security force field that marks the perimeter of the base. I try to ignore the guard towers looming over us, the sensation of being watched, not just by the sentries but by the blinking cameras all around us as well.

Kaine is quiet, too. I wait for a flirty remark, but his gaze is focused straight ahead, his hands tucked loosely into the front pockets of his uniform pants. I follow his lead and stay silent.

We meander our way toward the east quadrant, where several supply warehouses sit in the shadows. Beyond them is one of the base's delivery gates. As we approach, I finally hear some voices. Male. They waft through the open door of a small outbuilding with a gray exterior.

Tension snaps my shoulders straight. The door isn't the only thing that's open in our vicinity.

So is the delivery gate.

And there's a motorcycle standing unattended just beside it.

CHAPTER 14

This is my chance.

Unless it's a trap.

It has to be a trap, right?

Why else was the delivery gate left inexplicably ajar? Why is there a motorcycle here?

Either fate herself is extending a hand to me, or Cross Redden set a trap for me. A test. Will Recruit 56 stay put like a good little soldier or will she try to run?

I stop walking.

"You okay?" Kaine says.

Drawing a steadying breath, I glance at the motorcycle, then at Kaine. He's watching me with a mixture of amusement and concern.

"What's going on, Darlington?"

"You should go back to the barracks," I tell him.

My gaze shifts to the bike again, then conducts a scan of our surroundings, searching the shadows for any sign of movement. About fifty yards away, the nearest guard tower looms ominously, its searchlight sweeping the grounds.

Timing is everything.

"Darlington . . ." It's a warning. "Whatever you're thinking right now . . ."

"Just go back to the barracks, Sutler. I'll see you later."

"Wren," he growls, but I'm already darting forward, adrenaline sizzling through my veins.

I reach the motorcycle, my fingers trembling as I grasp the handlebars. A thumb pad is required to start the engine, but whoever the bike belongs to didn't lock it. I swing my leg over, straddling the machine, and, with a rueful glance at Kaine, start the engine.

It roars to life. Without a second of hesitation, I twist the throttle and the bike surges forward, the sudden speed throwing me back. The open gate is *right there*. I lean into the handlebars, urging the motorcycle faster, and the world blurs around me, only the narrow path ahead in focus.

I speed through the gate, the cool night air whipping against my face. It's an exhilarating feeling—freedom. A wild, intoxicating sensation that seizes my chest as I race down a long, paved road. Behind me, the Command base recedes into the darkness, the oppressive weight of its walls lifting from my shoulders. Ahead of me, the open road stretches out like an invitation to the unknown.

It takes a moment to gather my bearings when the road comes to an abrupt end. I need to turn. But do I turn left or right . . . Sanctum Point is east of here. It'll be impossible to stay hidden in the city. Too many patrols. Drones.

I go left. E Ward borders the Point, and all those boring geography classes I suffered through in lower school taught me that E is basically one massive forest. If I could reach the forest, I could disappear.

I give the bike more gas, but it's still not moving fast enough for me. I'd kill for a speed bike right about now. I've never ridden one, but Tana has. She said when that chemical thrust kicks in, it feels like a rocket ship launching into outer space.

The wind hisses and screeches past my ears, stinging my face, but I can't slow down. This was either the best decision I've ever made in my life, or the dumbest, and I'm rapidly leaning toward the latter. I can't shake the rising tension in my body, the fear that someone will come after me. I push the bike harder, and the engine's growl is like a defiant roar in the night.

The landscape blurs past in streaks of black and gray, illuminated only by the thin beam of the motorcycle's headlight. I've just glimpsed what look like treetops in the distance when I hear it.

A second engine.

"Hellfuck!" I shout into the wind.

I risk a glance over my shoulder and see the other motorcycle bearing down on me, growing larger with each passing second. It's moving *fast*. Speed bike, for certain.

Panic grips me, and I work the throttle harder, my engine screaming in protest as I try to outrun my pursuer. But he only keeps gaining on me. I see his headlight dancing in the corners of my vision. My pulse pounds in my ears, every muscle in my body coiled as I push the bike to its limits.

I look behind me again and stifle a scream of frustration.

Cross.

His face is barely visible in the shadows, but that smug smirk is unmistakable. He's enjoying this. The thrill of the hunt.

My fingers tighten around the handlebars, knuckles white with tension. There must be a way out, a path that doesn't end with my recapture. But the barren road stretches endlessly ahead. Where the hell is the forest?

"Darlington! Pull over."

His voice is muffled by the wind. He's closed the gap between us, riding alongside me now.

I clench my jaw and refuse to look at him. "Go away!" I shout back. "I'm busy!"

"You're really going to want to pull over," is his barely audible reply.

And then, in the distance, I see it. The faint, eerie glow of a force field.

My heart sinks. If I keep going, I'll crash into it at full speed and be electrocuted, fried to a crisp before I even have a chance to taste freedom.

But I can't stop, damn it.

"Stop, damn it," Cross growls.

The force field grows closer, its shimmering aura hanging like a curtain of tiny stars across the night sky. Maybe I could—

What? challenges my incredulous inner voice. *Kill myself via a deadly electric current?*

I realize Cross isn't beside me anymore. He decelerated. I guess *he* doesn't have a death wish.

The force field is less than twenty feet away now. Defeat and anger bubble up inside me, a fierce, helpless rage. With a desperate tug, I yank the handlebars, trying to stop. The tires screech in protest, the bike fishtails wildly, and I lose control, the ground rushing up to meet me as I'm thrown from the seat.

I hit the ground hard. A sharp pain slices through my cheek as it scrapes against the rough surface. The metallic taste of blood fills my mouth. I groan, pushing myself up on trembling arms, as my ears ring and my chest heaves for breath. The motorcycle lies a few feet away, its engine still rumbling softly before sputtering to a stop.

Cross's footsteps don't even make a sound as he approaches me.

"Really? A force field?" I mutter at him. "Seems like a colossal waste of resources to install a field out here."

"Actually, it's been a great investment. You'd be surprised how many deserters this thing has caught."

He reaches out to help me up. I slap his hand away, glaring at him.

"I don't need your help," I snarl, wiping the blood from my face with the back of my hand. "And I'm not a deserter."

That earns me a low chuckle. "No? Then what do you call this thrilling chase we just embarked on?"

I shrug, finally managing to rise to my feet. "I wanted to feel the wind on my face."

Cross steps closer. His dark hair is windblown, and he runs his fingers through it, drawing my attention to his inked arm. He has the kind of tattoos you need to study in detail. From far away, they appear like meaningless swirls and spirals, but standing this close to him, I realize I'm looking at wings and flames, with tiny lines of text weaving through the designs. I resent the curiosity they evoke.

This is General Redden's son.

I shouldn't care what his ink means.

I shouldn't notice how dangerous it makes him look.

I shouldn't find that danger embarrassingly sexy.

"So this was . . . what? A joyride?" His arched brow tells me he doesn't buy the horseshit I'm selling.

"Yep."

I wipe both palms on the front of my pants, then wince when I realize tiny pieces of gravel are embedded in my flesh. That skid across the road is going to leave more than a few cuts and bruises.

"But," I continue, dropping my hands to my sides, "for argument's sake, if I *did* try to escape, would you really blame me? I told you I didn't want to join the Program. I don't want to be here."

His eyes bore into mine with an intensity that makes me want to look away. "You want out that badly? Fine. You win. I'll release you from the Program."

"You will?" I nearly keel over with relief. "You'll send me back to Z?"

"No."

I nod at that, resignation settling. "A labor camp, then?"

"No. If you leave the Program, the only place you're going is back to the stockade."

"For how long?" I demand.

"For as long as I want to keep you there."

Cross walks over to my fallen motorcycle. I watch the strong lines of his body as he bends to right the bike. I can't escape the constant flutter of desire whenever I'm near that stupid body.

"Get on," he orders.

I stay rooted in place. The stockade? God. No. I can't go back there. Back to that small room with its tiny window and suffocating walls. He could keep me locked up in there for months, years even, out of pure spite. The prospect of losing what little freedom I have is terrifying. My mind races in search of an alternative.

"Please. Let me return to my ward." I almost cringe at the desperation I hear in my voice.

He hears it, too, because when he walks toward me, his expression softens just a fraction, a hint of something almost like sympathy flickering in his gaze.

Then he says, "No."

I gulp hard, the reality of my situation sinking in. "There has to be a way for us to reach some sort of agreement." I study him for a long moment. "There must be something I can do to convince you to send me home."

I don't miss the way his eyes flare with heat. At least I think it's heat. Could also be irritation. Revulsion.

But if that *was* heat . . .

I swallow again, this time to bring moisture to my suddenly dry mouth. I could do it. There's no reason why I can't. In fact, it would be easy to let myself become infected by the twisted morality that governs our world, where the ends always justify the means, no matter the cost.

I erase the distance between us. Neither of us says a word as we face off in the darkness. He's so much bigger than I am. Taller, broader, more muscular. I feel small and vulnerable standing here with him, in the middle of the empty road. I run my trembling hands through my hair, tucking the tousled strands behind my ears. Cross's gaze tracks my movements.

"Are you offering to fuck me, Dove?"

His visible humor has me tightening my lips. "If that's what it takes to strike a deal, then sure, I suppose that's what I'm offering."

That dimple grooves his cheek, but his smile is more taunt than agreement. "Really? You're willing to do anything to strike a deal?"

"Yes."

His gaze rakes down my body, lingering on the dust coating my clothes, the blood caked onto the skin of my left arm, the arm that dragged along the gravel after I was thrown from the bike. This time, there's no mistaking the desire in his eyes.

"All right." His voice is thick, rough. "Come here."

I can't will my legs to move. I stand motionless, my pulse speeding up as I watch Cross bring both his hands to his waistband. I can scarcely breathe. In one deft motion, he pops open the button of his dark pants and then slides the zipper down.

He gives me an expectant look. "I don't have all night."

I'm finally able to suck in a breath, but it only succeeds in making me lightheaded. I'm ashamed to feel my lower lip begin to quiver, and I slam my teeth down on it to stop the traitorous response. He's not allowed to see how shaken I am.

"I . . ." I inhale again, then wrest my gaze away from his smirking face. "I withdraw the offer."

"That's what I thought."

The asshole is laughing at me as he zips up his pants. He knew from the start I'd never do it. He was just toying with me.

I jolt when I suddenly feel him beside me. His hip jostles mine, our arms brushing, as his mouth hovers right above my ear.

"You'd make a terrible whore, Dove."

Indignation shoots through me. I shove him away from me, breathing through the anger. "Screw you."

"Yes, I'm already aware of how much you want that."

The arrogance dripping from his words grates on my nerves. "Don't flatter yourself."

His perfect face creases with amusement. "You're usually a better liar than this. I see the way you look at me."

A rush of shame floods my belly. The unwanted sensation combines with the fury twisting my insides. I hate that he's right. There's an awareness here. Of the sexual variety.

I . . . might be attracted to him.

So maybe it's myself that I hate. I've slept with soldiers before, but an attraction to Cross is a betrayal like none other. It's like spitting in the face of every Mod on the Continent.

His last name is Redden. There's no justification for falling into bed with him. I'd never be able to explain it to Tana, or Wolf, or all the other innocents who have suffered because of the Redden family.

Cross's lips curl at my silence. "My suggestion? Get that idea out of your head, Darlington. I'm your CO. I don't screw recruits." He stalks toward the bike. "Now move your ass. It's time to go."

"I'll stay in the Program." It takes some effort to grind out the words.

He stops, glancing over at me. "Is that so?"

"Yes. If my choice is between the Program or the stockade, I choose the Program."

"How magnanimous of you. Now get on the fucking bike."

———

I wake several hours later to the blinding glare of fluorescent lights. A chorus of groans echoes through the barracks as we all blink against the harsh brightness. I instinctively reach for a rifle that isn't there.

"Everyone up! Now!" barks Xavier Ford. His voice is a gravelly snarl, slicing through the fog of sleep.

I scramble out of bed, joining my fellows as we stand to attention at the foot of our bunks. My body is still sore from the fall I took earlier, the road burn on my arm stinging when I accidentally run my hand over it.

Ford isn't alone. Cross strides inside and stops beside his lieutenant. Both men wear black from head to toe. My stomach churns with dread as Cross's eyes scan the room, finally settling on me with a look that could melt steel.

"Sorry to interrupt everyone's beauty sleep," he says, his voice thick with sarcasm. "You can all thank Darlington here for this wake-up call."

I feel every head in the room swivel toward me. I clench my fists, wishing I could disappear.

"Darlington decided she wanted to feel the wind on her face tonight," Cross continues. "Stole a Command vehicle and went for a little joyride."

I don't need empath powers to sense what everyone is feeling. Their expressions vary from shock to fury and disgust.

"Are you fucking kidding me right now?" I hear Kess mutter.

"So now you're *all* going to feel the wind on your faces," Cross finishes. "Get your gear. You're running laps until sunrise."

A collective groan reverberates through the air. Waves of outrage are directed at me, but there's nothing I can say to make it better. I grab my boots and quickly lace them up.

"Joyride, huh?" murmurs Kaine from the bed next to mine. "Looked like a lot more than that to me."

"It wasn't," I mutter back, avoiding his prying eyes. "I just . . . I needed to get out."

From the bunk across from us, Bryce Granger overhears my statement. "Well, now we're all paying for it," she snaps. "Thanks a lot."

"Enough chatter," Ford says. "Move it."

As we file out of the barracks, the cold night air hits me like a slap in the face. The base is quiet save for the sound of our boots on the pavement. Ford and Cross lead us to the track that winds around the perimeter of the compound. An open-top truck waits there. Ford slides behind the wheel while Cross settles in the passenger side. Ford lights a joint, looking bored.

"All right, start running," Cross drawls. "And keep running. You stop, you're cut from the Program."

The smirk he aims my way tells me I'm exempt from that threat. If I stop, I go to the stockade.

We take off, a groggy, disorganized mass at first, but eventually we fall into a rhythm. The air is sharp, each breath burning my lungs. I can hear the ragged breathing of the others around me, can feel their resentment like a physical weight.

"Why would you do that, Wren?" Lyddie pants, her voice muffled by the sound of our feet hitting the ground.

Unlike the others, she seems more disappointed than mad. Ugh. I hate it when people are disappointed in me. That's so much worse.

"I don't know," I admit. "I guess I just . . . needed to feel alive." It's the best lie I can come up with, and it sounds hollow to my ears.

"Well, congratulations," I hear Ivy say from behind us. "We're all feeling real alive right now."

In front of us, Kess, who's running alongside Roe and Anson, twists to sneer at me. "Selfish quat," she hisses. "You're fucking dead."

Ford's voice wafts out of the truck that follows the group at a lazy speed. "Pick up the pace, assholes! You're moving like snails!"

My legs are screaming, my body pleading for rest, but I push on. The memory of the wind in my hair as I rode away from the base earlier seems so distant now.

"Hey, Darlington," Betima says with an irritated breath. "Next time you want to feel alive, try not to drag us all down with you, keen?"

Whenever the truck gets close, I resist the urge to look at Cross.

Each time we pass an exit gate, I force myself not to cast a longing look toward it. I slip up only once, my gaze lingering on the gates that lead to South Plaza, and I can almost hear Cross's voice inside my head. *Go ahead, try to escape again. I dare you.*

No. I won't be attempting another escape. There's no room for reckless Wren anymore. I need to be more restrained going forward. If I run, it can't be a spur-of-the-moment decision like tonight's haphazard move. It needs to be planned. Methodical.

It's time to play it smart.

SECTION   1

Instructor	HADLEY (O), FORD (LT)
Student	Wren Darlington, R56
Class	Hand-to-Hand Combat
Score	30%

INSTRUCTOR NOTES:

Darlington shows lack of coordination.
Insolent attitude. No upper body strength
or combat instincts. Borderline useless.

CHAPTER 15

B y the time I was six years old, I was an expert in survival.

Jim taught me how to build a fire and keep it burning. How to mend my clothes. How to stitch my own wounds.

He taught me to recognize the dangerous plants in the Blacklands and utilize their poisons to eliminate the prey that crept into our clearing when the sun left us.

He taught me to hide when we heard the infrequent roar of a fighter jet powering through the sky, because he wasn't sure if the gap in the mist was large enough to make us visible from above.

He taught me to defend myself using only my fists, my legs, my teeth. He showed me that any part of my body could be used as a weapon.

He taught me how to stay alive.

All this is to say—I can kick Lyddie De Velde's delicate ass without breaking a sweat.

And yet I'm currently lying flat on my back, pretending to gasp for air.

Each time she's come at me, her movements hesitant and clumsy, I've let her gain the upper hand. Most of our fellows are busy with their own sparring matches, but a handful gather around us. I suspect they're all hoping to see me get annihilated on the mat.

It's been days since we served our collective punishment for my individual infraction, and most of my fellows still haven't forgiven me for making them run endless laps. Three recruits got cut that night, including the ever-timid Pera. Although with her it was only a matter of time. She was never going to find her footing here. The teenager joined the Program directly out of upper school, which I think was a mistake. At least two-thirds of the other recruits completed a year or more at a job assignment before coming here.

Kess is especially keen to remind me that she hates my guts. But at least she loathes me out loud, whereas Ivy likes to whisper about it in the mess hall with Bryce. Ivy's always fucking whispering.

Both she and Kess are watching my sparring match this morning. Their laughter grates, but I ignore it, scissoring my legs to disrupt Lyddie's footing. I use hardly any force, so I expect her to hold her stance.

Instead she goes tumbling to the mat.

Shit!

Would it kill this woman to be *better* at this?

It isn't until I intentionally allow her to pin me, her legs straddling my chest, her elbow digging into my windpipe, that Ford allows me to tap out.

"Hell, Darlington, you're embarrassing yourself," he sighs as I step off the mats.

"It's almost as if I don't belong here," I say with a pointed stare.

We finish out the day in the shooting range, where our weapons instructor Ivan shows us a new sniper rifle the General is putting into circulation. When it's my turn to test out the weapon, I chide myself for the excitement simmering in my gut.

There's only one corporation on the Continent that manufactures firearms: Tecmel. I have a Tecmel rifle at home. Former home, that is. The home that Cross Redden and his despotic father handed to strangers. But this rifle bears a manufacturing stamp I don't recognize. REMM-4.

"What's REMM?" I ask Ivan. Nothing displeases me more than

conveying genuine interest in this program, but curiosity gets the better of me.

"Defense manufacturer," the older man replies. He's got a head of curly gray hair and the steadiest grip I've ever seen. "The General just awarded REMM a massive contract to develop a line of weapons for low-light conditions. We'll be testing this one in the field during your training ops."

He shows me the clip-on night sight. It's lightweight. Adjustable. Perfection.

I almost shiver in pleasure. I feel genuine disappointment when I must relinquish the weapon to Ivan.

Kaine pokes me in the ribs. "You look like you want to go to bed with that rifle."

"Shut up."

"Seriously. You're panting." He grins. "For someone who loves firearms this much, you would think you'd be a better shot."

I offer a sweet smile. "You don't have to be good at the things you love, Sutler. Sort of like how I imagine you love sex, but are terrible at it."

That summons a laugh. "Why don't you find out?"

"No, thank you."

"You're missing out."

"I really don't think I am."

Lyddie giggles. Everyone in Black Cell has naturally grouped off, and the three of us have formed an unlikely trio. I'm wary of everyone else, especially the Psycho Brigade, which consists of Anson, Roe, and Kess. Interestingly, I notice Ivy standing with their group today. She spends most of her time with Bryce and a male recruit named Jones, so it raises my hackles to see her with those three. They're huddled around like a pack of white coyotes.

"Your grip is all wrong," Ivan chastises me when it's my turn to shoot again. He's already demonstrated the proper two-handed grip half a dozen times, but silly me, I can't quite perfect it.

"I'm trying," I say, feigning helplessness.

"Sutler," he orders. "Go work with Darlington."

Well, that backfired.

A grinning Kaine joins me. He looks good today. He always looks good. The problem is, he knows it.

"So, we need to perfect your grip, huh?"

I sigh at his cheeky smile.

"Here, cowgirl. Let me show you." His hands lightly brush my shoulders as he moves to stand behind me.

"There's no reason for you to stand so close," I grumble. "Just show off your grip and be on your way."

"Nah. I think this requires some intensive hands-on training. Ivan agrees." Kaine calls over his shoulder, "Right, Ivan?"

The middle-aged man is busy with Lyddie. I don't think he heard a word Kaine said when he calls back, "Affirmative."

"See?"

I sigh again.

Kaine wraps both arms around me from behind. I instantly stiffen.

"It's just a demonstration, Darlington. Relax."

Easier said than done. My heart beats a little faster at his proximity. Kaine's hands slide down my arms, guiding them into position. His breath is warm against the back of my neck, sending a shiver dancing along my spine.

"Make sure your dominant hand is high up on the grip." His hand covers mine, adjusting my positioning. "Like this. Feel that?"

"Yeah," I manage to say.

His other hand comes around, settling over my left hand. "With your support hand, you want to wrap your fingers around your dominant hand. Keep your thumbs aligned. See?"

I nod, but my mind is more focused on the sensation of his body pressed against mine, his arms enveloping me. It's . . . distracting.

"Fix your stance. Wider."

I play dumb, spreading my feet farther apart. "Like this?"

"Perfect. There you go. Now, finger on the trigger. Focus on your target. And . . . squeeze."

I squeeze the trigger, and the recoil pushes me backward into Kaine's chest. Neither of us pays attention to where my bullet went. I'm far too fascinated by the way his fingertips graze my shoulder.

I twist my head up and find myself peering into a pair of heavy-lidded green eyes. His heated expression brings a tingle between my legs.

"See? Not so hard," he whispers, his lips dangerously close to my ear. "You're a natural."

"Kaine," I whisper back.

He licks his lips. "Mmm?"

"Stop fucking flirting with me." I shove him away, summoning a laugh from him.

"You're no fun at all, cowgirl," he accuses, still laughing as he saunters back to his own station.

———

Later, we file into the mess hall for dinner. I sit with Lyddie and Kaine at a table in the corner of the room, and we're welcomed by two new faces. One is Lash, or the Observer, as Lyddie secretly refers to him, based on his unnerving habit of watching everyone and rarely contributing to conversations. He sits across from me, silent, and I catch him glancing at me several times. When I raise a brow, he shrugs and looks down at his rations. We're also joined by Betima, who, as it turns out, is hilarious. She spends most of the meal regaling us with stories about the ghastly job assignment she'd received after upper school.

As I eat, I start to notice the whispers.

They're coming from Kess's table, which is unusual because those asswits aren't typically concerned about the volume of their voices. Ivy and Bryce sit with them tonight, once again triggering an alarm inside me.

The whispering continues throughout dinner, and I can't shake the suspicion it's about me, even though I don't appear to be attracting glares or sneers. It's just a gut feeling. A bad feeling.

I wait to shower closer to lights-out, because most of the other women shower before dinner and this offers me more privacy. Tonight, Lyddie joins me. She steps into the stall next to mine, and we chat over the partition as steam fills the fluorescent-lit room.

"Kaine is so on for you," she tells me, her eyes dancing.

"I think he's locked on anything with a pulse."

"No. He likes *you*. I can tell."

"Maybe."

She tips her head in challenge, causing water droplets to slide down her delicate throat. "Don't you dare tell me you don't like him, too. He's the best-looking guy in the Program."

"He's also the cockiest," I counter.

"What's wrong with cocky?" Lyddie shuts off the water and reaches for her towel. "Cocky can be fun."

She has a point. Kaine is certainly fun. I enjoy flirting with him, and the idea of falling into bed with him is tempting—if I didn't have to be on constant alert here. Sex is a distraction I'm not sure I can afford right now. Not when I'm in enemy territory.

I wrap myself in a towel and follow Lyddie to the wall of sinks. The terry cloth hangs to my knees, concealing the burn scars on my thigh, but when I lean forward to wipe steam off the mirror, my towel rides up and I hear Lyddie's breath hitch.

I give her a knowing look. "You can ask about it if you want."

She wrests her gaze away. Then glances back, sheepish. "Sorry. It's rude to stare."

"It's fine."

Biting her lip, she runs a hairbrush through her damp hair. I know she wants to ask, but it takes her forever to rustle up the courage.

"So, um, what happened?"

I shrug. "Accidentally dropped a pot of boiling water on myself when I was a kid."

"Whoa." She grimaces. "That must have been painful."

Excruciating. I still smell the burning flesh in my nostrils sometimes, that's how visceral the memory is. It's as clear to me as my reflection in the mirror. Running through the clearing, arms stretched out as I pretended to fly with the bluebirds flapping around my head. Then I blinked and Uncle Jim was grabbing me. He was frantic, ignoring my confusion, my protests, as he gripped my waist and pushed the waistband of my shorts down a couple of inches. He'd seen something when my arms were thrown in the air, when the hem of my shirt rode up to reveal a sliver of bronzed skin.

"When did this happen?" he demanded, and I remember peering down at the birthmark. A perfect circle right below my hip bone. About two inches in diameter.

Blood red.

"I dunno," I whimpered, because I truly didn't.

But he didn't like that answer. He grew agitated, displaying anger. Dread. "When did this mark appear, Wren?"

"I dunno," I insisted, and I watched as he drew a breath.

"Wren." He cleared his throat, softening the gravel from his voice. "I love you very much."

I frowned. This was so unlike him—emotion. He didn't show emotion, and he certainly didn't voice it. "Can I go back to the birds now?" I whined.

"No. Come stand beside me. Stand still. Don't move a muscle."

With one hand, he drew my shirt up to my navel, then dragged my shorts below my hip. And before I could grasp his intentions, his other hand was circling the handle of the steaming pot on the fire, and I shrieked as the scalding water poured over my exposed flesh. A high, bone-chilling sound that caused every bird in the clearing to take flight, flee in haste. He threw the empty pot aside and tried to reach for me. He said my name and I screamed for him not to touch me. Batted at his outstretched arm and scurried backward, my anguished sobs piercing the air.

"I'm sorry, little bird. I had to," he said roughly, as the skin of my thigh puckered and bubbled, charred and reddened. A piece of fabric from my shirt had melted into my burnt flesh.

I hated him that day. The kind of hatred that makes your hands shake and your breaths shallow.

My adult brain understands why he did it. He'd acted in my best interests. The bloodmark needed to be destroyed, plain and simple.

But I bear a different mark now. A badge of ugliness that brings pity to Lyddie's eyes before she shifts them back to her own reflection.

———

The whispers continue into the following morning. I notice Ivy frowning at me in the mirror before she leaves the lavatories. I catch Kess's smirk. Anson's dead stare. Roe's shrewd one. I've yet to decipher the captain's younger brother. He carries himself with an air of entitlement, treats our instructors with insolence and apathy. I sense a destructive petulance in him that makes me uneasy, but at the same time, I get the feeling he's far more intelligent than he lets on.

Pretending to look for my source, I linger in the barracks so I don't have to walk to the mess hall with them. Only after they shuffle out and I hear their footsteps retreat do I step into the corridor.

The clinking of utensils against plates fills the vast mess hall when I enter a few minutes later. I grab a tray, get in line, and dutifully accept my plate of scrambled eggs and bacon. Not synthetic bacon, either. I suppose the one upside to being held prisoner by the Command is that these jerks get to eat real meat.

I scan the room until I spot Kaine's blond head. He's with Lash, Lyddie, and Betima, but not at the corner table we occupied yesterday. Half a dozen Red Cell members beat us to it this morning.

Mess hall is the only time we see the recruits from Red Cell. They tend to stick to one side of the room and keep to themselves. It's interesting how we've naturally broken off into two opposing forces, mistrustful of each other despite us never competing, never even interacting.

I notice I'm drawing a lot of stares. The clatter of trays and hum of conversation remain constant, but I feel too many pairs of eyes on me, and I don't like it. Whispers tickle my wake, and by the time I reach my table, I'm annoyed.

"Any reason why everyone is talking about me?"

"Oh?" Lyddie's tone is suspiciously neutral. "I don't think they are."

"No, they are," Kaine corrects, and Betima snickers under her breath.

"What's going on?"

Silence falls. Even Kaine, who's never met a situation he can't find humor in, keeps his mouth shut.

"What's going on?" I repeat.

"Well. Um." Lyddie's doing that thing she does, where she tries too hard to be tactful instead of just stating what needs to be said.

"Spit it out, Lydia."

She pushes her eggs around her plate. "Some people are saying . . . that, uh, your uncle was Aberrant." She won't meet my eyes anymore. "And he was executed for concealment."

I slam my fork down on my tray.

"That struck a nerve," murmurs Kaine.

As bitterness whips through me, I grind my teeth so hard, I'm surprised nobody can hear my molars crunching.

Finally, I find my voice. Low and even. "My uncle wasn't Aberrant."

"Was he executed?" Lyddie asks. Beside her, Lash's gaze is unsettling in its intensity.

I nod in defeat. "He faced the firing squad. But what they're saying about him isn't true."

Even as the lie slips out, I feel the weight of the truth pressing down on me, amplified by the sidelong glances directed my way. Every single one of these people would happily see me dead if they knew what I was. They've been taught from birth that there's something wrong with me. I'm an aberration. I'm defective. I don't belong in society among the likes of them. We are not peers. They are better than me.

Except they're not. They're no better and no worse. We all live on this godforsaken Continent together, and we're all equally fucked.

"I don't know what's going on," I continue, "but they charged him with desertion and concealment. The desertion part, fine, I guess I believe it. They showed me his file and it confirms he was in the Command. I don't know why he left, but what I do know for certain is he *wasn't* Aberrant. I lived with him for twelve years. There's no way he could've been one of them all along without me suspecting."

Relief flickers through Lyddie's eyes. "I can't imagine how he'd even pull it off. Especially because of their veins. It's not like they can hide it forever."

"Exactly. It's impossible for anyone to maintain their cover for that long. I would've known." I shake my head. "I wasn't sharing a house with a 'fect."

My acting abilities impress even me. It almost makes me sick how easily I can spew this nonsense.

"At least it makes sense now, why you're here," Lash says with a rare contribution to the conversation. "Given that you don't seem to enjoy it much."

I give him a wary look.

"They're making you prove your loyalty, right?" He shrugs. "I've heard of them doing that before. Drafting family members of criminals as a loyalty test."

He's just provided me a great cover story, and I have no problem taking full advantage. "Pretty much, yeah. The Command probably wouldn't have been my first choice of life path. I miss the ranch. But if serving the General shows him that I can be trusted, then I'm happy to do it."

Lyddie nods her approval.

"How did everyone find out about my uncle, anyway?" I shove my tray aside. My appetite is completely gone.

Kaine fields that question. "Eversea."

It takes me a second to connect the surname with its owner. "Ivy?"

Irritation tickles my throat as I seek her out. She's sitting with Bryce and a few others. When her gaze meets mine, she gives a hint of a sneer. I remember her saying that one of her Copper Block fellows was in South Plaza for Uncle Jim's execution, but I wonder how she connected Jim to *me*.

Did Cross Redden tell her?

It annoys me that he might have.

Another silence settles over the table. From the corner of my eye, I sense movement. I swivel my head in time to see Kess sauntering toward us, and my fists clench involuntarily.

Ignoring her, I focus on my barely touched meal, hoping she'll take the hint and move on.

She doesn't. She stands directly behind me, breathing down the back of my neck. "Settle a wager for us, Darlington."

I don't turn around. "I'd rather not."

"Oh, but I think it will be fun."

"I think," I say, slowly shifting in my chair, "you and I probably have different ideas about what's fun." I lock my gaze to hers. "So maybe you should go back to your table now."

"I'm not going anywhere."

"Suit yourself. You can stand there like an asswit and watch me enjoy my breakfast." I hold eye contact as I lift my coffee cup to my lips. I take a long sip.

Kess's black hair ripples around her chin as she glances back at her friends. They're all watching in interest. Roe is leaning back in his chair, legs sprawled out in front of him, but his sharp expression belies the casual pose.

Knowing she can't be seen backing down, Kess kicks the leg of my chair, and my cup jolts in my hand. I manage not to spill a drop.

"Stop staring at me, bitch."

I can't help a laugh. "You're the one looming over me like a creep. You're free to walk away anytime."

Kaine chuckles into his coffee.

"Not until you settle something for me." She smirks, relishing the confrontation. "Did you know he was a 'fect?"

Don't you dare engage.

"Who?" I put on a bored voice.

"Your traitor uncle. The one who went down in a spray of bullets."

I can feel the eyes of the entire mess hall on us now, eager to see how I'll react. I breathe through my nose. Suppress the anger.

"What do you want from me, Kess?" I snap, my patience wearing thin.

"Like I said, our curiosity needs satisfying. Did his veins turn silver when he was banging you? I heard that happens to them in the bedroom."

My blood boils as the accusations echo in my ears.

I push myself to my feet.

"Darlington," Kaine cautions.

I ignore him. "You really don't want to piss me off this early in the morning," I tell Kess.

"Or what? You'll snitch on me?" She nods toward the instructors' table.

I know without a doubt that Hadley and Struck are aware of the storm brewing across the room, but they remain seated. Watching us over the rims of their coffee cups.

"Do it," she urges. "Go tell them your fellows are hurting your precious feelings. Saying mean things about your Aberrant uncle."

She's really not worth my energy. I start to turn away, but she's still running her mouth.

"Heard the 'fect adopted you when you were six or something. Seems a bit young . . . But I suppose the silverbloods aren't known for their morality, are they? And maybe you liked it when his hands were all over you—"

I spin around and strike, my fist connecting with Kess's jaw. She stumbles backward, caught off guard by the sudden attack. But she recovers quickly, launching herself at me with a snarl of rage.

"Wren!" I hear Lyddie shout, but I'm beyond listening. To Lyddie. To Kess. To anyone.

Screw these people. These smug Primes who think they own the world.

The mess hall erupts into chaos. Cheers and catcalls break out, and chairs scrape the floor as recruits scramble to their feet. I pay them no mind as I unleash all my pent-up grief and anger on Kess, defending Jim's honor with every blow.

My next punch sends her crashing into the neighboring table, but she pulls me with her. We collide into the chairs then go hurtling to the ground.

"*Bitch,*" she growls.

Blood pulses in my ears. Each strike of my fists is fueled by the burning desire to shut this woman's obnoxious mouth. I roll on top of her and slam my knuckles into her jaw, sending her head thumping against the floor. She hisses with fury and uses her right forearm to block, while her left fist swings upward and connects with my mouth. My lip catches on a tooth, and I feel moisture dripping down my chin. Before Kess can hit me again, I knock her hand away and drive my elbow into her face.

There's no more satisfying sound than the crunch of her nose as it breaks. No more satisfying sight than the two red streams that pour out of her nostrils.

Suddenly I'm hauled to my feet. Strong arms wrap around my waist, pulling me away from Kess. I thrash against my captor, my vision blurred with rage as I watch Kess being helped up by Roe and Anson.

"Easy, cowgirl." Kaine's voice. A warning in my ear.

"Let me go," I snarl.

"No." His arm is an iron band. My chest is heaving. I taste blood in my mouth.

Hadley and Struck run over, thrusting themselves between our two groups.

"Enough!" Hadley's voice roars over the din. "Break it up, both of you!"

Kess tries to lunge again. Hadley shoves her back with a firm hand.

"Save it for a pit night," he snaps.

As the adrenaline ebbs, I find myself panting for breath, my knuckles bruised and bloodied from the fight.

"Goddamn it, Darlington," Struck mutters, prying me out of Kaine's restraining arms. "Get over here."

She drags me away from the crowd, her face red with frustration. I hear Hadley addressing someone behind me. "Take her to Medical," he says, and I realize he's talking about Kess. Good. As I'm being led off, a sense of grim satisfaction settles over me. Fuck that bitch.

CHAPTER 16

CAPTAIN OF OPERATIONS.

For the second time in a week, I'm escorted to that dreaded door.

The sound of my boots on the polished floor seems louder than usual, each step bringing me closer to impending confrontation. This time, I won't let his chiseled face have an effect on me. Now that I know who his father is, now that he sold me out to my cell and made us run laps in the middle of the night, the attraction is gone anyway. There's nothing appealing about—

A bare chest assaults my vision when I step into the cavernous office.

He's in the process of taking off his long-sleeved shirt. The black fabric falls away to reveal a sculpted chest adorned with scars and weapons. Taut muscles. The faintest sheen of sweat glistening on his skin.

My cheeks flush as a wave of heat washes over me. There's sand in my mouth. I swallow, but it just scrapes its way down my throat. His chest is magnificent.

He eyes me without a word. Biceps flex as he tosses the shirt on the conference table.

It's still there. The undeniable attraction that bubbles beneath the surface. The attraction he mocked me about the night of my failed escape. I want to drown it out of existence.

Redden, I remind myself. Cross *Redden*.

His father is a monster, and by extension, so is he.

I watch silently as he reaches for the sheaths strapped to his body and begins to remove his weapons. Three handguns. Just as many knives. Each blade gleams in the dim light of the room. One by one, he sets them aside on the table with practiced precision.

I despise the way my pulse races at the sight of his chest. I resent the way my gaze travels over his broad shoulders and defined muscles. He grabs another shirt and glances at me as he pulls it over his head. It's his navy-blue uniform shirt, and I wonder where he came from, armed to the teeth, sweaty, and dressed all in black, this early in the morning. Maybe he never went to bed.

"Twice in one week," he says. "This is a record."

His eyes sweep me up and down, then focus on the corner of my mouth.

I run my tongue over it and feel the caked blood there. "I told you I was going to be a problem."

"So this is going to become a habit?"

"Honestly, it seems likely."

He nearly smiles. I know it because that dimple throbs just slightly before smoothing out. He walks to his desk and picks up his tablet. A second later, he starts to read out loud.

"'Lack of coordination. Insolent attitude. No upper body strength or combat instincts. Borderline useless.'"

"Don't be so hard on yourself, Captain. I'm sure you possess *some* redeeming qualities."

"That's Ford's opinion of your fighting skills."

I'm all innocence. "I faced some formidable opponents yesterday. Didn't stand a chance."

Cross studies me again, pensive. "And yet Kess Farren is one of our most promising recruits, and you just sent her to Medical."

"She didn't seem very promising when her face was under my fist."

His stride is pure arrogance as he walks toward me. I hold my ground despite my accelerating heartbeat, but then he touches my lips, and my heart stops in my chest.

"This mouth," he warns, his thumb scraping the seam of my lips until it reaches the cut in the corner, "is going to get you in trouble, Dove."

It's hard to draw a breath. When I finally do, my chest rises, and his gaze lowers to it.

Redden. Cross Redden.

Very slowly, I inch forward. He blinks in surprise. Our bodies are almost flush as I advance, walking him backward toward his desk. Until his ass hits the solid wood and he has nowhere else to go. I lick the corner of my mouth, and a coppery flavor coats my tongue.

"Cross," I say.

He blinks again, as if surprised to hear his name leaving my lips.

"I don't know how the General raised you, but where I come from, you don't touch a woman without her consent."

I rub the cut, scraping my nails over it so it spills open. Coating the pads of my fingers with blood. Then I reach out and drag those fingertips over the Silver Block emblem on his shirt. I smile as the silver coloring is stained red.

His nostrils flare.

"In other words," I finish, my voice cold, "don't touch me again without my permission."

Cross's gaze never leaves my face. "Or what?"

I frown at him.

"What are you going to do, Darlington? Hit me? Go ahead. Do it."

My hands curl into fists. I press them to my sides and take a backward step. "Don't tempt me."

"Do it," he repeats, baring his teeth in a dark smile. "I could use the excitement."

"You didn't get enough of it last night? Because those were a lot of weapons I saw you unsheathing just now." I slant my head in challenge.

Rather than shed light on that, he says, "Why did you attack Farren?"

My voice tightens. "Because she insinuated my uncle sexually assaulted me when I was a child. Among other things."

His eyebrows flick up. "You need to develop a tougher skin."

"Are we done here, or are you going to cut me for attacking your favorite recruit? Because I'm happy to accept that punishment."

"You've reconsidered the stockade, then?"

I clench my teeth.

"I'll take that as a no." Cross sidesteps me, his strides lazy but measured as he begins to circle me. "In regard to your punishment . . ."

He pauses. Pensive. But something else glints in his eyes. Something very unsettling.

"A slap on the wrist?" I suggest.

"You attacked one of your fellows. That can't go unpunished. Neither can your insubordination. You seem to forget the hierarchy of power in this room, Dove. You're not in charge. I am. Speak to me accordingly."

"Or . . ." I smile at him. "You can fuck right off."

He ignores that. "Insubordination has consequences. But I'll tell you what—I'll give you a chance to avoid punishment."

He opens his office door, then walks to his desk and leans against it, nodding toward the gaping doorway.

"Get to the door. If you can get through me, you're free to go. If not, every member of Black Cell is running laps again tonight from dusk till dawn."

My gaze slides from him to the door. We're equal distance from it. If I catch him off guard and break into a run . . .

He pushes off the desk and takes a few steps forward, closing the distance between us. "Let's see how uncoordinated and borderline useless you really are—"

I lunge at him, aiming a punch at his midsection. He deflects it effortlessly, his hand catching my wrist and twisting it behind my back. I wince but pivot my body, using the momentum to break free.

Cross smirks, but he's clearly impressed by my maneuver. "Nice try."

I spin around and aim a kick at his side, then hurtle toward the doorway again. But he catches my ankle and pulls me off-balance, sending me sprawling to the concrete floor. Before I can recover, he's on top of me, pinning me down with his weight. His face is inches away, eyes gleaming.

"You're going to have to do better than that, Dove."

I grit my teeth and buck my hips, trying to throw him off, but he holds firm, his grip like iron. I can feel every inch of his body against mine, and it . . . is . . . maddening. I twist, managing to free one arm, and swing at his jaw. He catches my fist, his lips curling into a smile.

"The door is over there. And you're down here. Doesn't seem like you're making much progress."

I glare at him. My breath escapes in short, ragged gasps. With a deep inhalation, I gather my strength, using my free hand to push against his chest. He's solid muscle, and for a moment, I'm distracted by the feel of him. He takes advantage of my hesitation, flipping me onto my stomach and locking my wrists behind my back.

"Looks like you're not reaching that door." His voice is a low rumble.

I thrash beneath him, my frustration mounting. "This isn't fair. You're like a hundred pounds heavier than I am."

He leans closer, his lips brushing my ear. "Life isn't fair, Darlington," he says coldly. "And neither am I."

Anger sizzles through me. With a sudden burst of energy, I wrench my body to the side, succeeding in releasing one leg and kicking him hard in the abdomen. He grunts, loosening his grip just enough for me to slip out from under him. I scramble to my feet, panting.

"Nice move," he remarks, rubbing his side.

I don't waste time with a response. I dart toward the door, but Cross is faster. He grabs me around the waist and hauls me backward, slamming me against the wall. Pain radiates through my body, which is already sore and bruised from Kess's blows.

I look up at him, my chest heaving. "You're such a prick."

"Just making sure you understand the consequences of defying me."

His words send an odd thrill through me, and I hate that he has the ability to affect me this way. I shove against his chest, trying to push him away. He doesn't budge.

"Stubborn," he mutters.

And that's how Xavier Ford finds us. The lieutenant enters the office with quick strides, then halts when his gaze collides with me and Cross locked in a showdown.

"Captain?" It sounds like he's trying not to laugh.

Cross glances over. "Black Cell is running tonight. Make sure the recruits know who to thank again."

Ford's dark eyes shift toward me. "Got it."

"And next time Darlington attacks one of my recruits, reward her with two nights in Stock C."

"Yessir."

Cross releases me and returns to his desk. "You're dismissed, Darlington."

———

At the end of the week, our scores for the first section are uploaded to our sources. I have to pretend to care like everybody else. Like Lyddie, who cares too much. During our afternoon break, when Hadley announces the scores are available, all my fellows become rabid wolves, pouncing on their sources.

My score is 49 percent.

I hide a smile. Perfect.

On the outside, I paste on a dejected face. Lyddie doesn't miss it. "Can I see?" she asks.

I angle the source toward her. She winces as if my score makes her physically ill. Or maybe she thinks it's contagious.

Lyddie grimaces. "I'm sorry." She's about to say more, but then hesitates.

"What?"

"Can I be blunt?"

"It would annoy me if you weren't."

She smiles faintly. "You don't apply yourself."

No kidding.

I offer another shrug. "I already told you, I'm not good at the classroom stuff. It's too hard."

It's actually very easy when you're not trying.

"You need to put in the work," she says with a serious face. "Even Kaine studies the maps after we're dismissed for the day."

I did notice that. He was poring over his source all night yesterday, reading up on the various outposts and installations throughout the Continent.

Lyddie takes my silence as offense. "I'm not trying to make you feel bad."

"Oh no. I don't. You're right. I should study harder."

She reaches across the table and takes my hand, squeezing it. "I'll help you," she says firmly. "An hour of studying before lights-out every night."

Her expression is so earnest it triggers a pang of guilt. Now I feel like a jerk.

"You don't have to do that."

"I want to. You're . . ." Her cheeks turn a little pink. "I know I'm being presumptuous. We don't know each other well yet, and you probably don't even view me as a friend—"

"I do," I assure her, and it's not entirely a lie. In here, I would certainly call her my closest ally.

"I consider you a friend, too. You're funny. And you're smarter than you think. You're a fast learner—look how much better your marksmanship is getting."

Sure, because it's difficult to be incompetent. There's a fine line between looking bad at something and looking like you're deliberately sabotaging.

"I don't want you to get cut. That means we need to get you studying, girl. One hour, every night. Keen?"

"Keen," I say, and her whole face lights up. At the notion of *helping* me. God, I wish I could dislike her, but I really don't.

Kaine and Lash join us, setting down their trays. From the Psycho Brigade table, I feel Kess's murderous eyes boring into the side of my head.

It brings me great pleasure that the bruising on her face still hasn't faded. Her skin was black and purple the day after I attacked her.

When the medics set her nose and sent her back to the bunks, I expected retaliation that night. She would try to smother me in my sleep. Drag me out of bed and hold me down while Anson did all the revolting things he imagines doing to me in his head.

But nothing happened. I don't know if the instructors warned her against it or if she's simply biding her time, but I'm not foolish enough to believe that Kess is going to let this slide.

"Well?" Kaine asks us.

"Eighty-eight," Lyddie says, then blushes when he answers, "Nice job, Lyds."

"I'm failing," I tell the guys and bite into a piece of bread.

Kaine grins. "If I didn't know any better, I'd think you were trying to get cut on purpose."

I freeze. "Of course not. Why would I ever do that?"

"Oh, I know you're not. You need to prove yourself to the higher-ups. But damn, cowgirl, you can't pass a test to save your life."

"Lyddie's going to help me study," I say, affecting a defensive tone.

Lash sits in silence as always. He rarely involves himself in our conversations unless they're about politics, and I try to avoid those at all costs. But he does have strong opinions when you get him going.

Betima joins us next, settling in the chair next to Kaine's. "What are you doing with your leisure pass this weekend?" she asks everyone.

Kaine shrugs. "Don't know yet. Maybe drink myself stupid to make up for this week."

He's not the only recruit who's been grumbling about the base's imposed limits on alcohol intake. We can use our credits to buy booze at the commissary, but we're only allowed to drink in the common room, and only on the weekends.

Me, I don't care about getting drunk, and this is the first I'm hearing about a leisure pass.

"We get a leisure pass?" I say, unable to fight a twinge of hope. This could be it. My shot to escape. They'll have a hard time tracking me once I leave the base.

"It's a Sunday pass. Came in on our source." Lyddie wrinkles her brow. "I had to scan my thumb to activate it. You didn't get one?"

Suspicion tightens my throat. I grab my source. "Where was it?"

"In the comm folder."

I open the folder and . . . there's nothing.

"My folder is empty."

She takes the source from me to investigate. The groove in her forehead deepens. "That's odd. You didn't receive one."

I glance at the others. "Did you all get a leisure pass?"

They nod.

What the hell. Why are they allowed to leave the base on Sunday when—

Cross.

Of fucking course. There's no way he's letting me step foot outside this facility.

"I'll be right back," I mutter, scraping back my chair.

I find Hadley and Struck at a table in the corner. They're not talking, each focused on their tablets, but their heads snap up at my approach.

"Why don't I have a leisure pass for Sunday?" I demand.

Hadley spares me a look before lowering his gaze to his screen. "You haven't been approved."

"Everyone else is approved."

Struck sounds amused. "Everyone else isn't you, Darlington."

I swear I'm going to splinter my enamel with the way I'm grinding my teeth. "I want to talk to the captain."

"No," Hadley says without lifting his head.

I turn to Struck. "Can you please take me to see the captain?"

"He's a busy man, Darlington. He doesn't have time to address every petty complaint from recruits."

"He makes time for me whenever I break your little rules." I glower at her unaffected expression. "Is that what it takes? Fine. Here you go."

I snatch Hadley's tray off the table and hurl it against the wall over Struck's head.

Chunks of beef stew splatter the wall and drip down it like thick globs of mud. A few peas fall into the instructor's dark hair.

The entire mess hall goes silent. She stares at me in disbelief. Then a chuckle breaches the silence. Cross's half brother.

I smile at her, all teeth. "May I see the captain now?"

She peels the peas off and flicks them onto the floor. "No."

———

I'm still fuming later in bed. I find no solace in the sounds of the dormitory, the even breathing, the snores coming from Glin Cotter's bunk. We're all starting to resent the poor guy. A few more days of those guttural honks and I fear Anson will slit his throat in his sleep.

I lie on my bunk, staring at the ceiling. Glin's arrhythmic snores fill the room, but my mind is restless. I twist my head toward Kaine's bed. The gray blanket is pulled up to his neck and cocooned around his body. He sleeps like a mummy.

It's late, so when I reach out to Wolf, I'm surprised that he links with me. Wolf tends to be early to sleep, early to rise.

"Why are you awake?"

"Stress."

"Stress," I echo, teasing.

"Yeah. I had a shit week. And then last night . . ." He doesn't continue.

"Last night what?"

"Nightmare. That's all."

"The drowning one?"

Laughter rumbles inside my head.

"What's so funny?" I ask, but the sound is so comforting. I've heard that laugh nearly my entire life. It's a reminder that while Jim is gone, I'm not entirely alone.

"Something just occurred to me," Wolf says.

"And what's that?"

I hear a rustling noise and glance over. Kaine shifts in slumber. His face is still turned in my direction, but his eyelids remain shut. He has no idea I'm carrying on an entire conversation beside him.

"That we know both everything about each other and nothing at all. I don't know your job assignment. Your family life. Hell, I don't even know your ward."

"I don't know yours, either." Although I can guess he's probably in the south since he talks about the ocean so often.

But he's right. We don't know the kind of information that's normally free flowing between close friends. Uncle Jim instilled in me the need for secrecy, and as much as I enjoy Wolf, I would never risk my safety or my uncle's safety on a stranger in my head. I omitted a lot of pertinent details over the years. The ranch. Jim. My real name.

"We don't know basic facts, yet you're an expert about my recurring nightmares." This makes him laugh again.

"Basic facts don't matter. It's the important things that matter."

His fears. His insecurities. That his favorite sound is rain hitting pavement, and the physical feature he likes best about himself is his hands. That he lost his virginity at sixteen, and the only woman he's ever given flowers to is his mother. What does his mother do for a living? I couldn't tell you. But it makes no difference at all to me.

"Did you wake up before the water filled your lungs?" I know sometimes he's jolted awake just as he's going under.

"No."

I shiver to myself. I've never drowned in a nightmare before. It happens to Wolf often. He described it to me once, and it sounded like pure torture.

"Don't want to think about it. Why can't you sleep?"

"Stress," I mimic.

He chuckles. "Feel free to elaborate."

"I feel . . . stuck." I'm careful with the details. Under no circumstances can I tell him I'm training for the Command. We trust each other, yes, but Mods get spooked about this stuff. "I'm not where I'm supposed to be, and it's suffocating. I hate feeling trapped."

"Then escape the trap."

"Easier said than done."

"Bullshit. Every trap can be escaped. It's just a matter of what lengths you're willing to go to."

"Oh really?"

"Mmm-hmm." His voice is a soft rumble in my head. I roll over and let it warm me like a blanket, turning away from Kaine. "Think about it. Animals get caught in traps all the time, keen? But the smart ones, the ones who refuse to be caged, they find a way out. White coyotes, for example. Unless you're right on their ass when they're captured, they're usually gone by the time you check your traps."

"Because they're known to chew off a limb to escape!"

"Like I said, it's a matter of lengths. The white coyote would rather sacrifice a leg than remain in a trap. What are you willing to give up?"

"Not my leg."

"All right. Then let the trap win. Or . . . I suppose you could always go the route of the horned bear."

I shiver again, because of all the predators roaming the Continent, the horned bear is my least favorite. They're rare, and certainly beautiful, but if you see one in the flesh, you're not likely to survive the encounter. They're angry creatures. Maybe because they came into existence because of a mutation. Victims of radiation. Like me, I guess. But the horned bear is far more vicious than I am. They're known to maul or gore without provocation. Uncle Jim killed one in the Blacklands when I was seven, but not before one of those lethal horns pierced his side, slicing off a chunk of flesh. We feasted that night, but I had nightmares about those horns for weeks.

"You know what a horned bear does in a trap, right? He could gnaw off a limb like the white coyote, but he doesn't. He stays alive for as long as he can, even if he's weak, even if he's on the brink of death. He hangs on, and then, when his captor comes for his body, he slices their throat with his horns. The white coyote escapes, but the bear stays just to kill the person who trapped him. He's taking his enemy with him."

I bite my lip. "I think I'd rather live than die for revenge. Wouldn't you?"

He's quiet.

"Wolf?"

"Revenge is overrated. Chew that leg off. Good night, Daisy."

I roll onto my other side, still restless. Glin snort-snores from his bunk, and I swallow a groan and sit up. *Chew that leg off.* No. I'm not quite there yet. But I have to do *something*. With Wolf's words echoing in my mind, I slide out of bed, careful not to disturb the others. I pull my uniform trousers over my sleep shorts and shove my bare feet into my boots.

For all I know, the doors are wired with alarms. Soldiers might swarm the hallway and tackle me to the ground. But I'm not trying to escape. Not tonight, anyway. If I'm caught wandering, I can say I felt like taking a walk. It's not entirely a lie. I need fresh air right now. I can't think in this stifling room with twenty strangers breathing the same air as me.

I reach the exit of the training facility and hesitate for only a moment before pushing the doors open. No alarms. Only silence. The cool night air rushes in to greet me. I glance behind me. All is quiet.

I slip out into the darkness.

CHAPTER 17

I wish I had more memories of my parents. I wish I could remember what they looked like, but their faces are nothing more than shadows in the recesses of my mind, half formed and elusive. Most of what I know about them came from Uncle Jim, but sometimes I'll have a blurry recollection of them. My mother's soothing voice, telling me it'll be all right. My father's laughter. The citrusy scent of his soap.

I don't even know their names. In the rare instances Jim spoke of them, it was "your mother," "your father," "your parents." I know she was a Mod. A Command colonel. I know he was a Prime. A soldier. I know they both served in Tin Block.

Uncle Jim told me once, after he'd knocked back half a dozen glasses of whiskey, that my mom was the bravest woman he'd ever known. That she was so cool under pressure, so rock-steady in the face of danger, you'd think she didn't possess a fear gene.

"So she was like me," had been my reply. A soft smile touched my lips, only to fade at *his* reply.

"No. You, Wren, are reckless. And reckless is not the same as brave."

My lips had tightened with offense.

"Rushing headfirst into danger is not an act of courage," he continued, gruff and impassive. "Your mother thought very hard about her every action. She went into every single situation with her eyes wide open. She knew exactly what she was doing and why."

I hear those words in my head now as I move like a shadow across the base.

The Uprising isn't saving me. That much is clear. They don't care that Julian Ash was executed, and they don't care that Wren Darlington is in the Command's clutches. I need to come up with a plan to save my own ass.

A real plan. One I think and rethink and then think about again before implementing. I need to take a page out of Uncle Jim's book, out of my mother's book, and use some restraint. I can't steal a motorcycle just because it happens to be left unattended. Finding a way off this base will require a good, solid plan.

And every good, solid plan starts with one thing.

Scouting.

I'm under no illusions about where I am. This is a military base. The perimeter is going to be beyond secure. Or . . . there might be a weak spot. Maybe two. Maybe someone makes a mistake one day. Leaves their post to take a leak. Forgets their keycard at the shooting range. Uncle Jim taught me to exploit other people's errors, capitalize on their shortcomings.

With each step, a new dose of adrenaline courses through my veins. There are cameras everywhere. Blinking red. There are guards stationed at the towers. I know they see me, but nobody acknowledges me. Nobody shouts for me to return to my bunk.

It's eerie.

I reach a courtyard and find myself staring up at a massive stone wall. At the bottom of the wall are two black metal gates. They're open, but all I can see beyond them is gaping blackness. I gulp when I realize I know where I am. I know what's on the other end of that tunnel.

I approach the gates at the same time a soldier patrolling the top of the wall notices me.

He jerks in surprise. "What are you—" Then he touches his ear and stops talking. Despite his narrowed eyes, he lets me pass through the gates.

It's not eerie anymore. I know what's happening. But at the moment, I don't care.

I walk down the dark, silent tunnel, focusing on the pale flicker of light in the distance. My footsteps are quiet against the paved ground. I reach the light and enter the South Plaza.

I stand in the center of the open courtyard. It's depressingly familiar. The red dirt beneath the soles of my boots. The platform. Floodlights affixed to the wall shine down on the wooden structure as if it's the stage for a Company theater production. It looks innocuous when there isn't anyone kneeling on it, begging for their life. Not that Uncle Jim begged. He had too much pride for that.

The memory of his rugged face flashes through my mind. I can almost hear his brusque voice ordering me to finish my chores.

Tears sting my eyelids. I turn away from the platform and glance at the gates behind me, then tilt my head to examine the wall, its stone ledge high above my head.

Wiping my palms on my pants, I approach the gate, plant my foot on the first iron bar, and start to climb. When I reach the top, I swing myself onto the wall itself. I find a foothold in the stone and feel for anywhere I can grip my fingers.

Still, nobody stops me.

I climb higher. My fingers curl into the rough surface as I pull myself up onto the ledge that spans the perimeter of the wall. It's several feet wide, allowing me to walk along it without fear of losing my balance. I go about fifty feet before stopping to take in the view. Beyond the base, the city stretches out before me like a black canvas waiting to be painted. Faint lights wink in the darkness. Proof of civilization.

I pivot and stare at the execution platform twenty feet below. Memories flood my mind. Memories of Jim's body crumpling to the ground full of bullet holes. The blood soaking his shirt. His last words whispering inside my head.

Goodbye, little bird.

The pain throbs like a phantom ache. I close my eyes, willing the tears away, but they threaten to spill over for real this time.

"Careful, Darlington. One wrong step and you'll end up a broken dove on the dirt."

I'm not at all surprised to hear his voice.

I sit on the ledge, letting my feet swing over the edge as I peer down at Cross. Bastard only seems to get more attractive.

Rather than respond, I shift my gaze away.

The gates don't creak as he climbs onto them. I find that disconcerting. They creaked when I did it. And his ascent of the wall is so silent I wouldn't have even known he was there if my peripheral vision wasn't clocking flashes of him walking toward me.

He joins me but remains standing. There's a gun holstered to his hip.

"You're not going to need that," I tell him in a tone laced with amusement. "I wasn't trying to escape."

"You can't escape, Dove. You wouldn't have made it out of the barracks if I hadn't let you."

I narrow my eyes.

"Every inch of this place is covered with cameras and silent alarms. My security team alerted me the moment they saw you exit the bunks. Same way they alerted me when they saw you stealing a bike in the east quadrant."

"Why did you order them to leave me alone?"

"Wanted to see where you'd go." His gaze fixes on the execution platform before he voices an unexpected question. "Did you witness the incitement?"

I ignore the tiny jolt of anxiety. "Honestly? I was too busy trying to figure out how to get up on that platform and save my uncle. I didn't notice what the squad was doing until people in the crowd started screaming."

Cross continues to observe me. I feel those blue eyes rake over every inch of me, including the parts made a little too visible by the thin white tank top they gave me to sleep in. I keep putting in re-

quests to have my belongings from Z shipped to me, and those re-
quests keep getting denied. I assume it's Cross's doing. No leisure
passes. No cozy pajamas. He has zero interest in making me feel
comfortable here.

After a brief silence, he slides his gun out of its holster. I stiffen.
But all he does is lower his tall frame and fold it into a sitting position next to me. He sets the weapon between us on the ledge, then
chuckles when he notices me eyeing it.

"Try it," he murmurs, the dimple making an appearance. "Liven up
my night."

I pretend that his nearness isn't affecting my heart rate. That his
woodsy scent isn't wreaking havoc on my senses. "You mean this isn't
lively enough for you? Traipsing after me in the middle of the night,
refusing to let me grieve in peace?"

"Is that what this midnight excursion is? A grieving session?"

"You sound like you don't believe me."

"I believe very little of what you say to me, Darlington."

I can't help a grin. Until my gaze focuses on the platform again,
and the humor dies. I gesture below us, a hard edge sharpening my
voice. "What you do here is barbaric."

Cross shrugs. "I don't do a godfucking thing. The squad isn't under
my purview. That's Tin Block's domain."

I think about those eight men and women who so willingly—
happily—fired bullets into my uncle's body. My fists curl, pressing
against my thighs. My need for vengeance hasn't dimmed, not even a
flicker, during this past week.

"With that said . . ." He slants his head toward me. "Ask yourself
what's more barbaric—ridding society of evil, or making innocent
people suffer in order to keep evil alive?"

"My uncle wasn't evil."

"What happens down there goes beyond your uncle. Before the
Last War, there were penitentiaries all over the world. As a society,
we housed millions of criminals. Clothed them, fed them. Cold-
blooded killers and child rapists living better lives than most free
people. Even the ones who were sentenced to death were allowed to

live for decades past their sentences. They ate three square meals a day while those who hadn't killed or raped anyone could barely afford to eat. Evil pilfering rare resources from innocent citizens."

I snort. "Weren't you the one lecturing me about how life isn't fair?"

"It isn't. All I'm saying is, the squad serves a purpose now. Maybe in the Old Era there was a place for mercy. But not anymore."

"My uncle never hurt a child or killed anyone." Anyone who didn't deserve it, anyway.

"Your uncle was a threat to the Company."

"He was a rancher."

"He was a deserter. He was Aberrant. And he jeopardized the one thing my father values above all else: order."

My father. It's the first time I've heard him say that. And it's the reminder I need to persuade my pulse that it really shouldn't be racing right now.

This man, no matter how attractive, is my enemy.

"The General is obsessed with correcting the mistakes of the Old Era. That's all my brothers and I ever heard growing up, how humanity destroyed itself. Letting chaos reign. Encouraging learned helplessness. Kids were in school until their twenties. Adults, too. All these pathetic assholes wasting time, wasting resources. If you're not productive, you're destructive."

"Is that what you believe? Efficiency and order above all?"

His voice becomes rough. "I believe that humanity is wired for destruction no matter the environment. Old Era, New Era. Aberrant on top, Prime on top. We will always find a way to destroy ourselves. We're a doomed species."

"That's really depressing."

He's quiet for a moment. This isn't the Cross Redden I've become accustomed to since I got here—mocking, ruthless, violent. This Cross is too introspective for my peace of mind.

When he speaks again, it's with a flat intonation. "I know what you're doing, and it's not going to work. You think failing your tests and sabotaging yourself at the range will get you cut, but it won't. I already told you, it's the Program or the stockade."

A knot of defiance twists my gut. "You know I don't belong in the Command. I'm only here because of my uncle's alleged crimes."

"Tell me, then—where *do* you belong? Where do you belong now that Julian Ash is dead? You'll never be allowed to return to your ward."

"You don't even want me in your precious Silver Block." Frustration clenches in my chest. "You said yourself you don't trust me."

"My trust can be earned."

Well, mine can't, I almost retort. Because I'll never trust Cross Redden. Or his father. Or any of the people on this base.

"Yes, I'm sure you plan to shower me with trust." I give a bitter laugh. "You won't even approve a leisure pass."

He returns the laugh, low and mocking. "Is that why we're out here? Does baby feel left out?"

"Screw you."

"You want a pass, you have to earn that, too. Your uncle's actions may have brought you here, but they don't define you. You have a choice now. You can either let pride and resentment hold you back, or you can rise above it and seize the opportunity you've been given."

I bristle at that. "The opportunity to be forced into a life I never wanted?"

"Sometimes we just have to accept our fate, Dove. Trying to fight against it only leads to headaches." He shrugs. "You have a chance to prove yourself, to forge a new path. I recommend you don't squander it."

I glare at him, anger boiling beneath the surface. "And what if I don't want to prove myself? What if I just want to be left alone?"

The question earns me a snort of amusement. "That's not going to happen. Not here."

He rises to his feet in one fluid motion, moving with grace you wouldn't expect to see from someone his height.

"You have an hour. If you're not back in the barracks by then, I've given orders to the sentries to drag you there by your hair."

"You're such a gentleman."

"No. I'm really fucking not."

Once he's gone, I stare at the execution platform again, and a spark of resentment ignites inside me, a whisper of defiance against this "fate" that has been chosen for me.

I've accepted a lot of fates.

I've accepted that my parents are dead.

That Jim is gone.

That my mind is a weapon and if people knew even half of what I could do, they would put a bullet in my brain.

I've accepted that I'm never going to trust anyone enough to show them who I am, because it will always be too dangerous.

But I will not accept *this* fate. I wasn't "destined" to be a Command prisoner. And I'll be damned before I submit to it.

CHAPTER 18

Nearly all my fellows leave the base on Sunday. In the hours I spend alone in my bunk, I'm startled to realize I miss Lyddie. I even miss Kaine's incessant flirting. My old life feels like it's slipping through my fingers. Tana is barely answering me. She must be sick of me only reaching out to beg her to contact the Uprising on my behalf, to champion my rescue. But I'm trapped and she's not. No matter what Cross advises, I'll never accept that this is my life now.

I kill time by searching things on Nexus. I know they'll be monitoring my searches, but my curiosity has always been a thorn in my side. Unfortunately, the results refuse to sate it. When I say, "Nexus, who is Julian Ash?" all I get are red letters flashing on the screen.

RESTRICTED DATA.

When I search for the phrase "Sun Post Bombing," which Struck and Ford brought up during my interrogation, I get the same message. When I search the name "Cross Redden," even the warning doesn't come up. It simply says:

SUBJECT NOT FOUND.

Annoyed with my dead-end research, I open a path and poke Wolf instead, but he doesn't let me link. Groaning, I roll onto my side and succumb to the boredom.

The next morning, we start the second section of the Program. I wait until the barracks clear out before grabbing my stuff to go take a shower. Everyone should be at the mess hall right now, so I freeze when I hear noises coming from one of the lavatory stalls.

A soft groan. A female voice gasping Roe's name.

Kess.

The door rattles on its frame as I tiptoe past the stall toward the showers. Of all the people I would've bet on to hook up during training, Kess and Roe wouldn't have been at the top of my list. She seems like she'd be more Anson's type. Two sadistic peas in a sociopathic pod.

During morning meal, Hadley announces we'll be running drills and small mock operations all week, as well as learning about the various technologies utilized in Silver Block and continuing to firm up our shields. Before we start the day, however, there's another test waiting for us on our sources.

This one is short and sweet.

What are your three biggest weaknesses?

I ponder the question. For once, I opt for honesty. Mainly because I don't think the truth can hurt me.

Impulsiveness.
Impatience.
Classroom learning.

They could probably figure out the third one based on my written scores.

After the test, each of us is given a radio call sign. It makes me feel like I'm in one of those spy movies they show in the theater in Hamlett. The Aberrant spies always lose, obviously. And if it's a Prime spy infiltrating an Aberrant cell, then the Primes win. Obviously. Propaganda is the General's favorite pastime.

Lyddie's call sign is Blue Jay. Kaine's is Condor.

Mine is . . .

I tap the icon in my profile.

My jaw drops. That fucking asshole.

Kaine leans over my shoulder and snickers. We're gathered in a large room in the tech wing of the main building.

"Broken Dove," he reads out loud. "I don't know if that's badass or just a bad omen?"

"Bad leadership," I mutter. "The captain's making a point."

Betima grins. "You're an expert on the captain's motivations now, are you?"

I notice Ivy frown at that. She's next to Betima and not being discreet about eavesdropping. She doesn't like me. But that's fine. I don't like her, either.

"All right, let's get started." Ford's deep voice booms from the doorway.

He strides inside, clad in a black shirt and khaki fatigues. It's the first time I've seen him out of navy blues, and I wonder where he's coming from this morning.

"This is Lieutenant Hirai. Communications."

A short, squat man in his late twenties steps forward. He's missing his two front teeth, but that doesn't stop him from flashing a gummy smile.

"Hiya," he greets us.

"Lieutenant Hirai knows everything there is to know about the tech on this base. Comms, cameras, signal jammers. Any tech questions should be directed at him. He'll be fitting you with the comms you're going to use during ops."

Hirai holds up a black case about the size of a sugar cube, then flicks it open to show us the item inside. The comm is no bigger than my pinkie nail. Flat, beige, and so tiny you can only see it when it catches the light.

"This," Hirai says, utterly delighted, "is not your average comm. It is every operative's dream device. I'm talking cutting-edge, extremely versatile, worth-billions-of-credits kind of technology. The kind of tech that makes you want to weep from its sheer splendor."

"This is weird," Kaine whispers to me, and I choke down a laugh.

Hirai presses his index finger into the small case then holds it up. The beige disk sticks to the pad of his finger.

"This little guy here was solely designed to give you a tactical edge in the field. It's got advanced audio processing capabilities that can filter out background noise and enhance speech clarity. It even detects enemy movements through sound alone."

I try not to raise a brow. Well, damn. Does the Uprising know about this thing?

Hirai grows more animated. "It's equipped with a built-in biometric sensor that's capable of monitoring your vital signs in real time, children. Real! Time! The data gets relayed to the Command Center. Gives us crucial insight into the physical condition of our operatives."

Still beaming, he distributes the comms to each member of our cell.

"The mic is voice-activated," he explains. "It stops transmitting and receiving after two seconds of silence. You can also start and stop transmission with voice commands."

Ford, who seemed bored until now, sweeps his gaze over the group of recruits. I swear it lingers on me.

"Every single op is recorded, logged, and evaluated. Every word you say is transmitted to the communications center. And at the end of every mission, you'll turn your comm in to Hirai. Same goes for any weapons. All guns are tagged and scanned back into the system once you return to base."

"We're leaving the base?" Bryce asks as a twinge of hope tugs at my belly.

"For some ops, yes. Not tonight." Ford glances at Hirai.

"Let's get you acquainted with your earpieces," the tech enthusiast says happily.

———

We're dismissed for the day but report to our cell leader again after dinner. Tyler Struck loads a 3-D map into the holoscreen and says we have five minutes to study it.

The projector shows a maze of steel and shadows. How the hell are we supposed to memorize this layout in five minutes?

Lyddie shares that sentiment. "I won't remember all these hallways, Wren," she hisses, sounding devastated.

"Don't worry. It's our first mock op. I'm sure they'll expect some mistakes from us." Or in my case, failure.

Since I plan to fail.

At this point, I don't think there's much I can do to convince Cross to cut me, but it still feels wrong to excel.

Our objectives are uploaded to our sources. Seems simple enough. We're to infiltrate a site without alerting the perimeter and interior guards, locate our target, and eliminate them. It's a timed mission, run in pairs, with two teams on the course at the same time.

I'm paired with Kess.

Kess, of all people.

I don't know what sadist decided it would be a good idea to put me with the victim of my right hook, but Struck explains that the pairings were picked at random, which sounds a bit too convenient.

Kess glares at me when I go stand beside her. There's still slight bruising around her nose, and I glean a perverse sense of satisfaction from it.

Kaine is on my other side. His partner is Roe, and they'll be on the course with us.

"I'm going to crush you," Kaine tells me, winking.

Meanwhile, my partner threatens me with a deadly look. "If you screw this up for me, I'm going to knock your teeth out," she mutters.

"How's your nose? Did Medical take good care of you when you were there?"

Her eyes blaze.

"The bruises are healing nicely," I add with a helpful smile. Kaine snickers.

Although every muscle in her body looks ready to pounce, she keeps her mouth shut as Struck and Ford stride over to us.

The mock op is taking place in a two-story warehouse on the out-skirts of the base. Kess and I are starting on the ground, while Kaine and Roe will infiltrate from the roof. We're told both pairs are an equal distance from the target on the second floor.

"First pair to reach the target gets five Lux credits in their ac-counts. After you eliminate the target, you exit the way the other pair entered. That means roof team uses the ground egress, ground team on the roof. Fastest total time gets another five credits." Ford smirks. "Worst pair in the group will run laps before lights-out."

"I don't get why we're not running all these ops as simulations," Lash puts in. "Wouldn't that be easier?"

Struck fields the question with the roll of her eyes. "Far easier," she agrees. "That's why we don't run sims. Virtual reality is no substitu-tion for real life."

We get into position, Kess and I stationed around the side of the warehouse, its shadowy exterior concealing who knows what within.

"Teams 1 and 2. Go." Struck's voice slides into my ear to signal the start of the op.

Palming our weapons, Kess and I move along the wall. She takes the lead. When we reach the end of it, she peers out, barely an inch, before pressing her back to the wall again.

She holds up two fingers.

Two guards.

I nod and edge closer to take a look. Two men dressed in dark uniforms walk the perimeter, blending seamlessly into the shadows. They scan the surroundings for any sign of intrusion.

This is supposed to be covert, so we don't want any fanfare. We haven't been tasked with killing anyone but the target. Which means we can't act until the guards have moved on.

The moment they disappear around the corner, Kess and I creep toward the door. Despite the fact that we're not supposed to be work-ing with the roof pair, Kaine's playful voice fills my earpiece.

"Broken Dove, come in."

I grit my teeth. Goddamn Cross.

"We've infiltrated the roof. Copy?"

"We're not working together, Condor!" I hiss, and his laughter tickles my ear.

Together Kess and I enter the warehouse. Various corridors snake away from the main entrance, disappearing into the darkness like veins in a giant, metal beast. Shit. I can only remember the path toward the stairs. Everything beyond that draws a blank in my brain.

Our footsteps are muffled by the thick layer of dust that coats the concrete floor. Every shadow seems to pulse with potential danger, every corner harboring unseen threats. I know it's fake, but I get caught up for a moment. Under other circumstances, I would thrive in this training program. My adrenaline is surging.

Kess and I move with silent precision. I glimpse the first alarm, a razor-thin blue line slashing across the floor. We carefully step over it. As we round a corner, a pair of guards materialize out of the darkness, armed. Without hesitation, we inch back, flattening ourselves to the wall. We wait for them to pass.

"Now," she urges, her voice barely a whisper in the stillness.

We press on, ascending a narrow staircase. Kess is in the lead again. She holds her weapon with ease and moves like a ghost. She's good. I hate admitting it, but it's true.

Halfway up the stairs, she steps on a tread that gives a loud creak. We freeze.

Everything remains quiet.

I release a breath and keep going.

Finally, we reach the top, our target tantalizingly close yet shrouded in darkness. According to the countdown on the source around my wrist, we're making really good time. I don't remember this part of the map, so I'm happy to follow Kess, who seems to know where she's going.

She halts in the middle of one hall, holding up her hand. I stop, too, following her gaze to the blue lines glowing up ahead. We'll need to crawl beneath them to make it to the end of the corridor. While a guard might be turning the corner at any second.

With a nod from Kess, I go first. Crawling on my elbows, keeping my head as low as possible.

"Hurry up, bitch."

My fellow, who's supposed to be watching my back, hasn't mastered the concept of camaraderie. Or encouragement. Or human emotion. I resist the urge to kick my foot back at her face.

After we clear the alarms, we hop to our feet and keep moving. For a second, I'm caught up in the exercise again. I don't know where Roe and Kaine are. Suddenly I want to beat them. I want to reach the target first. We're just turning the next corner when I hear, "Target eliminated."

It's Roe.

Kess huffs in displeasure and turns to glare at me as if it's my fault the guys got to the target first. But the op isn't done yet. We reach the door that was marked on the map. Kaine and Roe are already gone.

Kess eases the door open, locates the dummy that serves as our target, and presses her gun barrel to it to activate the sensor. Then she bitterly mutters into her mic, "Target eliminated."

Now it's a matter of getting up to the roof. We might be able to beat Kaine and Roe's time if we hurry, but I never had any intention of executing this mission.

The alarm is camouflaged in a layer of dust at the base of the staircase leading to the roof. It's easy to miss if you're not paying attention.

"Come on," I urge Kess. "Let's move faster. Run."

"Wait—"

Pretending not to hear her, I rush forward and trip the alarm.

The shrill sound pierces the air, echoing off the walls. Chaos erupts as the warehouse guards spring into action, footsteps pounding down the hallway as two of them descend on us.

Ford's sardonic voice slides into our earpieces. "Bang. You're dead."

"You dumb quat," Kess growls, her voice dripping with venom.

I shrug, trying hard not to laugh. "I'm sorry. I didn't see the alarm."

She's fuming the entire walk out of the warehouse. The moment she spots our cell leader, she stomps over.

"She screwed it up for me!" Her face is flushed with anger. She implores Struck with her gaze. "Can I run it again with a new partner?"

Struck laughs. "No."

By the time everyone's scores are logged into the system, Kess has not calmed down one iota. When she checks her source and sees the word FAIL under our names, she goes apoplectic.

"Stupid godfucking quat!"

She lunges for me, but Ford steps between us.

"Enough." He sounds bored. "Go disarm."

We're required to turn in our firearms at the end of every exercise, along with any weapons on our bodies. But . . . only the rifle is scanned, I realize, as I watch my fellows relinquish their weapons. Knives and sheaths are dropped on a long metal table, scattered in a disorganized manner.

Is anyone *really* going to notice if one measly blade goes missing?

Struck might—she's observing everyone unsheathe, eyes sharp as a hawk's, but when it's my turn, someone chooses that moment to call her name. She turns to address them.

I seize the opportunity, slipping one of the daggers along with its sheath under my waistband. It's thin, only about four inches. It certainly wouldn't be my weapon of choice—I feel naked without my rifle—but prisoners can't be fussy, now can they?

———

In the bunks, I hear Kess across the room bitching to the Psycho Brigade about our disqualification. Ivy is there too. She regularly associates with them now. And she always stares at me with distrust, as if I've personally affronted her.

Those same distrustful eyes find me in the lav mirror later before lights-out. She stands at the sink next to mine, brushing her pale hair into a ponytail. She's the kind of attractive that would jab at any woman's insecurities. I suppose you have to be to catch the attention of someone like Cross. Because he's the kind of attractive that doesn't exist in nature.

Ivy finally speaks. "Why are you still here?" Suspicion laces her tone.

"What do you mean?"

"I mean you can't shoot. You can't fight. You can't hold a knife properly—"

"I'm trying my hardest," I say innocently.

She ignores that. "Yet you strut around like you're better than all of us. It's the biggest case of unearned arrogance I've ever seen. You're one of the worst recruits in the Program."

"Huh. I've never viewed myself as arrogant." I purse my lips. "But I accept your constructive criticism and will do my best to grow from it."

Her jaw clenches. "Why isn't he cutting you?"

I raise a brow. I know who *he* is, but I feign ignorance. "Who?"

"Cross. He doesn't put up with this ineptitude from anyone. Why isn't he cutting you?"

"I don't know. I must be providing him with something he can't live without."

It's total horseshit, but she doesn't know that. The way her eyes flash tells me she doesn't love the idea.

"Enjoy it while you can. He'll drop you fast enough."

"The way he dropped you?" I smile at her reflection.

Her lips twist, cheeks flushing. I leave her glaring at me in the mirror.

SECTION   2

Instructor	STRUCK (S), FORD (LT)
Student	Wren Darlington, R56. Kess Farren, R22
Class	Drills and Mock Operations
Mission	Target Elimination
Objective	Infiltrate and navigate site undetected, secure and eliminate target, exit unde- tected.
Score	FAIL

INSTRUCTOR NOTES:

Pair was disqualified. Darlington tripped alarm.

CHAPTER 19

Our shielding classes continue to make me feel exposed. It's as if every question asked, every piece of information provided, is a direct attack on me.

"Can they read your mind if you're not in the same room?" asks a recruit named Minh.

Tyler Struck shakes her head. "No. You need to be sharing the same energy space."

"But they communicate telepathically over long distances."

"Telepathy is different than mind reading. Once a telepathic link is formed, they can access it from anywhere. But the initial link must be established in person."

Not always. Wolf and I linked spontaneously when we were kids in two different wards. Total strangers.

I'm not sharing with the class, though. I might be reckless, but I'm not stupid. I'm not giving these people ammunition they can use against me.

At the conclusion of each class, the Modified woman, Amira, appears to test our shields. Her presence has become easier for my fellows to stomach. Except for Bryce. Whenever Amira walks through that door, Bryce's faces puckers like she just bit into a lemon, as if she's appalled to be subjected to such atrocities. She's probably already lodged a complaint with her high-clearance father.

Me, I'm busy battling the impulse to reach out every time I see Amira. The temptation to link with the other Mod remains strong.

After dinner, Lyddie drags me into the common room for a study session, keeping her promise to help me raise my scores. I feel guilty that she's investing so much time and effort into me when I'm trying to fail. Though if I'm being honest, the reason I'm doing so terribly on my tests isn't entirely due to self-sabotage.

I'm an intelligent person. Observant. Strategic. I've got an excellent memory—I can take one look at the north pasture on my ranch and tell you if one blade of grass is out of place. But force me to memorize codes and coordinates and military jargon, and it all bleeds together into one boring jumble. I've never been good at staring at screens.

Lyddie enlists Kaine, Lash, and Betima to study with us tonight. Because "the more minds, the more knowledge." One of the many nuggets of De Velde wisdom. As obnoxious as she can be, I can't deny she's growing on me.

I've had Prime friends before. It's not as if Tana and I isolated ourselves in Hamlett and never spoke to a single Prime classmate. I've slept with Prime men. Exclusively, in fact.

But there's something different about befriending a Prime *here*. In a place that is designed to hunt, locate, and punish people like me.

We have another codes test tomorrow morning. Every Command installation is tagged with its own code. Red Post is P12. The weapons depot in Ward F is AF6. The airfield near the Blacklands is T299. I didn't realize how many outposts, depots, and airfields there actually are on the Continent, and I resent the fact that the Uprising continues to shut me out when I could be *helping* them, damn it.

"Whoa, there's a Silver Block outpost at the South Port," Lyddie exclaims, staring at her source. "That's where the trade ships to Tierra Fe dock."

I perk up. "Do you think we'll ever travel down there? Maybe for mock ops?"

I'd take that assignment in a heartbeat. Uncle Jim told me my mother's ancestors were from Tierra Fe, before it was ever called Tierra Fe.

Kaine laughs. "They'll shoot you on sight if you try to go there. We're godless heathens to them."

"I went there once," Betima surprises us by saying.

"Really?" Lyddie's eyes widen. "What's it like?"

"Unbearably hot. Very green. Menacing."

"How'd you manage that?" Lash asks.

"Well, my dad worked on a fishing boat," Betima starts.

Lyddie clucks sympathetically, but Betima doesn't seem offended by the response. It's no secret that in terms of desirability, commercial fishing is low on the list of job assignments. Fishermen are transported by helos and basically dropped in the middle of the ocean. With our ravaged coastlines sorely lacking in safe areas to dock, fishermen need to be delivered to their vessels. And fish processing plants don't operate on land anymore; everything is done on processing liners, which is yet another unfavorable assignment. I wouldn't want to live on a boat my entire life. No amount of shore passes can make that sound fun.

"When I was ten, maybe eleven, I joined him on a cod run, and our boat got caught in a storm. We drifted for days, and the next thing I know, there's a patrol boat speeding toward us and a bunch of angry men pointing guns at us. One of them got in my dad's face, accusing him of trying to break the treaty. But our boat was pretty banged up. Sails shredded. Engine flooded. They realized we weren't a threat and towed us to port." She rolls her eyes. "Wouldn't even let us step foot on land. We had to wait on the boat until a hovercraft from the Company picked us up. I'm assuming our boat went to a wreckage yard in Tierra Fe afterward."

"They really wouldn't let you past the port?" Lyddie says.

"Nope. They don't want us there. You should've seen how they looked at us. Like we were dirt. Like we didn't deserve to breathe the same air as them."

Sounds familiar.

I bite back my bitterness.

"I keep telling my father," drawls a new voice. "Those assholes shouldn't be allowed to have free rein down there."

I'm startled when Roe joins our conversation. He settles at another table, long legs stretched out in front of him. Then he lifts a slender metal tube to his nose and snorts, and I realize he's doing a stim.

I wonder how he managed to sneak recreational drugs onto the base. Stimulants aren't illegal, but they're wildly expensive, and I doubt the Command is allowed to use them during active duty. Doesn't seem like the General would be super keen having his soldiers high on missions.

Kaine voices my thoughts. "How the hell did you get stims on the base?" he demands, grinning.

"My last name might not be Redden, but I've got the General's blood running through my veins. They let me do whatever the fuck I want."

He clicks the tube and does another stim.

"Have you been to Tierra Fe before?" Lyddie asks, peering at him over her shoulder.

Roe nods. "Shithole. That whole continent. They claim we've lost God and that's why we don't belong in their holy presence, but that sounds mighty convenient, yeah? Wouldn't surprise me if they were cooking up a new toxin in some lab down there." He shrugs. "Or working on the existing toxin."

"The Aberrant toxin from the Last War?" Betima's forehead wrinkles. "It's all gone."

"You can't be stupid enough to believe there's no trace of the toxin left."

"There isn't," Lyddie says. "My mother is head of Biotech. She would know."

"Maybe she does and hasn't told you." Roe looks amused.

Lyddie is steadfast in her refusal to believe him. She picks up her source and says, "Nexus, what happened to the biotoxin that created the Aberrant?"

The screen comes to life, a monotone voice sliding out. "*All doses of the airborne biotoxin were destroyed in the Last War, more than a century and a half ago. The laboratory where the airborne biotoxin originated, located in the Lost Continents, was destroyed after radiation levels were deemed safe."*

"See?" Lyddie prompts, smug.

"What does that prove?" Roe challenges. "That a voice on your comm is asserting it to be true? Guarantee there's still some of that shit floating around. I bet they're colluding with the Aberrant, smuggling supplies to their secret base."

Betima looks doubtful. "The Aberrant have a secret base? Where?"

"Somewhere near the Blacklands, I heard."

"Sounds like a rumor to me," she says. "If there was an Aberrant hideout in the wards, we would've found it."

"Maybe not. They're rats, remember? And what do rats do best?" Roe chuckles, answering his own question. "They hide in the shadows like the rats they are."

He heaves himself off the chair. Rubs his nose. A manic glint enters his eyes, the stims clearly kicking in.

"You seen Kess?" he asks a young woman at the next table.

She shakes her head, a tad fearful. Roe has that effect on people.

"The toxin *was* destroyed," Lyddie insists once he's gone.

"It better have been," says Betima, and it isn't long before the discussion becomes political, which means Lash joins the fray. He argues that the Coup was necessary, even while relenting that the General's iron rule over our lives veers toward extreme at times.

When the topic of the Silverblood Purge comes up, I'm surprised to hear Lyddie of all people questioning the General's tactics.

"I don't know if they all needed to be *killed*. There had to be another solution. Especially what happened in Valterra Ridge. There were so many children there."

"Well, what about now?" Betima asks her. "Do you still think killing them is wrong?"

She bites her lip. "Maybe? I don't know."

Lash responds with the vehement shake of his head. "We continue to neutralize them because we refuse to go back to the way it was before the Coup. When Severnism was running rampant through the wards. When Primes were second-class citizens."

I roll my eyes at him. "You weren't even alive when President Severn was in power."

"No, but my parents were. My father is a surgeon, did you know that?"

"I didn't."

"He didn't start his training until I was born. And you know how old he was when I was born, Darlington? Thirty. From the ages of sixteen to thirty he cleaned sewers. He was the smartest kid in his class, and those Aberrant quats assigned him to Sanitation. Why?" Lash sneers. "Because he was a lowly piss-vein. His blood wasn't elite. He couldn't heal using some toxic fucking energy coursing inside him. He needed to use his brain for that. But Severn and his cabinet wouldn't let him."

"I'm not saying Severn's reign was a good one," I say, backpedaling, and we go back to memorizing codes.

———

It haunts me. The seething, disgusted expression on Lash's face. I can't get it out of my mind all night. I like Lash. He's levelheaded. Bright. Yet even *he* can't see we're not bad people.

I don't want to be here anymore.

Panic tickles my stomach as the thought pushes its way to the forefront of my brain.

I have to get off this base. I still don't know how, but I *have* to.

Lash isn't wrong. The Continent's former Mod leader treated the Primes abominably. I can acknowledge that, but Severn doesn't represent all Mods. His actions are not my actions. There are good people on the Continent whose only objective is to live their lives in peace. They don't want to oppress anyone. They don't want to feel superior. They just want to *live.*

Lyddie and the others are in the common room for another film screening, but I'm not feeling social tonight. Alone in the lavatory, I change out of my uniform and into my sleep clothes. I don't store anything in my bunk locker anymore. My meager belongings are all here in my lav locker, including the knife I lifted after our first op.

It's been a few days since I had a real conversation with Tana, so I reach out to her, desperation filling my throat the moment we link.

"I can't be here anymore, Tan."

"There's really no way for you to escape?"

"No. Cameras everywhere, alarms everywhere, and the captain is watching me like a hawk. I've fooled everyone into believing I'm a Prime, but he still doesn't trust me. He thinks I knew Jim was Modified. Probably thinks I'm helping the Uprising, too." I almost laugh in derision, unable to control my sarcasm. "I would love to help those assholes. But they won't let me help them! They don't care about me."

"Polly's not responding to me anymore, and I don't know who else to contact, babe. The network isn't running any operations through Hamlett because the village is being watched so closely. The Command thinks Jim had help here."

"Do they suspect you or your dad?"

"I don't know. But I just have a bad feeling. I feel like I'm always being watched."

I'm a bad friend.

I've barely asked how *she's* doing since I blew up our lives on Liberty Day. I've been so focused on my own predicament, my own imprisonment, that I didn't even consider what Jim's death meant to the people who knew him. Griff has been aiding the Uprising for almost eight years, from the moment Tana began manifesting her gifts at the age of twelve.

"Are you safe?" I ask her, worried now.

"As safe as I can be considering what runs through my veins."

"Fair point."

"I have to go. My dad needs me to help restock the bar. I'll touch base tomorrow, keen?"

"Keen. I love you, Tan."

"I love you, too."

I slump against my locker, utterly drained. I want to go home.

There is no home.

I don't care. I want my ranch. I want my uncle. I want my fucking life back.

"Look at you, all by your lonesome."

I startle when a low voice travels across the room.

Anson.

I smother a sigh. The last thing I'm in the mood for is this guy's predatory gaze and self-pleased smile.

"You know . . ." He tips his head, causing his long hair to slide over his shoulder. "I think this is the first time we've been alone."

I tense as he crosses the room, his easy gait belied by the gleam in his eyes. His grin widens with each step.

I force a tight-lipped smile, my skin crawling. "Is it? I hadn't noticed."

"I have. I notice you often, Darlington."

He moves closer, invading my personal space.

"Don't," I warn.

"Don't what?"

He smiles again, and my fists tighten at my sides. I stand stock-still as he bends toward me, his breath hot against my neck.

"I haven't done a thing."

Not yet.

When he takes a step away from me, I inch backward toward my locker.

"You know what I like about women like you, Wren?"

The sound of my name leaving his mouth makes my stomach churn with revulsion. But I refuse to show any weakness.

"I like how fiery you are." He licks his lower lip. "Roe sees someone like you and wants to put the fire out. He doesn't like the flames—he wants the ashes. He's a sick boy, in case you haven't noticed."

"And you're not?"

My instincts are screaming at me to get away, but I refuse to let him intimidate me. I do creep back another inch, though, until I feel the whisper of metal on my bare arm. My open locker door.

"No, I don't want to put your fire out."

I reach into my locker, my fingers wrapping around the cold steel of my stolen dagger.

"I want to watch you burn—"

I spring to action, grabbing his arm and pushing him into the lockers. At the same time, I press my blade against his throat.

Anson freezes. Caught completely unprepared.

"Don't test me," I warn, my grip tightening on the knife. "Because you're pissing me off, and I'm not afraid to use this."

Rage flashes in his eyes, but before he can react, we hear footsteps in the corridor and then a familiar silhouette fills the doorway.

Cross.

He stands there for a moment. Assessing. His gaze shifts between Anson and me, his expression unreadable.

"Either slit his throat or let him go," Cross finally says, his neutral tone betraying none of the tension in the room.

I shoot him a withering glare. "Go away, Captain. This doesn't concern you."

He glances at Anson. "Booth. You're dismissed."

"We're not finished with our conversation," I say, keeping the knife against Anson's throat.

"You're done. He's been dismissed."

I clench my jaw. Then I lower the blade.

Anson shoots me a venomous glare before slithering out of the locker room like the snake he is, his footsteps fading into the distance.

I turn to face Cross, angry at the interruption.

Unfazed by my thunderous expression, he steps closer, his gaze searching mine with an intensity that makes my breath catch in my throat.

"He started it." I don't care that I sound petulant.

Cross nods, his lips quirking into a wry smile. "Where did you get the knife?"

I could lie, but I don't. "I stole it from the warehouse after an op."

That makes him chuckle. I hate how much I enjoy the husky sound.

He stares at me, expectant.

Without a word, I grit my teeth and flip the knife in the air a couple of times. I catch it by the handle then spin it around and reluctantly hand it to Cross.

"So obedient," he murmurs.

"Don't get used to it."

"I wouldn't dream of it."

He continues to study me. Contemplative. When he speaks again, his tone is impossible to discern. "Tomorrow's a pit night. Recruits can go."

I stare at him.

"You should go."

To my shock, he hands the knife back to me. "Keep it in your locker. Only use it if he comes back."

I watch him stalk out of the locker room, unable to make sense of anything that just happened.

CHAPTER 20

P it night. I'm still not entirely sure what I'm in store for, but everyone in Black Cell is going, so I've agreed to join Lyddie. I heard Ivy tell Bryce earlier that the pit serves as both entertainment and release. With leisure passes scarce, it's a way to combat the perpetual boredom that naturally plagues the Command.

In the barracks, recruits are getting ready around me, and I feel a twinge of self-consciousness. It's quite unlike me, as normally I don't stress about my wardrobe or how I dress in comparison with others. But I'm seeing my female fellows slipping into short skirts, tight denim, tiny tops, and it triggers a rush of insecurity.

Lyddie has changed into jeans and a striped tee, her hair arranged in a braid. "You don't have to wear your uniform," she says, eyeing me. "You should put something else on."

I shift awkwardly on the edge of my bed. "I don't have anything else."

"Oh. Wait. Is that it? I thought you just preferred to wear the uniform all the time."

"Nope. They didn't let me bring any personal belongings. They gave away my ranch, my clothes. Everything I own is gone . . ." I trail off.

Sympathy fills her eyes. "I didn't know that."

"Yeah, well . . ." I gesture to my navy blues. "You're looking at my entire wardrobe."

"I wish we were the same size." She mulls it over. "I have an idea."

"It's fine—"

"Betima," she calls toward the front of the room. "We have an emergency!"

And then she drags me to Betima's bunk while I do my best to hide a smile. I do like how hard she tries to be my friend.

"Wren doesn't have any civilian clothes," she informs our fellow.

Betima is startled. "You didn't bring anything from home?"

"They wouldn't let me."

Because of my uncle. I see her making the connection as she offers a grim nod. "Got it."

"I thought maybe you could loan Wren something?" Lyddie sounds hopeful. "You two are about the same height and build."

"Except for the tits." Grinning, Betima gestures to her flat chest. "As in, I don't have any, and you have plenty."

I snicker.

"But yes, I think I can find something."

We walk to the rows of lockers on the far side of the room. She digs around in hers.

"Here. Try these."

A pair of dark jeans lands in my hands.

I usually avoid changing in the bunks, same way I shower at the most deserted hours, but Betima is waiting for me, so, with reluctant fingers, I unbutton my trousers. Our fellows across the room are paying us no mind, and if Betima is disgusted by the raised pink scar tissue covering my thigh, she doesn't let it show. She appraises me as I zip up the jeans. Her hips are narrower than mine, so the denim is tighter around my waist and rear. But they mostly fit.

"Outstanding," she says, then tosses me a top. "Try this."

I peel off my uniform shirt, leaving me in a bra. Fortunately, Anson's not in here. I know where his eyes would be if he were.

She's given me a black crop top with thin straps and a perilously low neckline. I slip it over my head but can barely tug it over my chest.

"Ditch the bra," she advises. "It's black. No one will see the nips."

Without the bra, there's a lot more breathing room, although I'm conscious of the way my nipples instantly bead against the fabric. The shirt ends just above my belly button, baring my stomach, and the neckline is racier than I prefer.

"You're pure smoke," Lyddie tells me, smiling shyly. "I love it."

"Thanks." I glance at Betima. "Are you sure you don't mind?"

"Not at all."

I sit on my bed to do up my laces. The black boots look good with the jeans and the top.

"Did you bring any makeup?" Lyddie asks Betima. "Wren's skin tone is probably closer to yours than mine." Lyddie's skin is whiter than our sheets.

Betima grabs her toiletry case. "Let's hit the mirrors."

She and Lyddie race off ahead of me toward the lavatories, and I have to jog to keep up. It's the first time in a long time that I've felt . . . young. Carefree. Like when Tana and I were just starting upper school and discovering how much we liked looking pretty and flirting with cute boys. Or cute girls, in Tana's case. For a second, I forget where I am, and I'm forced to rebuke myself. *You're not in Hamlett. You're a Command prisoner.*

But sometimes it's nice to forget.

———

This pit everyone keeps talking about is located inside a warehouse in the north sector of the base. As the three of us walk there together, I feel an aggravating sense of camaraderie with Lyddie and Betima that I wish I could ignore. There's a sense of community, too, as soldiers arrive in groups, pouring into the warehouse.

When we walk in, all I can make out is concrete pillars and shadows. Voices travel in the darkness, waves of laughter echoing off the concrete walls. My gaze tracks the bodies disappearing down a dark corridor.

"Come on, I think it's this way," Lyddie urges, her eyes twinkling in the shadows. She tugs on my hand, and we follow the crowd.

As we round a corner, the sound of raucous laughter grows louder, and now I hear the beat of a fast dance track and feel the bass line vibrating beneath my boots. A moment later, we emerge into a vast open space, a makeshift arena illuminated by flickering light fixtures dangling from black cords on the scaffolding along the ceiling.

I immediately see the pit. It's not deep, maybe five feet below us, ringed by a concrete ledge. There's no seating in the huge room, so soldiers are using the ledge. The bright lights cast shadows on the sand in the pit. It's a beige-brown color with patches of black. It isn't until we get closer that I realize those patches are bloodstains in the sand.

"Whoa, this is intense," Betima says, focusing on the spectacle in the pit.

A throng of eager onlookers are cheering for two male fighters whose bodies move in a blur of motion as they exchange blows. The crowd roars with every punch and kick, the atmosphere thick with excitement. There's no referee. There don't seem to be any rules at all, I note, as I watch one of the men elbow his opponent in the throat.

Betima passes me a whiskey bottle. She used her credits at the commissary for it, and I take a cautious sip before passing it to Lyddie.

I'm no stranger to drinking, but I need to keep a clear head every second I'm here. I can never lower my guard, especially after my encounter with Anson. I'm currently armed with the knife Cross allowed me to keep. I grabbed it from my locker when Lyddie and Betima were applying their mascara, and it's safely tucked inside my right boot. All I have to do is bend over and it's in my hand. I refuse to let Anson or anyone else on this base catch me off guard again.

A loud burst of laughter from across the pit catches my attention. I raise a brow when I spot Xavier Ford among the group. He's sitting on the ledge . . . with Tyler Struck in his lap.

I turn to my friends. "Did you know they were together?"

"I had no clue," Lyddie says. "They barely even look at each other in the training center."

They're doing a lot more than looking now. Ford's hand slides down the bumps of the woman's spine before slipping beneath her shirt. I glimpse him stroking bare skin, while his lips travel along her neck. She laughs and whispers something in his ear. Whatever she says has him lifting his head to grin at her.

One of the men in their group turns toward Ford, and my breath hitches when I realize it's Cross. Clad in dark pants and a white T-shirt, he holds a bottle between his long fingers, dangling it by the neck. I recognize the clear glass bottle. Vodka cider. I've noticed the alcohol selection on this base is very limited. All I've seen at the commissary is whiskey and vodka cider.

Lyddie and Betima drift closer to the edge of the pit, finding a spot by a pillar with so many cracks in the stone that it looks like it's going to crumble any second.

My gaze flits back to Cross. Drawn there as if by a magnet. Suddenly his head moves, and those blue eyes find mine. His expression is unreadable. But I don't miss the way his gaze travels from my face down to my bare midriff, then back up. It leaves hot shivers in its wake.

"The captain is staring at you," Betima says. She's smirking.

"Maybe he's staring at you," I counter.

"Definitely not. It's you."

I blanch, even as a teeny jolt of pleasure sparks in my belly. I'm embarrassed by the response. Resentful of it. I shouldn't be susceptible to this man, just because he happens to be attractive.

I don't want to be attracted to him. I don't want anything to do with him.

"All right, children! Who's next!"

A booming voice thunders through the din, drawing our attention back to the sand. The voice belongs to a burly man with a shaved head, who struts into the center of the pit, grinning broadly.

"Who's got a vendetta they want to pound out in the sand? Or who just feels like getting bloody?"

Laughter ripples through the crowd. My gaze flicks to Cross again. He has some company now.

A petite young woman with shiny dark waves streaming down her shoulders, long eyelashes batting up at the captain. She's midsentence when he shifts his gaze away from her. Toward me.

I lift the whiskey bottle and take a sip. When a drop of liquid clings to my bottom lip, I drag my tongue over it, and his eyes narrow.

"I got this!" shouts a female voice.

The crowd sways and then parts for a woman in ripped jeans and a high ponytail. Although she's lacking in height, she's so muscular I can't help but stare. Damn.

Her opponent is a tall girl as thin as the sweetgrass on my ranch.

"Five credits says Mel takes this," I hear someone declare.

"You're on," his comrade chortles. "Collie will snap her arm like a twig."

"Are they going to be breaking bones?" Lyddie sounds alarmed.

"I doubt it," I assure her. Then again, they might well be.

The guy with the shaved head shouts over the music. "Remember the rules—everyone leaves the pit alive. Good luck, girlies."

Rules, plural? Sounds like only one rule to me, but I'm relieved to hear that nobody is allowed to murder each other down there. I suppose the COs would never allow pit night to exist if soldiers were getting killed. The General needs his minions, after all.

The air crackles with anticipation. When the fight starts, I instantly comprehend why everyone waits with bated breath for a pit night.

These soldiers aren't here merely to spar. They're here for blood.

The women charge toward each other like frenzied beasts, fists swinging. I flinch as the sound of bone meeting flesh echoes throughout the pit. Before long, blood drips from split eyebrows and broken noses, yet neither woman shows any sign of backing down.

The entire time, I'm aware of Cross. His green-eyed companion is all over him, her fingers gliding over his bare arm. He doesn't seem overly interested in returning her advances.

It's odd to experience him in a social setting. To see him laugh. To see him make other people laugh. When he leans over to whisper something in Struck's ear, she throws her head back in delight. Is he funny? He's never struck me as funny.

In the pit, the skinny woman finally taps out when Ms. Muscles locks her in a submission hold that threatens to shatter every bone in her arm.

As a new match starts, Kaine and Lash push their way through the crowd and join us. Appreciation darkens Kaine's gaze when he notices what I'm wearing. It lingers on the swell of my cleavage.

"Staring is impolite," I chide.

Lips curving, he sidles closer to me. "Nobody ever said I was polite, cowgirl."

Kaine swipes the whiskey from Betima, then proceeds to shamelessly flirt with me until I don't know whether to throw him into the pit or kiss him senseless. I'm sort of leaning toward the latter when we're interrupted by more of our fellows. Someone drags Kaine away, and I'm left on my own as the next fight gets under way.

"You shine up nice."

I jerk when Roe comes up beside me. His dark eyes skim my bare stomach, and I feel it like the scrape of a jagged fingernail.

I don't respond to the compliment. I keep my gaze straight ahead. Unfortunately, straight ahead happens to be directly where Cross is standing, still talking to the girl with the shiny hair.

Roe follows my gaze and chuckles. "Don't bother. You're not his type."

I give him a sidelong look. "Oh no. I'm devastated."

"He likes them fragile," Cross's half brother continues, as if I hadn't even spoken. "That way he can take care of them, hold them close so they don't break. Be the hero." Roe laughs again. I think he's inebriated. Or high on stims. Probably the latter. "That's the irony, isn't it? Because he's the one who ends up breaking them."

Roe's view of his brother doesn't reconcile with the one I've slowly been forming. I can't picture Cross with a breakable woman. I suspect it would irritate him.

"Like poor Eversea. Tried so hard to please him."

"I can't figure out where you got the idea that I care about this," I tell Roe.

"You're the one staring at my brother." We both watch Cross

laughing at something Ford said. It draws another chuckle from Roe. "Don't let it fool you."

"What?"

"The jovial captain. He's a coldhearted bastard."

"I thought you were the bastard," I say sweetly, and enjoy how it extinguishes the humor on his face.

Before he can retort, a murmur goes through the crowd.

"Oh, this should be good," someone near us says.

I glance at the pit in time to see Xavier Ford hop over the ledge and onto the sand.

Cross is jumping in after him.

CHAPTER 21

Cross strides toward Ford with an easy grace. He exchanges a few words with the lieutenant, who chuckles and shoves Cross good-naturedly.

"He and Xav have been best friends since childhood," Roe says, bringing his mouth to my ear.

I shiver at his nearness. He's only eighteen years old, yet everything about him makes me uneasy.

"Watch how little that means to him."

I move a few steps to the side, hoping Roe will take the hint. He doesn't. He sticks close, clearly enjoying my discomfort.

My attention returns to the sand, my throat running dry as my captain and my lieutenant strip their shirts off. Fabric is tossed aside to reveal two bare chests. Sinew and muscle.

The men square off in the center of the pit. It starts almost like a tease. Their movements are fluid and practiced as they circle each other. Ford is grinning. Cross licks his lips. The air thickens with tension. Anticipation hangs heavy over the makeshift arena. Even the volume of the music seems to lower.

I hear Lyddie gasp when they suddenly launch at each other.

Holy hellfuck.

The ferocity takes my breath away. They're lightning-fast, trading blows with a savage intensity that borders on brutality.

I can't tear my eyes off him. He's ruthless. Unforgiving. Each blow is precise, delivering the damage he intends. He's the first to draw blood, cutting Ford's lip open and sending a red stream trickling down his chest. The lieutenant retaliates with a jab that has Cross's head rearing back, and while Cross is regaining his balance, Ford slams a knee into his abdomen with such force, I fear for his kidneys.

"This is savage," Betima breathes. She sounds impressed.

The fight rages on. The crowd's yells mingle with the frenetic bass line and the sounds of grunts and labored breaths coming from the sand. Each blow lands with bone-crushing force and sends shock waves of sensation coursing through me, igniting a fire that burns hot and fierce in my core.

I. Cannot. Look. Away.

I try to push the thoughts from my mind, but it's no use. The sight of Cross, his muscles rippling with exertion, his features twisted mercilessly, stirs something primal within me.

Hunger.

I hate both him and myself for it.

I gulp, my cheeks flushing, heart pounding with a rhythm that matches the violent tempo of the fight. It's vicious. I've never seen anything like this. Cross slams the other man's face into the sand. Ford curls over on his side, spitting out dirt and blood. Cross pounces, straddling the lieutenant, and lands a final blow to the roar of the crowd, so loud it seems to rock the entire building. Finally, he rolls off his friend and lies flat on the sand, breathing hard.

And then they start to laugh.

Ford kicks it off, wheezing out laughs as he scrubs a palm over his bloody face. Cross rests his knuckles on his forehead as his own body shakes with laughter. Then he gets to his feet and extends a hand. He helps Ford up, and just like that they're back to being best friends.

But I saw it. What Roe was trying to tell me before. *Watch how little that means to him.* Despite the levity at the end, there were moments during the fight when I knew, without a doubt, that Cross Redden is fully capable of killing his childhood friend.

Easily.

Without remorse.

I bite my lip as I watch him leave the pit.

Roe leans in again. "I'm sure he'll screw you if you ask."

"Shut up," I mutter. I twist away from him and find Kaine watching us.

"Little general bothering you?" Kaine asks.

It's what we've taken to calling Roe behind his back. I'm not the only one who's noticed his sense of entitlement. His unwarranted belief that he's in charge somehow, when in truth, he's just a teenage punk whose older brothers have a higher rank and their father's last name.

"Just being himself," I tell Kaine, who slings his arm around me.

"Come on, you have to hear this. Lash almost ran away to a Faithful camp when he was a kid."

I let him lead me toward Lash, because it sounds like a good story.

The fights last for hours. Match after match. Bloody nose after bloody nose. Lux credits transferring from account to account. Eventually I slip away to find a lav and use the toilet. I stare at myself in the mirror, at the gloss on my lips and the thick mascara coating my lashes. I feel like myself again, and at the same time, like a stranger is peering back at me.

I return to the pit, throwing some elbows as I attempt to push my way back to my group. I've just caught a glimpse of Kaine's blond head when Cross intercepts my path.

We study each other for a moment. I swallow hard, trying to school my features into a mask of indifference.

"Dove," he says in greeting.

"Captain." I pause. "Nice fight. I think you could've gone harder on him, though."

His eyes glint with amusement as he leans against the pillar behind him. A faint smirk plays at the corners of his lips before his expression darkens.

"What was my brother talking to you about?"

Blood seeps from his left temple, and he uses his shirt to mop it up.

He doesn't seem to notice or care that the white fabric is stained crimson.

"He thinks I'm on for you," I say with a shrug. "Little does he know, I don't screw assholes."

"Of course," Cross agrees. The smirk returns. "Just meek, insipid soldiers from Copper."

"Jordan wasn't meek." Now I'm the amused one. "At least not in bed."

"I highly doubt that."

"You seem mighty interested in what kind of lover he is." When he doesn't answer, I take a step away. "If you'll excuse me . . ."

He grabs my hand before I can go. My breath catches despite my best efforts to appear unaffected.

"Wren," Betima calls, and relief floods through me at the interruption.

Without another word, I sidestep Cross and rejoin my friends. But I can't concentrate on what they're saying. Or on the whiskey Betima passes me, or the next match that's beginning on the sand.

"I think I'm going to head back to the barracks," I tell the group.

Disappointment clouds Lyddie's eyes. They're glazed from the alcohol, and her cheeks are bright red. "Oh. All right. I guess we can—"

"No, you guys stay. I'll be fine walking back on my own."

"Are you sure?"

"Positive."

"Okay." She throws her arms around me in a tight hug. "I'm so glad you came!"

I nod. "See you tomorrow."

Bidding the others goodbye, I push my way through the crowd. I'm halfway to the door when the hairs on the nape of my neck tingle and rise.

I get the sense I'm being followed, but when I glance over my shoulder, all I see are soldiers laughing, chatting, and drinking. I quicken my pace to the exit, seeking solace in the deserted corridor.

I don't hear footsteps other than my own. I don't glimpse movement other than the shadows I'm casting myself. But the sensation that I'm not alone refuses to ebb.

And so I'm not entirely surprised when he grabs me.

I barely have time to blink before I'm pushed deeper into the shadows and suddenly there's cold concrete against the bare flesh at the small of my back. I know who it is. Even in the darkness, I recognize Cross's woodsy scent and broad shoulders. A large hand splays across my stomach, pressing me to the pillar. His other arm is above my head, palm flat against the stone.

It's too dark to read his expression, but I feel his eyes boring into me. His lips are millimeters away. For a moment, silence ripples between us, the air thick with tension.

I swallow through the lump in my throat.

"What did I tell you about touching me without permission?" It's intended to be a taunt. But we both hear my voice shake.

"It was just to steady you." He gives a deliberate stroke to my stomach before removing his hand. Then he leans close to my ear. His voice is velvet dipped in honey. "Tell me to put my hand back."

My breath is stuck in my throat. "You're drunk," I tell him.

"Maybe a little."

I choke down a laugh. "Is this what you do when you drink? You trap your recruits in the dark?"

"I've never even looked at a recruit before."

Before you. Is that what he's implying?

"I must be special."

He doesn't answer.

I could move. He's no longer restraining me. Yes, his hand still rests on the pillar. Yes, his tall frame is still inches from me, so close I can feel his body heat.

But I could move.

"I can't make sense of you, Dove."

"It's not your job to."

"Actually, it is."

Cross peers down at me. My eyes are adjusting to the darkness. I glimpse the shadowy planes of his face. The perfectly shaped lips. When I inhale, the scent of pine and spice fills my nostrils, along with the sharp smell of blood, a reminder that only minutes ago he was slamming his fists into another man's face.

He's silent for so long that I can't help but mutter, "What is it?"

"Any other woman would have asked me to kiss her. We'd already be heading back to my quarters."

My core clenches. Tempting. It's so tempting, my mouth runs dry.

Despite my better judgment, I reach up and touch him. "Is that what you want me to do? Ask you to take me back to your quarters?"

His breath hisses as my fingers trace the line of his jaw. God, that's a strong jaw.

"Because I can assure you, that's not going to happen. I'm not interested, Captain."

I see his lips curve before he leans in again. His breath tickles my ear. "Stop lying."

I open my mouth to protest, but the words get caught in my throat, choked off by the raw intensity radiating from him. There's no denying the pull between us.

Somehow, I manage to find it—control. Restraint. The strength to conquer the weakness that seems to grip me in his presence.

I square my shoulders. "You're drunk. Go find somebody else to bother tonight."

A mumbled curse escapes his lips. After a long beat, he steps aside and lets me walk away.

CHAPTER 22

For tonight's city drills, a Command craft flies us to the Point, landing on a paved lot with a backdrop of sprawling warehouses, small factories, and low-rise buildings. There's a heavy, oily scent to the air, a mixture of exhaust fumes and a burnt odor that makes me wonder what they're doing in those buildings. While my fellows gather around awaiting instructions, my gaze is busy searching for an escape. If the network wasn't ignoring me, they could have taken advantage of this. Attempted a rescue while I was off base.

You're not important enough to rescue.

Right. I forgot.

Kaine grins and sidles up to me. "Hope you're not scared of heights."

"No. You?"

"Not scared of anything, cowgirl."

I believe him. I've yet to see Kaine bat an eye during any of the exercises and mock ops we've done this week, even the ones that brought butterflies of trepidation to my stomach.

I shift my gaze to the task at hand. The night drapes over the two buildings like a heavy cloak. Tonight's mission is simple: climb the first building to the rooftop and jump to the second building one story below.

Did I mention we're doing both the climbing and the jumping without any safety gear?

Bryce balks at this. "In a real op, we would have a harness," she says with an irritated huff of breath.

"Would you?" An amused Struck glances at Ford, and I remember her on his lap. His lips kissing her neck. "Hey, Xav, did we wear a harness the night we scaled a cliff while tracking that Faithful camp?"

He snorts softly.

She refocuses on Bryce, her tone sharpening. "Listen, Granger, I know Daddy talked your way into the Program, but he's not here to smooth the way for you anymore."

I try not to raise a brow. Everyone whispers that Bryce is a staple, but this is the first time an instructor has stated it out loud.

"So climb the building or get out of my sight," Struck snaps at her.

Ford snickers. It's rare for Struck to lose her cool, but even I have to admit Bryce name-dropping Daddy is getting tiresome. Only so many times you can say "My father is in Command Intelligence" before people want to smack you.

We're divided into four heats and told the team that completes the mission the fastest wins Lux credits. This will be a hard one to sabotage, unless I purposely choose to plummet to my death, which doesn't appeal to me. I'm working with Lyddie, Roe, and a recruit named Jones. I can't for the life of me remember Jones's first name. All I know about him is that he's the male equivalent of Bryce, a staple whose father is one of the wealthiest capitalists on the Continent.

A metal ladder extends vertically along the side of the first building, only sections of it are missing. We'll have to climb the wall itself when we reach those gaps.

My team is up first. Ford nods at us as we get in position. "Time starts now."

Roe takes the lead, followed by Lyddie and then me, with Jones taking up the rear.

We ascend the ladder at a good clip. When we approach the first gap between rungs, my pulse quickens. The weathered exterior of the gray brick building doesn't appear very sturdy. Each handhold feels precarious, each step a gamble.

Below me, the heads of our fellows and instructors are getting smaller and smaller. Above me, the black sky stretches endlessly, indifferent to our presence. My heart pounds in my chest, the adrenaline in my veins heightening my senses.

Lyddie is slowing, and I offer some encouragement. "You got this, Lyds. Dig your nails into that hole in the brick and reach for the rung with your other hand."

But she's not as athletic as other recruits. Her strengths lie in the classroom. She struggles to find footholds, and even when she does, she has trouble heaving herself up to reach the ladder.

The cool summer air bites into my cheeks as I cling to the wall waiting for her to move, my fingers aching from the strain. Finally, *finally*, we reach the top. Lyddie heaves herself over the ledge. I swiftly follow suit.

When my boots hit the gravel that coats the rooftop, my heart beats even faster. The building is only five stories tall, so I can't see the entire city from up here, but I do catch glimpses of the skyline. Winking lights. Windows emanating a pale-yellow glow. I imagine all the obedient citizens in their tidy homes and apartments, going to sleep so they can wake up and go to their jobs in the morning. They earn Req credits to use for meals, necessities. Lux credits for the shinier things. They have schools for their kids. Safety on their streets. Maybe Cross is right. Maybe I should accept this life. There are far worse things than—

I shake myself out of it. What am I even thinking? There is nothing worse than serving the General. Nothing.

"Let's go." Roe's voice snaps me from my thoughts.

I approach the edge of the roof and swallow through the sudden dryness of my mouth. Oh. The jump is more daunting than I expected.

Lyddie's face turns ashen when she follows my gaze.

"It's fine," I tell her. "It'll be over in seconds."

Roe is irritated with Lyddie's hesitation. "Enough of this shit. You already slowed us down on the ladder. I'm not letting you lose this for us. Just run and jump."

She visibly gulps. "I . . . can't."

I don't even have to sabotage the drill myself, I realize. I could just let Lyddie give up. Yet as I see the anguish seep into her brown eyes, I suddenly think about all the study sessions she's foisted upon me. How freely she offers her help when I certainly don't deserve it.

"Hey." I nudge her with my shoulder. "You can do this. It's not a big drop. When you land, make sure you roll. Absorb the impact in the roll, keen?"

"Keen," she whispers.

"Hurry up," Roe spits out.

"She's coming," I growl. "Go. She's right behind you."

He scowls for a moment, then backs up, breaks into a run, and jumps. His black uniform blends into the darkness.

Lyddie is even paler now, her freckles becoming prominent.

"You can do it, Lyddie. I promise."

After a final beat of hesitation, she takes off. I can't stop the pride that fills my chest as I watch her fly through the night like a clumsy bird. She lands not very gracefully, but at least intact.

It's my turn now, and a rush of exhilaration races through me. I focus on the second rooftop, and then, with a running start and another surge of adrenaline, I jump off the roof, my muscles coiling like a spring as I launch myself into the void.

For a heart-stopping moment, I'm weightless. Free-floating as I arch through the air, and then time speeds back to normal, gravity takes over, and my feet land with a hard thump on the cold stone of the opposing rooftop. With a triumphant grunt, I roll out of the way so Jones doesn't barrel into me as he clears the jump.

We hurry toward the ledge and climb over it, descending another metal ladder. When all four of us are on the ground, Tyler stops our time.

Roe glances at me and says, "Wow. You didn't fuck it up for once."

"Must have been your incredible leadership skills."

He chuckles at that and wanders toward Anson and Kess.

Lyddie and I watch the other heats. Kaine and Betima are on the next team and seem to make good time. The third group features Ivy and Bryce, the latter jumping with ease and confidence I don't expect from someone wound up so tight.

As we wait at the bottom and watch bodies soar through the air, Lyddie links her arm through mine. "I can't believe we did that."

"I know."

She rests her head on my shoulder, her voice rippling with gratitude as she adds, "Thank you. You got me through that."

Oh hell. I'm softening to her. It's getting harder and harder to stop these little seeds from sprouting into a genuine friendship. It's the same with Kaine—I'm a victim to his charms. And Betima, who lures me in with her top-notch sarcasm.

In another life, an alternate universe, I could see myself being friends with these people. Or maybe that's where I am now, standing at the crossroads of some parallel universe, staring at divergent paths, one where an alternate reality is mine for the taking. Maybe I should not only accept my fate like Cross advised but *embrace* it.

Let myself care about these people with whom I've just spent three grueling weeks, truly care about them.

Give up my childish desire to become a valued member of the Uprising like Jim and my parents.

Forget that I'm Modified. I suppose that one won't be too hard. Telepathy is the only gift I rely on regularly, anyway. I can cut my links to Tana. To Wolf.

I can start fresh in this new reality. Why not give in to it—

A scream rips through the air, shattering the night like glass.

I can't quite grasp what I'm seeing. A blur above my head, moving so fast it's gone when I blink.

Then understanding dawns, and I watch in horror as the body falls out of the sky.

A recruit just plunged those five stories I promised Lyddie were safe. He lands not on the pavement but on the rusted steel fence separating the two buildings.

Impaled by one of the spiked posts.

Bile hurtles up my throat. It's Glin Cotter. I recognize his black curls and massive shoulders. Those shoulders are normally set in a proud line. Right now, they're slumped, his body grotesquely bowed over the post like a sick offering to the gods.

I start running, Betima and Kaine hot on my heels. Glin is still alive, but he's screaming. Crying out with the kind of agony that makes your body curl into itself.

Kaine reaches him first. "Hey, brother, it's okay. Don't move. Stop moving."

Glin continues to thrash, moans of pain ripped from his throat.

Roe joins us, helping Kaine try to keep Glin still. Betima's hands tremble as she touches Glin's shoulder to offer comfort, but there's little she can do. The young man's agony is palpable, his face contorted as he struggles to draw breath. We're helpless witnesses to his suffering.

Betima curls her fingers around Glin's flailing arm, but he slaps at her hand, his elbow snapping into her face. She makes a sound of distress but keeps attempting to console him.

"Help me!" Glin pleads between loud, agonized groans. "Get me off this thing. Help."

Struck and Ford move with urgency as they arrive to examine the wounded recruit. "Don't move, Cotter," Ford says in a low voice. "Let's have a look."

What's there to look at? There's a rusty metal spike protruding from the guy's chest.

Betima starts to back away. Hugging her arms to her chest and shaking as if she'd just entered a freezer. She pulls her sleeves down as far as they'll go and hugs herself tighter. She's in shock.

"Hold his arms," Ford snaps at her as Cotter continues to resist.

Although her face is green now, she leans in to help secure Glin's squirming arms.

Me, I slowly back away, because there's nothing I can do for him. He won't survive this. Nobody can.

Glin's screams have dimmed to whimpers. "H-help. Heeeeelp . . ."

He's fading.

Betima tries to soothe him, but it's a futile effort. He blinks at her, and then he's gone. Eyes glassy. Vacant. Dead.

A tormented moan escapes Betima's lips. She releases her grip on Glin's arm and stumbles several feet away, where she bends her torso and vomits all over the pavement.

"Poor Glin," I hear Lyddie whisper.

I hurry to wrap a consoling arm around Betima, smoothing her bangs off her forehead as she empties her stomach. When a prickly sensation travels through me, I lift my head and notice Roe standing nearby, suspicion tightening his brow as he watches me. He frowns, as if I'm somehow responsible for what happened to Glin tonight.

I break the eye contact and focus my attention on Betima.

———

The weight of tonight's tragedy hangs heavy in the air. Nobody says much when we return to the base. In the barracks, the usual chatter is replaced by somber silence. Betima seems especially haunted by Glin's accident. Her eyes held a dull sheen on the helo ride back, and she appears to still be in shock. While everyone else undresses and gets ready for bed, I notice her slip out the door, still clad in tonight's all-black getup.

I push away from my bed to follow her. Kaine gives me a questioning look, offering to come, but I shake my head.

She's halfway down the corridor when I exit the bunks.

"Hey, wait," I call after her. "I'm coming with you." I falter when I realize I'm being presumptuous. "Unless you want to be alone?"

Betima waits for me to catch up. "No, it's fine. I'm going up to the roof. I need a smoke."

We enter the stairwell at the end of the hall. I've never been to the roof of the training facility before, but evidently it's a popular spot, because tobacco butts and old joints litter the rooftop floor.

"Will this lock behind us?" I ask, holding on to the edge of the metal door.

She shakes her head, so I let it shut.

We walk to the ledge that overlooks the base. I scan the various outbuildings, then focus on the main installation in which I was held when I first got here. The interrogation room. The stockade. It feels like a lifetime ago.

A soft hiss breaks the silence. Betima flips the top of a metal lighter and sparks a joint that's neatly rolled in brown paper.

"Didn't know you smoked," I remark.

"I don't do it often. I like to save it for the nights I watch someone get impaled on a fence and listen to them shriek in agony."

"Seems like a good occasion for it."

She takes a deep hit. Her chest rises as she inhales, then falls on the exhale. A minty, medicinal odor floats in my direction.

"Do you want?" she offers.

I shake my head. I've never been a fan. Jim liked to smoke euca in the evenings sometimes, claiming it went down smoother into the lungs compared with the cannabis that used to be freely available all over the globe. I heard there's still a lot of cannabis production in Tierra Fe. Cocaine, too. But it's almost impossible to find it on the Continent, not without shady connections.

As she sucks on the euca joint, I tip my head up to the sky. "You can barely see any stars here."

"Too much pollution. You're from Z, right? You see the stars there?"

I nod. "The sky is gorgeous. All you see is stars."

She takes another deep drag. Blows out another billowing plume that's carried away by the breeze.

"You couldn't have saved him," I say quietly. "I hope you know that."

"I do. He was dead the moment that spike went through his body." She bites her lip. "I've just never held someone as they . . ." She exhales in a ragged burst. "I didn't realize how awful it was to feel someone die."

"Death is pretty awful." The memory of Uncle Jim hitting the ground flashes through my mind. Blood oozing from all the bullet holes in his chest.

"Have you dealt with a lot of it?"

"My parents are dead, but I was so young when they died, I don't know if it truly affected me. Losing my uncle was the first time I lost someone close to me. You?"

She nods. "I've lost friends."

The door creaks behind us.

We both spin around to see a figure appear in the doorway, the lightbulb above him casting harsh shadows on his already harsh features. Roe's expression is unreadable as he steps onto the roof, boots crunching on gravel.

I tense when I notice Anson trailing him. No Kess, though. I don't know if that's a good omen or a bad one.

"What do you want?" I ask the guys, suspicious of their sudden appearance.

Roe shrugs. "Saw you coming up here and thought it would be the perfect time to have a little chat."

Betima drops the joint and crushes it under the toe of her boot. She glances at me. I nod.

"Yeah, we were just finishing up," she says.

We head for the door. Anson moves in front of it. Smiling.

My muscles tighten when Roe approaches with his insolent stride, but he simply walks past us, wandering toward the spot where Betima dropped the joint.

"Now why waste good euca?" he tsks. He bends to retrieve it, brushing the dirt and gravel off. He reshapes the joint a little as he stands.

That's when I notice the sleek butt of a gun sticking out of his waistband.

Warning bells go off in my head, loud and persistent. My gaze shifts to Anson. "Move," I order.

He crosses his arms. Doesn't budge.

"Light?" Roe prompts, holding up the joint.

Betima frowns at him.

"I could get Anson to strip-search you for it," he offers.

She narrows her eyes. After a beat, she tosses him the lighter.

He catches it easily, then flips it open to light the joint. It glows orange at the tip as he inhales deeply. With a contented sound, he exhales a huge plume into the night sky.

"Tell your guard dog to move," I snap at Roe. "I'm not in the mood for your games tonight."

"Games, huh?" He pinches the joint between his thumb and forefinger. Takes another drag.

I step toward the bulky guy who's blocking our exit.

Anson's smile widens.

I could take him. Or at least push him aside so Betima and I can throw the door open. But I don't trust Roe with that handgun.

"Where did you get the gun?" I ask.

Roe ignores the question. "My father is fond of games—did you know that? There's this one party game in particular that he can't get enough of." He chuckles at my skeptical expression. "Can you believe it? General Merrick Redden hosting dinner parties and making his guests play games. Sadly, I don't get invited to his dinners anymore. Not after the last one."

Despite the tension thickening the air, I turn away from the door and slowly walk toward Roe. Betima follows. We haven't given up. We're both still on guard. But it's clear we're not going anywhere until Roe is finished with . . . whatever this is.

"Anyway, his favorite game is a murder mystery. Everyone draws a card, but only one is the murderer card. The rest of the players are supposed to guess who the killer is, while he methodically moves around the room killing their asses."

He offers the joint to Betima, who hesitates before accepting it.

"I was sixteen the first time the General issued me an invitation. His precious Cross and perfect Travis had been attending since they were kids. But not me. Took sixteen years before his little bastard got to come to dinner." He chortles to himself.

Betima tries to hand him the joint back, but he shakes his head.

"So I sit through that mind-numbing meal, pretending not to notice all the wives whispering about me, about who my mother was. Nosy little quats. Afterward, we're all ushered into the parlor. The guest of honor that night was this big-shot capitalist. I hate those assholes."

I don't love them, either. The capitalists are the richest of the elites, owning the bulk of the corporations on the Continent. A small group of men and women in the General's favor, always happy to collude with the Company.

"Travis pulls me aside before the game and says the capitalist is going to be the murderer."

I can't stop a snort. "The General fixes his party games?"

"Of course. And of course, we're supposed to let the capitalist win. Travis says Dad does the same thing every time with his important guests. Puffs them up. Strokes their ego so that they feel like a monarch from the Old Era. Even if it's just at a dinner party. But . . . me? . . . I don't let people win. They want to be better than me? Then they need to actually be better than me." He chuckles. "Why should they have it easy?"

"Because *you've* never had it easy, right?" This boy in front of me is both predictable and unpredictable. I hate paradoxical people.

"Exactly."

"Must be hard to walk upright," I say, "with that chip on your shoulder."

"The funny thing is," he says, ignoring the jab, "even if Travis hadn't told me, I would've guessed him as the murderer. Everyone has their tells. His was smoothing his left eyebrow with two fingers whenever he lied. And he kept slipping up, forgetting who he'd been alone with." Roe shrugs. "It's easy to tell when someone's trying to deceive you."

Something about his tone quickens my pulse. I look toward the door. Anson hasn't moved. He's picking at his fingernails, not paying us any attention.

"All right, Betima." I turn away from Roe, officially fed up. "Let's go."

I hear a rustling behind me.

"You're not going anywhere, Wren."

When I look over my shoulder, I freeze on the spot.

He's pointing the gun at me.

Ignoring my now-careening heartbeat, I put on an unbothered expression. "I don't know what you're planning here or why, but your brother's not going to like it when he finds out you're holding two of his recruits at gunpoint on a rooftop."

Betima nods in agreement. "We're going now. Enough of this shit."

We exchange a look, then glance at Anson again. We can take him.

There's a click. Roe releasing the safety.

"Actually, I think my brother will be more concerned with the fact there's an Aberrant bitch among us."

My blood runs cold.

By some miracle, I manage to keep my shoulders straight, my jaw locked, even while my knees are weakening and my breath thins from the panic flooding my body. Beside me, Betima goes stock-still. Her gaze darts toward me as if to ask, *What the hell is going on?*

"Okay, enough," I snap.

"Enough what? Enough lying? I agree."

Laughing, Roe saunters forward, closing the distance between us. He stops when we're a couple of feet apart, and a cold sweat breaks out across my skin.

He knows.

Somehow, he knows the truth.

"The thing about you people is that you look like us, you walk like us, you talk like us. But—and for once my father and I are in full agreement about something—you're *not* us. You're defective. You shouldn't exist."

He aims the gun at chest level, which tells me he's been paying attention at the range. Always go for the bigger target. The head is a sexy mark, but it's a lot easier to miss.

"Let's go, Betima." My voice is barely audible over my screaming pulse.

"But the one good thing about you," he continues, unfazed when we turn our backs on him to advance on Anson.

"Move, Anson," I growl.

"—is that eventually you slip up, too. Like the idiot at my father's dinner party. Thinks he's smarter than everyone, all the while broadcasting his identity to the group." Roe's cold chuckle chills my back. "It just takes a little while longer with you 'fects. Gotta be patient. Wait for the mistake. But you can't hide for very long. You never do."

I need to *go.*

My gaze shifts from Anson to Roe. Another wave of panic swells over me, threatening to drown out all rational thought. I'm seconds from lunging at Roe and batting the gun out of his hand. Or charging Anson and risking a bullet to the back of my head. Because standing here at either of their mercy is not an option. I ease forward an inch, my mind racing as I try to concoct a plan.

"Wren," Betima warns, as if she knows I'm about to do something reckless. She gives a shake of the head and I stop.

"Smart girl." Roe nods his approval. "But not so smart earlier, were you? You slipped up."

I blink. I don't know what he's talking about. I don't know what I did.

"I saw your veins when you touched him."

My veins?

Clarity strikes at the same time Roe's arm snaps out, and I watch in horror as he presses the gun barrel to Betima's forehead.

She freezes, all the color draining from her face.

And I suddenly hear her words buzz through my head.

I didn't realize how awful it was to feel someone die.

To *feel* someone die.

"Empath," Roe says, voicing my thoughts. "That's my guess."

Before I can process the stunning implications, I notice his finger tightening on the trigger.

"You're crazy," Betima says, her voice shaking.

"No. I saw your veins. And I saw your face. You felt what he was feeling. You *felt* it when Cotter died. That's why you got sick."

"No, I was sick because I watched one of our fellows get impaled by—"

"Would you just shut the fuck up already?"

The world shatters around me as Roe pulls the trigger.

CHAPTER 23

Time slows to a crawl. The gunshot echoes through the dark night. Betima falls to the ground, her blood staining the gravel like spilled ink.

I stand there, frozen in shock.

Betima had been hiding in plain sight. Raising her hand during class, playing dumb about Mods. *Can they plant images in my mind?* She had me completely fooled.

I don't wait to find out what Roe plans to do with me next. I shove Anson aside and throw open the door, then race down the stairs. My footfalls blast through the stairwell. I can't breathe. My heart feels like it's going to explode out of my chest.

I burst out at the bottom floor and hear the shouts in the corridor. Soldiers come running. I throw myself to the side, but someone grabs me. It's Hadley.

"What did you do?" he demands.

"Nothing."

"What did you do!"

"It was Roe. And Anson," I manage to whisper.

He frowns.

I nod to the door. "They're still up there. With her body. Betima's."

He blinks. Then he issues a command. "Go back to the bunks. Stay there until someone comes."

For once I don't feel rampant hatred for Hadley. I'm too busy thinking about Betima's blood pouring out of her skull.

He shot her.

He fucking *shot* her.

"Wren! What happened?"

The moment I stumble into the barracks, people are coming at me from all directions. My stomach starts churning, so I race into the lavatory, where I collapse onto my knees and throw up in the toilet.

I hear Lyddie's voice outside the stall. "Are you all right?"

After I've emptied my stomach, I rise to my feet and force myself to step out. I draw a breath, my gaze shifting toward the wall of mirrors, landing on my reflection. I look ashen. My eyes look dead. Dead like Betima.

A few other women stream in. Ivy. Bryce. Kess. Their expressions range from fear to confusion. Or in Kess's case, that smirk.

"What's going on?" Bryce asks.

I ignore her, focusing on Kess instead. It takes all my willpower not to lunge at her again. Beat that smirk right off her face.

"Did you know he was going to kill her?" I snarl.

"What the hell are you on about?"

"Betima. Roe." My hands start shaking, so I press them to my sides. "He killed her."

"Oh my gosh," Lyddie whispers. "Why? Why would he do that?"

"He accused her of being Aberrant and then put a bullet in her head."

"Betima was Aberrant?" Lyddie gasps. "No. I don't believe that."

"Roe's a smart guy," Kess says, the smirk resurfacing. "If he says it, then it's true."

I push past her, unable to stomach her horrible face a second longer. I stumble back toward the bunks. Each step feels like I'm moving through quicksand, my legs heavy with the weight of what I just witnessed. The memory plays over and over in my mind, a horrific loop of shock and finality. I can still hear the gunshot, the thud of

Betima's body, and the sickening silence that followed. Betima. Dead. Gone in an instant.

My fellows cast wary glances at me as I pass the rows of beds toward my own. Kaine's bunk is empty. I wonder where he went, but I'm too numb to ask anyone.

I sit on the mattress, my back slumped against the cold, concrete wall, and pull my knees to my chest, wrapping my arms around them. It takes everything inside me not to break out in sobs.

"Hey."

Lyddie's soft voice breaks through my haze of grief. I look up to see her standing a few feet away, her eyes filled with concern.

"Hey," I echo. Numb.

"Can I sit?"

"Sure."

She settles beside me but doesn't speak. She doesn't need to. Her presence alone is a comfort, a reminder that I'm not completely alone in this place.

We sit in silence for a while. The quiet voices of the other recruits travel through the room, but nobody comes to talk to us.

"He shot her in the head, Lyds," I finally say. The pain in my chest feels like a physical wound.

"I still can't believe it." She eases closer and rests her head on my shoulder.

It reminds me so much of Tana that I want to cry. I miss my best friend.

"Do you think it's true?" she asks. "That Betima was one of them?"

I'm one of them.

Betima was one of *mine*.

But I can't tell Lyddie that, and I'm not in the mood to spark some drawn-out debate about whether Mods should be allowed to exist.

Fortunately, we're interrupted by Kaine, who tosses his source on his bed and glances our way. His expression is serious for once.

"I guess you heard?" I say.

"Lash just told me."

I swallow. "She's dead."

"If she was Aberrant, it was bound to happen anyway," he replies, and once again I'm battling something inside of myself, because while I want to claw his eyes out for saying that, his response is exactly what it should be. For a Prime.

"Yeah," I say with a weak nod. "She would've been found guilty of concealment."

He nods back. "And faced the firing squad."

"Right."

Lyddie gives my arm a soft squeeze before climbing off the bed. "I'm going to sleep now. I'm sure we'll have more answers in the morning."

Betima will still be dead in the morning.

I feel Kaine's gaze on me, and when I glance back in his direction, what I see helps to pacify some of the nasty feelings I was having toward him.

Pain.

There's genuine pain creasing his features. Losing Betima hurts him. Maybe not as much as it hurts me, but I'm encouraged that at least on some level, he considers this a loss.

"You should get changed," he advises. "Lights will go out soon."

I've barely slid my sleep shirt over my head when his warning comes to fruition. Darkness engulfs the room, and I have to feel my way under my blanket.

I curl onto my side and resist the urge to cry. To weep until my eyes are raw and exhaustion claims me. But I can't show weakness here, so I pull the covers up to my neck and lie in the dark, feeling the crushing weight of my circumstances pressing down on me.

I'm in a room full of people, yet I'm completely alone. I've always been alone. Even with Jim in my life, the loneliness never abated.

I wish I had parents.

I wish I had a mother to comfort me and tell me I'll survive this.

A father to tuck me in and tell me he'll stay with me until I fall asleep.

But my parents aren't here. They're both long dead, and I can't help but feel I've let them down somehow. How does someone like me even measure up to someone like my father? My mother? I don't remember either of them, but from the meager details Uncle Jim provided, they were braver than I could ever dream of being.

They both sacrificed their lives for the Uprising. They both fought against the tide of oppression, refusing to back down. They weren't motivated by personal gain or glory. They dedicated their lives to a deep-seated sense of duty to stand up for what's right, no matter the cost. My father wasn't even Modified, yet he stood by my mother, by her people.

How am I supposed to follow in those footsteps when I'm pathetic in comparison? I just watched a friend get murdered in cold blood. My father threw himself in front of bullets to protect his allies. I ran. My mother faced a firing squad. I ran.

I can't follow in their footsteps.

They're far too big for me.

"Wren." Kaine's voice is a rough whisper. "You good?"

I don't know how he senses it. When I roll over and whisper, "No," he holds up the corner of his blanket in invitation.

I should decline. But I'm desperate for comfort, for a reminder that I'm not all alone.

I crawl into Kaine's bed and cuddle up beside him. He wraps an arm around my shoulder and then covers us with the blanket. His body is warm. His heart beats in a steady rhythm beneath my cheek.

I wish I could talk to him telepathically. Spill my thoughts into his mind, share my pain. For a moment I'm tempted to reach out to Wolf, but I'm distracted when Kaine takes my hand and laces our fingers together.

"It'll be okay," he murmurs.

Then he brings our entwined hands to his lips and kisses my knuckles. The sweet gesture unleashes a rush of emotion that floods my chest.

I rise on an elbow and gaze down at him. His handsome features are shrouded by shadows, but I don't miss the way he licks his lips.

"Wren—"

Before I can second-guess myself, I kiss him.

He makes a husky sound of surprise. Or maybe it's approval.

Approval, I decide, when he cups the back of my head and threads his fingers through my hair.

He kisses me back with an intensity I don't expect. In fact, we go about it a little backward. It starts with passion that makes me gasp, his tongue in my mouth and his hips arching toward me, my thigh draped over his. And just when I'm struggling for air, when my heart is beating so fast I fear it'll stop, the kiss turns infinitely gentle.

Kaine's lips brush mine in soft, slow caresses. His fingers stroke my hair while his other hand grazes my side before dipping beneath my shirt. When his palm reaches my breast, a jolt of desire sizzles through me. He squeezes, his thumb teasing my nipple, and I can't stop the desperate whimper that escapes my lips.

Whether it's my whimper that does it, or he simply comes to his senses on his own, Kaine wrenches his mouth away.

When he speaks, the words are hoarse and regretful. "As much as I want this, we both know now's not the time."

He's right. I want so badly to forget what happened to Betima tonight, but this isn't the way to do it. Not here. Certainly not now, when I can hear other people breathing around us and bedsheets rustling as someone shifts in their sleep.

Nodding, I sit up. Kaine brushes a kiss on my shoulder and then lets me climb out of his bed and back into mine.

———

I rise the next morning to the sound of Hadley's voice snapping for us to stand to attention. Everyone must not have slept as badly as I did—as in, lay awake staring at the ceiling all night—because nobody appears groggy or disoriented. Two rows of alert, albeit weary faces greet Hadley, who's joined by Tyler Struck at the front of the barracks.

A part of me prays they'll announce that Betima survived her head wound, wasn't an Aberrant spy after all, and would be rejoining Black Cell once she's released from Medical.

That doesn't happen. Obviously.

Instead, Hadley informs the group that "one of our own" was revealed to be working for the enemy and dealt with accordingly. Struck then tells us to put it out of our minds and resume our normal activities as usual.

The instructors leave, and I'm left staring at the empty doorway in disbelief.

Are. They. Fucking. Serious.

We're just supposed to act like Betima wasn't murdered? Resume our normal activities? Go to shielding class and the shooting range and prepare for another mock op tonight?

To make matters worse, my own friends, as subdued as they are, accept the orders without question and proceed to get ready for the day.

It's difficult not to scream at every single person in this room. But why waste my breath? They don't care that Betima is dead. And they certainly won't care when *I'm* dead. Which is the fate I'm looking at if I don't find a way out of here.

It's become even more imperative that I get out. Cross's psychopathic little brother shot a young woman in the head, and nobody is batting an eye. I'm in danger, and I'll always be in danger on a military base full of Primes who share Roe Dunbar's belief that the Aberrant must die. Must be made extinct.

"Coming?" Lyddie says from the doorway. She's heading for morning meal.

"How do you even have an appetite?" I ask her, trying to mask my disappointment.

"I don't. But we've got our orders." She bites her lip. "Come on, let's go."

I shake my head. "I'll be there soon. Just need to send a comm first."

To nobody. Because nobody cares about me. Tana is dealing with her own troubles. The network doesn't care about my existence.

"Hey."

Kaine returns from the lav clad in his short-sleeved navy blues, hair still damp from the shower.

The memory of what we did last night slides to the forefront of my brain, bringing a flush to my cheeks. "Hey."

He offers a rueful smile. "Are we good?"

It should feel awkward between us considering I crawled into his bed and mauled him, but it's surprisingly not.

"We're great. I'm sorry about last night."

"I'm not." Kaine approaches the foot of my bed where I'm sitting. As he gazes down at me, his voice thickens. "I like you, Darlington. You know that."

"I know."

And I like him, too.

But there's no guy on this Continent worth it enough for me to stick around here a second longer.

It's too dangerous, and last night proved it.

"All I'm saying is, if it happens again under different circumstances . . ." He shrugs, that trademark gleam dancing in his eyes. "I wouldn't be against it."

I fight a smile. "Noted."

"You coming to morning meal?"

"Soon. I'll see you there."

After he leaves, I duck out of the barracks and walk in the opposite direction of the mess hall.

I know my way to his office now. God knows I've been there enough times.

I'm going to ask to be dismissed. I'll go to the stockade if that's what it takes. But I know he doesn't want to imprison me, so maybe there's another solution. A compromise we can reach.

I slow down at the sound of voices beyond Cross's door. Someone is in the office with him.

"Absolutely not."

I recognize the booming, authoritative tone. It's the same one I've heard hundreds of times on Company broadcasts.

The General is here.

I move closer despite my better judgment. But their voices are low, and I can't make out exactly what they're saying. I press myself to the wall outside his door, straining to hear the conversation within.

I'm sure there are cameras watching me do this. I don't care. I'll own up to it if Cross interrogates me later. *Yes, I eavesdropped on you and your father. No, I'm not sorry. Please, cut me from the Program. Release me from this nightmare.*

". . . Aberrant bitch." The General's harsh oath travels out into the corridor.

My stomach clenches as I realize they're talking about Betima.

I inch closer to the door that sits slightly ajar. Then I take a chance, peeking through the open slit.

There he is. Merrick Redden, in the flesh.

I despise everything about his face. The severe features. The deep furrow running through his brow. His eyes, sharp and piercing. No hint of warmth or compassion in their depths, only a cold, calculating intensity that brooks no dissent.

". . . actions were unacceptable." Cross sounds calm, clearly not afraid to offer that dissent. "He poses a threat to the other recruits."

Roe. He has to mean Roe.

"Unacceptable? He did precisely what needs to be done to protect our interests. He eliminated a threat to our society, just as he's been trained to do."

My blood runs cold, because the General's endorsement of Roe's actions is a chilling reminder of the ruthless indoctrination that permeates every aspect of our society.

"He killed another recruit without just cause," Cross snaps. "We don't even know if she was a silverblood. There was no evidence to support his claim."

"He acted on instinct and trusted his training. He did us a service by eliminating a potential enemy. I know you believe they're useful for labor. You enjoy overcrowding our camps by sending the Aberrant there, recommending labor sentences over death to the Tribunal. But sometimes, son, death is the answer. Unlike you, Roe understands that."

"I want him out of my fucking program."

"Nonsense. He stays."

Frustration wells up inside me. The General is letting Roe stay? Just taking his word that he saw Betima's veins ripple silver? What if Roe was wrong?

"Sir. With all due respect, you instituted the Tribunal because you don't believe in vigilante justice."

"I believe my son."

"Roe is a punk."

I've never heard Cross sound so angry. And I can't deny I'm impressed that he's standing up to the man who runs the Continent. This man and his warped belief that he alone holds the key to preserving order and stability. That the whole world teeters on the brink of chaos, and only with him at the helm can we right that danger.

"He lacks discipline. He has no respect for authority. He spends more time snorting stims up his nose than studying. He's not ready for Silver Block. He's too young."

"He's a grown man."

"No, he's a liability." Cross makes a frustrated noise. "I want him gone."

"He stays," Redden repeats.

I've heard enough. I spin around and disappear around the corner, trying to contain the fury threatening to boil over.

What is *wrong* with him? He's making decisions based on the word of an eighteen-year-old boy?

My rage is abruptly doused by a bucket of desperation that almost knocks me off my feet. I regain my balance and hurry into the bunks. If Roe is staying, that means I'm leaving. I refuse to spend another night in this prison, waiting for trigger-happy lunatics like Roe Dunbar to figure out what I am.

I obsess about it at the range an hour later, my distraction causing me to miss all my shots. Luckily, Ford is accustomed to my incompetence. During afternoon break, I tune out as everyone has conversations around me, wondering what Jim would do if he were in my shoes right now.

Kill them all.

Uncle Jim would kill them all.

Sadly, this isn't a viable solution.

So then how? How do I facilitate my escape?

The conundrum sticks with me into our afternoon sparring sessions. I sit on the floor watching but not really seeing as Lyddie and Bryce exchange jabs on the mats.

This is what I know. I know Cross Redden won't cut me from the Program, no matter how low my scores are.

I know I don't want to go to the stockade again.

I know it will take more than a few hours to execute a foolproof escape plan.

My only move here is to force Cross's hand. Do something that will remove myself from the equation—today—without making it appear like I planned it.

Every trap can be escaped. It's just a matter of what lengths you're willing to go to.

I suddenly hear Wolf's voice in my head. I haven't thought about that discussion in weeks. Now, as my oldest friend's words replay through my mind, I see a solution in my grasp.

I'm not the horned bear.

I'm the white coyote.

"Darlington. Farren. Take the mat."

My head lifts at Ford's command. Kess is beaming like she's just been granted a leisure pass to a civilian beach. We haven't sparred since the morning I broke her nose during our unofficial mess hall match.

"Kess looks feral," Lyddie whispers as I hop to my feet.

She's not wrong. Our fellow is all but salivating at the chance to hit me again.

I take a breath. Rotate my shoulders and bounce on the balls of my feet, loosening myself up.

The air thickens with anticipation as Kess and I step onto the mat. Her gaze is fierce, exuding confidence.

"Been wanting this for a while, Darlington." She bares her teeth. "It's kept me up at night."

I smile at her. "That's really sweet that you think about me in your spare time."

"Shut up and fight," Ford says, rolling his eyes.

Kess is on me from the jump. She's a good opponent. Fast. Ruthless. Her fists fly like arrows, each strike calculated and precise. If I didn't hate her guts, I might enjoy sparring with her. And if I didn't have a firm objective right now, I might smash her face in, and with pleasure. But single-minded purpose guides my every move.

Sweat beads on my forehead as I block her blows. Only some of them; I let the others land because that's the precedent I've set since I arrived here. Each half-hearted strike of mine is met with a deadly counter from her, each dodge followed by a feint. Our breathing grows heavier.

Time to end this.

Chew the leg off.

With a sudden burst of adrenaline, I allow her fist to slam into my abdomen. Then I let the momentum knock me off-balance, and the second she has me on the ground, I twist my body, maneuvering myself into a vulnerable position.

"Protect your flank," I hear Ford snap.

"Get your arm out from under yourself," Kaine is shouting at me.

Too late.

In one swift motion, Kess is on top of me, her knees pinning my left forearm. I move my hand to the side, twisting my wrist, then use my other hand to claw at her thighs, all but inviting her to press her knees harder against me. I feel the sickening snap of bone as I force my wrist to bend at an unnatural angle.

Agony.

Searing, white-hot agony. It shoots through every nerve ending in my body.

I hear shocked gasps. Kess doesn't let up until Ford forcibly pulls her off me. "You broke bones, Farren. You're done. You win."

Lyddie rushes over, horrified. "Are you okay?"

I grit my teeth against the pain. "I think I broke my wrist," I manage to choke out.

Dizziness fogs my brain as I struggle to get to my feet. I breathe deep, glancing down at my hand. The obscene angle at which it dangles from the wrist makes me woozy again, and now I'm seeing stars.

Fucking white coyotes.

"Take her to Medical," Ford barks at Hadley while I try not to pass out.

CHAPTER 24

I sit on the uncomfortable infirmary bed, my broken wrist cradled against my chest. As far as chewing off limbs go, this wasn't so bad. The pain has dulled to a mere throb. It hurts, but not as much as before.

That could also be due to the fentaphine injection.

But still.

The door swings open. I look up, expecting the female doctor who took my X-rays.

It's Cross. He strides in, wearing his navy-blue uniform, a deep frown creasing his brow.

"Dr. Harumi says it's fractured in multiple places," I say helpfully. "One of the carpal bones is shattered completely."

He nods. "I heard."

"She's recommending surgery. And a cast. Eight weeks."

"Look at you, so educated about medical treatments." He approaches the bed. "Why didn't you tap out?"

"Couldn't. My arms were pinned."

"A verbal tap would've sufficed."

"She wasn't going to let me."

He nods again.

I don't like his lack of expression.

"Cross." I cringe at the pleading note in my voice.

A brow rises.

"I can't train like this."

"No," he agrees as he heads back to the door. "You can't."

His words are not at all encouraging. He wouldn't surrender this easily.

I'm not wrong.

I sit there for another two hours before someone returns. A man in his late twenties or early thirties with close-cropped hair and a lanky frame.

He's Modified.

I instantly clock that fact, as his short sleeves provide a clear view of his forearms and wrists. His right wrist bears the black band. No red to be seen.

I try to mask my distaste. A loyalist.

"Hello, Wren," he says, approaching the bed. His presence exudes an aura of calm assurance, but his piercing eyes seem to see right through me. "I'm Ellis. Heard you broke your wrist."

"Who are you?"

"I just told you." He chuckles.

"You know what I mean."

He notes my gaze on his wrist and smiles. Instead of answering my question, he says, "You must be very important."

"What makes you say that?"

"Because they dispatched a speed craft all the way to Red Post to collect me. Flew me back here without even letting me gather my gear."

I know from the study sessions Lyddie's been cramming down my throat that Red Post is the Command outpost that's farthest north. At the very tip of Ward A.

"Who are you?" I repeat.

He ambles toward the wall that contains the X-ray screen. He flicks on the light and studies my scan while I continue to study *him*. He's wearing khaki trousers and a white collared shirt. He's not a soldier. A doctor, maybe.

"Are you the surgeon?"

His lips curve. "Something like that." He's eyeing my injured wrist as he walks back to the bed.

The closer he gets, the higher my guard rises. Everything about this man unnerves me.

Ellis rubs his hands together. "They don't usually request my services for recruits," he admits.

His services?

My gaze sharply returns to his hand, but the black band is no longer the mark that matters. Another one has caught my attention: the bloodmark on the center of his palm, a perfect circle about an inch wide.

He offers a shrug. "Like I said, you must be important enough to merit healing."

I recoil at that, my heart pounding in my chest. "I don't need healing. I need surgery."

"Surgery to fix your wrist."

"Yes."

"The wrist I can fix right now in less than five minutes and with zero recovery time."

My mind reels from the implications of his words. I broke *bones* and instead of permitting me to undergo surgery for it, they flew in a healer to fix me.

Defeat crashes over me as I realize I'm out of options. I tried to chew my way out of the trap, and I failed.

I'm never leaving this base.

Cross isn't going to let me.

"May I?" Ellis nods at my arm.

Bitterness churns in my stomach. With it comes a sense of resignation and the urge to burst into tears.

I nod back.

Ellis places both hands on my forearm and gently pulls it straight. His movements are firm and measured, causing a bolt of pain to shoot through me.

"It'll stop hurting soon," he promises, then wraps his fingers around my wrist and forearm.

I hold my breath, waiting for the flow of energy I assume will come.

Within seconds, it happens. A tingling sensation washes over me, starting at the tips of my fingers and spreading up my arm like wildfire. I bite my lip as I feel the bones in my wrist realigning themselves, the pain melting away. A strange rush of heat penetrates my flesh, like the rays of the sun breaking through the clouds on a stormy day.

I've never been healed by a Mod before. It's astounding how quickly the pain begins to dissipate. The warmth flowing beneath my flesh. The pins and needles in my bones. I can *feel* them knitting back together with each passing second. The healing energy envelops me, sealing my fate.

"You don't have any questions," murmurs Ellis.

I lift my gaze to his inquiring one. "What?"

"Everyone I heal asks questions. How I do it. How my mere touch can mend bones and soothe wounds with nothing more than the power of my mind."

"I don't care how you do it as long as it gets done."

But I can't deny there is a sense of awe as he continues to work, his palms pressed over me as if, by sheer force of will, he can command the fabric of reality itself.

When he finally withdraws his hands, I flex my newly healed wrist, marveling at the strength that now courses through it. Then I remember why I broke it in the first place, and my spirits sink like a stone.

"Thank you," I say tightly.

"My pleasure."

Once he's gone, I close my eyes, fighting back tears of frustration. This isn't how things were supposed to be.

Dr. Harumi returns to examine me, clucking happily at my miraculous recovery, then dismisses me. I'm subdued when I return to the barracks. I missed dinner, but I don't care. My appetite left me around the same time as all my hopes of getting off this base.

"Wren!" Lyddie jumps up from her bed. "Your wrist!"

"All better," I joke weakly, holding it up.

Kaine, who was reading on his source, slides into a sitting position. He's bare-chested, his hair rumpled. "They have a healer on the base?" he says in surprise.

"They flew one in from an outpost."

"Whoa." Those green eyes, usually so playful, narrow at me. Kaine's a lot shrewder than those lazy smiles lead you to believe.

"I guess it's good to know they won't let us break bones here," remarks Lyddie.

"I'll just have to break it all over again tomorrow," a snide Kess calls from her bunk.

"Piss off, Kess," I mutter. I'm done with that bitch today.

"You okay?" Lyddie asks me.

"Just tired. I'm going to change for bed."

I hit the lav, where I stare at my reflection in the mirror. My face is . . . aglow. The dullness of my eyes contrasts with the sudden radiance of my skin. Whatever Ellis did to me, his energy seems to be flowing from the inside out.

I slide into bed, truly exhausted, ready to forget the entire world. But then I feel the poke in my mind, and I realize the world has not forgotten about *me*.

For the first time in weeks, since the night I arrived in the Point desperate to rescue Jim, I hear from Declan.

The network has decided to grace me with their presence.

I squeeze my eyelids shut, every muscle in my body trembling. That's how angry I am when I open the link.

"You fucking asshole! You left me here to rot!"

"If I'd known you were going to be this dramatic, I would have kept the link closed."

"What do you want?" I'm tired. Pissed off. Beyond betrayed. Yet despite that, a spark of hope flickers to life, eclipsing the despair that's threatened to consume me since the moment Roe killed Betima.

"Adrienne will meet you tomorrow night."

"Who the hell is Adrienne?"

"Midnight. The vehicle pool on the west end of the base."

"There are cameras everywhere—"

"There won't be tomorrow."

"How—"

"Midnight," he repeats before his voice floats out of my mind.

CHAPTER 25

I fear I'm walking into a trap. Despite Declan's assurances, I ruminate about it all day, wondering how this can bite me in the ass. He said there'd be no cameras. No alarms. But I'm supposed to blindly trust him?

Is this truly a risk I'm willing to take?

I consider that question during evening meal, and by the time I've finished eating, I decide that, yes, it's a risk worth taking. Last night, after Ellis healed me, I resigned myself to my fate. I gave in to defeat. But fate has other plans, it seems.

Based on experience, I know I have some leeway with the security men. Cross let me roam the base before. If they catch me on the cameras, I'm hoping he allows it again.

At quarter to midnight, I slip out of the barracks wearing my black op uniform and boots. If any of my fellows are still awake and notice me leaving, they don't raise an alarm. In the hall, I'm painfully aware of the blinking red lights in the corners of the ceiling. The cameras are operational, damn it.

"Declan," I gripe when he links. "The cameras."

"I promise you it's safe, Darlington. Go. She won't wait if you're late."

She. Adrienne. Whoever this woman is.

Heart racing, I scurry out the back exit of the training facility. Declan warned me not to use the front doors. I round the side of the building and follow the cold façade as I walk. "Stay close to the walls," he'd warned.

I feel the weight of the mission pressing down on me as I make my way across the base. Avoiding the sentries is easier than I expect. The ones in the towers all seem to be staring toward the south, and I wonder if the network arranged for a distraction that I'm not seeing.

Declan told me to go to the western vehicle pool, but I suddenly feel disoriented. Panic tugs at my belly as I hug the wall behind one of the guard towers.

I send a telepathic SOS. "I don't know where the entrance to that vehicle pool is."

A second later, a sharp pain explodes behind my eyes. He's projecting something.

"You could've warned me," I mutter.

"Who has time for that? Focus."

He's projected a simple map of the base. My destination is clearly marked.

"She'll be in the tunnel. Walk until you see her."

I continue walking, my pulse stuttering when I reach the massive chain-link gates. The vehicle pool features both an outdoor lot and a covered structure, and I creep toward the latter's entrance. Inside, I find rows of utility trucks and armored vehicles, illuminated by the greenish glow of the overhead lights. They sit silent and imposing, their sleek exteriors blending seamlessly with the shadows.

I have to pass a row of tanks to get to the transport tunnel. I stare at their gun barrels. They're pointed skyward, but I half expect someone to pop up, swing them downward, and begin firing at me.

At a shadowy doorway, my heart starts beating double time. The tunnel greets me with a warm breeze, yet somehow it brings a chill rather than heat to my bones.

He said to walk until I see her. I move cautiously, once again fearing a trap. With each step, the darkness swallows me deeper, the only sound the echo of my own footsteps against the paved ground.

Finally, I see her. A figure cloaked in shadows, beckoning me closer.

I swallow my nerves as I catch a dark blur of motion, and then blink at a sudden brightness.

She's projected a light onto the wall from the slender comm in her hand. Not the Company-issued one. It's something I've never seen before.

I study the woman who's summoned me. She's younger than I expected. Early thirties maybe. She's wearing all-black: leather pants, ribbed tank under a cropped jacket, and a knit cap covering her head. With her free hand, she slides the hat off, and a cascade of red hair tumbles onto her shoulders.

"Darlington." It's a statement, not a question.

Yet I still answer, "Yes."

"I'm Adrienne."

I'd never heard her name before last night, but I suspect she's important. And although I can't see a single weapon on her person—unless she's sporting some nasty surprises beneath that jacket—I get the sense she can kill me in a heartbeat.

I remain on guard, not taking that awareness of danger lightly. "The network has been ignoring me for weeks," I say in accusation.

"Because you're not important."

I bristle. "And I suppose Jim wasn't important, either?"

"You mean Julian?" She scoffs. "That man was nothing but a headache."

"You knew him."

"Of course. Julian Ash jeopardized the entire network with his actions—"

"What actions? Saving me?"

"—and then had the nerve to make demands. Set me up in an asset ward, he says. Get me travel passes at my command, he says." Her mocking voice floats through the tunnel.

"You gave it to him," I point out.

"It wasn't my call back then."

"But you call the shots now?"

"Lucky me. Tasked with deciding what to do with yet another headache courtesy of Julian Ash. The one he left behind for me."

"I thought I wasn't important."

"You weren't. But clearly, they like you. They flew in a healer for you. A recruit."

"How did you know that?"

"We have eyes all over this base."

Wariness creeps up my spine. "Should we be talking out loud?"

"We've got jammers up. Nothing's being recorded, and the cameras are on a loop within a two-mile radius. I'll link with you if I decide you're worth my time."

I try not to let my irritation show. "What can I do to convince you?"

"Make it into Silver Elite."

That startles me. "Why?"

"Because we have a hole to fill. We just lost one of our best operatives."

For a moment I'm confused. Then a gasp gets stuck in my throat as it dawns on me, the pieces clicking together.

"Betima."

Adrienne's lips curl. "I told them not to send in an empath, but I was outvoted." She makes a disparaging noise under her breath. "They're too much of a liability. Extreme emotions can spontaneously trigger their abilities."

I guess I shouldn't tell her about my ability to incite, then, seeing as how it only ever happens spontaneously. But I'm not about to blow my chances of getting out of here.

Although from the sound of it, she doesn't *want* me to leave.

She wants me to stay.

"If I make it into Elite," I say slowly, "then what?"

"Then you work for the network. You do what we tell you."

"And what will you tell me to do?"

"Anything. Everything."

"I don't take blind orders."

"Then you don't belong in the Uprising." She starts to turn away.

"Wait."

She turns back, eyes flashing with irritation. It's too dark to tell what color they are. "I risked my ass to come here tonight, and I don't need some twenty-year-old novice questioning our protocol. You don't have any say here. None at all. Fucking zero. You don't get to make a single decision. You don't get to use your brain to do what you think is right. Unless it's to improvise on an op so your cover isn't exposed. But the missions, the objectives—those are handed down to you by the adults, and, like a good little girl, you implement them. Your only job is to do whatever the hell you're asked."

I stare at her, jaw tightening.

"Do you support the General, Darlington?"

I recoil at the unexpected question. "Of course not."

"Well, his reign will come to an end—but only so long as operatives like you do as you're told. Do whatever it takes to save our people." She pauses, some of the bite leaving her tone. "Ash spoke about you over the years."

"Really?"

"He said he'd never seen anybody shoot the way you do. Told us to come find you if we ever needed a sniper."

I blink in surprise. I had no idea. Jim spent so much time trying to keep me *away* from the network, grumbling that he didn't want me running missions for them, and yet he was keeping them apprised of my sniper prowess? Emotion tightens my throat. I guess he always knew that one day I would work for them.

If I choose to work for them.

I study Adrienne's face. She's not the most beautiful woman, but her features are interesting. She's certainly not forgettable, and I wonder if that's why I've never seen her before. Unforgettable faces aren't exactly conducive to undercover work.

"You want me to make it into Silver Elite?"

She nods.

"There's no guarantee I even can. We won't find out who gets shortlisted until the last section, and my instructors said scores don't necessarily contribute to the selection process. And if the scores *do* matter, then . . ." I bite my lip. "That might be a problem."

"Why is that?"

"Because I'm failing the Program."

She falls silent several moments. I get the feeling she's talking to somebody else.

"If you're trying to talk to Tana or one of my contacts, they didn't know," I say. I don't want Tana to get in shit for this. "I didn't tell her that I was purposely sabotaging."

Adrienne looks annoyed. "There's five more weeks left. Turn it around."

I nod. But I have no idea how I'll convince Cross that now, out of the wild blue, I've developed a sincere interest in excelling.

Her eyes meet mine, and then I feel a tickle in the back of my skull. An invitation to link.

I accept it.

"Declan will be your handler. Orders will come from him."

Her voice fills my head. I'm startled, because it's one of those rare instances when her head voice sounds almost identical to her speaking voice.

"But just know he's not calling the shots. Everything comes from the top and gets filtered down to you. Understood?"

"Understood."

"Have a good night, Darlington."

She turns and disappears into the tunnel.

I stand motionless for a moment. Then I rub my forehead, wondering what I've gotten myself into. I could stay the course, try to fail out. Hope that Cross decides not to send me to the stockade or to face the Tribunal and lets me go back to my ward.

But what is there to go back to?

The ranch is gone. My village is being watched. People like Betima are being executed by an eighteen-year-old prick who's scared of her. Because that's what it comes down to. They can spew all the horseshit they want about our blood being toxic and how we're abominations who shouldn't exist, but the truth is, they fear us. That's why they're trying to get rid of us.

I won't let that happen.

I won't watch anyone else I care about get executed.

So. Silver Elite, it is.

CHAPTER 26

W e're shooting guns in the desert today. Sniper exercises. In other words, my chance to turn things around.

When we ran ops in the city, we took hover-helos, but for the desert we board a speed jet. It's my first time flying in a plane, which surprises my friends.

"Really? You've never been on a plane before?" Lyddie says from the seat next to mine.

"My uncle and I never had the Lux credits to spend," I admit. "We took the train if we ever needed to travel far distances."

"Eh, flying's overrated," Kaine says from my other side. "You haven't been missing much."

"Have you flown a lot?" I ask him.

"A handful of times. My mom liked to use her leisure passes to take us to Heath's End," he explains, referring to a small island in the southwest corner of the Continent, near Ward V. "You can only get there by air since there's nowhere to dock."

"You're so lucky. I've never seen the ocean," Lyddie tells him. "My parents like to leisure in the mountains."

"I love the ocean," Kaine says. "Although the first time I flew over it, I got the most intense motion sickness and threw up all over my mother."

I snort. "Sexy."

He bends toward me so he can whisper in my ear. "Sneak into my bed tonight and I'll show you sexy."

A shiver runs through me. Oh boy. It's been a few days since my grief-fueled visit to Kaine's bed, and other than the morning after, this is the first time he's bringing it up. I don't think he told anyone, because I haven't heard any whispers or received any questions. Me, I didn't breathe a word of it, not even to Lyddie. She would tease me relentlessly if she found out I made out with Kaine. In the barracks, no less.

I can't say I'm against it happening again, but not in a roomful of other people. And certainly not as a way to forget that one of our friends was killed.

We're in the air for less than an hour before it's time to land. We touch down on a narrow strip and climb into trucks that take us to the Command's desert camp. The area is not a flat expanse, but a lot of hills and craggy outcrops. We were given another set of uniforms this morning—desert fatigues. I have to admit it's nice to wear something other than navy blue or black. The new getup makes it easier to blend in to this landscape.

We start with easy targets, and I nail all my shots. I do well enough that Jones raises a brow and drawls, "Someone's been practicing after hours."

Someone's been making shots like that since she was ten years old.

Kess sneers. "It's just a fluke."

"I've been up all night reading sniper tips on my source," I lie. "How to account for the wind. Different magnifications. It's actually a lot more interesting than I thought."

Kaine's biting his lip like he's trying not to laugh. Lash looks doubtful. Meanwhile, Lyddie's eyes are bright with hope.

"See, I told you you've got potential! And sometimes books *can* teach you things!"

Oh, this girl. I always want to give her a hug. She's growing on me in a way I never thought possible. She's just so . . . positive. Yes, she likes to gossip, but her heart is enormous.

"Let's reposition to higher ground," Ford barks. "One pair at a time. Darlington, Eversea. You're up first."

Great. I'm paired with Ivy.

From her sour expression, she's not happy about it, either.

I sling the rifle strap over my shoulder and head for the path. The two of us make the climb up to the next perch, where I glance at her and say, "You want to spot first?"

"Fine," she mutters.

I position myself on my belly with the rifle in front of me. It's the REMM-4 that I'm obsessed with. I wish we were doing this in the shroud of darkness so I could test out that night sight, but I suppose a day exercise offers everyone a better introduction to the New and Improved Recruit 56.

Ivy settles beside me with a pair of binoculars as the blistering sun beats down on our heads. We lie prone on top of the outcrop, our camo uniforms blending seamlessly with the arid landscape. The desert stretches out before us, a vast expanse of hills, sun-bleached sand, and jagged rocks, the horizon shimmering in the relentless heat. Despite how barren it is, it's oddly gorgeous out here.

Squinting against the glare, I adjust the scope of the rifle, my fingers trembling with anticipation. It feels like forever since I've had the opportunity to shoot. I've been firing guns every day for weeks, yet there was no thrill. No excitement to take—and *make*—a challenging shot.

Now I've given myself permission to rely on my instincts. Or rather, the Uprising has.

I feel freer than I have in a very long time.

Ivy adjusts her binoculars, scanning the horizon for our first target. We don't know ahead of time where the targets are. It's the job of the spotter to locate them. We each get five shots, and all the targets are outfitted with sensors that will relay to our instructors where we hit.

"Target one acquired," Ivy says.

"Where?"

"At your two o'clock, about five hundred yards out." A hint of challenge laces her tone. "Might be too much for you. The wind sucks."

No shit. Tiny grains of sand keep flying into my face. This is a terrible day to shoot. Or maybe the windy weather is precisely why Ford chose today for long-range targets.

"I think I can manage." I locate the target in my scope. It looks like a sandbag on a pole.

With a steady hand, I adjust my aim again to compensate for the wind and the distance. The crosshairs settle on the target's chest, a perfect bull's-eye in my sights. My finger hovers over the trigger, waiting for the perfect moment. Finally, I squeeze the trigger, and the shot rings out across the landscape.

The bullet cuts through the wind with lethal precision.

Dead center.

Ivy swivels her head toward me.

"Been practicing," I say lightly. "Where's target two?"

"Six o'clock. Six hundred yards."

I lean forward, but before I can take aim, something else catches my eye.

A motorcycle is approaching the camp at the base of the hill, where the rest of our group congregates. Tires kicking up dirt. A sleek body curled over it. The rider isn't wearing a helmet or navy blues. He's in desert khakis and a white shirt, his dark hair messy from the wind blowing through it.

I find him in the scope and zoom in. That face. I focus on his lips, remembering how close they were to mine the night at the pit. His eyes are impossibly blue in the daylight.

I'm very aware of Ivy's presence. She raises her binoculars. "Captain is here," she says.

As if to punctuate that, Ford's voice echoes through our earpieces. "Be extra good today, kids. Got an audience. Don't make me look bad. First pair. Next target."

This second target is more difficult. The angle, and the direction of the wind, will be a challenge.

I steady my breathing and line up the shot. I feel Ivy's gaze boring into the side of my head, her silent scrutiny almost palpable. I push aside the pressure and focus all my attention on the target.

The report of my rifle echoes through the air. I connect with the target, another perfect bull's-eye boring into its center.

Ivy is gaping at me now. Once could've been a fluke. Twice? Not so much.

"Who was that? Eversea?" Ford's impressed voice fills my ear.

"Darlington," I respond, a bit smug.

"Well. I suppose even a broken clock works twice a day."

I glare at him even though he can't see me.

"Next target."

Target three is about eight hundred yards out. This angle is even more difficult. I glance at Ivy, who holds up her hand.

"No. Wind's shifting. Wait."

She's got good instincts, I'll give her that.

I wait, then take the shot.

Bull's-eye.

And then the next one.

Bull's-eye.

And the next one.

Bull's-eye.

Yet my comm remains maddeningly silent.

I shift the scope to where Cross stands with Ford near the white canvas mess tent. They're drinking coffee and laughing about something. The sight makes me bristle. I know they'll see my accuracy results later when everything is transmitted to their tablets, but I want them to pay attention *now*. Why am I even trying if not to impress these assholes?

Grumbling under my breath, I survey the camp. It's twelve hundred yards away, give or take. I sweep my scope over the area until I find a suitable target.

"Hey, LT," I say to Ford over the comm.

He sounds annoyed. "What?"

"On your left. The table near the firepit. Is that your canteen?"

"Yeah. Why?"

I lick my suddenly dry lips. Taking out a target from this distance, with the wind howling and the sun beating down on us—it's reckless, even for me.

I adjust my stance as I peer through the scope again. The canteen's outline is blurred by the heat haze that dances on the horizon. The wind snakes underneath my ponytail, adding another layer of complexity to an already daunting task.

You only live once, right?

I take the shot.

An explosion of water shoots out in all directions as I puncture a hole in the metal. Liquid pools on the table and splashes the dirt beneath it.

I smile.

Silence falls over the comm channel.

Ivy's expression is a mix of shock and disbelief. Through the scope, I see the surprise mirrored in Ford's eyes. But not Cross's. His lips curve, and then I hear his voice in my earpiece.

"Nobody likes a show-off, Dove."

I killed it today. Indisputably. And yet, when we check our scores for the day in the mess hall later, the readout staring back at me from the screen doesn't make a lick of sense.

Sixty-five percent.

I bolt to my feet and stomp over to the table where our instructors are chatting among themselves.

"Not a single other recruit in this class could make the shot I made today," I growl at them. "And you gave me a sixty-five? Are you joking?"

Xavier Ford lifts his head, dark eyes glinting with humor. "The captain was the one scoring you today. Take it up with him."

Fucking asshole.

I score a 70 after our next Combat class, despite slamming Ivy's ethereal face into the mats.

Seventy-two in Moving Targets, despite only missing three shots out of thirty.

Sixty-five in Archery. I deserve that one.

Knife Throwing? Sixty-two! That one is wholly unwarranted. My knives sank into every target like a blade through butter. Perfection.

"He's doing it on purpose," I complain at afternoon meal after enduring more than a week of mediocre scores.

Lyddie chews her mashed potatoes and tries to reassure me. "No. The instructors are fair. They wouldn't give you low scores for no reason."

That's exactly what Cross is doing. And he enlisted the other instructors to follow his lead.

It's infuriating. Now that I'm making a sincere effort, it isn't being recognized. I might not be an overachiever like Lyddie or Bryce, but I deserve recognition, damn it.

In shielding class, I'm somewhat mollified when Amira tells me I have the strongest shield of anyone in here.

"It's truly impressive," she says, and I pretend to blush at the encouragement when really, it had better be impressive. I trained with Julian Ash.

Every time I see Amira, the temptation to reach out gets stronger, but I refuse to endanger myself after what happened to Betima. I can't be too careful. Today, though, it occurs to me that I now possess the ability to verify the risk.

I check in with Declan after class to ask, "Is Amira a network operative? Is she undercover here?"

His response is not at all useful. "We cannot divulge the identities of our operatives."

At first, I take that to mean she's *definitely* one of us. But then I test that theory by asking, "Is Lyddie De Velde an operative?" and get the same generic rejoinder.

"We cannot divulge the identities of our operatives."

I try Bryce and receive the identical answer. I'm certain both those women are not Modified, especially since I've been in Lyddie's mind and she showed no reaction to the psychic intrusion. Unless, like me, she's mastered the ability to hide the physical shock, but I don't know many Mods who can actually do that.

In the afternoon, we run another mock op on the base. I'm paired with Bryce, which means for sure we'll score 100 percent. She's good, and she's *fast*. We have one minute to scale a wall, plant an explosive on a second-floor window ledge, and reach the safe zone before the charge goes off.

We nail it. Bryce even smiles at me in exuberance after we finish. That's how much we nailed this op.

And yet at dinner, when our daily results come in, Bryce scores 100.

I score 80.

Eighty! For doing the same thing.

I growl out loud and Kaine laughs at me. "All right," he relents, "I'm starting to think maybe it's a thing."

"I told you it was a thing."

I'm still fuming about it in the showers later. I *know* this is Cross's doing. And I know I need to fix it before I lose more time. Only a month remains of the Program.

I open a path and reach out to Declan again. "I'm not going to make it into Silver Block, let alone Elite. Captain hates me."

"Adrienne won't be pleased," is the response.

"But I have an idea. Can you get me schematics for the officers' quarters? All I know is it's a separate building somewhere on the base."

"See what I can do."

He contacts me as I'm sliding into bed, projecting a blueprint into my mind. It's a quick flash, and I make him do it again so I can try to memorize it.

"Thanks, I got it."

Now comes the hard part.

SECTION   3

Instructor	FORD (LT)
Student	Wren Darlington, R56
Class	Drills and Mock Operations
Score	60%

INSTRUCTOR NOTES:

Darlington might not be cut out for covert ops. Too cocky.

CHAPTER 27

In the morning, I pull Kaine aside on our way to the mess hall. "Hey, today in Tech, can you create some sort of distraction?"

Although his eyes sparkle with intrigue and his mouth lifts in a grin, he doesn't make it easy for me. "Sorry, cowgirl," he says in an overly stern tone, "but I don't do anything without knowing why."

Sighing, I lean in close and tell him. His smile widens.

"Your wish is my command."

It's a challenge to keep from laughing when I watch Kaine in action later. While we all gather around a table listening to Lieutenant Hirai prattle on about the intricacies of a voice-operated surveillance drone, Kaine winks at me, then deliberately bumps into Anson.

Excellent choice. Anson has the shortest fuse of anyone I've ever met. I think the guy just waits for an opportunity to blow up and hurt somebody.

"Sorry," Kaine tells Anson. "I tripped trying to get a better look at the drone." He claps the guy on the shoulder.

"Don't fucking touch me," Anson snarls. He shoves Kaine, because violence is coded into his DNA, sending Kaine stumbling backward.

The scuffle succeeds in diverting attention from the unlocked supply cage behind Hirai. I begin inching my way toward it.

Kaine feigns bewilderment. "Whoa, calm down. I didn't mean anything by it. Just my way of saying sorry."

He good-naturedly smacks Anson's arm, but since there's nothing good about Anson's nature, he gets directly in Kaine's face.

"I said don't touch me."

Kaine squares his shoulders, baiting Anson even further. "You've got some real anger issues, brother."

Hissing out a breath, Anson gives him another hard shove.

"Enough!" Hirai rounds the table and firmly plants himself between the two young men, and I take the opportunity to slip into the cage unnoticed.

I know exactly what I'm looking for, and it takes all of three seconds to retrieve it. With deft hands, I slip it into my pocket, then duck out of the cage and hurry over to pull Kaine away from Anson.

"Stop being such a troublemaker," I chastise him.

I can see him trying not to laugh.

That night, I wait until everyone is asleep before sliding out of bed, fully dressed in my black uniform. I activate the signal jammer and clip it to my belt. It'll stop the cameras from recording while I sneak out of the training facility. The moment it's out of range, they'll start recording again, but unless someone's paying extra-close attention, my bunk will look occupied at a glance, my pillow creating a human-like lump beneath the blanket.

Outside, the summer air is warm. Somewhere on the base, someone is smoking euca, because the minty scent floats in the breeze. The sentries must be bored on their graveyard watch.

With the jammer on my person, cameras won't catch me, and alarms won't trip. But the guards themselves aren't transmitting any signals that can be circumvented. I'll need to avoid their detection. I wait until the guard at the first tower turns his head before rushing forward.

With cautious steps, I make my way to the south end of the base, where the officers' quarters are located. Far from prying eyes. The soldier barracks are by the training facility, but the officers have their privacy.

A few minutes later, I reach the two-story building, eyeing the gray exterior and flat roof. According to the map Declan projected for me, my target is on the second floor.

I place all my trust in the device on my belt and enter the building, praying I'm invisible to the cameras mounted on the ceiling. So far, nobody has come running. No alarms blaring. I want to take this jammer back to the bunks and hide it in my locker, but I know that's not an option. It'll be confiscated from me soon enough.

One flight of stairs, and I'm stopping in front of Cross's door. I push on the handle with the lightest touch. Locked. A thumbprint scan is required to open it. It's fine. I expected that.

I freeze at the murmur of voices beyond the door.

Is he not alone?

I wait, letting a few seconds tick by, but there's only one voice now. Maybe he's talking into his comm.

I take the stairs up to the roof, where I peer over the edge to study the balcony below. The fire escape ladder from the roof doesn't reach all the way down.

Stifling a groan, I descend the ladder as far as I'm able to, then solo it the rest of the way. Scaling the wall like one of those monkeys in the Blacklands. God, I hated those things. They were so cute. Their little pink faces. Then they opened their mouths and revealed three rows of razor-sharp teeth that could rip your throat out.

There really is nothing left to fear after you've lived in that nightmare.

My boots barely make a sound as they connect with the balcony. The door's been left open to let in the night breeze. He's not worried about intruders, because he knows he'll be alerted by the alarms hardwired all over this building. Or maybe even earlier, the second a shadow crosses one of his precious cameras. The soldiers staffing the security center probably wake him if a recruit so much as sneezes. Which means I can waltz right in without a care in the world. This is what happens when people get complacent.

I pull out my knife, the same one he gave back to me. I enjoy the irony.

A soft moan echoes through the apartment.

Female.

My shoulders snap straight. So he's not alone.

Something sharp and unpleasant clenches in my chest, but I ignore it. Doesn't matter. It's probably better this way.

His quarters are spacious but not elaborate. A nice living area, tidy kitchen. I move like a ghost. I don't exist. He thinks I lack covert abilities? *Watch this, asshole.*

I follow the corridor off the kitchen, passing two closed doors toward one at the end that stands ajar. My heart beats faster as I peer inside.

They're on the bed.

"Wanted this for so long."

I don't recognize her voice. I'm grateful for that. I still don't like how hot my blood feels. I shouldn't care who he's with.

I creep closer, angling my body to get a better vantage point.

She's sitting astride him. They're both still clothed, but his long-sleeved shirt is unbuttoned, revealing tantalizing glimpses of his chest. He has one hand thrust in her long black hair. Strands of it fall into his face when she bends to kiss him. His other hand cups her ass as she starts to grind on him.

He releases a low, gravelly groan from the back of his throat, and I feel it everywhere.

I take a breath. I wait.

"Please," she begs. "I need you."

He rolls her over, pinning her beneath his strong body. Her arms loop around his neck.

I exhale. I wait.

When he rises on his knees and starts undoing his pants, I act.

Cross senses it at the very last second, growling in anger, but it's too late. The blade digs into his throat as I hold the knife against it.

His companion screeches and scrambles up the bed to the headboard. She presses her palms to her chest as if she's trying to cover herself, even though she's fully dressed.

I recognize her now. The shiny hair. She was at the pit a few weeks ago. Clinging to him. Batting her eyelashes. Doing everything in her power to capture his attention.

Guess she succeeded.

"What the hellfuck!" she cries out.

Cross remains on his knees while I crouch behind him, keeping the knife directly over his jugular.

Unfazed, he slowly twists his head. The blade digs into the tendons of his throat, and a line of red blossoms on his skin. His lips curl mockingly.

"Are you here to join or to watch?"

"You know why I'm here."

He turns back to the bed, and I lift the knife a hair so it doesn't cut him again.

"You need to leave," he tells his companion.

Her fearful gaze darts toward me.

"Relax, I'm not going to stab him," I say.

In a show of good faith, I lower the knife from his throat. I wipe the faint trickles of blood off the blade using my pant leg and tuck it into the sheath.

Shiny Hair glances between us, her eyes darkening with mistrust each time they rest on me. "You seriously want me to go?" she asks Cross.

"Yes."

I swallow my smile. I don't know why that satisfies me so much, the fact that he couldn't care less about keeping her around.

His lack of interest clearly grates on her. She slides off the bed, her short skirt flouncing around her firm thighs. She stops to snatch a pair of sandals off the floor and stomps away on bare feet.

"She really didn't have to leave," I say sweetly. "We could have talked while she was here."

"No point in letting her stay if you don't want to join us."

"I'd rather die."

Cross glances at my knife. "Am I going to need to confiscate that?"

"You had your chance. Now you have to fight me for it."

He sighs. Raking a hand through his hair, he slides off the bed and gets to his feet.

I avert my gaze when I realize his pants are undone. He zips them up, but rather than button his shirt, he peels it off his shoulders and tosses it on the tousled bedsheets.

I want to spend the next hour examining his tattoos and running my hands all over them. Ask him what they mean. *If* they mean anything. Maybe he just likes intricate wings and flames with cryptic lines of text snaking through them.

"Why are you in my bedroom, Dove?"

"Because you're sabotaging my chances of passing the Program."

To my surprise, he throws his head back and laughs. "Oh, that's rich coming from you. You've been sabotaging your own chances since the beginning."

"And now I'm doing better." I jut out my chin.

"Yes. Why is that?"

I knew he'd be suspicious. That's fine. I'm prepared for this.

"I have nothing to go back to."

The grim confession, spoken in my flat, discouraged tone, hangs in the air between us.

Cross eyes me for a moment before leaving the room and striding toward the kitchen. I trail after him, watching as he opens a cupboard and pulls out a bottle of whiskey. Another cupboard produces two glasses. He sets one down, then gestures to the other one with a questioning look.

I nod, even though I know it's a bad idea. I shouldn't be sharing a drink with him.

He pours. The dark liquid sloshes against the brim as he slides the glass across the counter toward me.

I pick it up, and he watches my lips as I take a tentative sip.

"You gave away my ranch."

"Yes."

"You're not going to let me return to Z."

"No."

"What happens if you send me to the Tribunal instead of the stockade?"

He considers the question. "There's not much evidence you were in collusion with your guardian, so they'd likely give you a labor sentence. Best case, a factory assignment."

"Not interested." I shake my head and take another sip. The alcohol burns my throat on its way down.

"You weren't interested in joining the Command, either."

"In case you haven't noticed, I'm stubborn."

"Oh, I've noticed."

I fall silent for a moment, studying his flawless features, the strong lines of his throat as he tips his head back to drink his whiskey. I'm trying very hard not to stare at his bare chest, and I'm grateful for the counter acting as a barrier between us.

Every time I'm in this guy's presence, I forget that I'm not allowed to be attracted to him. I keep waiting for it to go away. For me to be in the same room as Cross and not feel this magnetic pull toward him.

The fact that it seems to be entirely one-sided makes it all the more aggravating. I can't use his behavior at pit night as evidence of desire for me, because I'm not convinced it was. He was drunk. Men say ludicrous things when they're drunk, and any random person might seem attractive to them when alcohol's fueling their libido.

"I'm not like you. I can't just 'accept my fate,'" I say, quoting his own words back to him. "I have to think about it first."

"Really. You think before you act now? Is that why you're in my quarters?"

"I thought very hard about how to get into your quarters."

The dimple appears. "Went to a lot of effort to get me alone."

"Less effort than you think." I can't stop a smug smile from surfacing. "I'm better than all the other recruits here. You think Lyddie could have lifted a jammer right out from under Hirai's nose?"

I unclip it from my belt and set the small black device on the counter. Slide it toward him.

He catches it before it falls off the edge.

"I hope you know you just earned Hirai a reprimand," Cross says.

"Good. He deserves it. If someone is that unobservant, they should be punished accordingly. In fact, every single guard whom I waltzed right past tonight should be reprimanded. Whoever came up with the sentry schedule, too, because it's predictable as hell. A couple of nights of recon and anyone can figure out their routines. When Soldier 4615 is going to smoke his euca joint. When Soldier 380 will take a leak in the tunnel behind South Plaza."

Cross narrows his eyes.

"I wasn't trying before," I tell him.

"Clearly."

"But I'm willing to try now."

"You let Farren crush your wrist to get cut."

"That may have been a little . . . extreme."

"A little," he echoes in amusement.

"In my defense, I'd just witnessed your brother kill one of my fellows." My jaw tightens. "I don't give a shit what he says. I don't believe Betima was Aberrant. And I don't believe my uncle was, either. But if you insist he was, fine. I'll take your word for it."

I pick up my glass and swig nearly half of it before putting it down.

"You were right, okay? I can't go back. Jim is dead. And whatever he was, I'm choosing to remember him as the man who saved me as a child. I know you think I'm lying to you, but I promise you, I didn't know what he was doing. If he was an Uprising operative, I didn't know. If he was running missions for them, I—"

"We don't believe he was," Cross interjects. "He went into hiding after he deserted. Dormant for fifteen years."

"Why did he desert in the first place? I tried finding answers on Nexus—"

"I know. Your searches are flagged and sent directly to me." He cocks a brow. "You searched my name, too."

No point denying it. "You don't exist in the Command system. And on Nexus you're nothing other than the General's son."

He shrugs. "That's all I've ever been. The General's son."

I suspect he's right. The moment I found out who his father was, I stopped viewing him as anything but the offspring of Merrick Redden. Maybe that's a miscalculation on my part. If I'm to destroy this place from within, maybe I need to better understand its players.

His long fingers wrap around the whiskey glass. His hands are mesmerizing. Large. Radiating strength. I watch his throat dip as he swallows. And his chest is taunting me. Why does he have so many muscles?

"Cross."

We both hear the chord of desperation.

"Are you going to make me beg?"

I don't miss the flicker of heat in his eyes. "Sounds like something I'd enjoy."

I grit my teeth. "You win. *Please.* I want another shot."

"Do you now."

"You said you don't hand out second chances, but I'm still asking you for one. You said not to squander the opportunity you're giving me, and I'm promising you I won't. Not anymore."

Glass in hand, he rounds the counter toward me. My pulse quickens, but he doesn't linger. Instead, he walks toward the living space and leans against the side of the sofa, sipping his drink.

His gaze locks with mine, but he breaks the eye contact first, running a hand through his tousled hair. I try not to think about the reason his hair is messy. Or why I care.

I swallow my frustration and make another attempt to sway him. It's impossible to know what this man is thinking or if anything I'm saying even resonates with him.

"Cross," I say again.

Something flickers through his expression. I can't quite decode it, but it happens every time I say his name.

"As much as it pains me to admit it, I think you're right. Maybe it's time I let go of the past and look toward the future. Stop fighting against the current of fate and start swimming with it."

He licks a drop of whiskey from the corner of his mouth. "That's very poetic of you."

"I'm not a poet. I'm a pragmatist. I know what will happen to me if I fail the Program, and I refuse to let that happen. I want a post in Silver Block. And these bullshit low scores are starting to piss me off."

"Poor thing."

I glare at him. "Score me correctly or I'll file a complaint with Captain Radek."

"You think reporting me to the admin captain is a threat?" He chuckles. "I'm the General's son, remember? I can do no wrong."

"You're wrong to not evaluate me based on merit. Please. Let me prove I deserve it."

He's quiet for so long, I think he's going to shoot me down. He strides back to the kitchen to refill his glass, and I try not to notice the way his biceps flex as he pours.

Finally, he shrugs and says, "All right."

Relief floods my body. "Thank you."

"*If* you raise your written scores. Fieldwork and exceptional marksmanship alone aren't enough to get you into Silver Block."

"Exceptional, huh?" I can't contain the burst of pleasure I receive from hearing that.

His eyes find mine, and this time he doesn't look away. That magnet is back, trying to lure me toward him, but his next question jolts me out of it.

"Where'd you learn to shoot like that?"

Pain pierces my heart. "My uncle taught me. He started me off with a pistol, just slapped it in my hand when I was—" I catch myself before the real age slips out. *Five.* "I don't know, nine? Ten?" I play it casual, hoping he believes my abrupt pause was me trying to remember how old I was. "He used to set up targets all over the ranch—"

All over our little clearing in the Blacklands.

"And we'd stay out there for hours."

Until the light left us.

"He wanted me to be able to protect myself from the white coyotes, the wolves—"

The predators that roamed the darkness.

"—not to mention the Faithfuls that snuck onto the property and tried to steal our cattle. I took to it really well. He told me I have good instincts."

"You do." Cross clears his throat. "But I mean it. Start passing your source tests."

"I'll try." The words come out grudgingly, like a rotten tooth being forced out with pliers. But inside, I'm celebrating.

I wait until I leave his quarters—through the front door—before letting my smile surface.

CHAPTER 28

We're jumping out of a plane tonight.

This is amazing.

Not that I'm enjoying myself. I'm really, really trying to remember that the Command is an enemy institution and I'm here to destroy it from the inside.

But . . . this is fucking amazing.

The night stretches out before me as I stand at the open door of the aircraft. The sound of the engines drowns out the rhythmic thudding of my pulse. Below us, the desert lies bathed in the silvery glow of the moon.

"This is fucking amazing," Kaine shouts over the wind. His excitement matches my own.

My heart pounds in my chest, apprehension swirling inside me. With a deep breath, I steady myself against the rush of wind, the weight of my pack a reassuring presence against my back. We're doing parachuting drills tonight. In other words, there's no room for doubt and no space for hesitation.

"All right, listen up!" Ford says, his voice cutting through the roar of the wind. "Trust your equipment and you'll all make it down safely. Your landing zone is clearly marked. Aim for it and you'll be fine."

"I don't think I can do this," groans a male recruit from Red Cell. His face is turning green.

Ford rolls his eyes. "This is easy compared with the jumps you might be asked to make. In a real mission, you won't have the luxury of choosing where you land. You'll be parachuting directly into the heart of the city, a parking lot, a rooftop. Your life depends on your ability to adapt."

Lyddie's hand tightens around mine. She's been gripping it since we took off.

I see her chewing on her lip as she stares out into the darkness below. I can practically feel the waves of anxiety radiating from her.

"Hey," I say, placing an encouraging hand on her shoulder. "You've got this. You're stronger than you think."

"What if something goes wrong?" She releases a very un-Lyddie-like expletive. "Fuck! Why did I think Silver Block would be a good idea?"

"It's fine. You'll do fine."

"What if I miss the landing zone and end up stranded in the middle of nowhere?"

I squeeze her shoulder, my voice firm as I say, "It's too late to change your mind now. You're here. We all are. And the only way out is through. You can do this, Lyds. I believe in you."

For a moment, she wavers, her gaze flickering between me and our impending leap of faith. Then she gives a determined nod and squares her shoulders.

"Let's move!" Ford shouts, his hair tousled by the wind. He signals for us to line up. "Sutler, go."

I blink and Kaine is out the door.

Gone.

"De Velde!"

At her signal, I watch with pride as Lyddie steps up to the edge. She takes a deep breath and jumps.

"Darlington!"

Adrenaline sizzles through my veins. Without second-guessing it, I launch myself into the abyss, hurtling through the darkness with reckless abandon.

I. Love. This.

For a fleeting moment, I'm suspended between sky and earth, a gust of air tearing at my clothing and the roar of the engines fading into the distance.

Then, with a sharp tug, my parachute deploys, snapping open with a deafening crack that echoes through the night. As I slowly drift downward, the desert unfurls beneath me like a patchwork quilt. Silence envelops me, broken only by the occasional whisper of wind and the steady thrum of my own heartbeat.

With each passing second, the ground draws nearer. I scan the terrain below, searching for the designated landing zone. There's no margin for error.

Finally, my boots make contact with the soft sand, sending a plume of dust spiraling into the air. I stumble upon landing, fighting to regain my balance.

"I got you, cowgirl," I hear, and then Kaine's strong hand is there, steadying me.

"Thanks."

His gaze fixates on my face, a grin on his lips.

"What?" I say.

"You should see your face right now. Orgasmic."

"That was incredible," I declare, and he slings an arm around me as we go to join the others.

———

We're spending the night in the desert. The Command has a base out here, and as the adrenaline high from our nighttime parachuting begins to ebb, we hike to camp. Tents dot the sandy expanse, ocher-colored fabric fluttering gently in the night breeze. In the center of camp is an unlit firepit.

Ford, Hadley, and Cross are waiting for us when we walk up. My heart flips at the sight of our captain. Dressed in black, rifle slung over one shoulder, a day's worth of beard growth covering his jaw. I prefer him clean-shaven, but I can't deny I'm enjoying the feral look.

As it turns out, we're not done for the night. Our superiors make us run an obstacle course that leaves us grimy. We crawl like snakes through the sand and race over the jagged contours of landscape until we're exhausted. And then, when a recruit named Franks gripes about how we're never going to put this to use in real life, Cross smiles at him and makes us run it again. Fuck you, Franks.

Later, a crackling bonfire casts dancing shadows on the faces of my fellows as we gather around it, eating and drinking under the stars. For one brief moment, the world falls away, and I feel a glimmer of peace beneath the endless sky.

Until Lyddie says, "I miss Betima," and the spell is broken, replaced by a cruel dose of reality.

"You don't believe him, then?" Lash cocks his head across the fire to where Roe sits with Anson and Kess. "That she was Aberrant?"

Lyddie hesitates. "I don't know. He claims he saw her arms turn silver when Glin died, but I was standing right there. I didn't see anything. Wren, did you?"

I shake my head.

"Kaine?"

"I was too busy tending to the spike in Cotter's chest to pay attention to anyone else, Lyds."

I wince at the reminder. My gaze travels in Roe's direction, hardening to stone when he smiles at me. If you could call it a smile. His teeth are bared, but without humor. I haven't spoken a word to him since he put a bullet in Betima's head. Since I heard the General telling Cross that Roe did the world a great service.

Speaking of the General, his voice suddenly booms in the night.

I startle, thinking he's somehow parachuted his way into camp, until I realize the voice is coming from someone's source. They're projecting General Redden's latest broadcast to the wards.

" . . . the only way to ensure the destructive philosophy we call Severnism is rooted out," Redden is saying. I detest that stern, chilling cadence with which he speaks. "Ideas are like weeds. They emerge from the smallest cracks and thrive in neglect. And if they're not controlled, they spread. They grow. They invade. It's our role as loyal citizens of the Continent to pull out these weeds before they take hold. The Aberrant will not be allowed to poison our minds and seize our society—"

"I'm going to take that shower now," I say, getting to my feet.

Everyone else already took advantage of the outdoor showers to scrub the sand and dirt off, but I was waiting for the area to empty. With both Black and Red cells at camp tonight, the fewer eyes on my burns, the better.

The showers are on the outskirts of camp but in eyeshot of the fire. Just a row of simple stalls with wooden partitions between them, offering little privacy. I glance over to find them deserted, cementing my decision to go.

I reach the stalls at the exact moment Cross emerges from the other direction. He'd disappeared after the obstacle course, so I assumed he wasn't staying at camp with us. But here he is.

With a cursory look to acknowledge my presence, Cross walks past me toward one of the stalls.

Then he starts to strip.

My mouth feels like it's stuffed with a handful of the sand beneath my feet. I can't do anything but stare as he removes his shirt. His boots. I almost choke on my tongue when he drops his pants.

His bare ass taunts me. Tanned and muscular. I saw a lot of male recruits showering less than an hour ago, even caught a full-frontal glimpse or two, but nothing gets my pulse racing faster than the sight of a naked Cross stepping into the shower.

The partition mercifully blocks his lower body from my view, sparing me from making an even bigger fool of myself. I'm already gawking at him like a complete imbecile.

He turns the water on and tips his head toward the spray, soaking his face and hair.

Holy hellfuck, that body.

"Hasn't anyone ever told you that staring is rude?" He makes a tsking noise. "Where are your manners, Dove?"

I snap out of it to find his head turned in my direction, a smirk playing on his lips. And yet I still can't look away. His dark hair is slicked back, emphasizing his striking features. Rivulets of water cascade down the broad expanse of his shoulders and hard lines of his chest. Each droplet seems to accentuate the contours of his body, glistening on his tanned skin.

He exudes a raw masculinity that leaves me mesmerized.

"Were you going to shower or just stand there and watch?"

I clench my teeth, steeling myself against his potent sex appeal. So what if he looks good naked? Since when do I lose control of my faculties around an attractive man?

Without a word, I enter the stall next to his and get undressed there. It's a pointless stab at modesty—he's so tall, he can see right into my stall. I could have chosen one that wasn't right beside him, but I'm pretending to be unaffected.

I pull my shirt over my head and drape it over the wooden partition. When I take off my bra, I swear I hear his breath hitch, but a sidelong glance reveals his face is under the spray.

Despite my shaky hands, I manage to remove my pants. My underwear. I hang those up, too, and this time I know I didn't imagine his sharp inhale.

I twist the faucet on and position myself under the hot spray. From the corner of my eye, I see Cross dragging both hands through his hair to push it away from his forehead. He glances at me again, then slides a bar of soap between his heavy pecs.

His lips quirk when I visibly swallow. The bastard is taunting me.

Fine. I can taunt, too. As I tip my head back to soak my hair, I turn to face him fully and enjoy the way his eyes flash with heat. But then that hot gaze rakes over my body, branding every exposed inch, and my heart gives my rib cage a beating under his scrutiny.

His shameless gaze drifts lower still. I know the moment his eyes land on my thigh, because they narrow, sharpen. He doesn't ask about the burns.

Instead, he asks, "Are you fucking him?"

I wrinkle my brow. I was *not* expecting that. "Who?"

"Sutler. You spend a lot of time with him."

"Aw, Captain, that's sweet of you to notice." I lather the soap between my hands, then run them over my collarbone and breasts.

Cross's eyes downright sizzle.

"What if I was?" I can't stop the note of challenge. "Is there a rule against fraternizing?"

"Even if there was, I assume you'd break it." His voice is low. Raspy. But his face is unreadable. "So are you?"

I hide a smile. "No."

His expression doesn't change. He starts rinsing the soap off his body, and I can't help but steal another furtive glance.

I commit every detail to memory: the curve of his jawline, the ridges of his abdomen, the tantalizing hint of his ass beneath the partition. He's a work of fucking art, sculpted from marble, marked by ink, and bathed in moonlight.

"Are you sleeping with Ivy?" The question pops out before I can stop it.

Cross slides a knowing look my way. "No."

"Roe says she's basically the epitome of your type." A foreign entity has seized control of my vocal cords. *Shut the hell up, Wren.*

"Roe is the last person who should be speaking on my behalf."

Cross shuts off the water and steps out of the stall, grabbing a towel to dry himself with. I hear his husky laugh as he walks away, but I refuse to look over my shoulder. I'm breathing hard, shivering despite the warm water rushing over my body.

My heart is still pounding by the time I finish showering and return to the fire. We're bunking outside tonight. I unfold and lay out a sleeping roll next to Lyddie. Kaine is on my other side.

He gives me a thoughtful look. "Shower games over already?"

I flick him off, but he remains unfazed.

"Didn't realize the captain and I were in competition."

"There's no competition," I grumble.

"Wait, what?" Lyddie sits upright, her gaze sliding between us. "Is something happening here? Oh my gosh. Are you guys—"

"No," I interrupt, while Kaine grins at me.

Her forehead wrinkles. "Are you and the captain—"

"No." My tone is even firmer this time.

From across the fire, I notice a pair of pale eyes affixed on me like a leech. Ivy. I don't know if she heard any of that, but if Kaine saw me and Cross showering side by side, I'm sure Ivy noticed, too.

"I need some water," I blurt out.

Breaking eye contact with Ivy, I head toward the mess tent to refill my canteen.

When I emerge, I find Xavier Ford standing outside the canvas flap, smoking a cigarette. He studies me as he takes a drag.

"What?" I mutter.

"It's rare to see him like that."

We both know who he's talking about. "Like what?"

"Out of control." Ford drops his cigarette on the ground and extinguishes it with his boot. "You know, Darlington, there are very few things I like about you."

"Gee thanks. I'm touched."

"But this one . . . I find this one entertaining." Laughing, he strides off in the direction of the officers' tents, while I return to the bonfire and my fellows.

CHAPTER 29

Thanks to Lyddie's tutoring sessions, I improve on my next written test, scoring an 85. But I still prefer the mock ops. The drills. The exhilaration of jumping out of an airplane.

Sometime around Section 5, I start to wonder if I'm addicted to adrenaline.

Today we're running an exercise called Wait for Rescue. Kaine and I play the roles of hostages. We're being guarded by Roe, who checks on us every twenty minutes like clockwork. Our other fellows either serve as perimeter guards or form the team that's been tasked with freeing the hostages. Everyone wears sensor jumpsuits on ops now. If we take a fake hit, the sensor relays to our instructors where we're injured or if we're killed in action.

"This is boring," Kaine groans.

I stare at the slit of light peeking through the bottom of the metal door. Kaine lightly thumps his head against the cinder-block wall behind us, running his zip-tied hands through his blond hair. He's as restless as I am.

At first, we were thrilled to be paired together for this exercise, but as the minutes stretch into hours, impatience gnaws at us both. Each time our rescuers fail to infiltrate the warehouse, they're forced to start again. Kaine and I have been sitting in this cold, cramped room for an eternity, and so far, nobody has been able to rescue us.

"I hate placing my fate in other people's hands," I mumble. "We've been waiting all morning. Why are they so incompetent?"

"I say we just tag-team the little general next time he does his rounds." Kaine gives me a hopeful look.

I grin. "I'm down."

So that's what we do.

The next time the door creaks open to reveal the shadowy silhouette of our guard dog, Kaine and I spring to action. Our movements are synchronized as we dive forward, overpowering Roe before he can react.

We feel like a pair of badasses as we strut out of the warehouse a few minutes later, but our victory is short-lived. When we emerge into the daylight, Ford waits for us, arms folded against his chest. Hadley stands nearby, frowning at us. I hate the days when we train with Red Cell, because it means I have to see his face.

"Twenty minutes," Ford says in disapproval. "All you had to do was wait twenty more minutes and you would've passed this drill."

"We rescued ourselves," I protest.

"That wasn't the point, Darlington."

I glare at him. "The objective was to get rescued."

Our instructor makes an annoyed sound. "No, it wasn't."

"Then what were we supposed to do?" Kaine grumbles, equally irritated.

"Wait to get rescued! It's the name of the fucking op, Sutler. Wait for Rescue." Ford spells it out for us. "The whole point of this exercise is to teach you patience and discipline."

Well, when he puts it like that, I suppose I was always destined to fail. My impulsive nature chafes against the confines of those mission parameters. The desire for action will always burn like a wildfire inside me.

"Then why would you put us together?" I hook a thumb toward Kaine. "He's even more impatient than I am!"

Ford gives me a look as if to say, *Exactly,* then stalks off to address the rest of our fellows.

I'm confused for a second, until I suddenly realize what that look meant. We're being grouped for these drills not at random but based on the weaknesses we self-reported back in Section 2. This is why I'm constantly being paired with Kaine when it's evident we don't work well together. We're too similar.

"What did you enter as your weaknesses?" I ask him. "When that question popped up on our sources."

Understanding dawns in his eyes. "Reckless. Impatient."

"I said impulsive and impatient. And terrible at written work." I glance over. "What was your third one?"

"Too good looking."

I snort.

"So what he's saying is we need to think before we act and exercise more patience?" Kaine heaves a dramatic sigh. "That sounds so tedious."

"I know."

We rejoin the group for a debrief. Ford announces that all the Black Cell guards passed the mission. All members of the extraction team also passed.

"And our hostages, Sutler and Darlington," he finishes, his amused gaze flicking our way. "You failed."

"That's such horseshit," I grumble. "Technically the rescuers failed, too. Because they didn't rescue us."

From the extraction group, Kess presses her middle and pointer fingers to her thumb and flicks me off.

Ford practically growls with annoyance. "I told you, the rescue wasn't the point of the op. The purpose was to fulfill a role and follow directions. Everyone did that except you two assholes."

We're both suitably chastised. Ugh. I hate it when Ford is right. Turns him into such a smug bastard.

I'm fully aware that my weaknesses have the tendency to drag me down. I *know* I act on impulse, and I know it's stupid of me. I wouldn't even be on this base if I hadn't made the brash decision to race to Sanctum Point and try to stop Jim's execution.

Maybe if I'd listened to Griff, Tana, Declan, everyone who warned me not to go, then I'd . . .

Be right here anyway, I realize. Or end up in hiding. Maybe start my own Faithful camp somewhere in the mountains.

"Atten-tion!"

Everyone snaps to attention at Hadley's command, and the sound of footsteps on pavement has me glancing over my shoulder.

My heart freezes in my chest.

Jayde Valence.

She's striding toward us with purpose in her step. Her white-blond hair is tied in its usual low knot, her features pinched as always. The bloodmark on her cheek feels like a personal attack on me.

I'm on guard immediately. If she's here for me, I need to be ready to decoy my mind at a second's notice.

She moves with an aura of authority. There's something larger than life about her. Something terrifying. She's been marked by nature, but she's a formidable figure even without the red circle on her face.

I wonder how many abilities she has. Three? Four? Uncle Jim told me only the most powerful Mods bear a mark, and that he'd never known a marked Mod to possess any less than three abilities. I have four myself. That I know of, anyway. Perhaps there's a fifth or sixth or seventh lying dormant inside me, waiting to be unleashed at the most inconvenient of times. But another one would've manifested by now. I think. I hope.

Jayde comes to stand between Ford and Hadley, facing the recruits. A hush falls over the group as her piercing gaze bores into us with unwavering intensity that sends a shiver down my spine.

She's totally here for me.

She has to be.

I stand ramrod-straight, stoic on the outside, a hysterical mess on the inside. I inhale to regulate my unsteady heartbeat while I wait for her to say my name.

"You," she snaps.

The breath I'm exhaling stutters in my throat.

She's speaking to one of my fellows.

I don't know him. He's a member of Red Cell, a baby-faced guy named Peter with whom I've exchanged a total of zero words in five weeks.

"What's his name?" She addresses Hadley rather than Peter.

"Peter Berghman. Recruit 31—"

Jayde cuts him off with a wave of her hand. Returning her attention to Peter, she beckons him forward.

The kid steps out from the crowd, his eyes wide with apprehension. He's barely out of his teens, with a mop of unruly hair and a nervous twitch to his movements.

"Berghman. You're going to get six soldiers killed," she says bluntly.

A frown puckers my brow. I hear a few confused murmurs go through the group.

"W-hat?" he stammers.

"Eight months from now, you're going to make a grave error. Your actions will lead to the deaths of six Silver Block soldiers."

He shakes his head in disbelief. "I would never—"

"It's not a matter of intention. It's a matter of fact."

Peter's face pales, his mouth opening and closing soundlessly as he struggles to comprehend her words.

"But . . ." Finally, he finds his voice. "I don't understand. I would never do anything to harm my fellows."

"I've seen the outcome." Her tone invites no argument. "Your actions are irreversible."

"What actions? I haven't even done anything!"

His protests fall on deaf ears. Jayde nods at Hadley, who steps forward.

"Berghman, you're dismissed from the Program," Hadley barks.

Peter's jaw drops. "That's . . . crazy. I'm not killing anyone."

Ignoring him, Hadley takes Peter by the arm, and we all watch in stunned silence as he escorts the poor kid away.

Jayde turns her steely eyes back to the rest of us. "The lives of our soldiers are too vital to risk. Whether intentional or not, that boy was going to get people killed. Be grateful he's gone."

After she leaves, everyone starts talking among themselves.

"He didn't even do anything wrong." Lyddie is incredulous.

"What if her vision is wrong?" demands a male recruit.

Another one is quick to disagree. "From what I've heard, Valence is known for her accuracy. She's never had a false vision."

Shit. That doesn't sound good. For a second, I experience a twinge of fear, but I push it away, because I don't have time to worry about whether Jayde may or may not have visions about me. There are far more pressing dangers in my life right now.

"Freaks like her shouldn't even be allowed on this base," Bryce mutters.

Several people glance at her in surprise. It's rare to hear anyone criticize the Company.

When she notices the stares, her tone becomes defensive. "I would never question the General's leadership, but this feels like a dangerous gamble to take. Trusting one of them."

"She's served him for ten years," someone else points out.

A stubborn Bryce doesn't back down. "That doesn't make her any less dangerous."

It's funny to me how Jayde's abilities are feared and respected in equal measure. Hadley just cut a guy from the Program based on her word alone, which speaks volumes. Yet at the same time, everyone here is terrified of this big, scary power she wields. I find that part even more interesting.

As far as gifts go, I don't consider precognition much of a threat. Seeing the future isn't something I'd personally enjoy, but the worst damage I could do with it is, what? Tell someone they'll die in a horrible fashion? Shatter a recruit's dreams of serving the Command?

There are far more dangerous abilities to have.

———

Jayde's visit stays with me all night. I find myself climbing the stairs to the roof. It's my first time up there since Betima was killed, and the memory tightens my throat. I stare at the dark stain in the gravel where her blood had pooled.

I can't believe Roe is still here after killing another recruit.

I approach the edge of the roof. Today's drills were tiring, but I feel wired now. Peter's unexpected dismissal lingers in my mind. Everyone taking the word of a psychic who'd seen a grim fate awaiting him and made the decision to blindly trust that vision. I don't know any other precogs. I don't know how accurate they are. What if she's wrong?

And who's to say that by telling him of his error, he couldn't have corrected course?

I wish I could talk to Uncle Jim about this. Sometimes I still try to link with him, seeking out his energy signature only to find nothing but emptiness. I don't know why I keep doing it. It's a form of self-torture, but I can't stop.

I link with Wolf instead, because the loneliness is gnawing at me. I miss Tana. I miss my life.

"Hey." His voice surrounds me like a warm blanket.

"Hey. How's the ocean looking tonight?"

"It's always calm where I am."

"Do you ever see any boats?" I've never been on a boat. Doesn't sound too appealing if I'm being honest.

"I'm looking at one right now. Same one that's always there, anchored in the cove. White hull with a blue stripe. Red flag waving on the captain's perch."

"Does it have a name?"

"Too far away to tell."

"We should name it."

"I'm shit at naming things. You do it."

"All right. How about Knot So Fast?"

"Fuck's sake, Daisy."

"Finny Business?" I chortle at my own jokes, then slam my lips shut when I remember I'm in public.

His laughter tickles my ear. "You're not as funny as you think you are."

"You laughed."

"At you, not with you."

"Keep telling yourself that, Wolfie."

I fall silent for a moment, staring off into the distance. I remember Peter's heartbroken face over being punished for a crime he hadn't committed. Accused of killing six people who are still very much alive.

"Do you believe in fate?" I ask Wolf.

"I don't know... Maybe? Sometimes I feel like I have control over my destiny, but then something happens and I wonder if maybe there's some higher power pulling the strings."

"But if there is, then what's the point of even trying? If everything is already set in motion, then our actions, our choices, are meaningless, aren't they?"

He pauses in thought. "Maybe our choices are the catalysts that set the course of events in motion. Maybe our fate isn't so much predetermined as it is influenced by the decisions we make."

I frown, grappling with the idea. "So you're saying we do have some control over our destinies, but that control is limited by the circumstances we find ourselves in?"

"Exactly. Maybe we can't change the fundamental trajectory of our lives, but we can adjust the details along the way. It's like navigating an ocean current. We can't change its course, but we can choose which path to take as we flow along with it."

I run a hand through my hair as I stare out at the dark base. I suppose it's a comforting thought, the idea that we still have some control over our own lives. But deep down, I can't shake the feeling of unease that lingers in the back of my mind. I wonder what the future holds in store for me. Whether my path has already been laid out, or if I still have the power to shape my own destiny.

I return to the bunks. The lights are out, but some recruits are still up, their faces illuminated by the faint white glow of their sources. Kaine is still awake, the blanket pushed down to his waist. His chest is bare, a broad expanse of shadows and muscle.

He watches me lace up my boots.

"You okay?" he murmurs.

"I'm not tired. I'm going to take a walk."

"Try not to let Hadley see you."

Doesn't matter. I know those cameras will follow my every move. And I know Cross will know I'm out here.

What I *don't* know is whether I hope that he finds me, or that he stays away.

The night air is balmy as I exit the facility. My mind is so restless. I wander aimlessly, the soft tread of my boots the only sound in the stillness of the base. I end up near the South Plaza again, where I think about Uncle Jim and the morning he left me.

Just as I'm beginning to feel the weight of my solitude, I hear footsteps behind me.

"Always making me chase you." His low voice breaks the silence, sending a shiver down my spine.

I turn to face him. He stands several feet away, his silhouette illuminated by the pale silver of the moon.

"I'm not making you do that. You didn't have to come out. You know I'm not running."

Cross walks closer. "I should have stayed in my quarters then?"

"If you wanted to."

I'm indifferent on the outside. But despite my best efforts, I can't deny the way my pulse races whenever he's near.

I should step back, place some distance between us, but I can't bring myself to move.

"Doesn't matter to you at all then," he drawls, "if I weren't here right now."

"Not in the slightest."

"Doesn't matter to you if I'm with someone else. Ivy, maybe. If I walk away right now and find her. Bring her back to my quarters and strip her down. Put my hands and tongue all over her."

I ignore the hot clench of jealousy in my chest. "You're under the impression that I care what or who you do in your spare time." Our eyes lock. "I don't."

"I think you get off on lying to me."

The air thickens with tension, and the space between us seems to shrink with each passing second. I wrench my gaze off him, summoning a growled noise from his throat.

"You drive me crazy," Cross says, his voice rough.

"And?"

His expression darkens at my cavalier tone.

"I'm not trying to drive you crazy," I say, shrugging as if to prove how little I care. "You're the one who brought me here, remember?"

"Trust me, I remember. You've been a pain in my ass from the moment you broke into my room at the inn." He bites out an expletive.

"I have a job to do, a fucking block to run, Elites to supervise, and I spend all my time wondering what crazy stunt Wren Darlington is going to pull next."

It's hard to focus on what he's saying when my lips are tingling with the urge to find out what his taste like.

"I don't get involved with recruits." His jaw is clenched with frustration.

And now *I'm* frustrated. Frustrated and annoyed and so angry about how desperately every part of me craves him.

He doesn't get involved with recruits?

Well, I don't get involved with guys whose fathers are responsible for killing thousands of people like me.

I don't get involved with guys who think I'm defective and wouldn't want me if they knew the truth.

"Did I ask you to get involved with me?" In an impossible feat, I manage to keep my voice steady. Cool.

Those blue eyes flare. "No, you just take your clothes off and get in the shower with me. Daring me to lose control."

"I didn't get in the shower with you. I got in the shower next to you. And as I recall, you took off your clothes first." I lift a brow. "Seems to me like if anyone needs to gain control over their hormones, it's you—"

I blink, and I'm being backed into the tunnel, the moonlight abruptly swallowed by shadows.

Cross presses me up against the wall, his face inches from mine. I feel the warmth of his breath against my skin. The electricity of his nearness.

"You really want to talk about control right now?" he says, keeping me in place with a hand to my waist. "Because it seems to me you're the one with the control problem."

I try to ease out of his grip. "You're hurting me." He's not.

"No, I'm not." His laughter heats my cheek. "You're not timid or weak, Dove. You're a firestorm, and you're going to burn everything in your path if you don't learn how to restrain yourself."

I hate that he can see right through me. Right into the tumultuous storm of emotions raging beneath the surface. I'm always on the brink of losing control. I've felt it my entire life, that precarious sensation.

Cross trails his fingers along my hip, up my arm, toward my face. His thumb traces the curve of my cheek. I can't muster up the words to lecture him about touching me without permission, because I'm enjoying it too much.

"I'm not like this with women," he mutters. "I don't chase. I don't fucking beg." He groans. "But you . . . You make me want to break down your defenses."

A sliver of moonlight enters the tunnel, illuminating his face. Eyes smoky with desire, locking with mine. Daring me to act.

I twist my gaze away, unable to bear the intensity of his any longer.

"Look at me," he commands.

I do, giving an intake of breath when his thumb brushes my lips in a silent invitation.

We stand in the darkness, caught in a silent battle of wills.

"This is a bad idea." My voice is barely audible over my thrashing heart. It feels like it's trying to pound its way out of my chest.

"Probably."

His face is too close again, his mouth hovering over mine in a phantom touch.

The last threads of my willpower are unraveling inside me. When he releases a strangled noise, I feel it everywhere.

"I need to know what you taste like. Let me have it, Dove."

I lick my lips, and he groans again.

"Let me. Fucking. Have it."

I can't move. Can't look away. My breaths escape in shallow, rapid bursts as our lips linger just millimeters apart.

I swallow hard, the lump in my throat betraying my nerves as I lean in, drawn irresistibly closer. And then, in an explosion of pent-up need, the dam breaks and I'm reaching for him, my fingers twisting the fabric of his shirt as I yank him toward me.

His lips crash against mine in a fierce kiss. There's no hesitation. No restraint. In that single, electrifying moment, my entire body is alive with energy.

My hands tangle in his hair, and I pull him even closer, as close as

I can get him, my body straining against him. As his lips devour mine, every nerve ending screams with sensation, and the world around me fades into oblivion.

He drives the kiss deeper, his tongue chasing mine into my mouth. Greedy. Primal. Like he's trying to consume me. To claim me. His hands travel down to my waist, sliding over my ass, tracing the contours of my body, while his tongue finds mine and explores.

"Knew it would be like this." He's breathing hard.

I can only moan in response, kissing him again. Every brush of his tongue ignites a fire of need inside me.

I never want it to end, but the sound of voices breaks through the fog. It takes a second to realize it's just the guards in the tower by South Plaza, chatting to one another, but it's too late. Cross and I have already broken apart, and it's like time has stopped, leaving me suspended in a haze of pure, deep, helpless, hopeless lust.

As I struggle to catch my breath, an eerie sensation skitters through me. Fear. Not of him, but of how badly I want to keep kissing him. There's a rawness to our connection that defies explanation.

"May I be dismissed?" I whisper.

He looks as dazed as I feel. His head dips in a nod. I hurry out of the tunnel, leaving Cross Redden in its shadows.

SECTION	5
Instructor	FORD (LT)
Student	Wren Darlington, R56. Kaine Sutler, R42
Class	Drills and Mock Operations
Mission	Wait for Rescue
Objective	Fulfill the provided role and follow directions.
Score	FAIL

INSTRUCTOR NOTES:

Pair was disqualified. Cocky asswits rescued themselves. Likely would have gotten themselves and/or the extraction team killed during a real field op.

CHAPTER 30

They have us jogging early in the mornings now. Hadley got it into his head that some of his Red Cell recruits aren't in the shape that he expects them to be. And somehow that means Black Cell must suffer the same consequences, which means the two cells now have the pleasure of jogging at dawn.

"It's too early for this," I hear Kess mutter.

For once, I'm in agreement with her.

The sun is just beginning to rise over the base, casting a golden hue across the horizon. We jog in formation, trainers hitting the pavement, footsteps thudding in unison. It's a cool morning, and my breath emerges in a wisp of steam as I exhale with irritation. Who invented jogging? Is this not something we could have left behind in the Old Era?

I glance at Kaine. Beads of sweat glisten on his brow, but he's otherwise unbothered. The guy takes everything in stride, no pun intended.

Lyddie, on the other hand . . . Poor thing barely made it half a mile before she was gasping. When I poked her in the side to speed her up, she glared at me and said, "I'm here for Intelligence, not to join some sadistic running unit." The words were spoken on a wheeze, making me laugh.

A few others are like Lyddie, set on joining Intelligence, but I know a lot of them are like myself, eager to make it into a fieldwork unit, particularly Elite. The high-adrenaline, high-clearance ops. I only wish I knew what the criteria are for making it into Silver Elite. None of the instructors are too forthcoming with that information.

Only twenty of us remain in Black Cell. I think Red Cell is down to eighteen members. Of the thirty-eight recruits left, I have no idea how many will be selected for Elite. All I can do is work my ass off to make up for the first three weeks that I bungled.

We round a bend in the road, and now the base stretches out before us, a sprawling expanse of buildings and training grounds bathed in the soft light of morning. Alongside us, Hadley barks orders to move faster, to stay in formation. He's the worst.

By the time we return to the training center, the base is showing signs of life. Soldiers going about their morning routines. Vehicles rumbling to life in the distance.

Awareness floods my body when I notice Cross at the entrance. Dressed in fatigues, he's speaking to Struck, Ford, and a man with dark skin and a lot of muscles.

My traitorous eyes sweep over Cross, and a jolt of electricity shoots through me.

I can't get it out of my head. That kiss. His touch. His scent. The way his lips felt against mine. I swallow hard as every part of my body remembers him. My fingers tingle at the memory of how soft his hair felt sliding between them. My breasts remember the sensation of being crushed against his chest, the fast hammering of his heartbeat.

I shouldn't have kissed him.

Stupid fucking move.

As if sensing my presence, Cross's head swivels in my direction. His gaze meets mine, and my obnoxious heart flutters like a trapped butterfly in my chest.

Stupid fucking heart.

Our gazes hold for longer than appropriate. I glimpse a hint of his dimple before he breaks eye contact and turns back to his subordinates.

Hadley orders us to wait, then goes to join the small group.

"Wren?"

I glance over at the sound of my name.

Jordan.

It's been little more than a month, yet it feels like a lifetime ago when I was in bed with this man.

He strides up to me, clad in his uniform. It bears the Copper Block emblem along with two bronze stars—I remember him saying the night at the inn that he hoped to earn a third. He was planning to start officer school in the fall.

Kaine grins at me as I move away from the group to speak to Jordan, whose eyes fill with relief. He moves like he's about to hug me, but stops just short, arms dropping to his sides. His gaze flickers toward the Silver Block officers.

"I'm so glad to see you," Jordan says, keeping his voice low. "Are you all right? I was worried."

"About me?"

"I tried to find you after they executed your guardian. All I was told was that you'd been detained." He notes my workout uniform. "I didn't realize you were recruited."

"I wasn't at first. They held me for a couple of days, but after Lieutenant Colonel Valence confirmed that I didn't know what my uncle was, they allowed me to join the Program."

"I told them you were innocent," Jordan says, and I have no idea what I did to earn the conviction ringing in his voice. I'm not *that* good in bed.

"You spoke to them about me?"

"Yeah. After I found out you were caught in South Plaza. I told them there's no way you knew your guardian was a 'fect and that you were loyal to the Company."

Poor misguided Jordan with his poor misplaced faith.

He sneaks another glance at the officers, then raises his hand to my face. A quick brush of fingers on my cheek. I feel Cross's eyes burning into my back. Sure enough, the sharp tenor of his voice whips toward us.

"Darlington. Quit fraternizing. Rejoin your cell."

"Sorry," I tell Jordan. "I have to go."

"I'll track you down later, now that I know you're on the base."

I hesitate. "Maybe you shouldn't."

A slight frown mars his lips.

"I feel like it would make things worse for me," I clarify, giving a discreet nod toward the captain.

Jordan gets the message. "Right. I'll contact you on your comm first."

"Darlington," Cross snaps.

I edge away from Jordan and return to the group, where Kaine raises an eyebrow in question.

"Don't even ask," I say with a sigh.

Finally, the officers decide to acknowledge our existence. Ford does the talking. "Congratulations, ladies and gentlemen. We're starting UCOs this week."

Undercover operations. *Yes.* I've been looking forward to this section.

"Obviously we can't just send you into the wild without supervision, so you'll each have a handler in the field with you. We're doing this in stages. Five of you are up tonight. Schedule's been uploaded to your sources."

We're wearing our wrist sources for the run, so I check mine and brighten when I discover I'm in tonight's group.

"My name's not on this schedule." The accusation comes from Roe, who's openly glaring at his older brother.

Cross's expression remains composed. "As I told the General last night, we don't have a solid cover in place for you yet."

"That's bullshit, brother."

"It is what it is, *brother*," Cross says and dismisses him from his gaze.

––––––

When I return to the barracks, a dossier has been loaded into my source. It's a detailed biography of my undercover identity, and I've been given two hours to memorize it. That's not a lot of time, but I'm not too worried. Excitement tickles my stomach as I read my backstory.

Later, Tyler Struck comes to the barracks to collect the women who are on op tonight. Which is just me and Bryce. We drive to the building that houses Silver Block and follow her through a series of rooms until we reach the one she refers to as "Wardrobe." Inside, we find racks of clothing.

Bryce stares at a rack of dresses before turning toward the instructor. "Soldier Struck? I'm not entirely comfortable with my cover."

Struck laughs. That's her entire response. Laughter.

It sparks a flash of indignation in Bryce's eyes, and I resist the urge to say, *Aww, you couldn't have called Daddy to get you out of this section?*

If I had a Lux credit for every time I've heard *My father is in Command Intelligence,* I'd be able to buy out the commissary.

"How often does Silver Block go undercover?" I ask Struck.

She shrugs. "Depends on what's brewing in the wards."

"Is something brewing now?"

Another shrug.

Got it. I'm on a need-to-know basis.

"Pick whatever clothes you want," she tells us. "But keep your cover in mind and dress accordingly."

Despite appearing incredibly unhappy, Bryce selects one of the skimpiest dresses I've ever seen, which has me wondering about her undercover identity. Maybe her complaints are warranted.

"Will we have our weapons?" she asks, examining the silky fabric. "I won't be able to carry a gun in this."

"You'll get a small knife. Should be able to secure a garter sheath under there."

"A small knife? That's it?" Bryce is growing increasingly upset. "How do we defend ourselves?"

"What do you think we've been trying to teach you for the last month? You'll have a knife and your fists. That's it. Now are you done griping about every godfucking thing or do I need to hold your hand some more?"

Bryce flattens her lips. It's painfully obvious that Struck doesn't like her.

"Are you supervising both of us?" I ask as I flip through hangers.

Struck shakes her head. "You've been assigned to Hadley."

Ugh. Great. I turn my head so she can't see me making a face.

While I'm sifting through the racks trying to find a suitable outfit, she gets an alert on her comm and steps out of the room to check it. When she returns, her eyes gleam with amusement.

"I spoke too soon," she tells me. "You've been reassigned."

"To who?" I ask suspiciously.

"Who do you think?"

———

I'm alone in the back of a sleek black car, being driven to an unknown destination. As the lights of the city streak past the window, my wariness mounts. I have no idea where I'm going or what I'm doing. The only certainty at the moment is the backstory I memorized earlier.

"Broken Dove, copy?"

Ford's voice fills my ear, courtesy of Lieutenant Hirai's prized earpiece.

"Fuck off," I growl. "I want a different call sign."

He chuckles. "Take that up with the captain."

"All right, and where is he, exactly? Because I was told he's my handler, yet I'm sitting alone in this car with no idea what I'm supposed to do."

"He'll be in the field with you, but I'm the one running the op. So would you like to hear your objective, or do you want to keep whining?"

What does he mean, Cross will be in the field with me? The lack of details is making my skin itch.

When the car comes to an abrupt stop, I jump in my seat. I peer out the tinted window. We seem to be in an alley.

"Your op site is called Haven. Owned by a woman named Shenise Nelson. It's an illegal brothel masking itself as city lodgings with a pub downstairs."

"If you know it's a brothel, why haven't you shut it down?"

"Sometimes it's more advantageous to leave the criminals be. Nelson's a low-level threat and good for intel when we need it."

"So I'm hitting her up for intel? What do I need to find out?"

"Have you not been listening in class all week? Information gathering is a delicate matter. You ingratiate yourself. You mine out tiny little nuggets until eventually you find that one shiny stone you need. Your objective is to make contact and ask about a job. You're there because you don't want to apply for Human Services—it's too heavily regulated and there's no credits to be made there."

I nod even though he can't see me. "I'm going in alone?"

I'm surprised Cross trusts me to carry this out. To get out of the car and just walk down the street unaccompanied. What if I run? What if I manage to escape?

"You're never alone, sweetling. You should know that by now."

Ford isn't bluffing. I exit the vehicle to the sensation of a dozen pairs of eyes on me. I'm definitely being watched.

The street is busy for this time of night—it's past ten, which is nearing the city's midnight curfew. I've never been to Sanctum Point after dark, and I'm fascinated by the glow of neon lights and the blur of pedestrians. I'm in the heart of the Point's entertainment district. I scan the storefronts until I locate my target. Haven.

I'm halfway down the pristine sidewalk toward it when I hear a low hum from above me. Catching a flash of movement, I glance up and gulp. An automated drone buzzes overhead, its mechanical eyes scanning the street for any signs of unrest or deviation from the norm. It moves on but leaves me feeling unsettled.

I stop in front of Haven, a brick building with a façade adorned with polished brass fittings and frosted-glass windows on the ground floor. A wave of noise washes over me when I walk in. The main room is alive with the buzz of conversation, punctuated by bursts of laughter and the clinking of glasses. Round tables are scattered throughout the bar, occupied almost exclusively by men.

I make a show of glancing around uncertainly. Rub my arms in a self-conscious gesture. Drawing a few stares that I pretend not to see. The dress I chose for tonight's op is short but not too short—the hem hovers above my knees. It's sexy but not too sexy—the V neckline shows only a hint of cleavage. I've decided my alter ego is a blend of racy and modest, and this sleeveless dove-gray dress hugs my figure in all the right places without revealing too much.

I walk up to the bar carrying my evening bag. A slinky black thing containing the comm Hirai gave me on the base when I signed out my earpiece. I slide onto a stool, shifting awkwardly as I cross my legs.

The bartender wanders over. A woman with short hair and tattoos. "What do you need?" she asks in a husky voice.

"How many credits for something that isn't synthetic?"

"Probably a lot more than you can afford, darling."

"Oh. Okay. Synth whiskey then."

When she notices my disappointed expression, hers softens.

I pull my comm out of my bag and hold it out so she can scan it, removing five credits from my Lux account.

To my shock, when she turns toward the bar, she grabs a bottle of the pure stuff. Not the kind that's created in a lab somewhere in the capital.

She winks at me. "Our secret?" she says, and my chest squeezes, because those two teasing words bring to mind Morlee Hadley and the sweets she used to sneak into my hand when Jim wasn't looking.

I give her a grateful smile. "Thank you."

"Celebrating something in particular?"

"It's my birthday." I shrug. "Thought it would be nice to see how the elites live for a night."

"Well, happy birthday, darling." She slides the glass toward me.

"Thank you."

At my first sip, I almost moan out loud. Holy hellfuck. The taste of pure whiskey is a goddamn revelation. The rich flavor dances across my tongue with a fiery intensity and goes down so smoothly compared with the synthetic stuff I've only ever consumed.

"Good, right?" The bartender is grinning at my response.

"I believe that's an understatement."

I swirl the glass. Even the color of it is more . . . vibrant. The golden liquid gleams at me, its amber hues shimmering like captured sunlight.

The woman goes to serve another patron, and I swivel on my stool and watch the room. I spot more than a few Command soldiers, though I suppose that makes sense. Soldiers like to get drunk and laid.

From the corner of my vision, I see the bartender return. I turn around, hesitating before asking, "Do you know where I can find Shenise?"

She frowns.

"Someone told me I should talk to her," I add.

"What about?" She's very careful with her tone. It's evident she doesn't trust anyone. As she shouldn't.

"Job opportunities."

"All job assignments are provided by the Company," she says, as if reciting from a handbook.

"Well aware of that," I reply, donning a droll expression. "I already have an assignment. I'm looking for something off the books." I bite my lip. "Very off the books."

"Is it really your birthday?"

I nod.

"Funny thing to be doing on your birthday. Hunting for side gigs."

"Not really. What else am I going to do? I don't have any family. Don't have enough friends to justify applying for a gathering permit. I had a boyfriend, but he broke up with me last week, so . . . here I am." I take another sip of the most delicious liquid known to humanity.

She continues to study me. Her expression might as well be a concrete wall, that's how little it tells me.

"It's fine. Forget it." With the slight sag of my shoulders, I face the room again.

I sense her walking away. Hear her throaty voice addressing another customer.

Nursing my whiskey, I pretend to be lost in thought. Time passes.

Five minutes. Ten. Fifteen. My earpiece is recording everything, but Ford doesn't check in. Cross is nowhere to be found.

I'm debating whether I should just give up and return to the drop-off zone when another woman walks behind the bar. She has long hair and pouty lips, and is wearing denim that hugs her backside and a small top that barely covers her breasts. I can't quite gauge her age. Late twenties maybe, but she moves with an air of authority that makes her appear older.

The bartender whispers to her, nodding toward me.

My pulse speeds up when the newcomer walks around the bar to stand beside me. Suspicious brown eyes probe my face.

"Heard you were looking for me."

I fidget with the thin strap of my purse. "Are you Shenise?"

She nods. "What's your name?"

"Gilly."

"Do you live in the Point, Gilly?"

"I do. I was transferred from G about a month ago. I work in Administration."

"Pasha says you're looking for work." She purses her lips. "Why did you come to Haven for that? What gave you the idea we might accept workers who aren't assigned to us by the Company?"

"A friend of mine told me to find you if I needed anything."

Shenise doesn't let up. "What friend?"

I chew on the inside of my cheek, conveying reluctance. "I, um . . . I don't want to betray her confidence."

"Then I'm afraid we don't have anything to say to each other, Gilly. Perhaps you should look elsewhere for—" She stops midsentence, focusing on the door.

I follow her gaze, and my breath lodges in my throat.

Cross just walked in.

CHAPTER 31

The bar doesn't erupt in whispers. The chatter doesn't die. But I don't miss the way heads turn as Cross walks by them. In his navy-blue uniform, the four silver stars that flaunt how much power he holds, he makes for an intimidating figure.

That, and he's so devastatingly handsome that men and women alike have no choice but to stare.

His stride exudes confidence, every movement purposeful, as he makes his way to a table in the corner of the room. It's already occupied by two men, but that's no hindrance. At Cross's approach, their conversation falters, drinks paused halfway to lips. Then they set their glasses down and clear out so he can take their place.

My heart skips a beat as I watch him sit in one of the vacated chairs. He looks good. Edible.

"Excuse me," Shenise says before turning on her heel.

The moment she's out of earshot, I spin to face the bartender—Pasha. I fumble with the strap of my bag.

"What is this?" I hiss. "Some sort of trap?"

Her brow furrows. "What?"

I don a panicked tone. "Why is a Command captain in here? Did you call to report me because I asked—"

"Relax, darling," she interrupts, letting out a laugh. "You think he's here for you? Well, damn. You really are naïve."

I allow a mixture of relief and confusion to show on my face. "Why is he here then?"

"We serve a variety of customers, some of whom, as you can see, hold high positions in society. In fact, we've got a very loyal customer base within the Command. They're not here to cause trouble. They're here to unwind like everyone else." She shrugs. "He comes in every few weeks to blow off steam."

My jaw falls open. "He's a customer?"

"Indeed."

My gaze drifts toward the staircase that leads to the second floor. "But you . . ."

"Run a respectable lodging for travelers to Sanctum Point," she finishes primly. "Offering clean, comfortable accommodations."

I purse my lips in humor. "All right."

Across the room, Shenise is talking to Cross. He laughs at something she says. She reaches down to touch his shoulder, then leaves him to his own devices, hips swaying as she returns to the bar.

Pasha gives her a faint smile, nodding at me. "She thought you called the Command on her."

"Oh, sweetheart. You're not worth their attention. Or mine," Shenise adds pointedly. "Unless you've decided to tell me who referred you to us."

My dossier included an entire page about the source of my referral. I could have led with that information, but I thought I had a better shot of appearing trustworthy to Shenise if I showed some hesitation about snitching on my "friend."

"Do you promise they won't get in trouble?" I let my anxiety show.

"Of course." She's probably lying, but like Pasha said, my alter ego is a teeny bit naïve.

I lower my voice. "Her name is Olive. She worked here last year before she was reassigned and had to leave the Point. We worked together in G, and when she found out I was being transferred, she told me I should look you up." I lick my dry lips. "I'm sorry. Maybe it was a mistake."

"How is she doing?" Shenise surprises me by asking.

With a tentative smile, I say, "She's good. She's pregnant now."

This role is growing on me. I'm starting to feel like I'm actually Gilly, whose friend Olive from G is pregnant with her partner Jessa's baby.

Pasha leaves to deliver Cross's drink. The pure stuff, of course. Only the best for Captain Redden. She lingers at his table to chat, but I pretend not to notice.

"I'm really sorry for just showing up," I tell Shenise. "I guess I overstepped. But I'm all alone here. My Lux account is close to empty, and this new assignment they gave me pays next to nothing." Bitterness ripples through my voice. "If I'm supposed to build any sort of life in this city, I need credits. I need allies."

"That's an interesting word to use."

"I think you can have friends in the wards. I don't know if that's possible here."

She goes quiet for a moment, but just when she's about to respond, Pasha returns, a perplexed look on her face. "Shen," she says with a nod, and the two women disappear through a doorway beyond the bar.

I pull my comm out of my bag and pretend to read something, but it isn't long at all before Shenise returns. She studies me, and her amusement is unmistakable.

"The captain wants you."

My eyebrows soar. "I'm sorry. What?"

"He wants you to keep him company."

"Oh. What if I don't . . . want to do that?"

She starts to laugh. A low, melodic sound. "You said you wanted work. Let's call this a job interview."

"Um. All right. I guess I could do that." I gulp. "You want me to just walk over there? Should I say hello?"

Pasha looks like she's fighting her own wave of laughter. "Hello is a good start."

Shenise sighs. "You might find more success if you don't carry yourself like a frightened little mouse."

I take a deep breath, adjusting the hem of my dress, pretending to steady my nerves. Then, as if I've found a surge of courage from some bravery reserve deep inside me, I square my shoulders and push away from the counter.

He tracks my every move. I'm not trying to walk sexy, but he's looking at me like he wants to devour me.

When I reach him, I give a quick peek at the neighboring table where three soldiers sit. They regard me with curiosity before continuing their hushed conversation.

I shift my gaze to Cross. "I heard you wanted to see me?"

"Yes." His eyes gleam with undisguised interest. "Sit. Have a drink with me."

I'm about to lower into the chair next to him when he shakes his head and chuckles.

"Not there, sweetling." He pats his knee. "Right here."

I hear the soldiers snickering behind me. I hesitate for a moment. A glance at the bar shows Shenise watching me like a hawk.

Smothering a sigh, I settle onto his lap.

When my dress rides up, he plants his hand on my bare thigh, the one without the burns. The bottom of the scars on my other thigh is visible, a hint of pink, puckered flesh at the hem of my dress. I catch the soldiers eyeing it, and tug the hem down, ignoring the self-conscious flush that rises in my cheeks.

"Better?" I keep my voice steady as possible, but we both hear the tremble that sneaks through.

"Much better." His words are like a caress, soft and tempting.

Cross wraps a muscular arm around my waist, pulling me closer. "What's your name?"

"Gilly. What's yours?"

He doesn't answer. Instead, he reaches for his drink. My face is so close to his that I can smell the alcohol as he takes a sip. The pale liquid wets his bottom lip, and when he licks it away, I remember the feeling of that tongue exploring my mouth.

"Tell me about yourself, Gilly."

I feed him the same story I gave Shenise about my transfer from G. How I work in Admin. New to the city. Don't know a soul.

The entire time I speak, he's touching my leg. Stroking my knee. Squeezing my thigh over the thin fabric of my dress.

And every touch pushes me into a deeper state of arousal. I feel like I'm going to crawl out of my skin.

I'm unsure of the role I'm supposed to play. I'm here for a job, essentially asking to be a prostitute, but I'm also supposed to be new to this line of work, a naïve girl from the wards. I glance toward the bar.

Shenise doesn't look impressed by my performance. Damn it.

The young men at the next table scrape their chairs back. As they pass us, they nod toward Cross in a respectful gesture, one of them murmuring, "Captain Redden."

"Redden?" I echo in surprise.

He nods. His lips twitch with humor.

"Are you related to the General?"

"I'm his son."

Our eyes lock for a moment, and I feel his gaze like a physical touch.

With the hint of a smile, he brushes his hand over his ear and mutters, "Cease comm."

He's shut off our feed.

Which means we're no longer transmitting to Command when he leans in to drawl in my ear.

"I was wrong before. You make a very good whore, Dove."

I bristle. I wish I could punch him in the face. I stroke it instead. He tenses, just slightly, as I trace the line of his jaw, his stubble gliding beneath my fingertips. Then a lazy smile plays at the corners of his lips. The dimple appears, and I feel a sense of satisfaction that I'm the one who made it happen.

"The bartender says you're a regular customer," I tell him, quirking a brow. "I didn't peg you as someone who pays for it."

"For drinks?" He lifts his glass. "I can't exactly waltz in and steal them."

"You've never been upstairs?"

"No." He seems amused. "And if I had?"

"Whatever gets you off."

"I'm easy to please," he says, his lips brushing against my earlobe.

For a moment, I lose myself in the intoxicating allure of the charade. That I want to be on his lap. That I'm here to entertain him.

The heat of his body sears through the fabric of my dress. His hands find their way to my waist, pulling me even closer. His nearness is unbearable.

Pulse racing, I bring my mouth to his ear and whisper, "How long do I have to sit on you?"

"For as long as I fucking tell you to," he whispers back.

My jaw tightens. I force it to relax, pasting on a hesitant smile. A very sweet, proper Gilly smile. But the way he's looking at me is not at all sweet or proper.

As his hand strokes my thigh, he fixes his gaze on my face, and I see a flicker of bewilderment there.

"What?"

"Your eyes . . . That color. It's like . . ." He pauses, thinking. "Liquid gold," he finishes. "With flecks of sunlight dancing in it."

I can't help but laugh. "I was trying to describe a glass of pure whiskey earlier and I came up with a similar description. I think the whiskey is more impressive."

"No. It's not."

My breath hitches.

"You must have had all the boys in Z lining up to get with you, just so they could sit there and stare into those eyes."

"Hardly. I used to get teased about them," I confess.

"Bullshit. Why?"

"I guess in certain lighting inside the schoolhouse, they looked completely yellow. When I was twelve, this one kid, Oden, got it into his head that I was a witch."

Cross smiles, and it's a sight to behold. "A witch."

"Uh-huh. We were in the middle of a mythology unit in class, learning all about witches and werewolves and supernatural creatures, and our teacher projected a picture of this terrifying woman with glowing yellow eyes, casting a spell on a defenseless man. Oden and his obnoxious little friends started shouting *Witch!* at me whenever I walked into class." I grumble at the memory. "At first it really bothered me. I didn't understand why they were being so mean about something I couldn't control. But then"—I shrug—"my best friend Tana encouraged me to embrace it. She said witches were powerful, independent women who didn't conform to society's expectations. So the next time I came to school and he shouted *Witch*—"

"You beat the shit out of him."

My mouth falls open. Laughter tickles my throat. "How did you know?"

His fingers skim a path along my jawline, leaving prickles of pleasure in their wake. "Because I think even at twelve years old, you were a force to be reckoned with, Dove."

His fingertips graze my cheek with a featherlight touch. Each second stretches taut, the sexual awareness between us like a thread on the verge of snapping.

"Enough about me," I blurt out. "Tell me about you, Captain. Do you like your father?"

The abrupt subject change startles him. "What kind of question is that?"

"Just curious. You never speak about him."

"There's not much to say."

"That's a no then."

"I didn't say that." He leans forward to pick up his glass, and his body crowds me, his woodsy scent surrounding me.

I pause in thought. "I don't think I would want the General as my father."

"Why is that?"

"Too much pressure. He runs the Continent. A man like that must expect greatness from his children."

Cross's grip tightens over my thigh. I'm not sure if it's a warning or a reflection of his feelings toward the General.

"What about the rest of your family?" I ask when he doesn't respond. "Do you like your brothers?"

"Roe is a little shit."

"Can't disagree with that," I say, and Cross gives a soft chuckle. "What about the other one? Trevor? Travis?"

"Travis. He's . . . very driven."

"Interesting."

"What?"

"Of all the descriptors you could have used, you chose that one." I shrug. "And your mother?"

"Let's stop talking about trivial shit."

Disappointment flutters through me. It's rare for Cross to share any part of himself, and I want to know more.

Or maybe I don't. It's bad enough that I'm attracted to my enemy. Maybe it's better if I don't catch these glimpses into his humanity.

It's hard to focus with these conflicting emotions warring inside me. I wouldn't be having this problem if Hadley was supervising me. Then again, the idea of having to sit on Hadley's lap makes me nauseous.

I prefer Cross's lap.

A little too much.

Breaking eye contact, he touches his ear to reactivate the comm. Then, before I can blink, his hand slides beneath the hem of my dress and his mouth finds my neck.

I break out in shivers. It takes all my willpower not to moan out loud as his lips travel over the column of my throat. Kissing. Tasting.

"Fucking delicious," he mutters. He kisses his way up to my neck, my ear, then says, "Now push me off you. Tell them you can't do this, you're not ready for this line of work, and leave."

But I don't want to. It feels so good here in his lap. He's warm and hard and kissing my neck. I want to stay here forever, and I hate myself for it.

"Go to your drop zone and return to base."

He cups my chin and turns my face toward his lips, millimeters from mine.

"Push me off."

I slap his face away and scramble off his lap.

Anger sizzles in his eyes. "Get back here."

"I'm sorry." I snatch my bag and hurry to the bar where Shenise stands. "I'm sorry," I tell her, anguished. "I can't do that. I just can't. I'm not . . . Maybe one day, but not . . . not tonight. I can't."

I don't give her the opportunity to speak. I spin on my heel and leave the bar as ordered. My heels slap the pavement as I head toward the alley from which I came. The black car is still there, waiting.

I don't even know what the purpose of this op was. If I did well or not. All I know is that my body is still burning from Cross's touch.

As I slide into the back seat, I hear his voice in my earpiece.

"Dove. Report to my office for a debrief."

CHAPTER 32

I wait in his office.

It's late. I want to change into my sleep clothes and slide into bed. I want to shut off my brain so I can stop obsessing over my body's traitorous responses to him.

But his majesty, Captain Cross, wants a debrief.

I wander around the large space, not shy about being nosy. There are no personal items on his desk. Just a holoscreen and a tablet. The conference table was cluttered the last couple of times I was here, but tonight there's very little on it, only a stack of maps.

Paper maps, which I find fascinating. A projector sits in the center of the table, so I assume they use holo-maps as well, but the fact that there's any paper in here at all is odd to me.

Cross doesn't seem like an Old Era guy. And while I'm not an Old Era girl myself by any stretch of the imagination, I think it would be incredible to own a paper book. Flip through real, tangible pages. It's nearly impossible to procure paper products unless you're willing to pay through the nose for them. The Last War destroyed so much of the planet, and over a century later, lumber still isn't readily available. The trees that were replanted never quite grew as tall as they should have. There are entire "forests" east of the Blacklands that are nothing more than a sea of flimsy twigs.

The door swings open.

Cross notes me leaning against the map table. His eyes drift down my bare legs, my ankles, the low heels strapped to my feet. Then he raises them to my cleavage. I realize my left strap is falling off my shoulder and push it back up. He tracks that, too.

"You did good," he says, surprising me with the compliment.

"Really? Because I feel like I did nothing." Self-reproach darkens my mood. "I asked for a job and then blew it."

"You did exactly what you were supposed to do."

"But Ford said the objective was the job."

"No, the objective was to ask for it. To make contact. You weren't going to get that job tonight, Wren."

My heart does a little flip as my name leaves his mouth.

"Shen is not an idiot. She's not going to invite a random woman off the street into her inner circle."

"Oh."

"Oh?" He looks like he's trying not to grin. "You're not going to argue?"

"No. You're right."

"Say that again. *You're right.* I want to hear it again."

"Never," I vow.

He disarms, unholstering his gun before setting it on the desk. Then he stalks toward me. Stops when we're a foot apart. The awareness between us is thick and palpable, like a storm on the horizon.

"You're a dangerous woman," he murmurs.

More than he knows.

I laugh softly. "I think you're the dangerous one."

"I am," he agrees. "Especially right now."

"What's so special about right now?"

"Your dress. Those eyes." He scrapes his gaze over my body before returning it to my face. "That body rubbing up on me all night. Teasing."

"Seemed like you were the one doing the rubbing. And the teasing."

"You liked it."

"No. I was playing a part. I was picturing Jordan from Copper the entire time."

He growls out a noise. Ire-tinged exasperation. But it's quickly replaced by an arrogant smirk. "Too bad you won't be able to see him anymore."

I narrow my eyes.

"You didn't hear? Jordan was dispatched on a last-minute assignment. Headed for Red Post. Who knows when he'll return. The post could last months. Years, even."

My jaw drops. "You sent him away?"

"Yes."

"Why?"

"Because he touched you this morning."

I'm not supposed to be attracted to men like this. Possessive. Cocky. Ruthless. Yet the notion that I'd succeeded in triggering his jealousy sends a thrill shooting through me.

"You were jealous," I say.

"Yes. It's not an emotion I enjoy."

"I'm sorry."

"No, you're not."

"You're right. I'm not."

I grip the edge of the desk with both hands and slide up to sit on it. Cross's gaze lowers to where my dress is riding up.

"How did you get burned?" he surprises me by asking.

"A pot of boiling water fell on me when I was little. Accident."

"That must've been painful." His voice is oddly gentle.

"Excruciating."

He nods, still watching me. His gaze slides from my thighs to the swell of my breasts beneath my neckline.

I like the way he looks at me. I know I shouldn't, but I can't help it. My heart has never pounded this hard for anyone.

A strangled sound escapes his throat. "Darlington."

"What?"

"I'm so hot for you, I can't think straight anymore."

I know the feeling.

"I thought you don't get involved with recruits," I remind him.

"I don't."

He moves closer, until there's only an arm's length keeping us apart. I could reach out and touch him if I wanted. I could yank him toward me and give in to the palpable desire. *Mutual* desire, because if his strained expression is any indication, he's experiencing the same suffocating need.

"I've never jeopardized my post to fuck around." He shoves a hand through his hair, dragging it away from his forehead. "I don't get jealous of low-level asswits from Copper."

I have to bite my lip to stop a laugh.

"I wanted to tear his hand off for touching you. I want to rip Sutler's eyes out for looking at you."

The feral glint in his eyes sends my pulse careening again. I remember the unpleasant sensation in my chest when I broke into his quarters and found him in bed with Ms. Shiny Hair.

And I'm starting to wonder . . . maybe it's better to get it out of our systems. Face the tension head-on, surrender to it, and then it will dissipate. Then I'll be able to use my brain again without constantly thinking about this guy.

"Once," I burst out.

He blinks. "Once what?"

"I'm going to let you have it once. One time. Right here, right now."

Heat flares in his eyes.

"And then when I walk out the door, it's over. It's out of our systems. It doesn't happen again."

Silence falls as Cross considers my proposal. I find myself wishing, desperately, that he didn't affect me the way he does. But try as I might, I can't ignore the magnetic pull, the way his gaze strips away the layers of my defenses.

In that fleeting moment, surrender seems inevitable.

I lick my lips and that's it. He stalks toward me, pushing my thighs open so he can step between them, and brings his body flush to mine. He thrusts one hand in my hair and tugs on the brown strands, forcibly tipping my head back.

I gasp, my fingers clutching at his shirt, my body arching against his in a silent plea for more. A faint smile touches his lips as he pulls me closer, his hands trailing down my spine in a lazy glide that belies the fire in his eyes. He leans forward, his mouth approaching mine, teasingly, a heart-pounding, painstakingly slow trajectory that makes me whimper with impatience.

His smile widens.

"Stop teasing," I grumble.

His breath mingles with mine as our lips brush against each other in a fleeting caress. Meanwhile, his hands continue to roam, skimming my waist, scraping over my arms. Each touch sends sparks dancing along my skin. But it's not enough. I crave more.

With an irritated curse, I yank on his shirt and press my lips against his. Firm and insistent.

"You win," he mumbles before kissing me the way I demand to be kissed.

His tongue is hot and skillful, slicking over mine, drawing a moan from my throat. He swallows the desperate sound and deepens the kiss into something raw and primal. His teeth sting my bottom lip before that greedy tongue plunges inside my mouth again.

He kisses with the kind of intensity that leaves me breathless. And his hands aren't idle while he destroys me with his lips. He cups my breasts over my dress, squeezing, toying. The bra I'm wearing is so flimsy that his thumbs have no trouble teasing my nipples into two tight, throbbing buds.

I whimper against his lips, and he wrenches his mouth away to mutter, "Tell me not to stop."

I couldn't stop this now if I tried. All rational thought has fled my mind. The world has melted away, and my entire being has been reduced to *more*. I want more.

"Don't stop," I whisper.

Without warning, I'm off the desk and on my feet, being spun around as he bends me over. Cross bunches the material of my dress in one fist and drags it upward to expose my backside. One warm palm smooths over the curve of one cheek.

My skin breaks out in shivers when he eases my underwear down my legs. I kick it away. Holding my breath. Waiting for his next move.

I gasp when his hands return to squeeze my ass.

"Perfect," he rasps. "I wanted this from the second you were underneath me at the inn." He grinds himself against me. I can feel every inch of him. "Should've taken you then."

"I wasn't yours for the taking." My voice comes out breathier than I intend.

"Yes, you were. If I did this . . ." He brings his hand between my legs, and my whole body clenches for him. "Would you have stopped me?" He teases the warm, swollen flesh that is aching for him. "Or would you have begged for more?"

He slips his finger inside and I moan with abandon.

That makes him chuckle. "Begged," he concludes.

He adds a second finger, thrusting both inside me in a slow, agonizing tempo. His lips find my shoulder, kissing, tasting, and when he nips at my skin, it elicits a pain-tinged jolt of pleasure that makes me gasp. I push back against his exploring fingers, needing more. My body throbs in a silent plea for release.

"I like you like this." His taunt heats the back of my neck. "Bent over. At my mercy."

I swallow the moisture that floods my mouth. "Are there cameras in here?"

That gets me a chuckle. "No." He withdraws his fingers to tease my opening. "But goddamn do I wish there were."

I'm too mindless to respond. Pleasure dances through me each time those talented fingers fill me. And each time they retreat, I shake with desperation. Still he drags it out, moving his fingers in, out, unhurried, unbearable, and when I finally can't take it anymore, I twist around and growl at him.

"Stop. Teasing."

"Make me."

Arrogant bastard. I grab the bottom of his shirt and shove it up, practically ripping it off his torso. His chest, golden muscles and sculpted sinew, almost makes me whimper again. I run my palms over it, and he hisses out a breath, capturing one of my hands. He curls his fingers around mine. Tightly. For a second, I think he's going to stop me from touching him.

He does the opposite.

Keeping his gaze locked to mine, he drags my hand down the defined ridges of his abdomen until we reach his waistband.

"Undo my pants."

God. He's exactly what I hoped he would be. Commanding. Potent. Our eyes remain locked as I ease his zipper down, as I reach between the flaps of his trousers, slide my hand inside, find the thick, throbbing length of him. When I wrap my fingers around him, he betrays the first sign that he's not as in control as he lets on. His throat dips in a hard swallow. His chest rises on a ragged breath. I squeeze him, and he responds by thrusting into my fist.

I enjoy the choked, distressed noise he makes when I release him, but it's only so I can peel my dress off and undo my bra. Cross devours my naked body with his hot gaze, one hand coming out to toy with my breast, tease the nipple. His other hand shoves his trousers off.

I grip him again, anticipation building in my core, swelling, rising. His gaze lowers to the apex of my thighs, to the place that's aching for him. His eyelids grow heavy. Tongue comes out to lick his lower lip. Then, with a hint of a smile, he moves my hand away and takes over, guiding his cock between my legs and pushing the broad head inside.

We both groan at that first contact. He watches me adjust to him, his lips hovering over mine, and just when I part my lips to inhale, he's kissing me again. Hot and reckless, while his hips drive forward. While he fills me, again and again. Deep. Hard.

I wrap my legs around his waist and hang on for the ride. He feels so good, but it's still not close enough. I need *more*. Always more. I shove at the maps littering the tabletop and fall back on my elbows, pulling him down with me.

Laughing his approval, he covers me with his body, his full weight crushing me to the table. He fucks me harder, hips flexing, face buried in my neck. He's making sounds that heat my blood and make me tremble. Low, husky moans in my ear. A hiss of breath. A strangled grunt when I scratch my fingernails down his muscular back.

"*Yes*," he groans.

I suddenly remember him taunting me all those weeks ago.

I like it rough.

So I drag my nails over him again and enjoy the way he shudders.

My excitement falters when he runs his palm over the thick, raised scars crisscrossing my thigh. With a pang of self-consciousness, I move his hand to my other thigh. Smooth and unblemished.

"This one feels nicer," I say lightly.

"Every part of you feels nice, Dove," he whispers in my ear.

His lips capture mine again as he slows the pace. Pinpricks of pleasure move like static electricity through my body. For one reckless moment, I'm tempted to open a path and check if his shield is lowered, to find a crack in it and slide in, find out if he's telling the truth, if this feels as good to him as it does to me. But I banish the impulse. Even if his mind was open for the reading, I don't think I want to know. I just want to *feel.*

"I'm close," I tell him, rising up to meet his thrusts.

"Yeah?" His lips find my neck again. "Let me get you there."

Those clever fingers move between our bodies to find the tight bud that's pulsing in time to my heartbeat. He rubs circles over it, while his body continues to move, his cock easing out and then driving deep. The tingling starts in my core, taunting me, gathering into a knot and then twisting tighter and tighter until the tension becomes unbearable.

The moment Cross's tongue fills my mouth, the moment I hear him moan, the knot detonates into an explosion of pleasure. I cry out, squeezing my eyes shut as the climax rips through me. I'm vaguely aware of his fingers digging into my hip, his low groan as he finds his own release.

We're both breathing hard. His body collapses onto mine as we lie naked in the middle of the table, coming down from the high.

A high that evaporates so fast it gives me whiplash.

What have I done?

He's the General's son.

The shame that floods my body is so unexpected, I almost start to cry. There's reckless. And then there's this.

I'm not worried about pregnancy. All female citizens of fertile age get their yearly injections, a mandate the General implemented about a decade ago. We need to report to the Company when we're interested in starting a family. I'm worried about my judgment. My morality. My fucking soul.

What the hell.

Have I done.

I suddenly feel sick. And then I feel even worse when he withdraws and another rush of pleasure ripples through my body. I feel empty without him. I feel the need rising again.

"Wren."

He so rarely says my name that it startles me to hear it.

"Did I hurt you?" His voice is husky, his expression concerned.

"No. I'm good."

I scramble off the table, searching for my discarded clothing. He watches for a beat as I get dressed, then reaches for his own pants. I do my best not to look at him. I can't get distracted by his naked body. I can't allow myself to . . . *want* again.

"I meant what I said," I tell him.

"And what was that?"

"When I walk out the door, this doesn't happen again. So I hope you got it out of your system."

"Did you?" He tips his head, pensive.

I meet his eyes and say, "Yes."

———

When I return to the barracks, I head directly to the lav. I should take a shower, but I don't want to wash him off me. I can still taste him.

I'm startled to find Bryce at the sinks. She's changed out of her skimpy dress into a long-sleeved white sleep shirt and gray cotton pants.

She glances at my reflection in the mirror. "How did it go?"

I nod. "Good. You?"

"It was . . ." She smiles. "Exhilarating."

Swallowing, I shift my gaze away from hers. "Yes. It was."

SECTION 6

Instructor	FORD (LT), REDDEN (CAP)
Student	Wren Darlington, R56
Class	UCOs
Mission	Haven Undercover
Objective	Make contact with target and inquire about a job.
Score	PASS

INSTRUCTOR NOTES:

Darlington has great instincts in the field. Follows direction well but not afraid to take charge when needed. Bossy at times, but knows when to give up the reins. —CR

CHAPTER 33

"This is your starting zone," Ford says a few days later, pointing to the holoscreen. "And these two corridors over here—they're the danger zone. You don't want to be there when the timer goes off."

Today's drill is called Fallen Soldier. I'm paired with Lyddie, and we're supposed to run it twice. The first time, I'm going to be injured and she'll need to get me to safety. The second time, we'll switch roles.

I wish I could concentrate, but all I can think about is Cross Redden moving inside me. His teeth biting into my shoulder as he finished.

My body clenches and I smother a curse, forcing the memory out of my mind. Jim told me never to dwell on my mistakes.

"The charge you've set will explode precisely forty-six seconds after I say go. The enemy tossed some smoke bombs into the hallway, so visibility will be low. Oh, and you're not allowed to carry your fellow."

"You want us to, what? Drag each other across the floor?" I say in irritation.

"Do whatever you need to do. Just make sure you're out of the danger zone before the charge goes off."

Sounds easy enough. Except when your fellow is deadweight and you have less than a minute to complete the op, it's a lot harder than it seems. Throw in smoke so thick you can't see three feet in front of you, and two hallways to try to navigate before you reach the designated safety zone, and this exercise is damn near impossible.

On Lyddie's turn, we don't even make it five feet before the timer goes off.

Fail.

We switch roles, returning to the starting zone. When Ford barks "Go" over my earpiece, we snap to action, entering the smoke-filled hallway. Lyddie gets on the ground, fulfilling the role of fallen soldier.

I have no idea where I'm going. Can't see a damn thing. I'll need to feel my way against the wall and somehow also drag Lyddie while searching for the escape route. It's one thing to see the two hallways laid out on the holoscreen; it's another to navigate them while completely blind. We've barely made it down the first hallway when I notice the countdown on my wrist source revealing we have fourteen seconds left.

The smoke grows thicker with each step, making it harder to breathe, but I refuse to give up. "Come on," I urge Lyddie.

"We're not going to make it, Wren."

The countdown reaches zero.

Fail.

In the mess hall later, we hear some of our fellows discussing the drill. It's Bryce's table, and Ivy is there. Since she's not in the company of the Psycho Brigade, I feel a lot more comfortable intruding on their conversation.

"How do you know that?" I call out.

Ivy glances over, frowning. "Know what?"

"I just heard Bryce say there are two assignments with a mandatory pass. How do you know Fallen Soldier is one of them?"

"Because I've already gone through the Program." Her voice is curt.

"You made it all the way to the end?" For some reason I just assumed she got cut early.

"Yes," she says stiffly.

"And you failed Fallen Soldier?"

"No." Her pale eyes flicker with amusement. "Didn't fail it today, either."

"Wait, you passed?"

"We all did," Bryce chimes in with a smug look.

"But none of you got your partners out," I grumble.

"You know," Ivy says, "you come off as this coldhearted bitch—"

"Thanks."

"—yet you have a pathetic amount of compassion."

"What the hell does that mean?"

"It means they made it clear on the first day what they think about compassion. You're not supposed to get to the safety zone, at least not both of you. You're supposed to leave your partner behind," she explains in a condescending tone.

Shit. Yeah. Seems like something the Command would encourage. The officers here like to promote unity—until they don't. And then suddenly it's every man and woman for themselves.

I suppose this is why everyone at the Psycho Brigade's table is also in a good mood tonight. They all left their partners behind without batting an eye.

But I can't do that.

We run the same test again the following day. This time I'm paired with Kaine, and I give him a determined look as we wait for our turn.

"There has to be a way to pass this without just abandoning your fellow."

"You can abandon me," he offers. "I won't be insulted."

Sure, I could do that just to get a check mark on my source next to this drill, but I enjoy the challenge. I feel like I can beat this test. I can't carry him, and dragging him will be too damn hard, but there *must* be a way to beat it.

There isn't a way.

Even after memorizing the layout and counting the steps necessary to get from the starting zone to the safety zone, there's simply not enough time to pass this damn exercise.

When we're ordered to switch roles, my dear friend Kaine has zero qualms about deserting me from the word *Go*. He smacks a kiss on my cheek and says, "It's been nice knowing you, cowgirl." And then the asswit dashes off.

Following suit, Lyddie ditches her partner, Kess, although that's hardly an imposition. And with Ivy's prior knowledge of this drill spreading through Black Cell, all our other fellows abandon their partners, too.

Only one recruit fails the drill. Guess who.

I'm not surprised when I'm summoned to Cross's office later.

At this point, I could get there blindfolded. My boots thud on the polished walkway that leads to the building adjacent to the training center. Several corridors later, and I'm at the familiar door. CAPTAIN OF OPERATIONS.

It buzzes open before I can knock.

My breathing feels a little weak as I step into the office. He's leaning against his desk, clad in a black shirt and camo pants. I haven't seen him since the night we ran the UCO together, the night he made my body burn like nobody else ever has.

I swallow, pushing the memory aside. Steeling myself against it.

"You only have one more shot at Fallen Soldier," he informs me.

I blink. For some reason I expected him to bring up what happened. In this office. On that table. My gaze travels toward it, and when he notices, he offers a slight smirk.

"Tomorrow's your last chance," he adds.

"I'm not leaving my friends behind," I complain. "Pair me with Kess. Or better yet, Anson. I'll happily dance over his still-living body all the way to the end."

"That's not the point. It's not supposed to be easy to leave your partner."

The look I give him is loaded with challenge. "In all the time you've known me—I sure as hell spend enough time in this damn office— I'm surprised you haven't figured out by now what matters to me."

"Yeah?" He raises a brow. "And what matters to you?"

"Loyalty."

That gets me a snort. "Do you truly believe any of these people are loyal to you?"

"Some of them."

I know Lyddie is, without a doubt. Kaine, too. Yes, he left me today in the hallway, but I know in a real-life crisis he wouldn't.

"I think it's easy to desert your partner when it's a fake drill, but we're not here training to be fake. I'm thinking about what I would do, really do, if I was facing this situation in real life." I shrug. "And I know I would never leave a fellow behind. Not one I cared about or respected. I know you believe compassion is weakness—"

"It *is* weakness," he says bluntly. "And in this scenario, it gets you killed."

"Then I die with a friend. They don't have to die alone."

"You know what I think?" He pushes closer. "I think your confidence is misplaced. Your perceived sense of honor. I think it's easy to take a stand right now, because the danger to your life *is* simulated, but you might make a very different choice when your life is truly at risk. When self-preservation kicks in."

"Maybe. But here, in *this* situation, with this set of variables, I won't do it. I'll run your drill again tomorrow, but I can't see myself making a different choice."

"Even if it means failing out?"

Indecision slices through me. I'm the most stubborn person I know. If he pairs me with Lyddie or Kaine tomorrow, I don't know if I can leave them in that hallway.

But I also promised Adrienne and the Uprising that I would get into Elite.

Is one silly drill worth risking my place in the Program? If this is what keeps me from Silver Block, maybe I do need to set my principles aside and compromise my sense of honor.

But is it honor? Truly?

Honor is Uncle Jim facing his firing squad without flinching or begging for his life. Honor is my parents infiltrating the Company so they could make life better for the Modified.

I know what Jim would say to me right now—*do whatever you need to do to survive, little bird.* But my parents . . . I suspect they'd take it a step further. *Survive so you can help others do the same.*

"Are we done here?" I ask Cross.

"No."

It was too much to hope that he'd let me go without addressing it.

"I think about you before I go to sleep."

I blink in shock.

He stalks up, jaw set in determination. I blink again, and he's tugging me flush against his body. Letting me feel how hard he is for me.

"I think about this."

He drags his hand up my hip, skimming the side of my breast, my collarbone, until his fingers slide over the nape of my neck to wind through my hair.

I peer into his heavy-lidded blue eyes and say, "I don't think about you at all."

Rather than take offense, he barks out a laugh. He twists a hunk of hair around his fingers. "I'm not used to this," he admits.

"To what?"

"Being the one out of control."

"I'm not used to being the one *in* control." And I start to laugh, too.

His eyebrows lift in surprise.

"What?"

"That's the first time I've ever heard you laugh."

"That's not true."

"Without the sarcasm."

"Oh. Fair."

His lips curve. I like making him smile. I like seeing that dimple. But it's that warm burst of pleasure that reins me back in.

"We agreed it would never happen again," I remind him.

"Maybe we should reconsider that stance."

Slowly, he backs me into the door, surrounding me with scent, teasing my bare arm with his callused fingertips. I can feel his arousal, burning hot and fierce against my skin.

And oh, how I want to surrender to it, to lose myself in the heat of his touch.

"Or . . . maybe we should stick to the plan," I force myself to say.

I ease out of his grasp and push the door open, leaving his frustrated expression at my back.

———

Later, when I'm putting my source away for the day, I notice there's an update to my scores. I click it to discover my Fallen Soldier score has changed from FAIL to PASS. I wonder how he'll explain *that* one to his instructors.

I fight the smile that threatens to surface.

Kindness is weakness, huh? What does that make him then?

I wash the day away alone in the shower, thinking about Cross and how easy it would be to lose myself in him again. My body remembers that sensation. It craves it. But a small voice in the back of my mind whispers a warning. It could never work. Our loyalties can never be reconciled, and it scares me that every time his lips are on mine, I can't bring myself to care about that.

When I slide the soap over my thigh, it snags over the patchwork of pink and red scars, puckered and raised like the jagged peaks of a mountain range against the backdrop of flesh. I run my fingers along the contours of the scars, a clear, indisputable reminder of why I can't give in to Cross again. Even if I wanted to forget who I am and who he is, I can't. My body won't let me.

At lights-out, I settle under my blanket and manage to fall asleep faster than usual. Yet it feels like only minutes have passed when I'm suddenly yanked out of bed. Instinctively, I grasp for a weapon, but there's nothing within reach. My knife is in the lav locker.

A scream gets caught in my throat as I'm dragged onto my bare feet. I hear other noises. Gasps. Startled curses. A high-pitched cry.

Then I feel a sharp prick at the side of my neck, and everything goes black.

CHAPTER 34

I can't see a thing.

Not even my own hand when I lift it to my face to rub my temples. For a moment I wonder if I'm back in the Blacklands. The suffocating blackness feels like a trip home. But I can't smell the trees. The earth. When I inhale, it's the scent of metal and grease. I'm indoors. But where?

My heart is pounding. I'm lying on a floor that feels like it's made of metal and is covered with dirt. I wipe the grime off my arm as I attempt to sit up. The air is cold against my bare arms and feet.

It's some sort of drill. I know this because I remember the gasps and screams in the barracks. I doubt an Uprising operative just walked in and managed to kidnap the entire training class. I also remember reading through the list of sections when the Program first started. We've been learning interrogation tactics all week.

This must be the resistance part.

I groggily manage to get into a prone position. My head is splitting like someone tried to crack it open with a hammer. I take a breath, and it's in that moment that I realize I'm not alone. There's someone else breathing in here with me.

"Who's there?" I demand. Swear to hell, if it's Anson . . .

"Wren?"

Ivy.

A better alternative, but not by much.

"Yeah, it's me." I clear my throat, because it sounds like I'm speaking through a mouthful of dirt. "Are you okay?"

"Fine." She releases a pained groan. I hear the rustle of fabric. I think she's trying to sit up.

I rest my back against the cold wall and bring my knees up, hugging them. "Where are we?"

"If it's anything like last time, we're at the train tracks. Railway car."

"Last time," I echo. Wary.

"Yeah. That's where they took us for the RTI section."

I was right, then. This is Resistance to Interrogation. For once, I'm grateful to have Ivy around, because she can tell me what to expect.

"So how does it work?" I ask. "We just sit here, and they come in and try to make us talk?"

"Pretty much."

"How do they do that? Torture?"

"Nobody will be prying off your fingernails with pliers, if that's what you're worried about." She sounds unhappy. "But it's not going to be pleasant."

"Understatement much, Eversea?" another voice drawls, and I almost jump out of my skin.

Someone else is in here.

Roe.

"Damn it, Roe," Ivy grumbles. "How long have you been conscious?"

"The whole time."

Neither of us even heard him breathing. Maybe Cross is wrong, and the kid *can* be an asset to Silver Block.

"A warning would've been nice."

"Have I ever been nice, Eversea?" His chuckle travels through the darkness. "Also, in case I haven't said it lately, you're going to some pretty pathetic lengths to try to win my brother back."

Ivy doesn't answer.

"Won't work, by the way."

"Fuck you, Roe."

"Such animosity. Where was that hostility when you were kissing my ass over dinners with the General? 'Roe, you're turning into such a handsome young man,'" he mimics, chortling to himself.

I can't help but smile in the dark. I can totally see her sucking up to the General. Anything to win Cross's approval.

"You wasted your time," Roe tells her. "He was never going to stay."

"Yeah. Why is that?" She sounds tired now. There's a soft thud, as if she's resting her head on the metal wall behind her.

"Because you loved him too much. He doesn't want to be loved that hard."

Surprisingly insightful from the little general.

"Anyway, to answer your question, Darlington, this will not be pleasant at all. My brother prepared me for this."

"Cross?" Ivy snorts. "I highly doubt he helped you prep. He doesn't even want you in the Program."

"Not Cross. Travis. He warned me what to expect."

"And what can we expect?" I ask, since apparently Ivy doesn't want to share.

"Well, first off, say hello to the next five days of your life."

A shiver runs up my spine. "*Five* days? Ivy, is that true?"

"I don't remember how long it was last time. It felt like a long time," she admits. "Every hour felt like two weeks."

Neither of them is selling me on this exercise.

"They pull you out every few hours or so," she continues. "Ask you to reveal something about the Command. Then they throw you back in here. No food, no water, no light, no sleep."

"No sleep?"

"You'll see." She sighs. "No torture, though. Basic stuff. They slap you around, kick you. Sometimes waterboard you."

"Oh, waterboarding. Just basic stuff." I can't help but laugh, and to my surprise, she responds with one of her own. "If you last the full five days without talking, then that's it? They let you go?"

"Yep."

"Okay. I guess it can't be too awful, seeing as how you did this before and survived. So . . ." I shrug even though neither of them can see me.

Ivy goes silent. Roe seems to be done talking, too.

I lean my head back and prepare myself for what sounds like the worst party I've ever been invited to, with the worst guest list known to humankind.

Although I suppose it's better than being stuck in here with Kess and Anson.

————

The first time they come for me, they throw a black canvas sack over my head and haul me forward by the armpits. They don't say a word. I think it's two men, but I can't be sure. My legs drag behind me as I struggle to find my footing.

They throw me into another room. The bag is yanked off, and my eyes water from the sudden onslaught of light after hours of darkness. Ivy's right. We're on a train. A railway car that carries cargo. There's only a narrow strip of windows near the ceiling, but the slits of morning light they allow in practically blind me. Along the sides of the car, heavy-duty chains and tie-downs are secured to the walls, ready to anchor cargo in place during transit. Large metal hooks hang from the ceiling, and I'm wondering if they're going to string me up when I'm suddenly shoved onto a cold, metal chair.

I find myself staring at two men I've never seen before in my life. For a second, I question whether this is really a Command exercise.

"Where are Silver Block's black caches?" one of them asks. He's a muscular man in his mid-twenties with dark eyes and skin. His buddy looks older than that. A short, bearded blond man.

The black caches are weapons sites whose coordinates we had to memorize last week. They're totally off the books. Secret reserves of weapons that could arm the Uprising if they wanted to use them, or cripple Silver Block if they chose to destroy them.

I take a breath and say, "Wren Darlington. Recruit 56. Silver Block." That's the only information we're allowed to offer, according to what we learned in this section.

"That's not what I asked, bitch."

He slaps me across the face. Hard. My cheek throbs from the sting.

"Where are the black caches?"

"Wren Darlington. Recruit 56. Silver Block."

After ten more minutes of that, they shove the sack over my head and drag me back to the other car. The pitch black welcomes me once more, almost comforting. I'm not scared of the dark. This is just a nice morning in the Blacklands for me.

"That wasn't too bad," I tell Ivy.

"You say that now."

The door is wrenched open. Roe's turn.

"Get your hands off me, godfucker," he spits out as they manhandle him.

Once he's gone, I ask, "Did you really go to family dinners with him? Because that sounds like a nightmare."

Her snort of laughter echoes in the railcar. "Wasn't fun."

––––––

Those first eight hours aren't awful. Truly. The two men drag us out, repeat the same question for ten, fifteen minutes, slap us around, throw us back in the car. My stomach growls a little and my mouth is parched, but I'm otherwise unaffected.

Until I fall asleep. Somehow, my body succumbs to slumber, but not for long. I'm wrenched into consciousness by the sensation of being submerged in ice-cold water. No. I'm not submerged. It's coming from above me. Sprinklers. They've fitted the railcar with sprinklers. Assholes.

The three of us are now lying on cold, wet dirt. Shivering. And that's when I realize this is going to be a lot harder than I thought.

The worst part is the bucket. Every time I hear the loud, steady stream of Roe pissing into it, I want to vomit.

"How do you produce so much urine," I mutter in the darkness, "when you haven't had anything to drink in twenty-four hours?"

He just chuckles and returns to his designated spot. We've each chosen our corners, with the vile bucket taking up residence in the fourth corner. I pray I don't have to use it more than absolutely necessary. It's mortifying, and I now realize why Ivy hates this section so much. Taking care of your personal needs with two people listening—neither of whom likes you very much—is a form of humiliation. Though I suppose that's why they're doing it.

———

Day 2. I think. Every time I fall asleep, those sprinklers dump ice water on us, so I have no idea how much time has passed. My stomach hurts. When they drag me into the other car again, I feel a noticeable lack of energy.

The interrogation drags on. That same question over and over again. Where are the black caches. Tell us where the caches are. Repetition is a tactic. It's supposed to drive me mad, make me cave. And holy hellfuck, I want to scream for them to shut up. But I hold firm.

"Wren Darlington. Recruit 56. Silver Block."

Mr. Muscles spits in my face. The glob slides down my cheek and mingles with the blood pouring out of my lip. We've graduated from slaps to outright fists. He uses that fist now, slamming it into my jaw.

I fall off the chair from the brutal force. The metallic tang of blood floods my mouth. But still, I refuse to yield.

———

The hours and days blur into one another. I lose all sense of time. The hunger becomes a constant companion. I'm so thirsty. I could lick the floor, but the sprinklers have turned the dirt into mud, and I refuse to drink mud water. Besides, Roe tried it already and we heard him puking in our bucket the following morning. Or night. Time doesn't exist in this railway car.

I'm soaking wet because the sprinklers just went off again. My teeth chatter loud enough to echo off the metal walls. Loud enough that Roe lets out an angry curse and orders me to shut up. He's been very quiet today. Ivy, too. There's no camaraderie among our trio. We're not bonding. Swapping stories. We're wet, cold, hungry, tired, thirsty, and pissed off.

When our captors return Ivy to us, and I hear her defeated whimpering as she crawls back to her corner, I realize I can take advantage of this moment.

With their defenses stripped bare, their minds are mine for the taking.

I start with Ivy, whose mind is wide open. Not even a pretense of a shield. Guilt pokes at my gut, but I ignore it.

People have misconceptions about mind reading. They think it means a Mod can see their entire life. Their memories. But we can only hear what they're thinking in the moment. I'm not worried about lurid memories of Ivy in bed with Cross playing in color behind my eyelids. I do worry her thoughts will be consumed by him, though, which evokes a twinge of jealousy that annoys me.

But Ivy isn't thinking about Cross.

You can do this. You have to.

For Delia.

Ivy wants to join Silver Block for her older sister.

Delia. Died of a rare bone cancer that the regen chambers in the Point couldn't quite eradicate.

I retreat, the guilt intensifying as Ivy's grief surrounds my senses. I shouldn't have invaded her privacy. Yet even knowing I'm doing something wrong, I still shift my attention to Roe.

His shield is intact. Strong, too. I could try to prod at it, search for a crack, but I don't have the mental bandwidth right now, so I hug my knees tighter and close my eyes.

———

Ivy starts moaning sometime on Day 4. "I can't do this anymore. I'm so tired. My stomach is cramping."

Roe jeers at her from his corner. "Sack up, Eversea. You're tired and hungry. Big fucking deal."

He's such a prickhole that I feel the need to be the encouraging one. "Ignore him. You got this, Ivy. You were able to survive RTI before. Just gotta do it again."

"No," she mutters.

"No what?"

"I wasn't able to do it before. Why do you think I'm not in Silver Block, you dumb quat?"

I'm taken aback. Not by the verbal attack, but by her revelation. "You failed RTI?"

"I lasted three days."

I pause for a moment. "Okay. Well. I'm pretty sure it's been more than three days, so you're doing better than last time. You just need to power through."

Easier said than done, though. For me, too. I lie there shivering for hours. Sleep eludes me, those sprinklers ensuring I won't have any sort of respite.

The next time our captors come for me, my teeth can't stop rattling as I say, "Wren Darlington. Recruit 56. Silver Block."

I wonder how Lyddie is handling this. She's so delicate. Kaine, he could do this in his sleep. But not Lyddie. As the bearded man wrenches my head back by my hair so he can punch me in the face, I realize I desperately want Lyddie to make it. She might not be the best soldier, but she's smart. She could even be brilliant. I think she can excel in Intelligence.

When I'm thrown like a rag doll into the darkness, Ivy is still moaning in her corner.

"Eversea," I call toward her. "What's it like in K? I heard you telling Bryce that's where you grew up, right?"

"What?" She sounds dazed.

"I've never been there," I prompt. "I'm curious."

I think she knows I'm trying to distract her, because there's a trace of gratitude as she says, "It used to be a lot better."

"How so?"

"The controllers were nicer. Gave us more leeway, like looking the other way if we missed curfew. But it turned to shit when we got rezoned. After K merged with L, their ward chairman took over."

It happens often, the rezoning. There were twenty-six wards when the system was first implemented. I believe we're down to eighteen now. Some were integrated with their neighbors because of population decline. But most wards were swallowed up by natural disasters, as the coastline slowly tries to eat its way onto the Continent. The seawalls the General has the Company engineers tackling won't hold forever.

"It's really beautiful there," Ivy continues, sounding wistful. "You'd think being so close to the Blacklands would be creepy or something, but honestly? The black mist in the distance actually makes for some gorgeous sunsets."

"Did you ever go to the Blacklands?"

"No." She's horrified by the notion. "I don't know anyone who's gone in there and come out alive."

"Roe," I say. "Have you?"

His voice floats toward me. "Only to the edge. Maybe ten feet into the mist. It was Travis's idea."

"He took you there?" Ivy sounds surprised.

"The General had business in K when I was twelve. He brought us along, but we got bored and snuck off. My brothers dared me to walk in. Travis said it wasn't a big deal if you had your flashlight. Asshole didn't tell me they don't work in there."

Don't I know it. There's something wrong with the way the light reflects in the Blacklands. As in, it doesn't. Everything is black. Always. Jim and I learned that lesson when he tried to bring various light sources on our hunting excursions. Flashlights didn't work. Torches. Even his lighter.

It was fascinating to me. Each time he flicked that lighter, it wouldn't work, but when we were in the clearing's rare pocket of sunshine, he'd flick it to spark a visible orange flame. I wish we could study the phenomenon and find out why it's like that. Or maybe the Company already has, and they just don't want to share.

"Do you like Travis?" I ask Roe.

"I suppose." His tone is grudging.

"How is he different from the captain?" I hate revealing my curiosity about his family, but it's a dynamic I still haven't been able to figure out.

Roe thinks it over. "Travis is very practical. Calculated. He does shit to test you, to see if you'll be of use to him. He's got a scientific mind. He doesn't rely on emotion like Cross."

Ivy snorts. "*Cross* and *emotion* are not two words I'd put in the same sentence."

"You don't know shit about my brother. Either of them," he sneers. "You didn't have to grow up with them."

"You barely grew up with them. You lived with your mother until she died."

"I spent enough time at the estate to know what they're like. What all of them are like. Especially her."

I frown in the darkness. "Who?"

He makes a disparaging sound. "You know she never comes down when I'm over? Not even once."

"Who?" I ask again.

"The General's sainted Vinessa. My stepmother. Bitch won't even venture down the stairs when I'm there. Doesn't acknowledge my presence. When I visited as a kid, I remember being ordered to stay in the living room while the General was upstairs with his real family." Roe lets out a harsh laugh. "Sometimes he'd keep me waiting for hours. Sitting there like some unwanted guest."

Bitterness simmers beneath his words. I can hear the weight of years of hurt and rejection in his voice, but I can't muster up much sympathy. He killed Betima without a shred of repentance. This is not a misunderstood little boy. He's a dangerous man.

"I could never understand why she hated me so much. Sure, my mother worked in Human Services, but it wasn't Mom's fault the General developed a liking for her. Wasn't her fault he knocked her up. Birth control wasn't even mandatory back then." Roe makes a derisive sound. "He's the one who couldn't keep it in his pants."

"Will you be telling us your sob stories the rest of the time we're here or are you finished now?" I ask in a polite tone.

"You're a real quat, Darlington."

———

Mr. Muscles and the Bearded Man are jerks. They're eating thick roast beef sandwiches in front of me. Am I supposed to beg for the food? I sort of want to beg. My stomach hurts so bad, it's starting to cramp like Ivy's. At least I'm not completely dehydrated. Each time the sprinklers jolt me awake, I hurry to tip my head and try to capture some of that moisture in my mouth. But they stop so fast, it's only ever a few drops.

They throw me back in our car, which reeks of dirt, urine, and excrement. I settle in my corner and listen to Ivy's soft sobs. When footsteps approach the door a little while later, Ivy whimpers. It's her turn.

"You can do it, Eversea," I say, my voice ringing with confidence. "It's not that much longer."

I half expect her to not return from the interrogation. She's so broken down, it's only a matter of time before she capitulates.

But she comes back, and I'm almost disgusted at myself for the little spark of pride I feel toward her.

"Good job, Eversea."

"Thanks," she murmurs back, and there isn't a trace of animosity in her tone anymore.

CHAPTER 35

We emerge exhausted, completely beaten down. The light hurts my eyes. I squint against it the entire drive back to base.

First thing I do is take a hot shower. It lasts two hours. I scrub the mud off me and wash my hair. My scalp itches, and I don't even want to know what was crawling around on that dirty railcar floor.

After I've practically scoured my skin off, I go to the mess hall and am greeted by a sea of vacant faces. Everyone around me looks like they're in shock. Even Kaine is subdued.

"That sucked," he says dully.

"Wasn't that bad," I tell him.

"Fuck off."

Lyddie is pale, her hands shaking as she picks at her food. It's a good hearty meal. Real beef in the stew. Heady potatoes. Thick sauce. I gorge.

We have four days off before we need to report to class again. Everyone checks their sources to find they've been granted leisure passes for two of the days. An overnight.

Everyone except for me, that is.

I have to admit, it gets to me this time, not being able to leave the base. I don't want to be here right now. I want to be on my ranch. I want to ride my horse and feel the summer wind on my face. But I refuse to cry in front of these people.

While my friends take advantage of their freedom, I roam the base, trying to ward off the loneliness that threatens to suffocate me. Even Cross isn't here. He's not chasing me anymore, and I don't know if I should be disappointed about that, or relieved because it's what I asked for.

No, that's not true. I *know* which way I should feel.

But it's not what I feel.

On my evening walk, I reach out to Wolf, but he doesn't answer, so I try Tana instead. She lets me link, greeting me in a glum tone. She sounds as unhappy as I feel.

"I miss you," I confess.

"I miss you so much," she replies with a moan. "I hate it here, Wren."

"The soldier presence is still heavy?"

"Yes. So many of them that the barracks at Controller Fletcher's station are full, which means the overflow is coming to the inn. Which means I deal with them on a daily basis."

"Are they giving you any trouble?"

"Not yet. But they're constantly watching everyone. There's always at least half a dozen of them at the pub from open to close, watching my dad."

"Shit. Okay, well, let me know if you notice anything suspicious, or if they start harassing you."

I go back to the training center and read a mystery novel on my source. But I get bored fast, so I venture toward the common room, finding only a handful of Red Cell members I've never bothered getting to know.

Lyddie and Kaine return on Sunday. As does Lash, who tells us about his exciting visit home. Apparently, his parents secured a gathering permit to celebrate his mother's birthday, and one of the guests almost choked to death on a chicken bone at dinner.

The following day, we file into the cavernous classroom where two months ago I walked in wishing I were anywhere else. We're supposed to get our final scores for the Program today and find out who made it into Silver Block. Weeks of training have culminated in this moment, and there's an air of excitement as everyone remains standing, waiting for our instructors.

The room is not as full as it was that first day. Of the fifty-six recruits who started the Program, thirty-six remain. I remember Ford mocking that half of us would be gone by the end, but this is more than fifty percent.

I wring my hands together as anxiety swirls in my belly. I *think* I passed the Program. At least I hope I did. I don't know whether my poor performance from the first few sections will come back to haunt me.

My nerves intensify when Ford, Hadley, and Struck show up, and Hadley proceeds to list eleven names. Mine isn't one of them, and I fight a crushing sense of defeat as—

"Thank you for your interest in Silver Block," Hadley tells the eleven recruits. "However, you haven't been accepted at this time."

The relief almost knocks me over.

Hadley keeps his tone brisk, ignoring the disappointed faces. "Please report to your current COs or check in with Captain Radek about returning to your wards."

The rejected recruits march out the door. We're down to twenty-five, just under Ford's fifty percent cut rate. I guess he wasn't kidding.

The admin captain, Deron Radek, shows up then to address the rest of us.

"Welcome to Silver Block. You'll receive your posts and uniforms in the next couple of days," he says without preamble. "Until you're relocated to your new quarters, you'll remain in the barracks."

At that, he stalks out. I like the way Captain Radek operates. Efficient and to the point.

"Your final scores have been uploaded to your sources," Ford tells us. "If you have any questions about them, send a comm to Captain Radek. Dismissed."

That's it.

The three instructors leave the room, and I frown at the empty doorway. This whole affair feels incredibly anticlimactic.

Congratulations, you're in Silver Block, see you later.

Lyddie, however, makes up for our superiors' total lack of enthusiasm by letting out a squeal of joy. Turning toward me, she looks like she just won an exotic vacation to the Lost Continents.

"We made it!"

"We made it," I echo.

She throws her arms around me, hugging me tightly before doing the same to Kaine. Our other fellows are also celebrating. Lash. Kess. Anson.

Ivy.

I nod at her, my way of saying congratulations. Ivy nods back before turning to hug Bryce.

Roe made it, too, I note. Guess the General got his way.

"I want to see my final score," Lyddie says, scrambling to pull her source from her pocket.

Me too. I'm curious to see how I managed to turn things around, but at the same time disappointed because nobody said a word about Silver Elite, which was my only objective. I have no clue if I succeeded in doing the one thing the Uprising asked me to do.

When I open my source, rather than a score I find a screen that says:

available test: 1

I click on that, and another page pops up, a description of the test. This one says:

elite

There's a date and time beside it. It's scheduled for tomorrow afternoon.

I bite my lip to contain my excitement.

Lyddie peers over my shoulder and gasps. "You've been shortlisted! This must be the final test to get into Elite."

"I got the same message," Kaine says, twisting his source toward me.

A few others are now exclaiming over the message. The final count ends up being twelve. Twelve of the twenty-five recruits made the short list. The number seems quite high. How many of us will earn a slot?

I suppose I'll find out tomorrow.

On our way to the door, I catch a glimpse of Roe, and a shiver runs through me. His expression is murderous, which tells me that maybe the General didn't get his way, after all.

Roe wasn't shortlisted.

———

It's a pit night, so everyone decides to celebrate the end of the Program by watching our fellows beat the crap out of each other. I still don't own any civilian clothes, other than the outfit I borrowed from Betima, but it feels wrong to wear it tonight. My heart clenches at the memory of her. Lyddie told me the rest of Betima's stuff was returned to her ward. I wonder what happened to her family. Were they detained? Interrogated about whether they knew she was Aberrant?

Lyddie interrupts my thoughts. "Let's ask Soldier Struck if we can borrow something from the UCO wardrobe room."

Before I can protest, she dashes across the mess hall to speak to our now former instructor. Struck glances my way, then shrugs.

Lyddie returns to our table to say, "She says it's fine as long as you return it in the morning."

That's how I end up walking into the warehouse that night wearing a slinky red dress with a neckline so dangerous it would probably send me to the stockade if Cross weren't my captain.

Kaine's eyes nearly pop out of the sockets when he sees me. "Hell, cowgirl, are you trying to kill me?" Desire thickens his voice.

It's been a while since he's looked at me like that. I didn't think he'd lost interest, though. I've noticed that Kaine takes the Program seriously and always puts our training first. As much as he likes to flirt, he doesn't allow himself to get distracted, and these last few sections have been highly intensive, requiring all our focus.

Tonight his focus is on me.

"You know what I think?" He waits for Lyddie and Lash to walk ahead before moving closer to whisper in my ear. "I think we should turn around and go back to the barracks. They'll be empty . . ."

A week or two ago, I might've been tempted. Now . . .

Now I know what it feels like to have Cross naked and groaning in my ear.

I shake my head in regret, glad that he's not able to read my mind. It's too chaotic in there right now. "We have a test tomorrow. I can't afford the distraction."

Kaine purses his lips before nodding. "Good point."

I'm relieved he drops the issue so readily, though I wonder what I'll say next time it comes up. I can't tell him I slept with Cross, and I certainly can't tell him that our captain has completely messed with my head. That I wore this dress for Cross. That I—

Guilt jams in my throat and closes around my windpipe as something suddenly becomes apparent to me.

I've forgotten why I'm here.

What am I doing? This is not my life. I shouldn't be donning sexy dresses and celebrating with Primes. I haven't even made it into Elite, damn it. *That's* the objective. Not to drink whiskey and have a good time at the fights with my friends.

They're not my friends.

These aren't my people, and I'm not one of them.

This isn't my life.

I halt in my tracks, touching Kaine's arm. "I'm going to use the lav," I mumble, then pivot on the heel of my strappy silver shoe. I need to leave. Go back to the barracks.

I don't belong here.

Halfway down the corridor, I see him.

He's walking with Ford and one of the men who interrogated me in the railcar. Mr. Muscles, whose gaze flicks my way before dismissing me as if he's never seen me before in his life. As if he wasn't punching me in the face for five days straight.

My dress barely covers my thighs. I know Cross notices.

He says something to Ford and Mr. Muscles, who walk off without him. Ford smirks at me as he passes, leaving me and Cross to face off in the shadowy corridor.

Keep walking, orders a voice in my head.

Five seconds ago, I'd determined I shouldn't be here. That I'm in over my head and no longer have sight of the mission.

Of reality.

But one look at his piercing blue eyes and I'm frozen in place.

His lips turn up slightly. "Did you wear that for me?"

"Yes," I admit, and I hate myself for it.

"Are you leaving?"

I nod.

Then I shake my head.

The smile takes root, curving his mouth and softening his expression. "Which is it, Dove?"

Rather than answer, I plant my hand in the center of his chest and push him backward. His grin widens. In an atypical act of submission, he allows me to lead him. Down the hall, around the corner, until we're concealed behind one of the concrete pillars.

This is where he grabbed me the first time I came here. When he was taunting me. When he said I wanted him so bad I could taste it.

Well, I've had a taste. I've tasted his lips, and I want to taste them again.

One more time won't be the end of the world, will it?

His hands find my waist, pulling my body tight to his.

I fight to keep my composure, even as my blood burns with desire. Deep down, I can't deny the rush of exhilaration that courses through me at his touch. The anticipation coiling in my core.

"I want it," he growls in my ear.

"I know."

He laughs, and the husky sound triggers a jolt of electricity inside me. "Tell me you want it, too."

I respond by wrapping my arms around his neck and tugging his head down. His lips capture mine with a fierceness that steals my breath. I gasp and he takes full advantage by sliding his skillful tongue through the seam of my lips. I moan when the tip of it teases mine.

"I love that sound. The little noises you make, Dove, when I make you feel good."

He cups my ass and lifts me against him. I wrap my legs around his waist, moaning again as he rolls his hips. I feel every inch of him. He could take me right here—hell, he could take me out there, in front of everyone—and I wouldn't care. The need is too strong. I'm clawing at him, kissing him back with an urgency that makes me dizzy. Frantic.

We're both out of breath when he pulls back.

"Come to my quarters tonight?"

I nod. Because I want him more than I ever thought possible.

"Cross . . ."

And that's when we hear his name traveling down the hall. A sing-song voice.

We both frown. It suddenly registers. The silence. I can no longer hear laughter or music from the makeshift arena.

All I hear is, "Cross . . . Where are you, Cross?"

He sets me down. His lips are swollen from our kisses, but I can tell he's no longer here with me. Frowning, he stalks toward the corridor.

I hurry after him. His stride is long, purposeful. He's out of sight before I even step into the main room. I push my way through the eerily quiet crowd. When I reach the ledge, I peer down and spot him in the pit.

Roe.

He brightens at the sight of Cross, who's emerged from the crowd several feet away from me.

"There you are, Captain." Sarcasm drips from each word, especially *Captain*. I think he's on stims. He's always on stims.

Cross doesn't answer. He stares five feet below at his younger brother, waiting.

"I'm calling you out," Roe taunts.

"Are you now?" Cross mocks him.

The room is deathly silent. I notice a lot of wary, perplexed faces. But I know what's going on.

Roe's pissed about Elite and looking to take it out on his brother.

"We haven't knocked each other around in a while. Not since we were kids."

"Probably best to keep it that way," Cross says evenly.

"Nah. I think we're long overdue." Roe's eyes gleam, and suddenly he's addressing the crowd. "Captain of Silver Block, everyone!" He waves his arm in an extravagant flourish. "Come on, give him some encouragement."

Not a single person utters a word. They all feel the tension. It hangs over us like a storm cloud.

"Get down here, brother," Roe says, and I shiver at the sheer depth of the hatred darkening his face.

This is something that's been brewing between them for a long time. Their whole lives, probably. I remember the resentment lacing Roe's voice in the railroad car. *You don't know shit about my brother. Either of them. You didn't have to grow up with them.*

Cross is four years older than him. I wonder if Roe idolized him when they were kids. I wonder how Cross responded to that. I wonder if Roe's warning to Ivy during RTI was not about her, but himself.

You loved him too much. He doesn't want to be loved that hard.

"Are you scared, brother?"

I see the moment Cross resigns himself to the fact he needs to do this. Roe won't stop. He'll stay down there all night if he has to.

Cross's gaze flicks my way. Then, without another word, he heaves himself over the ledge and jumps five feet into the pit. His boots collide with packed sand.

"You really want to do this? Let's do this."

He doesn't strip off his shirt. Doesn't do anything but stand two feet from Roe and wait.

Roe frowns.

Then he charges at his brother.

Cross releases a right hook that catches Roe in the eye, followed by a jab so fast I would've missed it if I'd blinked. Roe barely has time to react before the second blow lands squarely on his jaw, sending him stumbling backward.

But the teenager refuses to back down. He's too proud. He throws himself back into the fray.

Blow after blow rain down upon him, each strike landing with bone-crushing force as his older brother unleashes a relentless barrage of attacks. Roe growls his rage. Spits out the blood that pours from his nose, his cheek, his mouth. He swings his fists in a wild, desperate attempt to defend himself, but no matter how hard he tries, he's no match for Cross.

It's embarrassingly obvious there is no comparison. At all. By any conceivable measure.

And yet he can't shut his mouth. Can't admit defeat.

"Is that all you've got?" Roe sneers, while his chest heaves with exertion and red rivulets drip down his face and onto the sand. "Pathetic."

Shoulders tightening, Cross puts an end to it.

With a final, brutal strike, Roe crumples to the sand in a bloody heap, his body battered from the onslaught. He peers up at his older brother through swollen eyes.

"Fuck you, Cross."

"You wanted it, brother." Cross is cold and unforgiving. "Consider this your education."

"You're a fucking asshole!"

"And you're a spoiled little prick."

"Fuck you!" Roe is screaming at him.

Cross just shakes his head and leaves him broken and defeated on the sand, gasping for breath.

A trickle of fear goes through me.

As Cross hauls himself up the ledge, his gaze slides toward me for a moment. Then he breaks eye contact and disappears into the crowd.

CHAPTER 36

The next afternoon, the twelve of us meet in the gym. None of the instructors have arrived yet, and my fellows hypothesize what's going on while we wait for direction.

"I think we all got in," says one of the female fellows from Red Cell.

"They're not letting twelve soldiers join Elite," Noah Jones replies. "I bet they shortlisted twelve knowing that some of us will fail the final test."

Standing beside me is Bryce. I can't deny I'm surprised to see her here, although I suppose she did excel in some of the training sections. And the girl is fearless, I'll give her that. She was the first to jump out of the plane during our parachuting drills.

"Daddy!" She lights up when a man suddenly steps through the door.

Bryce rushes up to a tall, dark-haired man with five stars on his Silver Block uniform. A colonel. He doesn't hug her. Rather, he greets her with a brisk nod, as if she's a colleague.

"You came to watch my final test?" I hear her ask, and on my other side, Kaine pokes me in the ribs.

"I didn't realize we were inviting people to this," he drawls, and I hide a laugh.

It doesn't surprise me that Bryce wanted her father to witness her glorious achievement. All she's done for two months is prattle on about how important he is.

I study the others on the shortlist. Me, Bryce, and Kaine. Kess. Jones. Anson, of course. That psychopath can carry out any mission he's ordered. The other six recruits are members of Red Cell.

I'm still wondering what the selection process was when Cross enters the gym, tailed by Ford and Struck. The trio salute Bryce's father, the colonel, who stands against the wall to give them the floor.

I haven't seen Cross since he stormed out of the pit last night. I think about how close I was to going home with him, seconds before he beat the shit out of his brother without batting an eye.

He doesn't even look my way as he addresses the group.

"You're all here because you're being considered for Elite. There are six available slots."

My heart sinks. Six slots, and twelve recruits angling for them. I'm starting to have a bad feeling about this.

"Who fills those slots is simple," he says. "Two of you are going to walk into a room, and only one will walk out."

Jaws drop.

"What? I'm not killing anybody," Jones balks.

"Did I say anything about killing?" Cross sounds bored. "Each room has two knives in it. Do with them what you want. If your opponent taps out, they're out." He sweeps his gaze over the room. "If you tap out, relax. You're still a member of Silver Block. You'll be assigned to a unit and be just fine. Victor is assigned to Elite."

It's so simple and so stupid.

"Why don't you just pick based on merit?" demands one of the Red Cell males.

"This is merit. Whoever's better will walk out of the room first. So be better."

Kaine and I exchange a look. Of the twelve of us, there are six males and six females, so unless they're using co-ed pairings, only three women will get into Elite.

I eye my potential opponents. I don't want to go up against Kess. Yes, I've kicked her ass before, but she's a vicious little creature. One of the Red Cell girls looks optimal. Short, slight, and nonexistent muscle mass.

But when my name is called first, it's followed by "Granger."

I'm facing Bryce.

Which does bring a twinge of relief. This'll be easy. I have every confidence I can get her to tap out. Bryce knows it, too—I see the defeat settle over her when she hears our names.

We're assigned a room number—3—and ordered to leave without getting to hear any of the other pairs. Bryce and I walk down the hall in silence. When we enter Room 3, we find it completely empty. No furniture, no windows. I assume the mirror against the wall is the kind they use for interrogations.

Two knives sit on the concrete floor.

I wonder who Kaine was paired with. I hope it's Anson and he slits the bastard's throat.

The door suddenly closes behind us. We hear it lock with an electronic beep.

Bryce glances up at the blinking camera mounted to the corner of the ceiling. She studies the mirror. Then, with a miserable expression, she leans closer to whisper in my ear.

"Please let me have this."

Pity ripples through me. "You know I can't."

I've been tasked with joining this unit. That's my one and only objective. Besides, we both know this girl wouldn't last a minute in an elite squad. She's not good enough.

Her jaw tightens. "Then I guess we fight for it."

"Guess so."

We eye each other for a moment. And I'll admit it—she completely catches me off guard when she blasts forward like a rocket, snatching one knife off the floor while kicking the other away.

I scramble after the skittering blade, managing to wrap my hand around the cold handle just as Bryce attacks. I dodge her, but she's good. Fast. She slashes the air, then pivots to protect herself from my blade. I grab her by the wrist and wrench her toward me as I jam my free fist under her chin. Her head rears back. She doesn't drop the knife, though.

"Bitch," she snaps.

She charges again. I trip her before the knife can sink into my flesh, and we crash to the floor, grappling for control. Her blade hisses past my ear. I curse when I feel a sting in my neck. She nicked me. I elbow her in the throat, and she gags.

I didn't expect such a brutal fight.

From Bryce, of all people.

With a cry of anger, I slam the knife handle into her face. I don't want to use the blade. I don't want to hurt this girl. But I have a sinking feeling there's no way she's ever going to tap out. Not with her father behind that mirror.

Panting, I get her beneath me, pinning her wrist under my knee, rendering her knife completely useless. Her gaze flits toward the mirror.

"Tap out," I beg her.

She keeps fighting. There's too much fight in her. She's better than she was when we sparred. I know her father's presence is fueling her actions.

I blink, and suddenly she gains the upper hand. She's on top of me, smashing her knuckles into my face. My cheekbone ripples with pain. She grabs my wrist and slams it against the floor, once, twice, hard enough that my fingers instinctively unclasp the handle. My knife goes clattering across the room.

Bryce releases a triumphant noise, but I manage to kick out from under her and roll away, crawling toward the knife. I've just reached it when the hot burn of pain hisses through my upper arm. She sliced me. Goddamn quat. A spray of blood blossoms from the gash in my arm. And then she's on me again, straddling my hips.

"Tap out," she growls. Feral.

"No," I grind out.

Her spittle wets my face. "I'm either leaving this room as Elite or dead, Wren."

I hear the truth in those words. That she would rather die than bring shame to her father. She would actually *rather die*.

But I'm equally determined. I *need* this. I need it for Uncle Jim.

Need it if I want my revenge against the people who killed him. If I'm going to bring this entire organization down from the inside.

Do you really want to die in this room?

My mother was willing to die for the Modified. Maybe I am, too. Maybe I need to take my own stand.

With a surge of adrenaline, I flip us over, tightening my grip on the knife. I need her to tap out. Somehow I have to *make* her. As Bryce slashes at me, I sink my blade into her thigh, summoning a strangled cry from her throat.

"Tap out," I plead.

"No."

She tries to thrust her knife at my throat, but I deflect. I pull my blade out of her thigh and implore her with my eyes. There's blood everywhere. All over the floor.

"Please, Bryce, just tap out."

Her breath escapes in shallow gasps. I suddenly notice she doesn't look too good. Her face is devoid of color, whiter than the walls.

That's when I realize how deep I cut her. The blood pours out of her wound like a steady stream from a faucet. She continues swinging at me, but half-hearted now. I see her energy draining, her eyelids fluttering.

"Bryce." I slap her cheek. "Bryce."

Her eyes close altogether. The pool of blood beneath us grows larger, spreading all around us.

Horror claws at my throat. I hit her femoral artery.

I've never seen anyone bleed out that fast.

I suck in desperate breaths, my lungs straining for oxygen. As my heart thunders against my ribs, I crawl away from Bryce, leaving her dead in the middle of the room.

CHAPTER 37

I stumble into the hallway, covered in blood.

Dazed.

Kaine is waiting outside another door, shocked at the sight of me. "Wren. What happened? Are you okay?"

"I killed Bryce."

My chest heaves on a ragged breath, the reality of what just transpired crashing down on me like a tidal wave.

And then the tears start falling.

Without a word, Kaine wraps his arms around me, pulling me close as I collapse against him, my body racked with silent sobs.

"She wouldn't tap out. I stabbed her and accidentally hit an artery." My voice is hoarse. I can't stop shaking.

He holds me tighter, one hand stroking my hair. "It's okay. You're okay."

"I . . . I didn't mean to . . . I was just trying to stop her."

"It's okay," he repeats. "You did what you had to do to protect yourself."

His words offer little solace. The weight of my actions presses down on my chest until I can no longer breathe, gasping for air, and the guilt, the shame, only burns hotter when a door opens and a man steps out. It's Bryce's father.

God. Her *father.*

Fear flickers through me when our gazes lock. My hands are stained with his daughter's blood. I know he can see it.

To my utter disbelief, he doesn't condemn me with his eyes or his words. He simply nods as if to say *Good work* and then marches down the hall, right past the room where his daughter's bloody, motionless body lies.

I let out an unsteady exhalation, sagging against Kaine again. I feel hollow. Broken.

"You're okay." His fingers thread through my hair, soft and reassuring. "I promise."

"Sutler. Darlington."

Cross's sharp voice echoes in the hallway.

Kaine and I break apart. My legs feel weak as I turn to find Cross in the center of the corridor. Face expressionless, he gives me a once-over. He focuses on the blood, then glances at Kaine.

"You're dismissed, Sutler. Report to your new quarters."

Kaine seems reluctant to go, but when I give him a slight nod, he walks away, leaving me alone with Cross. My heartbeat is not at all steady.

When Cross speaks again, it's brusque, impassive. "You had no choice. She was going to kill you."

"Fuck you."

"She wouldn't have tapped out."

"Fuck you," I repeat, and swallow hard. Another onslaught of tears threatens, but I refuse to cry in front of him. "May I be dismissed?"

"Report to Medical first. Get that stitched up." He nods at my arm.

"It's already stopped bleeding," I mutter.

"Get it looked at," he says in a tone that invites no argument. "Take her to Medical."

I realize he's addressing someone behind me. I glance over my shoulder to see Tyler Struck approaching.

Despite my protests, she escorts me to the Medical building. Outside the door, she stops and touches my arm, her eyes flickering with sympathy. "She was a staple, Darlington. She wasn't going to tap."

"I know that," I say flatly. "But that doesn't make it any better. Did anyone else die today?"

She shakes her head. "Everyone tapped."

"Oh great. So I'm the only murderer in the bunch."

I stalk past her into the Med ward, where one of the nurses cleans up the wounds on my arm and neck, rubs a regen ointment over them, and sends me on my way without so much as a bandage.

In the barracks I make a beeline for the showers, despite the nurse ordering me not to get the ointment wet for at least an hour. I don't care. I need to wash the blood away. The shame. I strip off my clothes and burst into the nearest stall, cranking the faucet. I stand under the hot spray and watch the blood spiral down the drain in swirls of pinkish water.

Why didn't she tap out?

Why didn't she *fucking* tap out?

Why didn't you tap out? demands an internal voice, harsh and unforgiving.

The voice is right.

Why am I blaming the dead girl?

I did this. I chose to kill her. I could have said screw Elite and not continued the fight. I could have let Bryce have it. But I didn't. I'm just as bad as she is. Just as pathetic.

I lean against the tiled wall, naked, defeated. Then I open a path and reach out to Adrienne, getting right to the point once she links.

"I'm in Silver Elite."

"Excellent. We'll be in touch."

That's it.

Excellent. We'll be in touch.

A woman's life in exchange for two sentences, five words. Five. Words. And all I had to do was kill someone whose biggest crime was wanting to please her father. Yes, Bryce could be insufferable at times. Smug. An entitled brat. But she didn't deserve to die.

I turn off the water and get dressed in the locker area. There's a message on my source telling me to pack my gear and report to a building on the base.

In the bunks, I find Kaine waiting by my bed. His gaze softens at my approach. "You all right, cowgirl?"

"No. But I will be eventually."

He watches as I zip my duffel. "There's a truck outside to take us to the new quarters. I waited for you."

"Thanks."

After a beat of hesitation, he pulls me into his arms. There's no hesitation on my part—I press my cheek against his muscular chest and wrap my arms around his waist.

"I didn't want to kill her." My voice is muffled against his shirt.

"I know." He strokes the small of my back. "We do a lot of things we don't want to do."

"Do you know who else made it into Elite?"

"Ugh. Yeah." I lift my head in time to see him grimace. "Kess. Anson."

Of course.

"Jones. You and me, obviously. And the sixth slot went to a woman from Red Cell."

He releases me from his embrace. "Come on, let's go check out our new home."

———

Our soldiers' quarters are in a three-story building on the other side of the base. I'm on the first floor. Kaine is on the third. We say our goodbyes downstairs, and he promises he'll find me later in the mess hall. I tell him I'll probably skip dinner. Stabbing someone in the femoral artery and watching them bleed out in seconds really kills your appetite.

I examine my new quarters and like what I see. It's a suite with a bedroom, a tiny living area, and a private bathroom. The bed is a double, which is an upgrade from the bunks. The armchair in the living space looks cozy. And in the bedroom closet, I discover hangers of clothes. Not just uniforms, either, although there are several new iterations of those with my new Command ID, a sole star to indicate I'm no longer a recruit, but a soldier. But I also find some plain cotton dresses, sweaters, a pair of jeans. Two drawers at the bottom of the closet contain socks, bras, underwear, and sleepwear. I don't know who picked everything out, but I'm grateful for them as I change into loose pants and a tank top.

I've just finished unpacking the meager belongings in my duffel when there's a knock on the door.

I open it to find Cross at the threshold.

Without a word, I let him in.

"Are you going to tell me to fuck off again?" he asks.

I shake my head.

"Are you going to tell me you got me out of your system?"

I shake my head.

"Good."

He strides forward with purpose, his tall frame towering over me as he backs me toward the small desk in the living area. He lifts me onto it while his gaze travels over me like a warm caress, gliding down my body, focusing on the way my tank top clings to my braless breasts.

His long fingers skim the waistband of my pants, dipping beneath it to tease my skin.

He gives me a questioning look.

I nod.

Neither of us speaks as I lift my hips so he can slide my pants off. He drags them down my legs, along with my underwear, and tosses them aside. He places his palms on my thighs, watching my face. Then, with his eyes on mine, he spreads my legs open.

I draw a deep breath. Waiting to see what he'll do next.

His voice is rough as he says, "Are you still thinking about what happened?"

"Yes."

"I'll make you forget."

He sinks to his knees, which brings a weak smile to my lips. "I like seeing you kneel."

A wicked smile tugs on his lips. "This is the only context in which you'll ever see me doing it. So enjoy it while you can."

As I watch, he kisses a path along my inner thigh, getting closer and closer to where I need him most. When his mouth finds me, I arch my back in pleasure and tangle my fingers through his dark hair to keep him in place.

He chuckles, glancing up at me. "I'm not going anywhere, Dove. Nowhere else I want to be right now."

Every stroke of his tongue, every brush of his lips over my sensitive flesh, succeeds in erasing the visceral pain and guilt that followed me out of that tiny room.

He's relentless. Attentive. Thorough. As if his sole purpose in life is to make me feel good, to make me forget. And he succeeds. My entire world has been reduced to what he's doing to me with his tongue.

He moans in approval when he brings his finger to my opening and finds me slick for him. He slips the finger inside. Gentle. A slow glide.

I bite my lip to keep from crying out in bliss.

Mesmerizing blue eyes focus on my face as his finger moves inside me. His thumb teases the sensitive spot that's swollen and aching for him.

"I told you I wanted you to find a way to control yourself. Do you remember?"

I nod. His gaze is hypnotic.

He slips another finger inside and I whimper.

"I don't want that right now."

"You want me to lose control?" My voice comes out hoarse.

"No, not lose it. Cede control to me. Give me what I want. Can you do that?"

He lowers his head before I can respond, sliding his tongue over that aching bud.

I sag back on my elbows. My head bumps the wall, but I don't care. All I can do is rock my hips in time to the strokes of his tongue and fingers, my heels resting on his broad shoulders. The tension builds inside me. Pleasure dances through my muscles, weakening them, laboring my breathing.

"There you go," Cross coaxes, then holds me steady as I completely come apart.

My entire world shatters. Nothing exists but the release shuddering through me.

I'm still floating down from the high when he stands up, tugging on the hem of my tank top. He drops it to the floor and I'm naked for him now. Exposed. I reach for his shirt, helping him pull it off, my hands exploring his hard male flesh. Chiseled planes and sculpted abs. His muscles quiver as I tease my hand up his chest toward his face. My fingertips scrape the whiskers on his cheek, the dark stubble coating his jaw.

"Take off your pants," I whisper.

His gaze never leaves mine as he snaps open the button. Tugs on the zipper. I help him shove the waistband down and squeeze his muscular ass when it's exposed to my touch. He plants kisses along my jawline, down my neck, leaving a trail of fire in his wake.

When his tongue finds my nipple, I momentarily forget I'm supposed to be getting him naked. He sucks it into his mouth, and I release a throaty noise of approval. He's still teasing my nipples when I remember I want him inside me.

"*Pants,*" I growl.

Chuckling, he kicks his pants away, and his cock springs out, thick and hard. He's given me an orgasm, yet he hasn't even kissed me, and suddenly I'm desperate to feel his mouth on mine. I yank his head down and he gets the hint, capturing my lips with his. Then he gathers me in his arms, and I hook my legs around his waist as our mouths fuse. He walks the five short steps toward the bedroom and lowers me onto the mattress, curling his strong body over mine.

"I've been thinking about this for days," he mutters. "You're all I think about."

When I reach between us to grip him, heat flares in his eyes.

"I've been thinking about it, too," I admit.

I guide him inside me, and we both curse when he drives his hips forward. My legs wrap around him, deepening the contact.

I mumble a happy sound. "About this exact feeling."

He withdraws in a slow, tormenting glide, then pushes back in. "This feeling?"

"Yes."

I close my eyes, submitting to the sensation of him filling me, teasing me. When I open my eyes, he's watching me. I don't like it. It's too much. It's just too much. So I tangle my fingers in his hair and kiss him again, our tongues desperate, greedy.

The bed shakes as he fucks me. The pleasure gathers again, twisting into a tight knot. I love the heaviness of him, his weight on top of me, his ass beneath my heels as I dig them in, trying to get him as deep as possible.

He pushes forward again. He's determined to wring every ounce of pleasure from me. His lips find mine, and he's kissing me when another climax rushes through my body. I gasp through it, and he moves faster, his thrusts becoming erratic until finally he plunges deep, his face buried in my neck, groaning in release.

We lie there for a minute. When he rolls over and pulls me on top of him, I let him, even though I know I shouldn't. I should ask him to leave. I shouldn't be setting a precedent for holding each other after sex.

But I'm too winded to move. Too blissed out. And I like the feel of his palm stroking my back. The scrape of calluses against my shoulder blade. It's a little too addictive.

There are so many things I want to ask, but I can't let myself get to know him, so I stick to business.

"You let Anson into Elite. You realize he's a soulless psycho, right?"

Cross chuckles. "Well aware. But he moves like a shadow and kills with no remorse."

"Is that what you want him to do, kill for you without remorse?"

"Among other things. Everyone was chosen for their own strengths. What I think they'll bring to the unit."

I figured Elite was responsible for assassinations, but his confirmation makes me uneasy. I wonder how many people Cross has ordered to be killed. How many times *he* followed orders to do the General's bidding.

The reminder is all it takes for me to sit up and hop off the bed. As I scavenge the floor for my discarded clothing, I feel his eyes raking over my naked body.

"Are you going to tell me you got me out of your system again?" he asks, sounding amused.

"No." There's no point in lying. The attraction between us only grows stronger. "I'm going to want to see you naked again."

"That's progress."

"It's as far as it will go," I warn.

"You trust me with your body but nothing else."

"Correct."

He props up on one elbow and runs his hand through his hair. "It should go without saying, but . . ." His expression turns serious. "This stays between us, Darlington. I'm your CO. Nobody can know that I'm—"

"Servicing your subordinate?"

He snorts.

"Don't worry, Captain. Your secret is safe with me. Now . . ." I give him an expectant look.

That gets me another snort. "Got it. My services are no longer needed."

"Also correct."

Laughing, he gets to his feet and searches for his pants. I try not to notice the way his muscles ripple as he moves. So graceful. Like the sleek cats in the Blacklands. A brave one made it into the clearing once, and I remember shivering as I watched him move. Muscles undulating beneath sleek fur. Almost rhythmic. That cat was so beautiful and so deadly. Just like Cross.

"I'll leave you to it then," he says.

I'm almost disappointed, but as much as I'd like to stay in bed with him all night, I need to set boundaries, manage his expectations. I'm using him. He needs to know it.

I walk him to the door, where he suddenly grabs me and pushes me up against it. One hand grips my ass, bringing me tight to his body. The other cups my cheek as he kisses me. I'm gasping for air by the time he pulls his mouth away.

"I'm doing it your way for now, Dove. But only until I no longer feel like it."

He smiles as he releases me. Hands shaking, I open the door to let him out.

Cross steps into the hall just as Ivy walks up.

We all freeze. His expression shutters, shoulders straightening. After a long, uncomfortable moment, he nods at Ivy and strides off.

She stares at me, then scans her thumb on the keypad at the door across from mine.

I had no idea her quarters were right there.

Shit.

Face devoid of emotion, she walks through the door and shuts it with a firm click.

CHAPTER 38

"I'm going to my first briefing."

I check in with Declan the following day on my way to the war room. Apparently, Silver Elite has an entire block of rooms on the base.

"Report when you're done," Declan says. "We need to know what their current objectives are."

"Copy that."

The Elite war room is dimly lit, of course, since windows play no role on this base. A long table takes up most of the room, surrounded by black padded chairs, and there's a holoscreen against the wall. I was excited to finally see who else makes up this mysterious unit, so I can't hide my disappointment when I walk in to find only Ford, Struck, and the other five new additions.

I take a seat next to Kaine and scroll through the new source I received last night. Which was another disappointing discovery— I don't have the kind of clearance I thought I would. When I searched "Julian Ash" last night, I received the same ACCESS DENIED alert. When I searched for myself, however, I discovered that my name is no longer in the system. Same for Kaine and the other Elite recruits. We've been wiped from the database. It's like we don't exist anymore.

Cross enters a moment later. Rather than sit, he stands at the wall by the holoscreen.

Kess glances around, her black hair swinging around her chin. "Is this the whole unit?" She also seems confused.

"No. I run a team of sixteen," Cross tells her. "Our fellows are currently in the field."

When his eyes land on me, I remember him moving inside me and have to tear my gaze away. I swear I hear him chuckle, but when I look back, his face is stoic.

I keep waiting for someone to confront me about Cross. Lyddie, maybe. Or Kaine, although I don't know how much contact he has with Ivy now that we're not all training together.

So far, nobody's come out and asked if I'm sleeping with the captain of Silver Block. Which tells me either Ivy has kept her mouth shut about what she saw, or people know and for some reason have decided to mind their own business.

"This," Cross says, activating the holoscreen, "is Jasper Reed. You'll find dossiers for him on your sources."

The photograph on the holo shows a man in his late twenties. A very handsome man, I can't help but notice. Reed has dark hair and an endearing dimple in his chin.

Ara Zebb, the Red Cell recruit who also made the unit, starts skimming through the file on her source. "He runs the black market?"

Cross nods. "Reed is a smuggler with fingers in every criminal pie in the Point. The bulk of his operation involves drug running. Used to bring opiates in from Tierra Fe, but we crushed that avenue last year. Yet the drugs keep flowing. We suspect they've set up a lab somewhere in the wards."

He swipes the holo, and a map appears in the ether, a close-up of the wards east of Sanctum Point.

"Farren. Zebb," he says to the two women, "you're going with Tyler to do some digging. Try to figure out where those drugs are being produced."

He replaces the map with a photo of what appears to be crates of medical supplies.

"Reed's other favorite pastime is smuggling supplies out of the Point and trading with the Faithful."

"Trading what?" I ask. "What could the Faithful have that's of value to Reed? It's not like they're drowning in credits."

Ford fields that one. "Favors. Escape routes. Places to hide if his people need them."

"We dismantled a Faithful camp last month and found a trove of medical supplies that could've only come from Company hospitals," Cross explains. "And the General doesn't enjoy having his resources stolen from right under his nose."

"Why can't we just eliminate this Reed guy?" Anson asks, sporting a creepy grin that tells me he'd love nothing more than to kill Jasper Reed with his bare hands. "Cut off the head of the snake."

"Killing him might seem like the easy solution, but it's not the right one. He's the head of the snake, yes," Cross agrees, "but cutting off one head won't kill the beast. There are others waiting in the wings, ready to step up and take Reed's place."

Ara Zebb hesitantly speaks up. "But if we take out the head, won't it at least disrupt their operations?"

"Maybe temporarily. But sooner or later, someone else will fill the void. We need to dismantle Reed's operation piece by piece, from the ground up. Cut off their resources, disrupt their supply chains, take down their lieutenants." He shrugs. "The head can wait while we chop up the body."

"Darlington, Sutler, you're with me," Ford says, glancing in our direction. "We leave for Ward C in the morning. One of our informants says he might know where they're storing the med supplies."

Cross nods at Anson and Jones. "You two will be with me."

"Doing what?" asks Jones.

When Cross sends a quick glance my way, apprehension knots my stomach. I get the feeling I'm about to be tested.

Sure enough, he swipes his finger through the holo ether. The Jasper Reed intel disappears, replaced by a photograph of Hamlett.

"That's my village," I blurt out. "What does Silver Block want with Hamlett?"

"Z is the suspected location of an Uprising cell. We were already keeping an eye on the ward, but after we learned Julian Ash had surfaced in Hamlett, we redirected most of our surveillance there."

I try to maintain a neutral face, despite his gaze boring into me. "I'd like to be assigned to this op instead."

"No."

I can't stop the protest. "But it's my ward."

"Exactly. That's why it's a no. You and Sutler are going to C with Xavier." His hard tone brooks no argument.

"What are Anson and Noah going to be doing in Hamlett?" I push.

Cross folds his arms to his chest and gives everyone in the room a stern appraisal.

"Here's the deal. You guys might belong to the same unit, but this isn't a team effort. Everyone here is still on need-to-know. You don't concern yourselves with what your fellows are doing, keen? The specifics of their ops make no difference to you or your mission."

My stomach sinks like a stone when I realize he's really not going to tell me what he plans to do in Hamlett.

After the briefing ends, I linger in the war room, waiting for Ford and Struck to leave before I stomp over to Cross.

"It's my home," I snap at him. "I have friends there."

He lifts a brow. "If your friends aren't part of an Uprising cell, then they should have nothing to worry about."

"You're the one who said my uncle wasn't working for the Uprising anymore. You said he was dormant."

"This has nothing to do with your uncle. We've been watching Hamlett for six months."

Six months?

My mind starts racing. That's long before Jim was executed. Long before I killed a white coyote with a shot that caught the Command's attention . . . Suddenly it dawns on me. That's why Cross was there that night. He wasn't celebrating Liberty Day. He was on Elite business.

The knowledge that there'd been eyes on us for six months makes me sick to my stomach. Griff uses the tunnels to smuggle Mods out of the labor camps. Tana works at the inn and provides intel to the network. They're both in deep with the Uprising.

"Your helo leaves in an hour. You should go now."

I glare at him.

"What?" he says.

"I prefer you when you're making me come."

His lips twitch. "Dismissed, Darlington."

I'm turning to the door when someone raps on it. A man in his mid-twenties and bearing a strong resemblance to Cross enters the room.

Travis Redden. The colonel.

"Am I interrupting?" Travis asks.

He's not in uniform but wears a gray shirt and black trousers. His hair is a few shades lighter than Cross's, but his eyes are darker, an intense midnight blue. Although he's not as tall and muscular, he is just as handsome as his younger brother.

"Soldier, this is Colonel Redden," Cross tells me.

When I start to salute, Travis grins and says, "Don't bother. I'm not about the formalities." He studies me for a moment before addressing his brother. "New member of Elite?"

Cross nods. "We filled six slots from the summer session. Darlington is one of our best."

I remain on guard, scrutinizing Travis the way he did me. I remember Roe calling him practical, Cross saying he's driven. I note the sharp intelligence of his eyes. This is a man who takes everything in. Doesn't overlook a single detail.

"But not Roe," Travis murmurs with a knowing smirk.

"No. He'll find a good post in Silver Block."

That makes the colonel chuckle. "You're cold as ice, brother."

They seem unbothered that I'm standing there, but I still begin to edge away. "May I be dismissed, sir?" When Cross nods, I direct a polite smile at Travis. "Nice to meet you, Colonel."

"Likewise, soldier."

The first thing I do when I return to my quarters to pack is report to Declan.

"They've assigned me to a smuggler named Jasper Reed. I'm supposed to go to Ward C and track down where Reed stashes the stolen medical supplies he gives to the Faithful."

"Have fun. Reed is a pain in the ass."

"You guys don't like him, either?" Look at that, the Uprising and the Command have something in common.

"We would like nothing more than to tie him to a rocket ship and launch him into the sun. Or recruit him. But he's not amenable to the latter."

"Elite is also running another mission in Hamlett. You need to warn Griff and Tana."

"They're already aware."

As disconnected as I've been from Tana lately, I'm fairly certain my friend *isn't* aware of this new threat. Yes, she's noticed the increased soldier presence and senses she's being watched, but I don't think either she or Griff recognize the extent of the Command's efforts.

"This is more than extra surveillance. Cross has people—"

"Cross?"

"Captain Redden," I make the hasty correction. "He just assigned two Elites to join him on a mission there. He wouldn't give me the details."

"Do you know when it's happening?"

"No. I'm assuming sometime soon. Please, just tell Griff to be on guard. I'll warn Tana myself."

"No. You will not."

Indignation rises inside me. "She's my best friend."

"You no longer owe loyalty to anyone but the Uprising."

I bristle.

"You answer to Adrienne," Declan continues. "You answer to the network. Everything you learn in Elite is relayed to us, and if we decide the information needs to go elsewhere, then we will be the ones to provide it. You keep everything to yourself, understood?"

I bite my lip. "Understood."

But when he severs the link, I decide I don't understand. What would it hurt to warn Tana and Griff to be more careful? To alert them that Silver Block is running an op in Hamlett?

I'd never forgive myself if something happened to them and I could've prevented it.

It's not even a question in my mind as I open another path.

———

"This assignment blows," Kaine says a few days later.

I glance at him, grinning at his glum expression. We're in our lodgings in C, sharing a room with two single beds. We've been here for three days already, and I can't disagree with Kaine's assessment: This blows.

So far, Silver Elite is a massive letdown.

All we've done since we arrived in this ward is visit seedy establishments to dig for intel or wait around while Ford speaks to his various informants. Or rather, Xavier. We're allowed to call our former instructors by their first names now, which I'm still not used to.

I lean back on the headboard, scrolling through my source. "He's so attractive."

"Who?"

I touch the screen to project the image of Jasper Reed's rugged face.

"He's all right," Kaine says.

"But you're better, right?"

"Of course."

I'm reading through Reed's dossier. He's an interesting guy. Doesn't seem to have loyalty to anyone but the person who's paying him the most credits in the moment. There's nothing more dangerous than a person whose loyalties shift like the wind. It's also interesting that his network is smuggling supplies into the lawless lands. Most citizens don't care one way or the other whether the Faithful survive.

I flip through pictures of the Faithful camp that Silver Block destroyed six months ago. They'd been found living in a cave system in Ward G.

"Do you ever feel bad for them?" I can't stop the question from slipping out. "The Faithful?"

"What do you mean?"

I tap the screen to project the photograph. "These people . . . They just want to be left alone. Sometimes I wonder if it's fair for us to impose the General's idea of society on them."

Kaine frowns, considering my words. "That's not for us to decide. Our duty is to follow orders."

"They're just trying to live free."

"They're stealing from the Company."

I can't push him any further without casting suspicion on myself, so, with a shrug, I swipe at the air and the projection disappears.

Fortunately, Xavier's voice over my earpiece saves me from having to explain why I'm suddenly feeling sympathy for the Faithful.

"Intel came through," he says. "Let's go."

———

The hospital is a small nondescript building. A sad-looking place compared with the one in Sanctum Point with its gleaming windows and high-tech wings. The Point hospital has two regeneration chambers. Here, it's like they're using barbaric Old Era medicine. Offering rudimentary heart transplants when they could be growing a new heart in a lab. But to the Company, these people aren't worth it, I suppose. Save the perfect new hearts for the elites. Let these ones take their chances with a harvested organ that their bodies may or may not reject.

Xavier's informant said Reed is moving his contraband through this hospital with the help of workers who stash supplies in the basement. Kaine and I access that basement from one side of the building, while Xavier enters solo from the other. We creep down a long hallway, where the tubes of fluorescent lighting crackle too loud for my comfort. Sounds like they're going to burst into flames at any second and set the entire hospital on fire.

Our quiet footsteps echo off the concrete walls, muffled by the worn linoleum floor. The informant said there's nobody down here during the day, that the supplies are moved out at night, but I still tighten my grip on my weapon, my senses heightened as we approach a fork in the corridor. Kaine and I exchange a silent glance. Without a word, we split up, each taking a different path.

I move cautiously, scanning every shadow for any sign of movement. The smell of disinfectant hangs in the air.

Suddenly, a faint sound catches my attention—a low murmur emanating from behind a closed door up ahead.

I touch my ear. "Condor, I have signs of life."

There's a window in the door. I peek through it and frown. There are people inside.

"Broken Dove," Ford says in my ear, and I curse the stupid call sign for following me from training to real life. "Report."

"There's people here, LT."

"We're not looking for people. We're looking for supplies."

"I know, but . . . This is . . ."

I can't quite fathom what I'm seeing. These people . . . Some of them are strapped to hospital beds, restrained by leather cuffs around their wrists. They appear to be not in pain but in a state of agitation. A patient in a gray hospital gown wanders past the window.

Despite my better judgment, I pull on the door handle. It moves, the door inching open. I half expect an alarm to blare, but nothing happens.

I forget my objective. The mission. I enter the large room, which seems to be an entire ward of gray-gowned people. Around twenty of them. The ones walking around are completely oblivious to my presence. Across the room is a wall of cabinets and what appears to be a freezer. Through the glass I can make out tubes of blood and vials of clear liquid.

Drawing a breath, I approach the bed of a brunette with bony shoulders and long fingers she twists together in her lap. Her eyes widen at the sight of me, but I don't think she's truly seeing me. She senses my presence, though. Her dazed demeanor shifts into one of distress.

She starts speaking. No, mumbling. Repeating the same phrase.

"Shut up. Shut up. Shut up. Shut up. Shut *up*."

Whimpering, she covers her ears with her palms and rocks cross-legged on the bed.

My heart stops when I notice her arms. The veins.

She's Modified.

"Shut up. Shut up. Shut up shut up shut up *shut up shut up.*"

Her veins are glowing and moving, undulating as if thin eels are slithering beneath her skin, but it's not consistent. The silver flickers in and out. Stops and starts. Her body, her mind, is shorting out like an appliance.

The woman at the next bed is silently clawing at her own temples. Unlike her neighbor, she has a black band tattooed around her wrist to confirm she's a Mod. No red band, though.

My gaze travels down the row of beds, the ones that are occupied. I can't find a red band among any of the tattooed patients. These aren't slaves.

But they're Mods. Most of them, anyway. Not everyone's veins are rippling, but I can't be sure if that's because they're not using their gifts. The veins that are visible seem to be in a constant stop-and-start motion. Like flickering lights.

"Wren?" Kaine's puzzled voice comes from the door.

I ignore him. I approach the next bed, where a young man with dark hair lies flat, staring at the ceiling with vacant eyes. It's so eerie and unnerving that I hurry past him. The next patient is restrained. She's incoherent, rambling under her breath.

"In the garden with the windows, but I saw—when he saw—sometimes in the mountains—Henry, but then no one. When she died—and then together, water for Keren . . ."

Literal nonsense.

Each patient seems more dazed and disjointed than the last.

"Darlington." Ford's voice now.

I spin toward the doorway. "What is this?" I ask the lieutenant.

I'm surprised to see sadness flicker in his eyes.

"What *is* this?" I repeat. "Why are they here?"

"They're fragmented."

Understanding dawns. I remember sitting with Jim a long time ago in the Blacklands while he tried to explain what happens when a mind isn't strong enough to withstand our gifts. It didn't quite sink in back then, that opening paths and linking to other minds could overwhelm anyone, could break them. That some mind readers were unable to filter or link willingly, that their shields weren't good enough to dam the barrage of voices from foreign minds.

Now I'm surrounded by an entire room full of people with fragmented minds, and the fear that weakens my knees is impossible to ignore. What if *my* brain hadn't been strong enough? What if I'd ended up in a place like this?

Why are they in a place like this?

The question gives me pause. Yes. Why? Mental illness isn't well tolerated on the Continent; the General considers treating it a waste of resources. Schizophrenia is probably the closest thing to what the fragmented experience, yet it's rare to encounter a schizophrenic. If the General doesn't tolerate mental illness in Primes, why would he keep Mods, of all people, alive in a hospital ward?

"Why don't you just kill them?" I ask Xavier, but I'm able to answer my own question when my gaze returns to the wall across the room.

The freezer.

The blood vials.

A tsunami of horror slams into me. "They're *experimenting* on them?"

"I have no idea what goes on in here," he replies. "And it's none of my godfucking business. We're here on an op. Let's go, Darlington."

Reluctant, I turn away from the fragmented Mods. I've taken three steps to the door when one of the unrestrained patients snaps out her hand and grabs my arm. She starts screaming. A bloodcurdling, ear-splitting, never-ending scream. When I try to escape her grip, she starts clawing at me, jagged fingernails scratching down my arm, breaking the skin.

There's a commotion from the doorway as a trio of orderlies in white scramble inside to pull her off me.

"It's all right, Eleanor. It's fine. You're fine."

Two men lead her to a bed while the third orderly, a large woman with beefy shoulders, turns to glare at us.

"Get out of here!" she barks. "I don't care what block you're in. You don't belong here."

I suck in a breath, my heart in danger of bursting out of my chest, because no, I *don't* belong here. I don't. As I race to the door, I pray to a god I'm not allowed to believe in that this never happens to me. That there'll never come a day when I can't close a path or shut out the voices.

The words Jim spoke in the clearing that day travel through my mind. *Our gifts aren't always a gift, little bird. Sometimes they're a curse.*

————

We find the supply room. Xavier calls in a unit from Gold Block to dismantle it, cordon it off. After what I saw in the hospital basement, everything else seems pointless. I check in with Adrienne in plain sight of Xavier and Kaine as we drive to the airfield. I tell her about the fragmented ward, and while she sounds disgusted, she surprises me by not being at all surprised.

"I know."

"What do you mean, you know?"

"There are places like that all over the Continent. This isn't anything new. Not everyone can cope with the gifts we've been given."

"So that gives the General the right to experiment on them?"

"Of course not."

"I want to kill that man," I growl to Adrienne.

"Control yourself. You are not there to be the fire that burns down the world, Wren. You're just a piece of kindling."

Kaine glances at me as we strap into the helo. "You good, cowgirl?"

"I didn't enjoy that op," I say flatly.

"I don't think anyone did."

"On a related note," Adrienne is saying, "we do need you to keep an eye out when you're in the wards. Our investigation into Julian's execution has officially stalled."

"What's there to investigate? They fucking killed him. The end." I can't stop the bitterness from seeping out.

"We heard rumors there was an inciter in the crowd that day."

My lungs seize, making it impossible to draw oxygen into them.

"We've been trying to verify the claim, but it's basically one dead end after another. You were there that day—did you see it happen?"

"No. Like I told Tana, I noticed the firing squad was experiencing some weird moment of confusion, but it didn't look like someone was controlling them."

Somehow a sliver of oxygen makes its way in. My desperate inhalation sounds more like a wheeze, causing Kaine to reach over and take my hand.

"Darlington. Look. I know it was . . . well, sort of horrifying. But you need to put it out of your mind," he says in a gentle tone.

"I'll try," I say out loud.

Silently, I say, "If an inciter was there that day, all I can be certain of is that it wasn't me. If that's where this conversation is headed."

"No. We already know that."

They do?

"The network keeps records of all known inciters. Every operative is required to disclose their abilities and those of their family, especially if it's one of the rarer abilities. Julian reported your gifts when you manifested at age twelve."

I don't know how I manage to stay upright when there's a wave of emotion threatening to knock me to my knees.

Julian Ash.

Uncle Jim.

I don't know what I did to deserve that man, but it never fails to amaze me how much he'd looked out for me over the years. How far he'd gone to protect me. Even behind the scenes, the man was trying to keep me safe.

I've never missed anyone the way I miss him.

We're only a few minutes into takeoff when Xavier gets an alert. He touches his earpiece, then unbuckles himself and marches toward the cockpit.

"Change of plans," I hear him tell our pilot. "We're going to Z."

My spine snaps into a rigid line. "Z?" I echo when he retakes his seat.

"Cross requested backup." He smirks at me. "Looks like you're going home."

CHAPTER 39

The controller station in Hamlett is a modest brick compound about a mile from the town square. It houses Controller Fletcher's office, a small dormitory for visiting soldiers, a conference room, and a handful of cells and interrogation rooms. It's so strange to be back here, driving down the narrow roads where I used to ride my bike. The square looks tiny now. Maybe I've outgrown it. Which is ironic, because it's not like I've been exploring the great wide Continent all these months. I've been isolated on the base.

Yet Hamlett feels smaller now.

Insignificant.

Cross meets us outside the compound, but rather than provide a single detail, he and Xavier march away to talk between themselves. My anxiety is only heightened as I'm forced to stand there and wait, not knowing why we're here.

Despite my nerves, I can't help but notice how good he looks. Command fatigues and a black T-shirt cling to his tall frame, and the sweat glistening on his brow speaks of how hot it is tonight. Summer's over, yet Hamlett is always scorching well into the fall.

When the men return, Cross addresses me in a clipped tone. "How well do you know Griff Archer?"

The blood freezes in my veins. I consider how to best answer that, but I don't have much time to think it through.

"He owns the pub. And he's my best friend's father."

"Right. Your friend. Tanya, is it?"

"Tana." I grit my teeth. "What the hell is going on here? I thought you needed backup."

"We do. We'll need a team once we break Archer."

It feels like an icy explosion just blew into my chest. I take a steadying breath. My hands feel weak. "What do you mean, 'break' him?"

"We've been questioning him all day."

My gaze darts to the building. "Why?"

"Archer and his daughter tried to run. They managed to dodge our surveillance a few nights ago and somehow made it out of Z without detection. Last night they were stopped at a checkpoint in S, where Archer tried to mow down two Copper soldiers with his truck. We brought them both back to Z for questioning."

Guilt pulls at my insides. This is my fault. I'm the one who warned them about Silver Block being here. They must've made plans to escape right after I spoke to Tana.

My stomach churns, bile burning my throat. I thought I was helping her with the warning. And now . . .

I might actually throw up.

"We believe they got out using a tunnel."

It takes extreme effort not to react.

"We've been searching for it for weeks now, with no results. We even conducted several flybys with thermal imaging. Couldn't find a single heat signature belowground."

Yeah, because the entire tunnel is reinforced with steel. Thermal imaging can't see through metal.

I'm surprised, though, that Command Intelligence is unaware of a tunnel that was built by Primes. Granted, it was a hundred years ago. Records get lost. Maps get burned. Mods take advantage of ignorance.

I gulp through my queasiness. "Where is Tana?" I ask Cross.

"She's being held at the inn."

"Who's serving as sentry?"

"Booth."

Anson? No. No fucking way. I don't want that creep anywhere near my best friend.

Panic threatens to overwhelm me, but I take a breath and think through my options. I need to make contact with Tana. Right now.

But my attempt to link yields no response. She's being watched, then.

"Let's go inside," Cross says. "Tyler and Hadley should be finishing up with Archer."

My legs tremble with each step. I hope my attempt at masking my terror is working. I think it is, because nobody gives me a second look or asks if I'm all right. Although once inside the station, I receive a funny look from a young man who's vaguely familiar to me. It takes a moment to place him. He assists the controller.

"Wren!"

Speaking of the controller.

The big, bearded man lumbers into the lobby and surprises me by giving me a hug. Fletcher and I have never been close. I don't think we've ever shaken wrists, let alone hugged.

"We were worried about you," Fletcher says.

"'We'?"

"Everyone in the village. You never responded to my comms."

"I didn't receive anything from you."

I resist the urge to glare at Cross. Because if anyone from the outside world had tried to contact me through proper channels, then he's the reason I never got their messages.

"I've been training in the Program," I tell Fletcher.

"So I've been told." His wary eyes shift toward Cross. Fletcher clearly doesn't trust him. "Anyway, it's good to see you." He squeezes my shoulder. "I'm glad you're all right."

"Can we save this reunion for another time?" Nobody misses Xavier's sarcasm.

Leaving Fletcher and his people in our wake, Cross leads us to a small briefing room, where Tyler and Hadley fill him in.

"He still won't give up the location of the tunnel," Hadley reports.

I maintain a neutral face. I know exactly where the tunnel is. I used it to leave this very town when I went to rescue Jim. I could probably draw them a map of the entire system.

"He's not talking at all," Tyler says. "If he's a silverblood, he's not using his gifts. We made sure his arms aren't covered. Same for the girl."

I feel sick again. Tana is alone at the inn. With Anson watching over her with his creepy snake eyes. His revolting leer.

I reach out to her again, hoping maybe Anson stepped out to urinate, but her link remains closed.

"Let me talk to Griff," I blurt out, cutting Tyler off midsentence.

Cross arches a brow. "No."

"I've known him since I was eight years old. If he's going to talk to anyone, he'll talk to me," I insist. "I promise you, if there really is a tunnel, he'll tell me."

"Or," Cross counters, "we use the daughter as leverage to make him talk."

I glower with indignation. "You're not using my friend as leverage."

His expression sharpens like a knife's edge. "These people are part of an Uprising cell. These are not your friends."

"I get it. I understand what you're saying to me." I clench my teeth. "But I've known them almost my whole life, and if you're right and they are working for the enemy, I can get them to talk. If I promise Griff that Tana will be safe, he'll tell me whatever we want to know."

"Who says she's going to be safe?" Xavier drawls.

I level him with a deadly look. "You're not hurting her."

"It's not your call. They'll both be sent to the Tribunal for sentencing."

"*No*," I implore Cross. "Please, if I can get him to give up the location of the tunnel, can you promise me they won't face the squad?"

From across the room, Hadley speaks up in typical stern fashion. "Aiding the enemy is treason, Darlington. It's punishable by death."

"Sometimes people go to labor camps," I shoot back. "Sometimes they're more useful alive than dead. Like your mother."

His breath sucks in.

"Yeah, I heard all about your Aberrant mother," I say coolly, enjoying the way he blanches. Then I refocus my attention on Cross. "Why can't Tana and Griff be sentenced to labor?"

"Because we don't know the extent of their crimes yet."

Cross is visibly losing patience with me, but I give him one last push.

"If I get him to reveal where the tunnel is, will you spare their lives? Can you make that deal?"

He hesitates.

"Please."

After a beat, Cross caves. "Let me talk to the General."

———

The fact that Griff isn't restrained tells me he hasn't put up a fight. He wouldn't, though, not with his daughter's life at risk. He'd never take any chances with Tana's well-being or safety.

He's shirtless. They want to be able to see his arms if he uses an ability, which is a waste of time because Griff isn't Modified. But they don't know that.

He watches me approach the table, and although his square jaw remains tight, I notice his expression softening.

"It's good to see you, kid." Griff's familiar baritone voice makes my heart ache.

"Are you okay?" I ask him. "Did they hurt you?"

"No."

I don't care that our conversation is being recorded, that we're being watched. Touching the prisoner isn't a standard interrogation technique, but I still squeeze his hand as I sit in front of him.

"I just got here," I say. "They said Tana is at the inn. She's okay." I hope.

"Have you spoken to her?"

The question has a double meaning. When I shake my head, I know he understands that her link is closed. It's going to be impossible to have this conversation with everyone listening. There are too many things I want to say and can't.

"It's over," I tell Griff.

Surprise flickers in his eyes.

"Whatever you guys are doing here, it can't continue. We're going to find the tunnel."

I say "we." But he knows I mean *they,* or at least I pray he knows. I pray he trusts me enough to believe I would never betray our side.

"I got my captain to promise that if you give us the information we need, you and Tana won't be harmed."

His loud snort reverberates off the walls. "Yes, kid. I'm sure the General is going to let a couple of suspected network cell operatives waltz out of here."

"No. But his son is willing to deal."

His bushy eyebrows soar.

"Captain Redden," I clarify. "He's out there right now. And he gave me the authorization to offer you a deal. It's a real one. You know I would never screw you over."

I squeeze his hand again.

"It's not a trick. It's not a trap. I just stood out there fighting on your behalf. But if you don't help them—us," I hastily correct and hope nobody noticed the slipup, "they'll send both of you to the Tribunal. And you know the Tribunal's favorite sentence is the firing squad."

I see the pain in his eyes. He knows what his daughter is, and he knows what will happen if it's revealed that she's Modified.

"Labor, huh? You think I want my daughter slaving away in a salt mine for the rest of her life?"

"At least she'll have a life. Please, Griff. Cut a deal. Tell us how the Uprising operates here in Hamlett. In Z Ward. Give us the location of the tunnel they use to smuggle the Aberrant, and I promise you, your life and Tana's will be spared."

"Wren!"

Her voice slices into my head so abruptly that it catches me off guard.

For a second, I'm unable to hide my surprise. The last time someone linked without me explicitly allowing it was when Wolf thrust himself into my mind as a child.

"Are you okay?" Griff asks, frowning.

"I'm fine." I swallow the lump of fear in my throat. "Sorry, I was just thinking about Tana. I don't want anything to happen to her, Griff. And the only way it won't is if you talk to me."

"Wren! I need you."

CHAPTER 40

With telepathy, sometimes it's hard to interpret someone's exact emotions. Yes, you can pick up on tone depending on how hard you're concentrating, but you might lose nuance. What you hear doesn't always translate into what they're feeling.

There's nothing lost in translation right now.

Terror and despair.

That's what Tana is feeling.

It's impossible to concentrate on Griff, so I lean back in my chair, rubbing my temples as if I'm warding off a headache.

"What's going on?" I ask Tana. "Are you okay?"

"I need you. Where are you? I don't know what to do."

"I'm in Hamlett."

"You are?" Her relief hits me like a gust of wind. "Please come. I'm at the inn. You need to come as fast as you can."

I tamp down the rising panic. I don't know how I'm going to make that happen.

"Why don't I bring the captain in here and he can verify the deal?" I say to Griff, scraping my chair back. "And I'll grab us some coffee. I need the caffeine fix. My head feels like it's going to explode."

Griff is not a stupid man. He knows me well, and he understands what my pointed look means.

"You can trust Captain Redden. I promise you, the deal is real."

At least I hope it's real. Cross said he would spare their lives, and I have to believe he'll keep his word.

Griff nods. When our gazes lock, I hear his unspoken plea. He knows I'm going to Tana.

I step into the hall to find Cross frowning at me. "Why did you walk out? What the hell was that?"

"He needs to hear you confirm the deal," I lie. "I could see it on his face that he needed to hear it from an authority figure. He still views me as a kid. Probably thinks I don't have the power to grant deals."

It's a believable excuse, and Cross buys it.

"I'll talk to him," he says. "And those coffees sound pretty fucking good. Get me one, too."

"Wren! Please. Help."

"I'm trying. Tell me what happened."

"I need you. Room 4."

"I need some air first," I blurt out.

Cross's frown deepens.

"Only for a minute. I just . . . It was hard seeing him in there like that. I need a minute to regroup before I continue."

"Don't take too long."

"I'll be right back," I assure him.

I keep a measured stride until I round the corner. Then I bolt forward like my horse whenever she hears thunder, tearing for the exit.

Outside, the controller station is deserted. From here, it's about a mile to the town square and the inn. I could try to run, but I worry I'll get caught before I get there.

I can't risk taking any of the Command trucks, so I scan the area until I spot a dusty black motorcycle parked against a wall. The lock on the thumb pad isn't engaged.

With only the briefest of hesitations, I throw one leg over the bike.

I'll return it. I'm not stealing it. I just need to get to Tana.

"Tana, talk to me," I say as I speed away.

She doesn't answer, but our link remains open. I know she can hear me.

"I'm on my way."

"Please hurry." Her voice is a whisper. The anguish in it spreads through my mind like a pebble skimming the water, creating ripples.

I still have my earpiece in, but the feed stays silent. No Xavier or Hadley or Cross barking in my ear, ordering me to get my ass back to the compound. They haven't noticed I'm gone yet.

Within minutes, I'm at the inn, ditching the motorcycle in the square. There are no guards stationed outside. I walk inside and find the front desk empty. The place is too quiet, and that chills my blood.

I hurry up to the second floor. Room 4 is at the end of the long corridor. At the top of the staircase, I slow my pace, reverting to my training. I have no idea what I'm going to find in that room, and I don't want to burst in gun blazing.

Creeping along the carpeted hallway, I let Tana know I'm here.

"Almost at your door. Let me in."

I hear a rustling of sound. The knob begins to turn, the door opening a crack.

Big, terrified brown eyes meet my gaze. A second later, Tana releases a choked sob and pulls me into the room, locking the door behind us.

The sight that greets me freezes me in place.

There, sprawled on the bed in a pool of crimson, lies Anson.

Dead.

Completely, thoroughly dead. Lifeless eyes staring into nothingness.

My breath catches in my throat as I stumble backward. "Oh my God. Tana . . . What happened?"

Her hands are shaking uncontrollably as she hugs herself, rubbing her upper arms. "I . . . I didn't mean to . . . He . . . he attacked me."

I take a hesitant step forward, my gaze sliding between Tana and the body on the bed. His long hair is wet. Soaked in blood. The bullet hole isn't quite between his eyes. It's closer to his left one, toward his forehead. There are no splatters on the headboard, only the sheets, and the direction of the blood castoff is toward the foot of the bed, which tells me he was probably on top of her, facing the headboard. Looks like Tana rolled him over when she crawled out from under him.

His uniform pants are undone.

Her dress is torn.

Vomit bubbles in my throat, and my heart shatters into a million pieces as I grasp the gravity of the situation.

"I killed him." She's clearly in shock. She stares at me, unblinking, her cheeks stained with tears.

"Hey. Tana. Listen to me. It's okay. You're okay."

I pull her into a tight embrace, and the moment my arms wrap around her, she starts to shudder. Uncontrollably. Her breaths escape in unsteady wheezes.

"It's okay, sweetheart. It's going to be okay." The assurance feels hollow against the weight of the truth.

"I waited until he was . . . until he was . . . distracted. It was the only time he let down his guard . . ."

She's mumbling. Panting. Trembling in my arms, and the rage cracks through me like a whip.

I can scarcely breathe. I'm so angry. He put his hands on her. He . . .

I twist away from the sight of Anson. I knew he was dangerous from the moment our eyes locked on orientation day, and I'm glad he's dead. I just wish someone had killed him before he hurt my best friend.

"I grabbed his gun." Her tears soak into the front of my shirt. "I shot him in the face."

I stroke my hand through her dark hair. "It's okay. We're going to handle this."

How? my brain is screaming.

How the hell are we going to "handle" this? She killed a Silver Block soldier.

Pulling back, I cup her cheeks and wipe her tears with my thumbs. "Tana. I need you to listen to me right now, keen?"

She's not blinking again. She looks dazed.

"You didn't kill him."

"What?" Confusion etches into her face.

"You didn't kill him. *I* killed him. I walked in and found him on top of you. And I killed him. Okay?"

Her shiver fits return. "Wren, no. You'll get sent to the Tribunal."

"Not if I claim I was defending myself." I go to the closet, searching for something she can wear. I find a man's cardigan sweater and hand it to her. "Here. Put this on. You're shaking."

I don't know how I'm managing to keep my composure.

She dropped the gun on the floor after she shot Anson, and I bend down to pick it up. I walk around the bed toward Anson's right side. He was right-handed, I remember. I wrap his fingers around the weapon and curl his finger over the trigger. He died recently, so his fingers aren't stiff yet. I'm easily able to maneuver them.

I straighten up and unholster my own weapon. I don't have a silencer on it, and I pray that nobody hears what I'm about to do. If they do, we'll have to act even faster.

"Move over here." With a gentle touch, I nudge Tana toward the armchair in the corner. "Stay there for a second."

She gives a fearful look as she watches me raise my gun.

"What are you doing?"

"Setting the scene," I say, then fire one shot at the door.

The story unfolds in my head.

I left the station to check on Tana. I couldn't bear the idea of her being detained.

I walked into the room and found Anson assaulting his prisoner.

When he saw me, he fired. Thankfully, he missed and the bullet struck the door.

I fired back. Kill shot. I take self-defense very seriously.

Anyone who looks too hard at this scene will note that the blood spatter won't match my story, but the only good thing about the General's system of justice is that no one will dig too deeply into it. Suspected criminals aren't given the benefit of the doubt, and there's no time or resources for lengthy, drawn-out investigations.

All I need is for Cross to take my word for what happened.

As if on cue, his furious voice suddenly rumbles in my earpiece.

"Where the hell are you, Dove?"

I glance over at Tana. "Are you going to be able to follow my lead?"

Despite her tears and the wild shuddering of her body, she responds with a nod.

"Good." I tap my earpiece. "I'm at the inn. There was an incident."

"What incident?" Cross demands.

"I killed Anson."

———

Cross doesn't buy it.

I can tell he doesn't, as he surveys the scene. His blue eyes slide back and forth from me to Tana. Skeptical. Shrewd. But those eyes soften when he notices the state of her dress. Sighing, he turns toward the bed, assessing the blood on the sheets. The hole in Anson's head.

Xavier stalks in a moment later and curses loud enough to startle Tana, who's in the armchair hugging her chest.

"What the hell, Darlington?" Xavier demands.

"He shot at me," I reply, my voice cold. "I came to check on my friend and heard her screaming. I threw open the door, found Anson on her, and ordered him to stop. He twisted around and fired at me."

To drive that home, I point to the bullet embedded in the door behind us.

"I fired back," I finish.

Silence falls.

The two guys exchange a look. They focus on Anson's body, then Tana shivering in the chair.

I wrap a protective arm around her shoulders. "It's okay. You're safe now." My gaze seeks out Cross. "He attacked her. It was self-defense." I realize how that sounds and add, "I was defending myself after he fired at me."

He rubs his forehead. "Fucking hell."

"Captain?" Xavier's tone is wary.

Finally, Cross activates his earpiece. "Hadley, we need a sanitation squad at the inn."

I hear Hadley's response over the feed. "Copy that."

"Where's my father?" Tana asks. She's starting to look less dazed. More present.

"He's being transported as we speak," Cross says. He glances at me. "He gave up the location of the tunnel."

Fear fills Tana's eyes. "Transported where?"

"He's being taken to the mine in Ward D. He was sentenced to labor."

A strangled noise leaves her lips, and I give her shoulder a soft squeeze.

"You'll be going to X to serve your sentence," Cross tells her.

Her gaze flies to mine. "What is he talking about?"

"I'm so sorry," is all I can say, but with her cardigan on and her arms concealed, I'm able to express more than an apology. "It was the only way to save you from the firing squad. You guys were being charged with treason. I'll contact the Uprising as soon as I can and try to get you out."

She gapes at me. "I'm not going to a labor camp."

Cross shuts down her protests. "You have no choice."

Her focus remains on me. "Wren. You can't let them do this."

"You can't fucking let them take me away!"

"I don't have a choice, either. I fought to get you this deal."

"This is bigger than both of us, Tan. You know it is. I'll find a way to get you out. I promise."

"You . . ." Her breathing quickens as she stares at me in horror. Sheer betrayal.

For a moment, I'm afraid she's going to reveal what I am. That we're communicating telepathically.

Then her gaze shifts to Anson's body and she jerks as if she's received an electric shock. It's as if she suddenly remembers what happened, what he did to her, and the last shards of my heart crack off when I see all the light drain from her eyes. She's broken. Ravaged.

It's an expression I can't erase from my mind, staying with me long after Xavier escorts her to the door.

———

It's late when we return to base. I don't speak to anyone. I've tried to link with Tana a hundred times, but she's not letting me in. Either she doesn't want to speak to me, or she can't. I'm leaning toward the former.

I allowed them to take my best friend to a labor camp. I stood there and watched. Hell, I facilitated the deal.

Standing in front of my bathroom mirror, I stare at my reflection and say, "Who the fuck are you?"

The Wren from a couple of months ago would have fought to the death to save her friend.

But the entire time Tana had been pleading with me, I kept thinking about my parents and how much they sacrificed to help the Uprising. I worked my ass off to make it to Elite, and fighting for Tana would have meant destroying the solid cover I'd built, the trust I'd earned.

If anyone even trusts me after tonight. Covering up Anson's death was beyond reckless.

I stuck my neck out as far as I was able to for Griff and Tana. How will it serve the network if I'm at a labor camp, shoveling salt or coal alongside them? I can do more good here, undercover in Silver Elite.

And so I continue to stare in the mirror. Into the yellow-gold eyes and bronzed skin I'm told I inherited from my mother. The brown hair and cheekbones I got from my father. The longer I look, the more of a stranger the woman in the mirror becomes.

This woman, who convinced Griff to take a deal rather than fight, who let Tana be led away, who killed Bryce Granger.

I don't know who I am anymore.

Fighting back tears, I get in the shower and blast the temperature as hot as it will go. Until my skin is red and scorching. I imagine my identity being burned off, along with the shame of what I've done.

"Dove? What are you doing?"

Cross appears as a hazy silhouette in the curtain of steam. When he comes into focus, I make out his concerned expression.

I don't know how he got into my quarters. I don't question it. He's a better soldier than I'll ever be. As he peers at me through the foggy glass door, his features soften. Then he peels off his shirt and undoes his pants. Naked, he steps into the stall and comes up behind me. I don't turn to face him. I don't want to see his eyes. He folds his strong arms around me, forearms over my breasts, muscular chest pressed against my spine. I'm not sure how long we remain there, surrounded by steam and silence. He holds me, and I let him.

Until I remember who's bringing me comfort.

I turn off the water, then shove past him to get out of the shower. As I fumble for a towel, he watches me with an array of emotions. Worry remains one of them. Suspicion is more prevalent.

"You're going to have to stop lying to me one of these days."

"I didn't lie about anything. He hurt her." The words taste bitter on my tongue.

Cross steps onto the bath mat. With tenderness I haven't seen from him before, he pushes wet hair off my forehead, tucking it behind my ears. His thumb strokes my bottom lip.

"I know. I saw. But I also know that if I run ballistics on the bullet in Anson's head, it won't have come from your weapon. And if I test the bullet from the door, it won't be from his."

I raise a brow. "Do you really want to go through all that trouble? There's one less sadistic creep on the Continent, and my best friend gets to spend the rest of her life in a salt mine. What other resolution do you want?"

A muscle tics in his jaw.

"Do you want to keep talking about it? Dissecting it? Why are you here, Cross?"

"I came to make sure you're all right."

"Well, as you can see, I'm all right. So if you don't mind, I'd like to be alone now."

His cheeks hollow as he mutters, "Fine."

After he leaves, I curl up on my bed, tucking my knees to my chest. It occurs to me, as I lie there numb and exhausted, that there's nobody left.

Jim. Tana. Griff. Even Betima, the only person on this base I could have conceivably revealed myself to, is gone.

I am all out of allies.

I am all alone.

CHAPTER 41

I've barely heard from Tana in two months. It breaks my heart. I want to know how she's doing. I want to tell her I love her. I can't even imagine how she's processing what Anson did to her. Alone. With nobody to talk to about it.

I've checked in. She links every now and then, just to tell me she's okay, but I sense she's not.

As Elite, I have clearance now, and I've checked in with the guards at the salt camp. I can access the camp's daily logs. I can see when Tana scans into the mine, and when she scans out. They work twelve-hour days out there. I've seen photos of the women's quarters. They look comfortable. Everyone gets leisure time. The food seems decent.

But a gilded cage is still a cage.

And I put her there.

She should never forgive me.

"We need those coordinates, Wren."

Adrienne's voice is in my head. After Tana and Griff were detained, she usurped Declan as my silent contact. I suspect they don't trust me. They shouldn't. I'm the one who warned Tana that Silver Block was running ops in Hamlett. I'm the reason they tried to escape, and the reason they got caught.

All I can do now is focus on fulfilling my role here. Because if I don't get the Uprising the information they require, if I don't sabotage and sneak around and do whatever the hell they ask me to, then this was all for nothing.

I have to make it worth it.

But I miss my best friend. I miss Jim. Even Wolf is out of touch. It's not unusual—sometimes months elapse before we speak. Still, his silence is equally oppressive, only compounding the demoralizing sense that I'm completely alone.

Except I'm not alone.

I have Kaine. Lyddie.

Cross.

Yes, I definitely have Cross. Almost every night. He's an addiction I can't conquer, and these days, I don't want to conquer it. When I'm in bed with Cross, it's the only time I'm able to shut off my brain and just . . . feel.

I don't have to think about how I'm surrounded by Primes all day, every day.

I don't have to worry about how I'm going to maintain my cover.

I don't have to do anything but lose myself in sensation. And the fact that Cross has wisely learned not to make things more serious than they are is just a bonus. He doesn't try to offer me comfort anymore. He knows I won't accept it if he does.

Today I've been tasked with securing the coordinates for a black cache in the west. The infamous Silver Block black caches that my fake captors tried to real-beat out of me during the Program. I know those captors now. Mr. Muscles is Theo, who's serious and soft-spoken when he's not slapping people around. The bearded one is Ezra, a lieutenant who tells the most groan-inducing jokes.

One of the perks of being part of an elite unit is that we don't follow a set schedule. No sentry post or regular assignment where I must wake at a certain time, perform my duties, and return to my quarters.

I can sleep when I want. Go to the mess hall when I want.

Stroll into the war room when I want.

It's not locked. It never is. It's not as if they expect any of us to be actively plotting against each other.

The dim glow of the holoscreens illuminates the otherwise darkened room, casting ghostly shadows across the large table. Doing this in the dark would pretty much be advertising my clandestine motives, so I switch on the overhead lights, then approach one of the holos.

I can't be too obvious about it. Can't actively type in specific coordinates, or the search will be logged. What I can do is pull up a map of all active black caches and project it to Adrienne using my mind.

"Incoming," I tell her.

I focus on the caches for less than five seconds before she says, "Got it."

"You don't need more time?"

"Photographic memory. I can recite them back to you if it makes you feel better."

I ignore the condescending tone. "No need. Anything else?"

"No. We'll be in touch."

She cuts the link, and I flip to a different map. This time, I input a search command. An informant told us yesterday that she thinks Jasper Reed moves his drugs through the coast. I zoom in, scan the area, and click a random site. There. If anyone wants to know why this map was activated, that's the reason.

"I'm sorry, I didn't know anyone was in here."

I stiffen when Travis Redden enters the war room.

The resemblance really is remarkable. And unnerving. I know what it's like to have his brother's lips on mine, and now I'm staring at lips that are eerily similar.

His demeanor is harder, though. Not that Cross is soft; he's equally inflexible. But I pick up on a hint of cruelty in Travis. Same way I think Cross can kill without batting an eye, I think this man can, too—only Travis would enjoy it.

"Darlington, right?"

"Yes. Good evening, Colonel. If you're looking for the captain, I don't know where—"

"He's meeting me here," Travis interjects.

"Oh. All right." I close the map and move away from the holoscreen. "Sorry, I just needed to grab some grids. I have suspicions about—" I stop. "Right. I just realized I don't know what kind of clearance you have."

That makes him laugh. "The highest kind. But it's fine. I don't need the details of what you're working on." He leans his hip against the edge of the desk. "How are you enjoying your new unit?"

"It's great."

His gaze begins a slow perusal that makes me uncomfortable.

I force a smile. "Anyway, I should go."

Travis continues his visual exploration, focusing on the hair I wore loose today. "You're not his usual type."

"Whose?"

"My brother's."

Roe said the same thing. Although I suppose I understand where both are coming from, when Ivy is who Cross dated before. But Ivy is not as fragile as they clearly believe. She's in Silver Block, after all. She persevered through the Program for a second time and excelled in it.

"I don't know why you would bring that up," I lie. "I'm not with your brother."

Unless . . . did Cross say something to him?

Or maybe Ivy did? I swear to hell, if she reported seeing Cross in my quarters and this jeopardizes my place in Elite . . .

I'll be calling her out on the next pit night, that's for hellfucking sure.

"Captain Redden is my commanding officer," I add. "He doesn't fraternize with subordinates."

Travis chuckles again. "Right, my mistake," he says smoothly.

"Have a good night, Colonel."

I step into the hall at the same time Cross rounds the corner.

The way his eyes smolder at the sight of me, you'd think I was naked rather than in full uniform.

"I haven't seen you all day," he accuses.

"You've been off base all day," I remind him.

"You're right. It's my fault." He inches me toward the wall, his voice lowering to a wicked pitch. "I've been a bad boy."

The moment his body touches mine, my brain completely melts

and I forget my own name. I forget everything except for how much I want him. It happens all the time. It catches me off guard during the day. I'll be talking to Kaine, or reading a dossier on my source, and suddenly I'm thinking about Cross's intense gaze, his skillful touch. It's maddening, this relentless pull that seems to grow stronger with each passing day.

As much as I try to deny it, I can't ignore the truth any longer. I am hopelessly, helplessly infatuated with Cross Redden.

"Wait while I grab something and then we'll go to your quarters?" he says, his breath warm against my skin.

I nod toward the war room. "Your brother's waiting for you in there."

"Shit. Right. We're supposed to discuss security for the Silver Jubilee. Okay. I'll come by in an hour or so." He brings his mouth close to my ear. "Be waiting for me in bed."

I know I should say no. But we both know I'll be waiting.

————

I have breakfast with Lyddie in the mess hall the following week. It's good to see her, and I love watching her grow into her own. This morning, her hair is not in a braid but streaming around her shoulders. She's practically glowing as she tells me about the colonel she's working under in Intelligence. She loves her new assignment.

"I miss you so much," she says.

"I miss you, too," I answer, and I actually mean it.

We manage to catch a meal here and there on the base, but the Elite schedule is so inconsistent. I'll be assigned to a three-day op out of nowhere, or randomly spend an entire day undercover in the Point with Kaine, so it's difficult to make time for her sometimes.

Lyddie studies me over her coffee cup. "Kaine thinks you're seeing someone."

I tense slightly. "Why does he think that?"

"He says you look like you're getting laid." *She* looks like she's trying not to grin.

"Tell him to mind his business."

"So it's not true?" she pushes.

"Nope. My sex life is painfully nonexistent. How about you?"

Lyddie's cheeks turn pink. "Same."

Our meal is interrupted by a summons from Xavier. It comes via my source, since we only wear our earpieces out in the field.

War Room. Now.

"Shit. I have to go." I chug the rest of my coffee before getting to my feet.

"Everything okay?" she frets.

"Just a briefing."

"I'll comm you later. We need to plan our shopping trip for Jubilee dresses."

The last thing I'm thinking about is the General's ridiculous Silver Jubilee. Who wants to celebrate twenty-five years of that man's iron fist up our asses?

Everyone here.

Right.

Sometimes I forget that I'm surrounded by Primes who actually like and respect General Redden.

I reach the war room at the same time as Kaine. "How's Lyds?" he asks.

"Nosy." I give him a pointed look. "She says the two of you discuss my sex life."

"Obviously."

"Careful or I'll start gossiping to everyone about *your* sex life."

"You don't have that kind of time on your hands, cowgirl."

I'm not at all surprised to hear he hasn't been celibate during our time here. In an alternate reality, he and I would be finishing what we started the night Betima died. Multiple times a day, no doubt.

But in this reality, I've been caught under Cross Redden's spell. No matter how much I fight it, I can't stay away from him.

I suspect Kaine knows our moment has passed. He still flirts with me, but lately he seems far more concerned with serving in Silver Elite.

And, apparently, sleeping his way through the base.

"Ooh," I tease. "Anyone special?"

"They're all special to me." His lips twitch. "In the moment."

When we enter the war room, the tension is palpable. Cross stands at the front, his expression grim. He waits for us to take our seats, then fills everyone in.

"We just received reports that the Uprising bombed one of our weapons caches."

My pulse speeds up. Holy hellfuck, they did it. The network made use of the coordinates I gave them last week.

"The damage to the cache itself was minimal—the idiots missed."

Xavier chuckles from his chair.

"But they took out half the nearby forest," Cross says, projecting a live feed of the forest in question.

My jaw drops. It looks like the entire area was flattened into a pancake.

"Sugar bomb?" Ezra rubs his beard as he studies the screen.

"What the fuck is a sugar bomb?" Kaine asks with a grin.

Theo, whom I've discovered has a scientific mind, fields the question. "The enemy's been testing out a new incendiary device."

Cross flattens his lips. "Using tech they stole from us."

Theo nods. "We call it a sugar bomb, but I think the scientists in the capital gave it some other, more sophisticated-sounding name. Can't remember what. Anyway, our people developed a process to extract and refine natural sugars into a compound that releases immense amounts of stored energy upon detonation. When this shit is ignited, the reaction generates a blast wave comparable to the atomic bombs they used in the Last War. Not in scale, but intensity."

"Is there radiation?" I ask.

"Nope."

"The bomb didn't hit our cache, though," Tyler prompts, glancing at Cross.

"Correct."

Ford gives a sardonic laugh. "Guess their hotshot pilot must be losing his touch."

Kaine leans back in his chair. "I bet it was some rookie. From what I've heard, the famous one never misses."

"He missed this morning," Cross says with a shrug. "And it's clear they're escalating their efforts. Picking more high-level targets. We need to figure out how they found that cache."

I hope nobody can see through my neutral expression. Beneath it, I'm fighting my excitement. The knowledge that I played a part in the bombing, that I'm the reason we're all sitting in this war room right now, makes my heart beat a little bit faster.

There's something incredibly thrilling about the notion that I helped create chaos.

———

Two days later, I run into Ellis outside the mess hall. The presence of a Mod on the Command base is never a good omen, but there's something doubly unsettling about Ellis. I still remember the spooky sensation of my bones literally knitting back together because of this man.

No human should have that much power.

Not that my power is any less dangerous. The ability to incite is far more destructive. Ellis heals, making things better.

I break them.

He nods at me as we pass each other in the corridor. I force a polite smile, then keep walking.

I raise my coffee to my lips, savoring the rich flavor. Every time I grab a cup from the mess hall, I refuse to let a drop go to waste. The stuff here on the base uses real coffee beans from Tierra Fe, the one export I hope never runs out, which is a valid fear given how it's no secret the trade treaty between the Continent and our southern neighbors has been on shaky ground for years.

At least it prevented a war, though. When those first Mods started coming into existence in the years after the Last War, Tierra Fe almost waged another one on us. They thought we were demons from hell, and a religious war nearly broke out among the remaining continents. It was the Continent's ruler at the time who managed to thwart it. A Prime who assured Tierra Fe's leadership that the Aberrant would be contained.

And contain them he did.

The thought of those early Aberrant asylums reminds me of what I saw in that Ward C hospital. A roomful of people with fragmented minds.

Sadness lodges in my throat. It's devastating to me that they're trapped there. And they have no idea, their minds too broken to grasp what's happening to them. But perhaps that's better. Maybe oblivion truly is the more blissful state of being. Those fragmented people have no idea they're trapped, but people like Tana, like Morlee Hadley, who are working at a labor camp—they *know* they're prisoners.

Thinking of Tana brings a stab of pain to my chest. Our telepathic conversations are few and far between these days. She won't admit it, but she blames me for where she is.

An alert comes through on my source, drawing me from my dismal thoughts. I stop walking to pull it out of my pocket.

Report to Medical

Instantly, my hackles are raised. I'm in perfect health. Although I did hit my head while sparring with Kaine in the gym the other night. For fun. Truth is, Silver Elite is not as exciting as it's been made out to be. It involves a lot of waiting around. A lot of surveillance. I'd kill for some action right now. I can't even remember the last time I got to shoot my rifle.

Wariness lines my steps as I make my way to the Medical building. I reach it at the same time Kaine emerges from the opposite hallway.

He grins at me. "You were summoned, too?"

"Yep."

Turns out we all were. All the Elite members who are currently on the base.

Kess walks in alone. She's cut her hair since the last time I saw her. Given herself bangs. It's a severe look but suits her perfectly. Since Anson's death, she's lost her biggest ally, and she's been keeping to herself during briefings.

Ara Zebb and Noah Jones arrive together, nodding in greeting.

Several soldiers I don't know too well yet linger at the door. Theo is among them, his huge biceps flexing as he runs a hand over his buzzed scalp.

Cross enters with Xavier and Tyler. My heart rate kicks up a notch when he comes to stand right beside me. But then I notice Ellis walking in, and my pulse races for another reason.

"Let's get started," Cross says without preamble. "Theo, you're up."

"What is this?" I ask him.

"Mandatory wellness checks."

Trying not to frown, I watch Theo stride toward one of the narrow hospital beds. He strips off his shirt but doesn't stop there. The pants come off, too. In nothing but boxer shorts, he sits on the bed as Ellis approaches him.

Alarm ignites inside me. "Shouldn't they be doing this in a private examination room or something?"

Cross shrugs. "Not necessary. Only takes a couple of minutes. It's not like he's performing surgery."

I stand in the medical bay, my anxiety growing with each passing second as I watch Ellis attend to Theo. Everyone else keeps their distance, giving Theo his privacy, but I can't help listening in on his "wellness check."

Ellis runs his fingers over Theo's left arm. He focuses on a jagged cut on the forearm.

"How did this happen?" I hear Ellis murmur.

"Nail ripped through the skin when we were hopping a fence in the Point."

"This is infected. You didn't put any regen ointment on it?"

Theo's expression turns sheepish. "Nah, I did. But I kept getting it wet."

"Don't worry. I'll patch you right up."

I give Cross a sidelong look. "Isn't this a waste of his skills?"

"No. We need all our soldiers in tip-top shape."

"We already have regen balms and lasers to heal most things," I point out.

"This is faster," Xavier cracks.

He's not wrong. Even I can't hide my wonder as the nasty red gash on Theo's arm literally disappears in front of our eyes. The skin changes. Swells. The puckered edges smooth out as Ellis runs his palm over them, a furrow of concentration in his brow. When he lifts his hand, it's as if the cut was never there. Smooth, dark skin is all that's left behind.

"I mean, that's impressive," Kaine remarks.

Kess is up next. I'd prefer nobody healed her ever, so I turn my gaze away from her session.

I'm intensely aware of Cross's presence. He doesn't say a word, but I feel his eyes on me. The heat.

"Stop," I warn, using a soft voice only he can hear.

"Stop what?" he murmurs back. "I'm not doing anything."

"You're thinking. And I always know what you're thinking."

"I'm always thinking about getting you into bed."

"Exactly."

The charged moment dissolves into another wave of anxiety when Kess is dismissed and Ellis says, "Who's next?"

"Might as well get this shit over with," Xavier says, peeling off his shirt on his way to the bed.

When he drops his pants, I don't miss the way Tyler's eyes flicker with approval. I can't blame her for enjoying the view. Ford's body is nice to look at.

"Are you having any pain here?" I hear Ellis inquire a few moments later. His hands are on Xavier's abdomen. "Something feels off."

Xavier winces. "Yeah. It's been feeling tender lately. I think it's still sore from last weekend's pit night."

"No. I suspect you have a kidney stone forming."

"How the hell can you tell that without some sort of ultrasound?"

"I've done this enough times to know. Let's take care of this, keen?" Ellis presses his palms against Ford's tanned flesh, concentration once again creasing his face.

By the time my name is called, the knot of dread in my stomach is coiled around every inch of intestine.

"Is this really necessary?" I ask Cross in a last-ditch effort. "I'm not injured. Not even a scratch on me."

"Sutler slammed your head against the floor last night."

"Sorry about that," Kaine calls out. He's standing nearby with Ara and Jones now.

"My head is fine," I insist.

"I'm not sending you into the field concussed, so just let him do his job, Darlington. Stop being so difficult all the time."

Xavier snickers again.

Gritting my teeth, I join Ellis at the bed. I've gotten used to the complete lack of modesty on this base, so I don't even hesitate before removing my shirt. My pants, on the other hand . . .

My fingers tremble as I unsnap the button, and a wave of self-consciousness washes over me when my thighs are revealed to the room. Not everyone has seen my burns.

"Your head, you say?" Ellis prompts when I sit down.

"I don't have a concussion."

That doesn't stop him from cupping the back of my skull and conducting his own investigation. The warmth of his touch seeps into my head, and I didn't even realize I had a headache until suddenly it's gone.

Well, shit. I can see why the General keeps Mods like Ellis alive. We can be very useful assets to him, especially in the military.

With my head taken care of, Ellis proceeds to run his hands over my body.

I hear a low noise from Cross's vicinity. Oh, he doesn't like Ellis touching me? Too bad. He's the one who facilitated this.

When the healer's gaze reaches the ugly puckered scars marring my thigh, I shift in discomfort. I feel more exposed than ever under his probing eyes.

"This is very old burn tissue," he remarks.

I nod. "From childhood."

He doesn't touch the scars. Instead, he tips his head and says, "I can get rid of all this scarring right now if you'd like."

CHAPTER 42

Fear explodes inside me.

"It won't take long at all," Ellis assures me while my heart careens inside my chest like a runaway horse. Thundering off a cliff of panic. "If you just want to lie back—"

"No!"

I don't mean to raise my voice. It causes everyone to swivel their heads toward me. No one was paying attention before, but now all eyes are on me, and I curse myself for losing my cool.

I can't let him heal me.

There is no fucking way I can let him heal me.

I swallow hard, my mind searching for a way to deflect his attention without raising suspicion. I know exactly what lies beneath all this scar tissue. A bloodmark that will expose me as their enemy.

Or at least the mark *used* to be there. I have no way of knowing whether it was fully burned off, or if it's lying dormant beneath layers of skin like that famous underwater volcano that, according to the history books, swallowed half of the Lost Continents in less than an hour. I know of one Mod who tried cutting their bloodmark off and it turned out to be so many layers of skin deep that it left a hole in their hand.

Either way, I can't take the chance that it's still there. It exposes me not just as a Mod, but also as one of the most powerful Mods in existence. Uncle Jim went to great lengths to erase it.

And now this nosy asshole is about to undo all that hard, painful work in a heartbeat.

"No," I warn when Ellis starts to place his hands on me. I shrug them off.

His eyebrows arch in surprise. "It must be painful."

"It's not."

I'm not even lying. Yes, my thigh aches on rainy days, which I'll never understand. Sure, there's discomfort when the skin is stretched taut, and fine, sometimes the nerves in there forget they were incinerated and I'll feel a phantom shock of pain if I move my leg wrong. But I can live with it. The pain has never been bad enough that I can't ignore it.

I grab at my clothes. My hands are shaking. I feel the weight of Ellis's gaze and it makes my skin prickle.

"If you don't want me touching you so close to an intimate place, we could bring Soldier Struck over here. She can make sure nothing untoward happens."

"That's not the reason I don't want it. I don't mind the scars, okay? Go treat somebody else."

"What's going on here?" Cross strides over.

"He wants to heal my burns," I snap.

"Okay . . . Is there a reason you're resisting?"

"Yes. I don't want them removed."

Cross searches my face. "Darlington. Not sure I see the issue here."

Panic claws at the edges of my consciousness as I scramble for an excuse, any excuse, to justify my refusal.

"With all due respect, I'd prefer not to," I finally say, my voice wavering despite my best efforts to control it. My throat is so tight I can barely swallow around it. "I'm not going to pretend I didn't have an accident as a kid."

"This isn't about pretending. It's about healing you," Ellis says.

"No, it's about erasing a part of myself."

My brain finally sees it. The way out. And my voice stops shaking. Growing steady.

"I know they're ugly, but they're part of me now. They remind me of where I've been, what I've endured. All these scars, and not just the burns, are memories." I point out the faint white scar on the left side of my collarbone. "Like this one. I got it when this horrible kid, Oden, pushed me into a thornbush. A thorn ripped right through my shirt and tore a chunk of flesh when I was trying to crawl out. Later, when I was in upper school, Oden asked to take me on a date, and for a moment I forgot about how nasty he was in lower school. And then I noticed this scar in the mirror one day and it reminded me I couldn't trust that asshole."

The thornbush story is true. Everything else is horseshit. I didn't need an old fading scar to tell me to reject Oden. But the story sounds good.

I stare down at my thigh, where the burn tissue crisscrosses the skin like a map of my past.

"These are part of me," I repeat. "I would feel weird without them. So please, keep your hands off me."

I hold my breath, willing them to see my sincerity, to take it for conviction rather than desperation.

Ellis nods. "As you wish, soldier," he says, and relief floods my body when he moves on to treat the next soldier.

———

Later that night, Cross knocks on my door. Tonight is a pit night, but after fighting to save the scars Uncle Jim had inflicted on me, I felt oddly emotional, so I decided to stay in. I spent most of the night lost in memories. Those three years we spent in the darkness. The twelve years on the ranch. I miss him. So damn much.

Cross walks into my quarters, dark hair rumpled, a bottle of vodka cider in his hand. He's a little unsteady on his feet.

"Are you drunk?" I ask in amusement.

"No, but I feel good."

"So that's a yes."

He laughs. I enjoy that sound far too much.

"I've been thinking about something all day," he says, setting the bottle on my desk. "Since the wellness checks."

The next thing I know, he's pulling off his white T-shirt. He tosses it on the small armchair where I like to curl up and read at night.

"Is there a reason you need to tell me your thoughts while shirtless?"

He grins, that dimple digging a deep hole in his cheek. He's so sexy when he smiles. It makes him look so much younger. His usual expression—mocking and apathetic—lends him an air of maturity, but then he smiles at me, and I remember that he's twenty-two.

"Give me your hand," he says.

I play along and place my hand in his. It looks tiny in his palm, with his long fingers stroking my shorter ones. He presses my palm over his right pec and moves it back and forth.

"Am I supposed to be feeling anything?"

"Two years ago, there was a scar there. The size of a bottle cap." He snickers. "Looked like I had two nipples."

I can't help but smile. "You asked Ellis to make it go away?"

"Yes."

"How'd you get the scar?"

"My brother shot me with an arrow."

My jaw drops. "What? Which brother?"

"Which one do you think?"

"You're right, stupid question. Obviously it was Roe. How did it happen?"

"Hunting trip a couple of years ago. I was twenty, he was sixteen. The General wanted us to have some brother bonding time. I guess Roe complained that I never spent time with him. So we went into the woods with a couple of crossbows, split up to track a deer, and what do you know? Oops. He mistook me for a white coyote. Accidentally shot my ass."

"Accidentally."

"So he claims. With Roe, it could really go either way. I don't think he hates me enough to kill me, but . . ."

"He's jealous of you."

"Always has been. My father . . . He worships my mother in a way that he never, ever did with Roe's. He took care of her when she got pregnant, but he never gave a shit. There's only one woman Merrick Redden will ever love. And that's Vinessa."

It's the first time I've heard Cross say his mother's name.

"That's such a pretty name." I hesitate. "How come she doesn't go out in public?"

"He doesn't like to expose her to that. He never did with us, either."

I nod. The General always delivers his broadcasts alone. I don't think I've even seen photos of him with his family at celebrations. I saw Vinessa Redden standing with him on the balcony of the Capitol once for Liberty Day fireworks, but other than that, the General keeps his family out of sight.

"He doesn't take chances. He's scared of assassination attempts. But I digress."

"Right. Your psycho brother shot you in the woods."

Cross snickers. "He did. And I always had this scar as a reminder I couldn't entirely trust my brother. Either one of them."

"Travis shot you somewhere else?"

He smiles faintly. "Something like that. Anyway, after the scar was gone and I wasn't seeing it in the mirror every morning, I forgot about it."

"The fact that he shot another recruit in cold blood wasn't a good enough reminder?"

"No, and stop being a smart-ass."

"Sorry."

"All I'm saying is, you got me thinking earlier. About how we can't erase our scars because we need them to remember."

I realize I'm still touching his bare chest and can't help but stroke his heavy pecs. He makes a sound of contentment.

"If you keep touching me . . ." he warns.

"What?" I say with a taunting smile. "What are you going to do?"

His eyes smolder. "I wasn't done talking."

"Oh, now you're Mr. Chatty?"

"I guess you bring out that side in me."

He captures my hand beneath his. Then, keeping it pressed to his chest, he slides it to his other pec, directly over his heart. I feel it hammering against my palm.

"They're not ugly," he says. "You said earlier that you know the scars are ugly, but they're not."

He gently pushes me toward the bedroom. The backs of my knees bump into the bed. I sink down onto the edge, and suddenly Cross is on his knees in front of me, pulling at my loose linen pants.

He licks his lips when my bare legs are revealed, but his eyes focus on my thigh. The puckered skin, the pink ridges.

"They're not ugly." His fingers skim over the burn tissue, tracing the textured ridges.

A wave of insecurity washes over me. "Got it," I say, trying to shift away from his touch. "You don't think they're ugly."

"I think they're beautiful."

"Now you're messing with me."

"No." He runs his palm over the scarred expanse. "I don't care if you got this from a pot of boiling water or an enemy attack in the Last War. It's still a battle wound. A testament to how strong you are. It's goddamn beautiful."

My throat is dry now. And my heart stutters when he kisses the scar tissue.

It's so intimate that it triggers a pang of discomfort, so I try to lighten the mood by saying, "Just so you know, there's zero sensation there."

Chuckling, he rests his other hand on my other thigh. The one unmarked by burns.

"How about over here? No sensation?"

"All the sensation," I whisper, falling back on my elbows as he glides his hand between the juncture of my thighs.

His mouth is still on my burn when his finger slips inside me. I cry out from the pleasure that rocks my body.

"Goddamn beautiful," he repeats, and then kisses his way to where I want him most.

———

He stays the night. It's a rare occurrence. But he's in my bed when I wake up, lying on his side, his arm crooked under his head. My gaze fixes on his tattoos. I've been up close and personal with them plenty of times since Cross and I started . . . enjoying each other. But my resolve to keep an emotional distance means refraining from digging deeper. It means I can't ask why he chose wings and fire, or what those mystifying lines of script signify.

Memories of eternal snow.

When the wind turns against you.

A single second.

I'm an obnoxiously curious person, so the fact that I can't make sense of those cryptic words eats at my brain like a worm in an apple.

What does it mean, damn it?

When I shift on the mattress, his eyes slit open.

"Did I wake you?" I murmur.

"No, I wasn't asleep."

I reach out and rub my fingertips over the stubble on his face. "You look messy in the morning."

His lips quirk. "Yeah, I need a shave and a coffee."

"You look tired. Did you have a bad sleep?"

"No. But I didn't sleep much."

"What kept you up?"

Rather than answer, he searches my face, those blue eyes flickering with an emotion I can't read. "We'll never fully trust each other, will we?"

The question takes me by surprise.

"Where is this coming from?"

"I don't know. Just a thought I had during the night. Whether it's possible to trust someone completely."

"Cross. You're too smart to ask a question like that, when we both know the answer is no, you can't."

"I know." He rolls onto his back, sighing. "But man, imagine how fucking nice that would be."

It would be more than nice. Trusting someone with my entire being. Ripping my chest open and letting them see inside. All the dark, ugly, twisted parts. All my secrets and fears and crippling insecurities. Showing them every part of me without fear of judgment or betrayal.

But the world doesn't allow for such luxuries.

"You can trust me," I tell him, nestling at his side. "Mostly."

He snorts. "Mostly."

"Uh-huh. You can mostly trust me." I run my hand along the warm, sculpted flesh of his chest and enjoy the way he shivers. "You can trust me not to lie to you. Sometimes."

"I'm honored." His laughter is choked.

My fingers dance down his body, teasing his abs, following the tantalizing line of hair that arrows southward. "You can trust me to make you feel good."

"Is that right?"

"Uh-huh."

My mouth follows the path of my fingers, until I find him, hot and hard for me. I wrap my lips around him and am rewarded with a low moan.

In the back of my mind, I'm unable to shake the nagging feeling that I'm nearing a point of no return with Cross. That soon it will be too late to turn back, and this warm bubble that surrounds me when I'm with him will burst and destroy everything around me.

But for now, I push aside my doubts, choosing instead to focus on the fragile illusion of happiness.

CHAPTER 43

"Is this a date?" The question pops out of my mouth before I can stop it. For a second, I hope he didn't hear me over the sound of the rotors and rush of the wind at the open sides of the helicopter. But then he chuckles, and embarrassment warms my cheeks.

Cross glances over at me. "No."

"Then why am I wearing a dress?"

"Did I ask you to wear a dress?"

I falter as I realize that no, actually, he didn't. All he'd said was, *We're going off base. You don't have to wear your uniform.*

I smother a groan, but it slips out anyway. "Hellfucker. I made it into a date."

"It's okay, Dove. You wouldn't be the first."

He pats my arm in reassurance, and I glare at him.

My stomach suddenly flips as the helo banks hard to the left before straightening out. The late-afternoon sun is creeping toward the horizon line, bathing it in a haze of pinks and oranges. It's beautiful. We're flying somewhere over Ward S, and my head instinctively turns toward the west. My throat tightens with longing. For my ranch. My horse.

"You miss it," Cross says, as if reading my mind.

"Yes." Then I tear my gaze away.

I don't know where he's taking me, but I'm not complaining because it's nice to get off the base for something other than a mission. It's also nice when he reaches over and covers my hand with his. The pads of his fingers are rough as they stroke my knuckles.

I tip my head toward him. "What are you doing?"

"Touching your hand . . . Is that allowed?"

"I suppose."

He seems to be fighting a smile as he turns his gaze toward the open door. Meanwhile, my heart is doing ridiculous things in my chest. Somersaults. Flips. An asinine dance.

I stare at his chiseled profile and bite my lip. There are so many things I want to say to him, but I force myself to stick to the facts.

You're my enemy.

Your father hates me.

You would kill me if you knew who I was.

We could never have a future.

We will never be together.

I slide my hand out from under his and fold both of mine in my lap. I refuse to check what his expression is.

A vehicle waits for us on the tarmac after we land. It's got an open top, and once we're on the road, the wind whips through my hair, sending it blowing behind me. I slip the elastic off my wrist so I can tie my hair back, but Cross says, "No. Leave it down."

And for some reason, I do.

I wonder if this is what normal people feel like. The ones who aren't always peering over their shoulders, the ones who are happy with their lives, their job assignments, their quarters. The ones who have willingly submitted to the General's way of life. Accepted every part of it—the checkpoints, the broadcasts, the rules. They're all in for the greater good, and by surrendering to it, they take drives like this out in the country and allow themselves to enjoy it.

Cross parks in a wooded clearing and announces we need to walk the rest of the way, but when I ask where we're going, he refuses to share. Just says to trust him and it'll be worth it.

Trust.

Such a big word to be throwing around. Our talk in bed last week about it still lingers in my mind. On some level, I do trust him. Maybe not with my secrets, but I certainly trust him with my body. I trust that he would protect me in the field the way he would any other Elite operative.

Considering his last name is Redden, that's a lot more trust than I ever believed myself capable of giving to him.

I'm wearing sandals with my dress, not exactly hiking shoes, so I only make it about ten minutes before I'm grumbling with irritation and cursing every time a twig stabs me in the toe.

Cross stops walking and grins. "Come here."

He gestures to his back, and the next thing I know, I've got my legs wrapped around his waist, my arms looped around his shoulders, and we're laughing as he carries me through the woods. It's the youngest I've felt my entire life. Even as a child, I felt like an adult. I hate that Cross Redden, of all people, brings out this side of me.

"I could get used to this," I tease in his ear. "You carrying me around."

"Don't tell anyone. It will ruin my manly reputation."

"Nah, it'll just make the women swoon harder."

"Probably," he says arrogantly, and I punch his shoulder. "All right. I'm going to need you to walk the rest of the way. Think you can manage?"

"I'll do my best."

We trek through the trees and brush until we reach a rocky cliff, looming above us. Holes and cracks in the rock make for great footholds, but there's no way I'm climbing this.

"I can't scale that in these shoes."

"Don't worry. We're not going up." Cross points to the ground. "We're going down."

That's when I see the hole near the base of the cliff.

I glare at him. "Did you bring me here to kill me?"

He snickers. "No. There are a lot easier ways to kill you. Bullet in the head. Smother you in your sleep."

"You're so romantic."

That gets me another laugh. "I like this."

"What?"

"This less bitchy side of you."

"Don't pretend you don't like the bitchy side."

"I love it. But this is nice, too." He wipes his palms on the front of his camo pants. "Come on. I promise you, you're gonna want to see what's down there."

"All right, let's go."

He blinks. "That didn't take much convincing."

"In case you haven't noticed, I don't require a lot of convincing to do stupid things. Reckless is my middle name."

"Do you have one of those?" he asks.

"What?"

"A middle name."

I shake my head. "I don't think so."

"You don't think so?"

"I only knew my first name when Uncle Jim found me on the side of the road."

Cross hesitates, eyeing me as if he wants to ask a hundred more questions. Instead, he crouches in front of the shadowy crevice and starts to ease himself down. His dark head disappears over the edge, his fingers the only visible part of him left. He hangs for a moment and then he's gone. I hear a soft thud as he lands below.

I peek into the opening to find his beautiful face peering back at me, framed by shadows. "You know, I could just walk away right now . . ." I call toward him. "Leave you here to die."

"You know," he mimics, "I could climb right back up."

"Let me have my fantasies, please."

"You coming or what?"

I kneel, then twist around so I can slide my body along the edge of the craggy wall. I move lower, until my legs are dangling and I'm fully hanging.

Cross's muffled voice drawls up at me.

"Yes. Stay just like that. I'm enjoying the view."

"Fuck off."

I make the six-foot drop, my sandals landing with a thud on the rocky floor. I look around to examine what appears to be a cave system, various gaping openings in all directions, while Cross presses his finger to the source around his wrist. A moment later, a torch illuminates our path.

"Where are we going?" I ask as he takes the lead.

"You'll see. Just stay close and watch your footing. I really should have told you to wear boots."

"I think you did this on purpose. You want me to be helpless."

"There is nothing helpless about you, Wren."

My heart flips. He rarely calls me by my name, and when he does, it sends ribbons of warmth unfurling through me.

As we descend deeper into the cave, his source shuts off abruptly, and the darkness envelops me like a shroud, filling the narrow passageway with an unnerving sense of isolation. The only sound is the steady drip of water echoing off the walls.

"Sorry." His torch comes to life again, but the darkness hadn't bothered me. I'm at home in the dark.

Anyone else might have felt claustrophobic as the twists and turns get narrower, but I stay on Cross's heels, driven by curiosity. After what feels like an eternity of winding tunnels and precarious ledges, we finally reach our destination, and when we emerge into the cavernous chamber, I gasp at the sight that greets me.

"What is this?"

I sweep my gaze over the cave walls, stunned. The sea of flowers takes my breath away. They're everywhere. Vibrant blooms sprouting from every crack and crevice, their petals unfurling in a riot of colors that paint the cave in a kaleidoscope of hues. And they're *glowing*. An ethereal radiance casts the chamber in iridescent light. It's extraordinary.

"How are they growing in the dark?" I demand, spinning to face Cross. "And how are they glowing? Are they creating their own light?"

"They thrive in the darkness. Some sort of mutation," he explains. "And they're not glowing. It's the daggerstone."

My brow wrinkles. "What?"

He beckons me closer. When he plucks one of the flowers, I realize it's growing between cracks not of rock, but of gemstone. Dagger-stone. I remember learning in school how these cave systems began to get discovered about fifty years after the Last War. So many things died from the bombing, the radiation, and never grew back. In the Blacklands, I saw hybrid plants that never existed before the war. Bears with horns. Trees whose roots grew up and outward, rather than into the ground. Daggerstone is one of those anomalies. Cavers stumbled upon entire walls of these gemstones shaped like gnarled daggers, long and pointed and shimmering like white fireflies. Dag-gerstone is almost always white, although I did see someone with a blue daggerstone pendant once. Several shades darker than cobalt.

More daggerstone hangs from the ceiling like crystal chandeliers, their icy tendrils sparkling in the light. Across the cavern is a pool of water that glimmers like liquid silver, like Modified veins, reflecting the dazzling array of colors that dance across the walls.

"This is incredible."

I reach out to touch a delicate blossom. The petals are soft beneath my fingertips as I breathe in the sweet scent. It's like the cave itself is alive. A living, breathing entity that pulses with the heartbeat of the earth.

A sense of awe tightens my throat.

"I've never seen anything like this. It's so beautiful."

I turn to find Cross watching me.

"What?"

"I thought you might like it. I could have bought you synthetic flowers. A nice little bouquet in a vase of water. But that's not you." He gestures to the flowers that are practically exploding from the cave walls. "This is you. Wild. Mysterious."

I laugh. Yet part of me is melting.

This is the most romantic thing a man has ever done for me.

I close the short distance between us. "I don't need flowers."

"I know you don't. You have no expectations, and you always keep people at arm's length. But that only makes me want to impress you."

It's uniquely vulnerable coming from Cross. And it's becoming evident that this guy is not at all what I thought he was. He's rough, but he's also tender. He's lethal, but he has compassion, even if he claims it's a weakness.

"You want to impress me?"

"Yes." His voice is thick.

He tugs me toward him, and his lips are millimeters from mine when his wrist vibrates, causing us to jump apart.

"Sorry," he says, glancing down at his source. "Alert." A frown instantly puckers his brow. "Give me a second."

He walks several feet away, and I watch as he taps his ear. He's rarely without an earpiece, I've noticed. I don't think I've even seen him take it out at night when he's sleeping. *When* he sleeps. He rarely does that, either.

"Shit," I hear him swear. "I'll be right there."

I frown at him when he rejoins me. "Is everything okay?"

Cross shakes his head, moving toward the entrance of the cavern. "We need to go."

"What happened? Where are we going?"

"I have to go see my mother."

———

He won't drop me back at base. He says it's an emergency, and so I'm strapped in the helo again, heading for his Sanctum Point estate.

The General's house.

I feel queasy, but the sensation is accompanied by a burst of anticipation. This is the kind of access the network can only dream of. And there's only a tiny twinge of guilt as I reach out to Adrienne in the car at the airfield. It feels wrong sitting beside Cross and using telepathy to report to his enemy, but I silence my conscience and capitalize on the moment.

"I'm about to go to the General's mansion."

"What?" I can hear her excitement. "How?"

"I'm with Cross."

"And to think we didn't want you at first."

"Yeah. Thanks."

I'm still bitter that they left me to rot for three weeks. If Betima wasn't killed and there'd been no hole to fill, they'd probably still be ignoring my SOSs.

"I assume I'm not going to be able to walk around freely, but . . ."

"Do what you can. Any intel is an asset. Anything you think might be important."

"And if he's there?"

"Assassinate him."

"What?"

"Joking. That won't accomplish anything."

"It won't?"

"A dead General doesn't dismantle the system. If you want to enact change, you need to do more than just take out the leader. You need to deprogram the minds. Root out the ideology."

I wonder if she recognizes the irony. If she realizes she's repeating the same things General Redden says during his broadcasts. Ideas are weeds. Don't let them spread. Although I suppose Adrienne's take has a slight variation. She doesn't want to simply pull the weeds. She wants to plant something new in their place. I suppose I can admire that.

"We're here," Cross says.

"I have to go. I'll report afterward."

The General's house is not what I expect. You hear *mansion* and *estate* and envision turrets and gables and beautiful gardens. But not this house. The sleek mansion looms like a monolithic fortress, all sharp angles and sterile lines. The exterior is a sea of glass and concrete. It doesn't feel at all warm, just cold and hostile.

I give Cross a wary look. "This is where you grew up?"

He nods.

It's a far cry from my ranch house, and I feel a pang of sympathy for him. I knew the General was an austere man, but this is a mausoleum.

We walk inside, where I continue to be struck by the oppressive atmosphere. The ceilings are higher than you'd think from the outside, but that's the only redeeming feature about this place.

Cross leads me into a living room. It's a massive space, but the furnishings are sparse and minimalist. No plush couches or cozy armchairs. No soft rugs or knit throws. Instead, everything feels impersonal. Even the art on the walls is cold and detached. Muted colors and shapes that offer zero insight into the personality or tastes of the house's inhabitants.

I expect staff to come out and greet us. This is the General of the Continent, after all. He should be living a life of luxury, waited on hand and foot, yet the house is as silent as the mausoleum it resembles.

"Is nobody else here? Housekeeper? Butler?"

Cross shakes his head. "The General doesn't allow anyone to freely roam the house. Staff is allowed in only when his guards are here to supervise."

"Sounds like a prison."

"It is," he says simply. "If you don't mind waiting here . . ." His forehead creases with reluctance, as if this is the last thing he wants to be doing right now. "I need to go up to see her."

"Sure."

Leaving me alone is a huge sign of trust.

Or so I think.

Once he disappears up a staircase with a metal-and-glass railing, it doesn't take long to realize there's nothing to be gleaned from this place. No true intel to be gained. The kitchen looks as if no one's ever cooked a meal in there. It's utterly pristine, the counters bare. I wander through the first floor, and while I'm sure cameras are capturing my every move, I don't care all that much. The curiosity has taken hold.

The more I wander, the bigger the glimpse into Cross's life. And it's really sad. It's really cold. Every door I come across is closed and requires a fingerprint scan to enter. Every handle I push buzzes to indicate there's no access. I find myself at another staircase on the other end of the house. After a moment of hesitation, I take the first step.

I hate everything about this place. It's like every inch of it has been carefully curated to convey a sense of detachment and isolation. To be honest, I think Roe dodged a bullet by not growing up here.

Upstairs are two wings, and I walk in the direction of the staircase Cross took. Some of the doors in this wing are open. I peek in and see a bedroom, then another one, and another one. Nothing is out of place. Neatly made beds. Modern furnishings. I wonder which room was Cross's. Travis's. Roe's when he came to visit. There are no personal items to be found anywhere. No photographs or mementos to offer a window into the General's life or his family's. I'm walking through a hollow shell of concrete and glass.

When I hear a low murmur somewhere ahead of me, I follow the sound. The worst that will happen is he'll yell at me. Order me to get out. But I'm too curious to avoid a scolding. Besides, he should know me better by now. Of course I'm not going to stay put and wait for him. Not after he drops a cryptic *I have to see my mother* and then leaves me to fend for myself in his house.

I follow his voice to a tall archway with a set of slate-gray doors. Peering through them, I find the one room in this mansion that has any sort of character.

It's luxurious, the walls painted a pale blue rather than the whites and grays of the rest of the house. In one corner is a cozy sitting area with plush armchairs and a white chaise longue. In the center, a huge four-poster bed, its towering frame draped in billowing white silk. The bedspread is a vibrant shade of royal blue, and both nightstands display porcelain vases overflowing with red flowers.

I venture deeper and realize the room is L-shaped. Around the corner is another sitting area, with double doors opening to a stone terrace, and a wall of windows overlooking the manicured gardens, still green despite the winter chill. I read that the plants in this area used to die when winter came, that the trees lost their leaves, the soil turned to frost. But it's been decades since the Continent experienced those kinds of temperatures.

A woman stands at the windows, her back to me. She's clad in a white shirt and a flowing blue skirt that reaches her ankles. Long dark hair cascades down her back.

Cross is beside her, his voice laced with frustration. "You have to eat. You can't do this again."

She doesn't answer.

"Mom. We're not doing this again. I don't want to hook you up with tubes again. Please."

As if sensing my presence, his head swivels toward me.

"Fuck's sake, Wren. I told you to wait downstairs."

"I'm sorry. I just . . ." I trail off. There are no excuses. I was being nosy.

His mother doesn't turn at the sound of my voice. Doesn't seem to care there's a stranger in her bedroom.

Frowning, I edge closer.

"Wren. Go downstairs." He sounds tired.

"Is she okay?"

"No, she's not."

"How can I help?"

"You can't."

"Cross—"

The woman spins around so fast I jump in surprise. A pair of wide-set blue eyes meet mine with an empty stare that sends a shiver skittering down my spine. The complete absence of emotion is unsettling as hell.

But it doesn't remain that way. For a moment, I can tell she's registering my presence, because confusion etches into her face. Then she blinks and shakes her head, and her gaze shifts from confused to vacant. Back and forth. Confused. Blink. Vacant. Blink. As if her brain is struggling to keep her present.

Unease churns in the pit of my stomach. I've seen that expression before. Those same erratic blinks.

Either I'm completely crazy, or Cross's mother is Modified.

CHAPTER 44

Before I can even begin to make sense of that shocking notion, Vinessa Redden slaps both hands over her ears and lets out an anguished moan.

"Mom," Cross says urgently.

She ignores him. Her slight shoulders start trembling. The moan dissolves to soft whimpers while her mouth keeps opening as if she's trying to speak but can't. I stare in disbelief.

"Mom, come here. It's okay."

He leads her by the arm toward the sitting area, helping her into a chair. With infinite tenderness, he pries her hands from her ears.

"It's okay," he repeats. "Wait here. I'll be right back."

The whimpers fade. She looks at him, the blank stare returning.

Cross turns on his heel and heads for the door. I hurry after him.

"Cross. What the hell is happening right now?"

He quickens his pace.

"Is she Aberrant?" I demand.

He stalks down the hall toward another door, scanning his thumb to open it. It's a study, with an entire wall of glass bookcases and a full bar in the corner. Without a word, he pours himself a drink and takes a long swig.

"How long has she been like this?" I ask from the doorway.

He finally acknowledges my presence. "Catatonic? Maybe the last five years."

"And before that?"

"She had to be sedated all the time. She was too violent. The voices made her angry."

I walk over and take the drink from his hand, gulping the rest of it before passing it back. He swiftly refills the glass.

"She's Aberrant?" I prompt, because he didn't answer me the first time.

Cross shakes his head. "Schizophrenic."

The response surprises me. It doesn't feel right. Yet I don't get the sense he's lying to me.

For a moment, he buries his head in his hands. Then he lifts it and meets my baffled gaze. "She was fine for most of my life. It started off slowly. I think I was around twelve when she started getting irritable, paranoid. Said her thoughts felt scrambled. She was having trouble concentrating. And then one day, she said there were voices in her head. She was hearing and seeing things that weren't there."

"And you're sure she's not Aberrant?"

"Her veins don't turn silver, not even when she hears the voices."

That doesn't mean anything. Yes, if Vinessa is Modified, she would be the first Mod I've met whose veins don't turn silver, but I know Mods like that exist, because, well, I exist.

And if she is a Mod . . . Well, the irony that the General's wife is one of the toxic 'fects he despises is almost comical.

"What did your father do when she was diagnosed?"

"He hid it. Hid her away." Cross gestures in the direction of her suite. "She hasn't left that room in years, other than to go for walks in the garden with the General."

"Do you have staff to take care of her?"

"She takes care of herself. Most of the time, anyway. She gets up. Gets dressed. She eats the meals that are delivered to her. She walks in the garden. She just hasn't said a word since I was seventeen years old."

"But before that, she was hysterical and paranoid?"

He nods. "When the voices were louder. Before she went completely catatonic, she told us they were getting quieter. Whispering rather than shouting."

I think about the fragmented people in the hospital ward, the ones who are still violent and fighting whatever is happening inside their minds.

"The voices eventually drove her insane, and now she's like this. She doesn't speak. She's confused. And every now and then, she stops eating out of the blue. Our cook called and said she hasn't eaten in two days. Usually when that happens, we need to bring a doctor to put in a feeding tube. But she doesn't enjoy that." His expression pains. "I don't want that for her."

"I'm . . . so confused. How does he deliver those broadcasts and talk about rooting out weakness in society when his wife is mentally ill? Didn't he euthanize like thirty people when the Command busted that illegal psychiatric center in Ward B?"

Cross's answering chuckle lacks any trace of humor. "He loves talking about weakness, doesn't he? He might not admit it, but he knows what *his* weakness is. My mother. He would never allow anyone to euthanize her."

When Cross tried to hold my hand in the helicopter earlier, I pulled away. This time, I'm the one reaching for his hand. I lace my fingers through his and touch his cheek with my other hand, stroking his jaw.

"Cross. I'm really sorry."

Several seconds tick by. Then he lets out a breath.

"I need to go back and make sure she's okay."

"Do you want me to make her something to eat?" I offer. "Soup? Maybe if I try to feed her, she'll think I'm a nurse or something and be more receptive."

"You would do that?"

"Of course. I don't want to see anyone suffer. I know I come off as a bitch, but I'm not heartless."

We go down to his sterile kitchen and into a walk-in freezer. He grabs soup that's already been prepared, thaws it, and we heat it over the stove before carrying it upstairs on a tray.

"Mom," he says. "This is Wren."

She's back at the windows, staring outside.

"She brought you some soup. Do you want to try it?"

There's something incredibly tender about the way he speaks to her. The way he pushes a strand of hair away from her face.

She blinks.

"Why don't we try some soup, keen?"

He leads her toward the table where I set down the bowl. She doesn't object.

"This is a good sign," he says gruffly.

"I'm glad. Do you want me to try?" I gesture to the bowl.

"Let's see how I fare first." He dips the spoon into the bowl, then brings it to her lips. "Try this," he urges.

He nudges her lips, and her mouth automatically opens and closes around the spoon. When she swallows, relief floods his face.

"Do you want me to wait downstairs?" I ask.

"No. I don't know why, but you're calming her. Will you stay?"

"Sure."

I hate this. I hate how connected I feel to him right now, how gentle he is. How vulnerable. I hate that I feel sympathy for the General, of all people.

And although I hate to do it, I open a path to Vinessa Redden's mind, because I need to know for sure.

A hot stab of pain instantly jolts through my own mind. I sever the path, shaken by the attempt. I've never tried to read a fragmented mind before, and it's . . . pure chaos. I can't even confirm whether she's a Mod—the frequencies in her mind are so *off*, so volatile, it's impossible to stay in there for more than a second.

I rub my temples and approach the terrace doors. Beyond the glass, I see a manicured lawn. A rectangular pool. Iron benches situated an equal distance apart along the stone walkway lining the grass. It looks like a mini military installation.

I shift my gaze to the wall, where an oil painting hangs. It features a tranquil sea in a little cove. Beautiful and soothing. I wonder who chose it.

I glance over my shoulder. Cross is still spooning the soup into

Vinessa's mouth. Infinitely patient. This hard, ruthless man I've spent months with, softening. A boy trying to help his mother.

From the credenza, I pick up a small figurine of a lighthouse. Examining it.

"Is she a fan of the ocean?"

"She grew up in F, before the entire ward was flooded. It was her favorite place on earth. That painting is the town where she grew up." He nods toward it.

This time, I pay more attention to the details. It's quite lovely. A serene ocean cove done in soft pastel hues. Blue sea and cloudless sky. A lone sailboat glides across the tranquil waters. It has white sails and a white hull, with a navy-blue stripe running along the bottom and a red flag fluttering atop the captain's perch.

I can't make out the boat's name because it's too far in the distance—

A shock wave rocks my body as I realize I'm staring at a scene that was described to me before.

Many times.

By Wolf.

CHAPTER 45

I t can't be.

There's no way Cross Redden is Wolf.

There's no conceivable way that could be possible.

He's not Modified.

But his mother is.

I'm almost certain she is, but that doesn't mean anything. A Mod parent is not guaranteed to produce a Mod child. Hell, two Primes aren't even guaranteed to produce a *Prime* child. The mutation caused by the biotoxin lies dormant in some people. Anyone could be born like me, like her.

Like him?

No. There's no way.

But that painting is . . . uncanny. It's—

A coincidence. The world is full of coincidences. Like the fact, for example, that one of the Command officers who came to my ranch to watch me shoot just happened to know Jim from fifteen years prior and just happened to recognize him. That was a coincidence. A random twist of fate.

But this . . . Believing that Cross could be my oldest friend, the person I love most in this world after Uncle Jim, is so preposterous, it makes me want to laugh.

Yet it eats at me for days following our visit to the General's estate.

Cross leaves the base on an assignment, which comes as a relief because I don't know what to do with these suspicions floating around inside me. I move on autopilot. I share a morning meal with Lyddie. I run a recon mission with Kaine. I share an evening meal with Kaine, Ivy, and Lash, which ought to be uncomfortable, but I'm so preoccupied I don't even care I'm eating with Cross's ex-girlfriend.

I think about his mother hidden away in that concrete prison and wonder if Ivy ever met her. Seems unlikely. If anyone outside the family knew that Cross's mother was schizophrenic, it would've come out eventually.

Does Roe know? I ran into him in the mess hall last night and almost blurted out the question. But I suspect he's in the dark about it. I remember his bitter voice in the railcar, griping about how Vinessa Redden never came down when he visited. If he knew she was ill, I think it would've given him perverse satisfaction. *His* mommy was better than Cross's mommy. He would've shouted it from the rooftops.

I search for Vinessa on Nexus. Pull up pictures of her when her sons were younger. She made some appearances with the General, but even back then they were scarce. He was always strict about his family's security, so I suppose it wasn't unusual when she dropped out of the public eye entirely. Now she's hidden away in his concrete mansion, catatonic and vacantly staring at a scene that Wolf has described to me.

There's no way.

I have to find out if it's true.

But how can I possibly do that without revealing myself? I can't just come out and say, *Hey, are you my telepathic friend?* without alerting him to the fact I have fucking telepathy. And that's not information I should be providing without confirmation that *he* has it, too.

By the time he's back on the base, seeking me out in the mess hall, I'm no closer to a solution. A plan.

All I know is that my heart swells at the sight of him striding toward me. He's tailed by Xavier, who nods in greeting as he passes me. Cross stops.

"You're back," I say.

For a moment, I think he's going to kiss me, but then his demeanor becomes professional. "We just got in. There'll be a briefing tomorrow in the war room."

I nod.

"Come to my quarters tonight?" His voice is low. Husky.

It's rare that he invites me into his personal space. But we haven't been alone since I found out the truth about his mother, so maybe he's hoping for more privacy in case I bring it up.

I nod again. "I'll comm you before I leave."

I leave him to join Kaine, who's once again eating with Lash and Ivy. Before this week, I felt like I hadn't seen Lash in ages.

Halfway through the meal, I realize Lash is only eating with one hand. His other one is resting under the table on Ivy's knee.

I try to keep my eyebrows from soaring. Is that a thing? Because I'm not entirely against it. I like Lash. I think he's a good man, aside from the fact he'd strangle me with his bare hands if he knew I was Modified.

Anticipation flutters in my stomach when I walk toward the officers' quarters later that night. The jeans I'm wearing are the ones that belonged to Betima. I still think of her often. I didn't know her as well as I would've liked, but I know she didn't deserve to die.

Cross opens the door and greets me with one of his mocking smiles.

"I was hoping you'd be naked."

I snort. "You wish."

"Desperately."

"Successful op?" I ask as he lets me in.

"Very. We found a Faithful camp in the hills near D."

"They're working with Reed?"

"Well, they have supplies they could've only gotten from the city, so I assume the answer to that is yes. I don't want to talk about it, though."

"What do you want to talk about?"

"I don't want to talk at all."

And then his mouth is on mine.

Are you Wolf? I want to ask as he kisses me. *Are you? Are you Wolf?*

I'm not suicidal. I can't just blurt it out, not without a plan. But the idea that I could be kissing Wolf right now elicits a thrill. A rush of joy I didn't see coming.

The realization hits me hard and fast.

I *want* him to be Wolf.

So badly. Because other than Uncle Jim, Wolf is the one person I trust most in this world. I don't want him to be a voice in my head anymore. I want him to be this living, breathing man. Muscle and flesh and bone and a beating heart beneath my palm as I press it to his chest.

He walks me into the bedroom. His shirt comes off. My clothes follow suit. His pants. He throws me on his bed, downright feral.

"I think about you every second of the day," he mutters, kissing my neck. "It's a weakness."

I dig my teeth into my lip. "I don't want to be your weakness."

"Too late." He rises on his elbows, his blue eyes piercing into me with such intensity, I start to look away, because it's the kind of intimacy I can't reciprocate.

Normally he lets me avert my eyes, but not tonight.

Tonight, he cups my face with one hand, his strong thumb keeping me in place while his other hand reaches between us to grip himself.

"Look at me," he says.

Once our gazes lock, he brings the broad head of his cock between my legs.

"Look at me while I do this. Just one time, Wren."

I bite my lip again, and his thumb slides up to unsnag it from my teeth, smoothing out the seam.

"Don't hide from me anymore."

For a moment, I let myself believe I'm peering into Wolf's eyes. I melt beneath him, and we both moan when he pushes himself inside me. My legs wrap around him, and soon we're moving together in perfect unison. We're so in tune with each other.

"It's never been like this with anyone," he admits.

"I know."

When I close my eyes again, he rumbles in disapproval. "No. Don't hide."

It's unbearable. It feels like he's staring into my soul, and I don't want to know what he sees. I just don't. I betrayed Tana. Let them take her away so my cover wouldn't be blown. I let them kill Jim. Stood there and watched him die. I—

"Hey. Where are you?"

I blink.

"Come back," Cross whispers. "We're right here."

His hand slides between us to stroke my most sensitive spot, and a bolt of pleasure travels through my body. The tempo quickens. Faster and faster. Deeper and deeper strokes, while his thumb teases the tight bud that's throbbing for him.

When I cry out, he nods with approval. "That's it. Give it to me. Give me everything."

Not everything. I can't give him everything. But this . . . This I can give him.

I gasp as release finds me, rocking my hips to wring every ounce of pleasure from him. It's not long before he finishes, too, shuddering, his lips finding mine in a blistering kiss.

We lie there afterward. Both breathless. He rolls us over so I'm curled beside him with my head on his chest. I hear his heart rate begin to regulate, only to speed up when I say, "How's your mother?"

"Good. Eating again. I'll go see her this weekend and take her for a walk." He pauses. "Thank you for being so kind to her."

"Of course."

Silence settles between us.

Are you Wolf?

I'm desperate to ask him. I need to know, but short of outright telling him who I am, I'm unsure how to find out. I lie there, enjoying the steady rise and fall of his chest. I feel myself getting sleepy, but I try to stay awake, because I know he will. He hardly ever sleeps—

My breath gets stuck in my throat. I think . . . there might be a way.

I drag my fingers up and down his chest in lazy strokes. "Are you still only getting three or four hours of sleep?"

"Sometimes five."

"That's not terrible. Have you always had insomnia, or did it start when you joined the Command or something?"

"Always, I guess. But it's not a big deal. I've never needed much sleep to function."

"I went through a phase where I wasn't sleeping either," I confess. "But that's because I was having a recurring nightmare."

"Yeah?" He's absently stroking my hair. My bare shoulder.

I give a shudder. "It was horrible. I used to get it all the time. It's been a while, though."

"What was it?"

There's my opening.

I steel myself for what I'm about to do.

"It always starts the same way. I'm swimming in a beautiful cave. Exploring. And then I see something sparkling in the water. I can't make out what it is, so I start swimming toward it."

He keeps stroking my hair. His body is warm. Relaxed. I wonder if maybe his mother's painting meant nothing and I'm going in the wrong direction. But it's too late to correct course.

"I swim deeper into the cave, and all of a sudden everything becomes disorienting, and I don't know where I am, which way is up. I'm starting to lose my breath."

His hand stills in my hair.

"I'm trapped in the cave, and it's like the entire weight of the ocean is pressing down on me. I'm frantically searching for an escape, but the walls just stretch on endlessly. My lungs are burning. I don't know how much longer I can hold my breath."

His fingers slip out of my hair.

"The panic sets in. My vision is blurring, darkness closing in around me. And there's this sinking sense of dread because I know I have no choice but to inhale. I *need* to breathe. I open my mouth and take a deep breath, and the water rushes in, filling my lungs. My whole body starts convulsing, fighting it, but there's no relief. I'm choking, dying—"

He moves so fast that I don't see it coming.

In a heartbeat, I'm flat on my back with a knife at my throat.

Cross's eyes are wild. Blazing. Every muscle in his body coiled tight as he peers down at me and snarls, "Who are you?"

CHAPTER 46

I can't stop myself.

I start to laugh.

Deep, gasping, shaking giggles. He blinks in shock, but my laughing fit is uncontrollable. All I can do is shudder beneath him as he straddles me with a blade to my throat. Each time I laugh, I feel a sting against my flesh. Soon it's going to draw blood. That just makes me laugh harder.

"Who are you?" he repeats, his breath escaping in a hiss. "Who told you that story?"

"Can I . . ." I try to speak through the laughter. "Can I ask you something?"

He raises the knife. Just millimeters. He's still wound tighter than a cobra. He can slice my throat at any second.

"Is your favorite animal still a wolf?"

He freezes. Staring at me, as if he can't comprehend what I'm asking.

"Because mine isn't a daisy anymore. My favorite flower, I mean."

His breathing becomes ragged. The knife rises another half an inch.

"It was, at one point." When I lived in the Blacklands, but not even

Wolf knows where I came from. "Except then wild daisies started taking over the north pasture of the ranch, spreading like a weed, and the cows didn't have enough grass because of those stupid daisies. So it stopped." I giggle. "Being my favorite flower, that is."

Sensing I'm no threat to him, Cross lifts the knife. It hangs loose from his fingers now. I can see his brain working, trying to make sense of this.

When he speaks, it's one hoarse word.

"How?"

"I don't know." I sit up and lean against the headboard. "I only figured it out the other night."

He gives me a questioning look.

"Your mother's room. Her painting. The white hull, the blue stripe, the red flag." I start to laugh again. "All this time I thought you lived by the ocean. I didn't realize you were describing a painting."

Cross studies my face as if he's never seen me before in his life.

"Daisy?" he finally says. His voice shakes slightly.

"Wolf." A smile spreads across my lips. "It's nice to finally meet you."

We eye each other.

I blink and I'm in his arms. They're wrapped tightly around me, as if he's trying to melt me into his body.

"I don't know how the fuck this is happening. Is this actually happening?"

He's in my head now. Wolf. He sounds different, though, because I know what *Cross* sounds like.

"Your voice is not as raspy as you think it is."

He grins at me. "Yours is higher than you think."

"I do not have a high voice," I say out loud, trying to hear it for myself. It sounds deeper to my ears.

"Yes, you do." He shakes his head in amazement. "How is this possible?"

I know exactly what he's feeling. It's strange and exciting. Terrifying, too. I've known him since I was six years old, yet this is the first time we're meeting.

And he's Cross Redden.

He's Cross Redden.

The implications race through my head. For a moment, I worry he might turn me in, until I remember that turning me in means turning *himself* in.

"You're Modified," I accuse.

His expression pains.

"Does anyone else know?"

"No."

"How? How were you able to keep it a secret?"

Cross moves to sit beside me, long legs stretched out in front of him. "I don't know. I guess even at the age of eight, when I was suddenly inside someone else's head, I wisely knew never to reveal it to anyone."

"Nobody in your family knows?"

"No, you're the only one."

"What gifts do you have?" I ask curiously.

"Only telepathy, and I don't think I'm very strong. I've only ever done it with you. I have no idea how I managed to connect with your mind all those years ago, but I'm glad I did. It made me feel less alone."

"My uncle told me it's common for children to form spontaneous links when they're first manifesting their abilities. They don't know how to use anything properly yet. It's almost like their minds freaking out."

Cross is equally curious. "What do you have?"

"Just telepathy."

Guilt embeds into my stomach. He doesn't need to know that I'm also a mind reader and projector. That I can incite. Or rather, that I can sometimes incite at random and inappropriate times, with no rhyme or reason to how I've done it.

But Cross isn't stupid. "Julian Ash's execution," he spits out.

I'm quick to deny it. "It wasn't me."

For the first time in my life, I'm actively lying to my closest friend. It rips a hole in my heart. I never thought I would lie to Wolf. Only by omission. But I'm unsure about our level of trust now. Because Wolf isn't Wolf anymore. He's Cross Redden.

He eyes me skeptically.

"It was Jim," I tell him.

"Ash? Jayde didn't get any indication he was an inciter when she was reading his mind."

"Well, I don't know what to tell you because it was him. I don't think he had much control over it. I only saw it happen one other time over the years, and even then, it wasn't successful. He said inciting required a lot of control, and it wasn't something he wanted to practice. He didn't like interfering with people's free will." I swallow. "But he interfered at the execution. I guess when your life is in danger, you'll go to any lengths to save yourself."

"So. You *did* know your uncle was Aberrant."

"Obviously."

A faint smile touches his lips. "I knew you were lying to me. But for a while there, you even had me convinced."

His breath suddenly hitches.

I frown. "What is it?"

"Your shield held up against Lieutenant Colonel Valence. Wren. Do you realize how extraordinary that is?"

"Maybe she's not as good as she claims to be."

"No, she's better. I've seen her read the mind of someone a thousand yards away. As long as she has them in her eyesight, she draws their energy to her."

I shiver. It's a menacing, foreboding thought. For once, I'm grateful I have my own internal alarm system that allows me to feel it when someone tries to penetrate my mind.

Silence drifts between us. We continue to study each other. He reaches over, touches my face. He traces every line and curve as if he's trying to memorize it with his touch.

"I can't believe it's you," he says.

"*I* can't believe it's *you.*"

He pulls me into his lap, and I rest my head against his chest. There's something so comforting about this. It's rare that I feel safe. Protected. But I do in this moment. With Cross holding me. Wolf holding me.

Emotion wells up in my throat. There are so many things I want to say, to ask, but he speaks before I can.

"Are you working for the Uprising?"

My head snaps up.

"Shit," he says, noting my expression. "You are."

"Yes, but it's sort of a recent development. I only started after Jim died."

He's skeptical again.

"You need to stop that," I chide.

"Stop what?"

"Doubting what I say now. When I was Daisy, did you ever doubt me?"

"Never."

"Then don't start now." I smother the rush of guilt that tries to surface. I lied to him about the incitement, I know that. But that's a secret I'll take to the grave.

"What have you done for them?" Cross asks before biting out an expletive. "The weapons cache. You gave them the grids?"

I offer a rueful nod.

I want to ask him what side he's on, if he believes in his father's vision for the Continent. I want to ask him how he can stomach it when he sentences Mods to death. When he sends us to labor camps. I want to know how he feels about people like us, especially since his mother . . .

I can't stop my next words from popping out.

"She's Modified. Your mother. You know that, right?"

He rubs the bridge of his nose. He looks like he'd rather be talking about anything but this.

"The General might be in denial about it, but I think deep down you know what she is. Have you ever met a Mod whose mind has been fragmented?"

His head dips in a nod.

"Do you not see the similarities?"

"Her symptoms are close enough to schizophrenia—"

"That's not schizophrenia, Cross. Her mind is fragmented— because she's Modified. And I think you damn well know that. How does the General not see it?"

"Her veins don't ripple."

"I don't have to tell you that means nothing. Some Mods, a rare few of us, don't have the silver veins." I switch to telepathy to prove my point. "Like me." My gaze drops to his arms. "And apparently like you."

He curses under his breath.

"You suspected she was Modified despite her veins, because yours don't do it, either."

Tension hardens his jaw. "Wren. You can't tell them."

"What?"

He switches to telepathy. "You can't tell the Uprising I'm Modified. If they use that information against me, if it gets back to my father, my brothers . . . They'll kill me."

My heart twists in my chest. "So what do we do now?"

"I don't know."

"Why don't you speak to them? Maybe you can join the network, too."

The idea fills me with hope, but he's quick to shoot it down. Incredulous.

"I'm not working for the Uprising."

"But you'll work for the Command? You'll help your father kill all the people who are like you?" Anger rises inside me.

"Have you ever seen me kill a Mod?" he challenges.

I falter. Thinking. The General's words buzz through my mind. Accusing Cross of overcrowding the labor camps with the Aberrant. His brother killed Betima without hesitation. But Cross . . . He spares their lives.

"I do more good here than I would anywhere else," he says out loud. Groaning, he rakes both hands through his hair. "This is . . . a lot. It isn't something we can talk through in one evening, Wren." He pauses. "Daisy." His features soften as he touches my face again. "This is unbelievable."

Yes, it is. I think back to our talk about free will and destiny, and for the first time in my entire life, I wonder if maybe some events are inexorable. Predestined.

Maybe I was always supposed to end up here with him.

His lips are nearing mine when the alert sounds. Cursing, he grabs his comm from the night table and checks the screen.

"Shit. We have to go. Now."

"Why? What happened?"

"An Uprising fighter jet just crashed near one of our weapons depots."

CHAPTER 47

Cross briefs us in the bomber jet. It's the B-8, a new tactical aircraft we learned about during the Program. Our instructor spent a lot of time raving about this experimental three-seat model with its brand-new, cutting-edge air-to-ground weaponry system. We take two of them for the op, with me, Cross, and Xavier in one; Kaine, Tyler, and Jones in the other.

"Our radar caught a solo jet flying erratically at low altitudes," Cross says over the comm feed. "By the time we got a drone out there, the fighter had already crashed in the forest. Drone shows the engines on fire, cockpit empty. Marks in the dirt indicate the pilot dragged himself away from the crash site."

"Is he still in the area?" asks Xavier from the pilot's seat. He skillfully propels the jet through the black sky, making me wish I'd paid more attention in Basics of Flight. New operatives to Silver Block aren't allowed to fly any aircraft without extra training, though, so I'm not worried about being thrust into the pilot role anytime soon.

"That's what we're going to find out," Cross replies. "The plane is one click from our depot, which was decommissioned a few years ago. They might have old intel and think it's an active one. Intelligence thinks they were trying to bomb it when the plane crashed."

The B-8 banks as we near our destination. From the air, the weapons depot is barely visible. Not until Cross points it out to me.

It doesn't resemble a military installation. Nestled in the rugged terrain of an isolated valley, the depot is small and unassuming, little more than a collection of nondescript buildings hidden among the trees. The main warehouse looks like a barn. Squinting, I make out old crates stacked near a sagging chain-link fence and other random pieces of debris littering the dusty ground.

"Anyone can waltz up to this," I say in surprise. "That warehouse doesn't even look like reinforced steel."

"The whole point is that it's in plain sight. It's supposed to look inconspicuous. When it was operational, the entire compound was wired with explosives. Crawling with land mines. Motion sensors. Drone security. It used to contain an arsenal of weapons and munitions. But it's been abandoned for years."

Once we're on the ground, we split into two teams. One to investigate the plane, the other to secure the perimeter of the depot. I'm with Cross and Xavier again, delving into the forest in search of the fighter jet.

Something feels . . . off. I wonder if the guys agree, but I don't ask them as we move through the darkness. I smell the smoke when we're about half a mile out. Jet fuel.

As we near the crash site, a knot of foreboding tightens in my stomach.

"Keep your eyes open," Cross murmurs. "We don't know what we're walking into."

I readjust my grip on my weapon. A sniper rifle is too cumbersome for this op, so I'm outfitted with the smaller version of the REMM-4. The 3. It's equally delicious and fixed with the same night sight that the other model uses.

My senses remain on high alert as we approach the smoldering wreckage of the downed jet. Cross signals for me to venture to higher ground, gesturing that he and Xavier will investigate while I cover them. I nod and move up the rocky outcrop. They don't move until I'm in position, covering them as they creep closer to the plane. Thanks to the rifle's night sight, I see them clearly in the dark.

I scan the area for any signs of movement. All looks calm, yet still I feel vulnerable, exposed.

"Clear," Cross says a few minutes later.

"We've got a trail of blood." Tyler's voice comes through the comm. "Heading for the main building now."

"Be careful, Dixie," Xavier warns, using her call sign.

"Dove, are you seeing anything?"

It took a while, but Cross finally dropped the "broken" from *my* call sign, which has been a relief.

I sweep the area again. "There's nobody here."

"Well, there's definitely somebody *here*." Kaine's voice now. "Bloody footprints everywhere."

"Dixie. Proceed with caution," Cross says. "Any hint of trouble, retreat and wait for us."

"Copy that."

The line falls quiet. But only for a few seconds.

Tyler returns, her unease unmistakable. "Captain, something's not right here—"

An explosion goes off in the distance.

I hear it in my ear, too, just a split second of deafening thunder before the feed cuts and the silence returns. I'm already on my feet. Cross and Xavier come running.

"Dixie!" Xavier shouts. "Come in."

No response. The channel is completely silent, eerily so.

Without delay, the three of us race toward the source of the blast. I see the flames the moment we reach the depot, burning hot in the side of the main building, smoke gusting out of the gaping hole left by the explosion.

"Condor," I say urgently, tapping my earpiece.

Silence.

"Kaine, come in. Please."

"Tyler." I hear the note of fear in Xavier's voice.

"Kaine."

"Jones. Tyler, damn it."

We've abandoned call signs as we plead for our fellows to answer.

Silence.

Despite my instincts screaming *danger!* I run toward the warehouse, but I only make it five steps before I'm being yanked backward. Cross shoves me behind him moments before a second explosion rocks the night.

A blinding burst of light illuminates the darkness like a thousand suns, sending shock waves of embers and debris hurtling in our direction.

We flatten ourselves to the ground, and I watch in despair as the weapons depot is transformed into a hellish inferno, flames licking hungrily at it, thick plumes of black smoke billowing into the sky. The force of the blast shattered windows and sent broken glass raining down like deadly shrapnel. A shard of it is lodged in Xavier's cheek.

When he tries to get up, Cross issues an order. "Stay down."

A sickly scent fills the air. Sweet. Mingling with the acrid stench of smoke. As the fire rages unchecked, the walls of the depot begin to buckle and groan. With a series of earsplitting cracks, they give way, collapsing in on themselves as flames continue to consume everything.

"What the hell bomb was that?" My eyes water as I stare at the building, utterly helpless. "I've never seen an explosion like that."

"Sugar bomb," Cross says.

The building has been reduced to a smoldering ruin. Nobody could have survived that second explosion. The first one, maybe.

But not the second.

The stinging of my eyes gets worse, and it's no longer from the air quality. Battling my tears, I jump to my feet. "We need to . . . They might still be . . ."

I take several steps toward the raging inferno, but even from twenty feet away, the sheer heat of it singes the tiny hairs on my face.

Cross pulls me back. "Stand down. Do you want to burn alive?"

"*They're* burning alive." Vomit bubbles up my esophagus. "We need to get to them."

"They're gone, Wren," he says, confirming my grim thoughts. "Nobody survives that."

Xavier is the one trying to make a run for it now. When Cross locks his arms around him from behind, forcibly restraining him, Xavier unleashes an elbow into Cross's throat.

Cross growls. "Stand down, Lieutenant."

"Tyler's in there."

"I know." He sounds utterly defeated.

Several long, painful minutes pass. The fire continues to rage. We continue to stare at the scorched ground where a whole building used to be.

Hope bursts inside me when I suddenly hear static in my ear. I suck in a breath, waiting for Kaine's lighthearted voice to assure me he's okay, that no explosion could stop someone so dashing and handsome.

But the crackling ends as abruptly as it starts.

"The hell was that?" Xavier demands. "Did you all hear that?"

"Something's not right." Cross's features sharpen.

"Of course something's not right! You fucking prickhole. You just stood there and let them die. You should've let me try."

"Would you have preferred to die, too? Is that it?"

As they face off, I register another sound. A gust. The faint roar of an engine. I tip my head, and I swear I see a shadowy blur in the sky.

I frown. "We need to get to the airfield."

Cross arches a questioning brow.

"I think I just saw a plane."

Without further discussion, we take off, hiking through the brush in the direction of the airfield. When we emerge from the trees, we stop in our tracks.

Of the two B-8s that brought us here, only one remains.

It was a trap.

The pieces of the puzzle click into place. They crashed their fighter on purpose. Their pilot was never inside the depot. He sprang the trap and then waited. Waited for us to go to the crash site, for Tyler's team to investigate. They used the crash as a diversion, a smokescreen to cover their true objective, and while we were distracted by the chaos of the explosion, they stole one of our most advanced bomber jets.

Our?

Confusion fogs my brain. I realize I'm thinking of myself as part of the Command.

Their jet, I mean.

My people stole *their* jet.

But the lines are blurring. God, they're blurring.

"The planes are fitted with cameras," I say. "There'll be footage of it, right? Showing whoever took it?"

Cross responds with a cynical look. "They just lifted our bomber from right under our noses. You think they didn't come up with a plan to disable the cameras?"

Beside him, Xavier has fallen silent. His gaze is unfocused, face drained of color. I'm confused for a second until the reminder slaps me in the face.

Tyler's gone.

Jones.

Kaine.

A sob gets stuck in my throat.

"Check the perimeter," Cross tells Xavier, who nods dully.

The second he's out of earshot, Cross's voice rumbles inside my head.

"Did you know about this?"

I gape at him. "What?"

"You're working with them. Did you know what they were planning?"

A slice of hurt penetrates before I'm able to steel my expression. "I swear, I had no idea."

"You expect me to believe you were just as blindsided as the rest of us?"

His doubt is unambiguous. So is the anger.

"I didn't."

He grabs my arm. Hard. Holding me in place as his gaze bores into mine. He doesn't believe me.

"I promise you, Cross. I didn't know. I would never, ever have led them into an ambush. Not Kaine." Agony rips through me at the notion of never seeing Kaine's impish grin again. "He's my closest friend here."

My eyes feel hot again. I shrug his hand off me.

"I didn't know."

At that, I spin on my heel and go help Xavier secure the perimeter.

The funerals are held two days later in a small cemetery on the grounds of the base. It's a depressing affair. Three flag-draped caskets sit side by side. They're empty, of course. Our three fellows were nothing but ashes by the time we were able to send a team to go through the bomb site.

My gaze falls on the Company flag, its navy backdrop with the white crest in the center. Everyone stands in respectful formation, but most faces are bereft of emotion, including grief. *They* might not care, but I'm grieving. Grieving for a golden-haired young man with mischief in his eyes.

I cry for my friend. I don't care if it's wrong. I don't care that six months ago, I would've secretly been cheering for the deaths of three Primes. Three Command soldiers, for that matter. Bonus! Tana and I would've shared a drink in the town square and toasted to their deaths.

But Tana is not here.

And there's nothing to celebrate.

The loss weighs heavily on me. I know he was the enemy . . . but he didn't feel like it. I stare at Kaine's portrait being projected from behind his casket, and my chest clenches with sorrow. My gaze shifts to Tyler's image. That doesn't make it better. I didn't know her well yet, outside the context of instructor, but she was someone Xavier cared about.

He doesn't cry for her like I cry for Kaine. He stands in his dress blues. Expressionless. Jaw hard.

When their commanding officer is asked to step forward, Cross moves in front of the three caskets. Rather than deliver a speech extolling their virtues, he simply recites their names, rank, and ward.

"Tyler Struck, 2nd Soldier, Ward A. Kaine Sutler, 1st Soldier, Ward D. Noah Jones, 1st Soldier, Sanctum Point."

There's a low growl at Noah's name, and I turn to see a man with jet-black hair and murder in his eyes. He wears a tailored suit, impeccably fitted to his lean frame, and the expensive clothing and diamond-studded watch speak to wealth and privilege. He exudes power. He's also one of the few people here who is visibly overcome with grief.

This must be Jones's father, the capitalist. I wonder why he gets to attend when Kaine's and Tyler's families are conspicuously absent. Lyddie, who's clutching my hand like it's a life preserver, told me that the General doesn't like "emotional fanfare" with his funerals.

Noah's father stands next to Travis Redden, who seems to be having trouble maintaining a composed expression. Flashes of barely restrained fury keep breaking through the mask.

With a sinking feeling, I realize that heads will roll for this.

The burial is short and concise, just the way the General likes it. He's not even here, our esteemed leader who values his military above all else. The ceremony draws to a close with the slashing of the flags. Two honor guards step forward in unison to hold the Company flag taut for Cross. He reaches into his belt and slides a knife out of its sheath, the silver blade winking in the morning light. His face has been impassive since we got here, but when it's time for him to slash the flag, I notice his throat dip, the first hint of emotion.

I never understood this tradition. Slicing the flag down the center but stopping short of tearing it in half. It's supposed to represent resilience or some shit. *Damaged yet not destroyed.* I remember the General uttering those words during a televised funeral for a colonel from Tin Block. I suppose a few paltry dead soldiers don't warrant his attention the way a colonel does.

One by one, Cross slashes the navy and white pieces of fabric. The guards' movements are synchronized as they carefully drape the flags over the caskets again. And that's it. We're dismissed.

I want to talk to Cross, but he's intercepted by various officers. I keep my distance, waiting for him to be free, despite the fact that he glances over his shoulder at one point to pin me with a hard look. We haven't spoken in two days. He's kept his distance. I sent him a message on his comm, and he ignored it. He won't come to my quarters. He won't let me link with him as Wolf, and he won't let me talk to him as Cross.

He thinks I knew about the ambush, but I wasn't lying to him when I insisted I didn't. For the past two days, I've been cursing the Uprising for keeping me in the dark, and the conversation I had with Adrienne about it after we returned to base that night hadn't done shit to appease me.

"I don't appreciate being kept out of the loop," I'd snapped at her. "I'm Elite. I could have—"

"What? You could've done what? Made the operation go even smoother than it did? We got what we wanted without you."

"The plane."

She neither confirmed nor denied it. "You don't call the shots. We do. If we had needed you for that mission, you would have been part of the mission. And we didn't need you, Darlington. In fact, prior knowledge of it might have endangered the whole op."

"What? You don't trust me?" I said bitterly.

"It's not about trust. It's about sincerity. Your reactions. The entire operation was exactly what we needed it to be. You were going in to investigate a fallen aircraft. If you'd known it was a decoy, you might've tipped them off."

"I'm better than you think."

"And worse than *you* think. You're young and you're arrogant. With that said, there are some things coming down the pipe. We'll need your help with the Jubilee."

Anticipation tightened my gut. "What are you planning?"

"We'll be in touch," was all she said, and I haven't heard from her since.

I try to act nonchalant as I trail after Cross at a discreet distance. Like a lovesick puppy.

My spine stiffens when he stops to speak with Jones's father. The man is clearly livid. Whatever Cross is saying, Mr. Jones is not having it. When the volume of his voice rises, Travis touches the man's arm and leads him away from his brother.

Nearly fifteen minutes pass before Cross breaks away from the crowd and stalks toward the entrance of the building.

Anxiety flutters through me. I need to talk to him. He has to know

I had nothing to do with that ambush. I stride after him, watching him disappear through the door. I've lost sight of him, but I know where he's going. Our war room isn't in this building, but his office is.

I reach that door—CAPTAIN OF OPERATIONS—in time to hear glass breaking. I'm about to push it open when I realize he's not alone.

"How the hell did you let this happen?"

Travis.

"What the *fuck* is the point of your godfucking elite unit if you let your own people die in a fucking ambush?"

"You might want to take a look in the mirror, Colonel." Cross's voice is pure ice. "You're the head of Intelligence."

"You're my boots on the ground! You should have known about this. How am I supposed to explain to Wexton Jones that his only son is dead? Died because my brother walked him directly into a trap."

Cross doesn't say anything.

"Fix this," Travis snarls.

"I'm sorry that this is inconvenient to your friendship with Wexton Jones." Cross is mocking him now. "I know you had big plans for him for when the General retires and you take your place at the helm. Is that still your dream, Trav?"

His brother doesn't answer.

"Because you're fooling yourself if you think the General will ever hand over the reins to either one of us. For someone who outlaws God, his God complex sure is big enough. He thinks he's the only one who can lead the people. Keep the order. Contain the Aberrant."

"The hell are you babbling about? *Fix* this. Find the people that stole our plane. Do your job."

At the approaching footsteps, I duck into the open doorway nearest me. I wait until Travis's angry footfalls disappear around the corner.

There's a moment of silence, then another crash from Cross's office. More broken glass.

I bite my lip. It's evident this isn't the time to talk. Maybe that's for the best, though.

There's something I need to do first, anyway.

CHAPTER 48

The sun has set by the time I find the courage to go to his quarters, and a part of me is surprised that he lets me in. Without a word, he holds the door open. I walk inside and he closes it behind me.

I'm in civilian clothes. I shrug out of my jacket, leaving me in jeans and a tank top. His gaze flicks toward me before he sinks into the chair by the sofa.

Anxiety mingles with frustration and squeezes my throat. This is unbearable. It hurts knowing that Wolf—Cross—is mad at me. I'm still struggling to shift the way I think about him. But I'm going to have to evolve because he's not quite Wolf anymore. Wolf is my childhood friend. Wolf is a boy. Cross is a man.

"My uncle didn't find me on the side of the road."

Cross swings his gaze back to me.

"He smuggled me out of the city when I was five years old. My parents were Uprising operatives. Working to take the system down from within. My father died in the field. My mother was executed for concealment."

I sit on the sofa and offer a contrite look.

"Whenever I spoke to Wolf about my 'father,' I was referring to

Jim. The truth is, I don't remember my parents. I never knew them. I don't remember anything, really, before Jim took me to the Blacklands."

His mouth falls open.

"Yeah," I confirm in a dry voice. "We lived in the darkness for almost three years. Well, it wasn't always dark. We found a sun pocket in a grassy clearing that got about five hours of light a day. My parents asked him to protect me, so that's what he did. And when he deemed it safe, we returned to the wards and set ourselves up in Z. We really have been ranching these past twelve years. I knew he was Modified." I don't say Aberrant because Jim was not an aberration. He was not defective. "But he didn't work for the Uprising. Neither did I, not until after his execution. They recruited me not long after I joined the Program. Or rather, after you forced me into it."

Amusement tugs on the corners of his mouth.

"I lied to you when I said I only have one ability."

His smile fades.

I get to my feet and start to undo my jeans.

"What are you doing?"

"I went to see Ellis earlier." I bite my lip in humor, hesitating only briefly before asking, "Did you know he was working for your enemy?"

Cross hisses through his teeth. "Fuck's sake."

"I'm sorry. I confirmed it with my contact before I reached out to him. He's been undercover here for years."

I tug my zipper down.

"I asked him to heal my scars. I wasn't sure if it would still be there. But . . ."

Beneath the denim I wear a pair of white underwear. Palms damp from nerves, I remove my jeans, leaving them in a pool on the floor.

Cross sucks in a breath when he sees my bare thighs.

The burns are gone.

The bloodmark is still there.

"I don't have one ability. I have four."

"Four." He looks like he's trying not to laugh. "All right. Well. I know what one of them is. What are the other three?"

"I can read your mind." I purse my lips. "Actually, no, I can't read *your* mind—your shield is phenomenal. Maybe lower it for a second?"

His gaze turns distrustful.

"Please. I won't abuse the privilege."

When he nods, I peer past him toward the balcony, focusing on the view beyond the glass door. I push the image into his mind.

He sighs.

I give a sheepish shrug. "I'm a projector."

"Clearly."

"And . . ." I gulp. "I can incite."

"Fuck, Wren."

"I know. If it makes you feel better, I can't control that power at all."

"How would that make me feel better?" he balks, then draws a calming breath. "So that was you, then, at the execution?"

"I'm sorry I lied to you. I wasn't sure if I could fully trust you." I nibble the inside of my cheek. "But yes, it was me. I didn't do it on purpose if you can believe that. It's sort of like how you and I accidentally linked as kids. You opened a path and blindly reached out without even realizing what you were doing. That's what occurred at the execution. I was watching in horror as the squad lined up in front of Jim. I was pleading with them in my mind to put their guns down. And then . . . it just happened."

"Just happened," he echoes in disbelief.

"That wasn't the first time, either. It's happened here and there over the years. Usually when I've been angry or panicky about something. I was inciting the night I told you about, when my father—Jim—drove us off the road. I told you I was driving. I wasn't. I accidentally incited him to turn the truck around and we almost died."

"Shit."

"Jim tried to train me in it, but it wasn't his strongest suit. And there are so few known inciters on the Continent that I can't even, you know, call someone for advice." A laugh slips out. "I don't know how to use it." The laughter fades. "I wouldn't use it even if I did."

He slants his head. "Really."

"Really. Remember when we talked about free will? Well, it's sort of an important concept for me. I like the idea that I'm making my own decisions. That my actions are my own. There are very few people I hate enough to want to take that away from them."

Cross's features soften.

"I lied to you about some things as Daisy, but always by omission. But you did the same." I give him a pointed look, and he nods. "As me, as Wren, I've lied about so much since I got here. I've hid from you."

I touch my thigh, directing his gaze to the red circle imprinted there. To the reason I didn't want Ellis to heal me.

"Jim burned this off me when I was a child. It appeared when I was seven. He didn't want anyone to know what I was, including the Uprising."

That makes him frown. "He kept it from them?"

"Yes. He knew I would be used as a pawn. My mom knew, too. That's why she sent me away. She was the first person I incited, when I was five. She recognized the danger in it, especially in the hands of a child, so she begged Jim to take me far away. Other than him, you're the only one I've ever told."

"Your friend didn't know?"

"Only you. And now Ellis, I suppose."

There's a beat of silence.

Then his jaw clenches tight, and I'm startled by the flash of ire that ignites his eyes.

"Damn it, Dove. How could you do such a stupid fucking thing?"

My mouth falls open. "You're angry at me for telling you the truth?"

"I'm angry at you for exposing yourself. For removing the only godfucking layer of protection you had between you and your enemies."

I blink.

He's right.

My chest rises as I draw a shaky breath. "I know it was reckless."

"You think?"

"But it seemed like a good idea at the time."

"Why would you ever put yourself at risk like that?"

"I . . . I wanted to show you that you can trust me. I wanted to show you . . . me." The lump of emotion in my throat is liable to choke me. "I wanted you to see what I am."

"I see exactly what you are, Daisy. I always have."

I barely have time to bask in that before he's kissing me. We don't even make it to the bedroom. Our clothes are ripped away. We start off on the couch but it's too small for us, and with a hiss of frustration Cross pulls me onto the floor, falling back on his elbows, eyes gleaming as I settle astride him.

I pull him free, giving a slow, thorough stroke that makes him curse. Then I sink down on him, and we both groan.

"Best feeling in the world," he mumbles.

Time seems to stand still, my surroundings fading away until there's only the two of us. It's always been that way. The two of us.

He reaches up to cup my breasts. Squeezing. Toying with my nipples. I shiver. Then shiver harder when those strong hands travel downward. He runs his fingers over my newly healed thigh, and it feels weird to . . . well, feel. There'd been no sensation there for so long that it's like discovering a new erogenous zone. The unfamiliar sensations are delicious.

"I didn't know about the ambush."

It's probably the worst time to say it, but I can't stop the words from popping out of my mouth.

"I believe you," Cross says, then thrusts upward and fills me so deep I gasp.

His eyes grow hazy with pleasure as he watches me ride his cock. My own pleasure rises at the sight of his pulse hammering in the base of his throat, at the feel of his hands roaming my body. His lips on my nipple when I curl over him, losing control of the rhythm.

Release finds us within seconds of each other. I moan against his neck, and he groans against mine, giving one last thrust while I feel him throbbing inside me. We're both breathing hard when I roll off him. We're too lazy and sated to move. We lie on the floor, staring up at the ceiling.

"I love you," he says.

I press my lips together to suppress the smile that's tickling my lips.

"I've loved you since I was eight years old. And I'm still adjusting to all of this. Trying to merge the two of you. Daisy. Wren." Regret thickens his voice. "I'm sorry I lashed out after we lost Tyler. Sutler. Jones. They were my responsibility. I was pissed at myself, not you. Travis is right. I led them into a trap."

"You didn't know."

"I would have if I hadn't been so distracted."

"By me." My heart sinks.

"Yes, but that's not your fault. It's not your fault you've been Daisy all along, or . . ." His voice grows even hoarser. "Or that now that I know the truth, I've never been more fucking terrified in my life."

"Terrified?" Frowning, I sit up. My hair has grown so long since I got here that it falls like a curtain over my breasts. "Terrified of what?"

"Of what I feel for you." His gaze seeks out mine, holding me captive. "You're in my soul, Wren. I take a breath and feel you in my chest. You're inside of me. You have been since I was a kid, and the thought of losing you . . ."

My throat is entirely constricted, but somehow I manage to whisper, "You're not going to lose me."

"You make it very hard to keep you safe."

"You don't need to keep me safe."

"You're reckless. You would've raced into that burning depot if I hadn't stopped you."

"He was my friend—"

"Your life is more important to me," Cross interrupts. "Don't you get that? Sutler was a good guy, but his life is irrelevant compared to yours. Yours is the only life that matters. I will rip anyone's throat out, burn the entire fucking world down, if it means keeping you safe and—"

"I love you, too."

He stops, a grin playing on his lips. "I know."

Cocky bastard. I've never said those three words to anyone before, and here he is taking them for granted.

But then he pulls me on top of him again and I forget why I'm annoyed with him.

———

Later, as we're lying in his bed facing each other, I run my fingers over the warm flesh of his arm.

"These . . ." I lightly stroke the ink. "Are dangerously close to being religious. They could be mistaken for angel's wings. I'm surprised your father allowed it."

One corner of his mouth tips up in a crooked smile. "He didn't. At least not the first time. I got the first tattoo when I was sixteen. It was just a small wing on the inside of my wrist. Nothing to lose his shit over. But he took me to the hospital in the Point and threw me into the regen chamber. Made it disappear."

"Somehow that doesn't surprise me."

"Pissed me off so bad I went back to the ink parlor the following night and got an entire sleeve tattooed."

I snicker. "Very impulsive of you. That sounds like a Darlington move."

"Fuck. You're right."

"So are they angel's wings?" I trace the detailed feathers. The thin lines and delicate curves.

"No."

"Then it's birds? Really? You made fun of my bird name, yet you have bird ink?"

He grins.

"Why wings?" I push.

"I don't know. I guess they remind me of freedom."

My eyes move to the flames. "And the fire?"

"Destruction. A reminder that this whole world is always on the verge of total destruction."

I nod slowly, studying his arm. It's the words woven amid the artwork that intrigue me the most.

"What do all these lines of text mean?"

His voice is deep, reflective. "Just words, phrases, that have stuck with me over the years. Lessons I've learned. Moments that have changed me."

I want to spend the rest of the night poring over every word, but instead, I decide to ruin the peaceful moment by doing something reckless again.

"The Uprising has something planned for the Silver Jubilee."

He stiffens. "And you're only telling me this now because . . . ?"

"I only just found out. And I don't even know what the plan *is*. I am so low on the food chain that it would take an infinity ladder to see the top."

"There'll be civilians in attendance at the Jubilee."

"I assume whatever they have planned won't involve the guests. The network would never harm innocents."

"They harmed innocents at the weapons depot," Cross says tightly.

"Three. That's minimal casualties."

"Wow, Dove. I'm sure your good friend Sutler would love to hear his death was 'minimal' in your eyes."

I stumble into a sitting position. "That is *not* what I'm saying at all. I'm not excusing it, and it kills me that I lost Kaine. If I'd been involved in the planning of that op, I would've tried to talk them into setting off the bomb when the warehouse was empty. All I'm saying is, large-scale casualty events are not the way Mods operate. They don't bomb large groups of people—that's the General's MO. How many were killed in the Silverblood Purge? Tens of thousands? And what about the bombing of Valterra Ridge? An entire Mod community wiped out. The Uprising doesn't target innocents."

When his dubious expression lingers, I voice a challenge.

"When has there ever been a high-casualty event caused by the Uprising?"

"There've been bombings."

"How many civilian deaths?" I push.

He grumbles under his breath. "All right. It's true. They don't target civilians. So what the hell are they planning for the Jubilee, then? Is my father the target?"

"Would you care if he was?"

Cross hesitates, then says, "I don't know."

———

It's difficult on the base without Kaine. I didn't realize what an integral part of my life he was, how much I enjoyed his teasing grins, his shameless flirting. It's been a week and I still expect to walk into the mess hall and find him there, handing me a cup of coffee. I have to settle for Lyddie, who's been clinging a little tighter lately, making more of an effort to share meals with me since Kaine's death.

"I miss him," she says today at morning meal.

My heart clenches. "I do, too."

She hesitates. "Can I ask you something about Elite?"

I furrow my brow, wariness flickering through me. "Sure, but I can't promise I'll be able to answer."

"Have you noticed any tension between Captain Redden and the colonel?"

"The colonel as in Travis Redden?"

"Yes. Things have been really tense in Intelligence since the bomber was stolen. Travis is on edge."

"I thought you didn't work directly under him."

"Oh, I don't." She blushes. "I delivered a coffee to him once, but that's about it. I hear murmurings from the other soldiers, though. And yesterday I walked by his office and heard him talking to someone on his comm about Elite."

I frown. "What was he saying?"

"He said the unit has gotten complacent, but he's going to change that. And then"—she lowers her voice—"he's putting together a shortlist of high-ranking officers."

My jaw drops. "You think he's trying to replace Cross?"

"I don't know. But I thought maybe I should tell you."

For someone who works in Intelligence, Lyddie has a big mouth. It's the one dangerous trait of hers that she was unable to conquer during our training. For once, though, I appreciate her gossipy tendencies. I waste no time reaching out to Cross right under her nose.

"Your brother might be looking to replace you as leader of Elite."

He snorts in my head. "He'll have to go through our father first.

The General's not going to let someone he doesn't explicitly trust take over."

"Your father trusts you explicitly, huh? He says as he speaks telepathically to his Modified girlfriend."

That gets me Wolf's trademark laughter. I didn't realize that the entire time Cross was teasing me with his stubborn dimple and infrequent laughter, I'd already been hearing him laugh my whole life. It's pretty fantastic. We linked spontaneously as children and now here we are, bound even tighter. It speaks to the undeniable truth of our connection. We're two halves of a fractured whole, drawn together by forces beyond our control.

He's right.

It's terrifying.

"Are you going to wear the dress we picked out in the city?" Lyddie interrupts my thoughts.

"What?"

"For the Jubilee."

"Oh. Yes."

For the first time in my life, I used Lux credits to purchase clothing, and I even managed to find a fabric that isn't gray, black, or blue. The dress I bought is a deep emerald green that complements my eyes and makes my skin appear luminous. I looked like a stranger in the mirror, but I felt beautiful. I want Cross to see me in it.

"I'll come by your quarters before the party tomorrow. We'll do our hair and makeup together."

"Sounds great." I squeeze her hand, and it feels bittersweet.

We started off this journey. Me, her, and Kaine. Now there's only two of us left. But I suppose it's better than being alone.

———

That night, Adrienne reaches out and tells me what I need to do. It's a simple objective, and one that gives me hope I wasn't lying to Cross when I said they wouldn't target civilians.

The following evening, I make my way to the outskirts of the base and the tunnel off the vehicle pool where I first met Adrienne. The package they've left for me is inside a sleek black pack bearing the Silver Block logo, identical to the packs we carry on missions. I don't know how she got it. Don't care.

I fit the straps over my shoulders and then skulk back into the lot, making a show of looking around. I'm here under the pretense of tracking down Yemi, one of the officers in charge of signing out vehicles.

"There you are," I call, smiling at the burly man as he hops out of the driver's seat of an armored truck. "I wanted to talk to you about borrowing a car this weekend. I have a leisure pass."

It's not a lie. I do have a pass. I told Lyddie I'd visit her parents in the city with her, which anyone can verify by asking her.

"Sure thing," Yemi says, leading me toward his booth.

I shift the pack on my back, hoping whoever is monitoring the cameras and may have seen me enter the vehicle pool without a bag, doesn't notice that I'm leaving with one.

CHAPTER 49

I t's time.

The Jubilee starts soon, and I have less than an hour to execute my mission. With my pack in the passenger seat, I drive my borrowed vehicle across the base to the large, sprawling venue where the General hosts all his events. The capitalists and other Continent elites prefer the only hotel in the city grand enough to host large gatherings. The Elysian. They purchase permits to celebrate the most frivolous things—a daughter graduating from upper school. A son landing his first job assignment.

The General, of course, is not about these frills. His trusty Command base will do, even for celebrating such a monumental feather in the cap of his rule. According to Cross, he doesn't care one lick about this Jubilee. The General believes all parties are self-indulgent, period, but hosts them for appearances' sake. Tonight he'll be giving a speech. There'll be dancing. Refreshments. And then everyone will be dismissed in military fashion before midnight and ushered off the base.

Copper Block is overseeing transportation. Civilian vehicles will enter the base from the checkpoint near the venue. Searched and scanned, of course. I ran into Lieutenant Hirai in the mess hall earlier, and he told me he was responsible for strengthening the force field surrounding the venue. If any guests ignore the multiple warning signs and try to step foot beyond the designated area, they're in for a nasty surprise in the form of electrocution.

"We really hope we don't have a lot of dead civilians on our hands tonight," he said ruefully, and I had to giggle.

"Do you have the package?" Adrienne asks.

"Yes."

This will be the tricky part. I need to set the charges inside the caterers' quarters. Not in the kitchen, but a large supply room two doors down. Adrienne projected the blueprints to me last night.

"There won't be anyone in here?" I ask her, the same way I asked yesterday when I was told my objective.

"There shouldn't be."

Good. I'm assuming my role in the plan is to create another decoy. The explosives taking up residence in my bag are nowhere near enough to do much damage to the supply room, let alone the entire base. But I'm still on need-to-know footing, with no directive other than to plant these explosives.

Silver Elite comes with the kind of security perks that make the lower blocks jealous. My movements hardly ever get questioned, and if I do happen to get stopped, I scan my thumb, they see my unit, and there are no questions asked. Today, luckily, not a single soul notices me.

The venue is chaotic. Catering trucks parked outside, soldiers with guns watching the staff unload items and scanning each one. I keep my head down and slip into the building, averting gazes in the hallway. I haven't activated my jammer yet—it'll draw too much attention if all the cameras in the building suddenly stop working—so I'm very aware of the blinking red lights in the ceiling following my every move. I enter the kitchen, and only then do I remove the jammer from my bag, activate it, and scurry back into the hall, invisible to the cameras.

In the supply room, I make quick work of the charges, setting them around the room. Every sound, every rustle of fabric, sets my nerves on edge. I want to hurry, to rush what I'm doing, but I can't afford to be careless. Adrienne is counting on me.

I haven't been asked to arm the explosives, only to position them at strategic points and connect them to the ignition system. I assume the detonation will be remote. After I stick the remaining silver pod on the wall inside a slatted wooden closet, I slide the now-empty backpack over my shoulder, the jammer peeking out of the side pocket.

I breathe a sigh of relief.

I did it.

Done.

Time to get the hell out of here.

Halfway to the door, I hear footsteps directly outside it. I freeze.

Keep walking, I implore whoever it is. *Just keep walking.*

The doorknob begins to turn.

Shit.

I shove the top of the jammer deeper into the pocket, out of sight, just as the door swings open and Jayde Valence appears in the doorway.

My heart stops.

We stare at each other for a moment, until her cool, crisp voice breaks the silence.

"What are you doing in here, soldier?"

"Oh, I was looking for the caterer. I think his name is Eman?" I gulp through my bone-dry mouth. "The kitchen crew said he might've ducked in here to grab some supplies."

"The caterer."

"Yes."

Jayde closes the door behind her and steps deeper into the room, scanning her surroundings. My heart promptly starts beating again. Loud and persistent.

The charges I've set are invisible to the eye. Strategically placed. I should be fine so long as she doesn't take a closer look. Particularly at the window. All she has to do is raise the blinds and she'll find those two small silver pucks I affixed to the frame.

"But as you can see," I finish lightly, "he's not here. I guess I need to keep poking around."

I take a step toward the door. She doesn't move.

"Lieutenant Colonel?" I prompt.

She smiles. The bloodmark on her cheek appears even more menacing when paired with an expression of mirth.

"It is very rare," she says, "that I misjudge people."

"I'm sorry?"

"I saw you set the charges. The General will not be pleased."

Panic sparks inside me. "I don't know what—"

"My mind has never failed me," Jayde interrupts. "Even in childhood. Every vision I've ever had has been confirmed with unerring accuracy. This evening's vision . . ." Her lips tighten. "I recognized your face immediately. I interrogated you after Julian Ash's execution."

"You did. And you cleared me," I remind her, squaring my shoulders. "Because I didn't do anything wrong."

Even as I speak, my mind is already decoyed in preparation for her penetration. It doesn't come. She simply stands there, shaking her head in bewilderment.

"How?" she asks.

"How what?"

"How were you able to keep your mind controlled for so long? It's extraordinary."

"I honestly don't know what you're talking about." I try to keep my voice steady despite the fear coursing through me.

"Don't lie to me, soldier. I might have erred during your interrogation, but I'm not a fool."

We stare at each other. My stomach is churning, twisting with anxiety. I throw out a desperate link to Cross, who responds immediately.

"What's wrong?"

"I need you. Now. Jayde Valence just had a vision of me aiding the Uprising."

"Where are you?"

I give him my location and say, "Hurry."

My fingers tingle with the urge to reach for the gun on my hip. But nothing's happened yet. She isn't reaching for her own weapon, and I don't want to reveal my hand too soon.

Even more telling is that no one else is rushing into this room. No footsteps thundering in the hallway. I suspect there's nobody outside the door. The question is, why didn't she bring any backup? How the hell did that vision of hers end if she felt this comfortable coming alone?

As I watch her, my nerves are stretched taut like a bowstring, ready to snap at the slightest provocation.

"Normally I would dispatch a squad to collect you, but I had to see for myself." She shakes her head again. Astounded. "The vision was so preposterous. I *cleared* you. And yet here you are."

Hubris, I realize.

That's why she's alone.

She was so confident in her mind-reading abilities that she couldn't fathom how she could've possibly been bested by me. She had to investigate. And maybe there's some embarrassment driving her actions, too. She'd been so colossally wrong about me; would she really want an audience while her shortcomings are being aired?

Or—I wryly acknowledge, as she gets her hand on her gun so fast I barely have time to blink—maybe she's a highly trained lieutenant colonel who trusts in her ability to take care of herself in the field.

"I haven't done anything wrong," I protest as she points the gun at me. Its steel barrel is affixed with a silencer.

"Tell me how you did it. Who trained you? That kind of shielding requires extensive training. Years of it. Decades."

"I don't know what you're talking about. I just have a regular shield that I learned in lower school and then shored up in the Program."

Her lips curl in a condescending sneer. "Fine, then. I'll find out for myself." She jerks the gun barrel toward my hip. "Unholster your weapon. Lay it on the floor and kick it toward me."

It's clear she's not playing around, so I follow her instructions. When I squat to put the gun down, my other hand inches toward my boot.

"The knife, too. Kick it toward me."

Shit.

She chuckles. "My visions are very detailed, soldier. I know every move you're about to make."

"Cross. Hurry, damn it."

"Trying."

I'm weaponless as I rise to my feet. Keeping her gun trained on me, Jayde's emotionless eyes seek out my gaze. I feel it the moment she penetrates my mind, but I don't react.

"Fascinating," she murmurs. "You don't feel the shock?"

"No, I feel it." I've officially given up on denying the truth. At this point I'm only insulting her intelligence.

"You do?"

"Yes. I just ignore it."

Amazement floods her expression. "We've performed tests on other Aberrants. Do you realize the shock you receive when another Aberrant infiltrates your mind is the equivalent of almost five hundred volts?" She starts to laugh. "You just ignore it."

I shrug. It's hard to focus with the itchy sensation crawling all over my body. She's in my mind, and I'm having trouble keeping it decoyed while trying to come up with an escape plan at the same time.

Jayde is nodding with approval. "There you go. I hear you now."

"Because I'm letting you." My icy tone belies the thundering of my heart.

I need to find a way out of this.

"Cross, where are you?" I plead.

"Moving as fast as I can."

"Move faster."

"You're communicating with someone," she accuses. "Who is it?"

I decoy my mind before she can figure out it's Cross. My gaze darts toward my discarded gun. It's in the corner of the room, maybe three feet from Jayde. She'll shoot me before I reach it.

"Yes," she says, answering my thoughts. "I will."

I could lunge at her. She'll still fire at me, but if I can get her to lower the weapon, even a few inches, I'll have a better shot of not taking a bullet to the chest.

At this point, there's no harm in trying.

"And what are we trying?" Jayde's tone is distracted. Her forehead has a deep groove in it as she concentrates on pillaging my thoughts.

I take advantage of that. The only time the shield of a Mod as powerful as her might show any weakness is when she's using those powers. When all her concentration is directed elsewhere. Directed at me. I reach out with my mind, opening a path to hers. When I encounter her shield, I start pushing.

"Your veins . . . They don't change."

She's still reading my mind. It makes me sick to have her poking around in there, but I continue to use it to my benefit. In fact, I help her out, bringing certain thoughts to the surface, making it easier for her.

"You're working for the Uprising. Oh, you stupid, foolish girl."

I throw all my mental force against her shield. I slam into it as hard as I can. In my mind I imagine a crack form. Widen. Splinter at the sides. For some reason her shield looks gold now, but I go with it. I've found that fighting your own mind is a futile exercise. The gold shines brighter, flecks of it dancing through my head like dust motes. Long, thin fissures form across Jayde's shield, spreading outward, like the surface of ice that's about to break and—

I'm in.

Am I?

I don't feel the pressure of her shield anymore trying to repel me. But she also doesn't jerk in surprise. I didn't get the feeling that she'd mastered the ability to ignore those five hundred volts. She seemed too stunned that it was even possible. Unless she was shocked because she believed she was the only one who could do it?

Setting my questions aside, I focus on pushing a command into her mind.

Lower your weapon.

"Stop straining yourself. You don't need to try to read my thoughts," Jayde assures me. "I'll enlighten you myself. You're fighting for the wrong team, Darlington. We're not the villains here."

That momentarily makes me lose my focus. I stare at her, incredulous. "You've murdered thousands of your own people."

"They are not my people. Especially not the ones you're working for. They're unnatural. They're corrupting minds." Her gray eyes become oddly magnanimous. "If you surrender right now, I won't kill you."

I can't stop a bark of laughter. "Uh-huh. I'm sure."

"I won't." I glimpse a spark of excitement. "I want to study you. I want to work with you."

My jaw falls open. "I would never work with you."

Lower your weapon.

Jayde lowers the gun, just slightly. I don't think she even realizes it. What I learned from my experience with the firing squad is that they couldn't hear what I was saying. I was in their minds, but my commands weren't translating into something they could consciously interpret. They didn't *hear* me telling them to pull the trigger—they just knew that they should.

"I wish you would reconsider," she tells me. "You're extraordinary. I've never encountered someone with such a strong mind."

"Yes, I'm sure this is a sincere offer and I'll just skip into the Capitol, where you and I will work together happily, our offices side by side."

"Of course not. You would be a prisoner. At first," she emphasizes. "But I think once I teach you everything there is to know, once I show you the possibilities, you'll understand why I'm working with the General."

I want to command her to lower her weapon again, but her animated voice, her palpable enthusiasm, triggers a cold rush of unease. It roils in my gut. An eddy of fear. I could stomach being a prisoner. Getting thrown into the stockade again.

But I can't stomach being *her* prisoner.

My mind flashes to that hospital full of fragmented Mods. The freezer of blood vials that makes me believe something horrific is happening there.

This woman wants to study me.

I refuse to let that happen.

"We could accomplish great things. Imagine the possibilities."

"I will never work for or with you. You're the reason my uncle is dead."

"He's the reason he's dead." Her expression clouds at the notion she's not getting anywhere with me. "Your mind is the strongest I've ever encountered. I would hate to let that go to waste."

Turn the gun on yourself.

She's such a strong Mod that I expect her to smile and say, *Nice try.* But she doesn't. She's still in my head, though. Why isn't she aware of what I'm trying to do? I wish I knew something about this ability of mine. Anything. Does it work on a different frequency?

Do I care right now as long as it's working?

Turn the gun on yourself.

Jayde's brow knits as her hand twitches, the gun trembling. I feel her losing her grip on my mind as she fights whatever impulse I'm feeding into hers. She tries to resist it, but my determination is stronger than hers. I'm not going to let this woman study me or sentence me to death. I refuse to face the squad. I refuse to leave Cross. I refuse.

Turn the gun on yourself.

"If you're not going to work with me, then this is the end of the road for you." She's angry now. "But it really is a shame."

Turn the gun on yourself.

She clicks the safety off, her exterior once again icy as she realizes I'm not going to "work" with her.

Frustration gathers inside me as my commands continue to go unobeyed. Why isn't it working, damn it? I'm experiencing that same surge of energy I felt at the execution. My mind is alive with a kaleidoscope of gold dust. And I know she feels *something*. She thinks I'm reading her mind. She senses I'm doing something. So why isn't—

"Try saying it out loud. I heard that helps sometimes."

Uncle Jim's voice rumbles through my head. Advice uttered a long time ago, during one of our many training sessions. He seemed so sure that vocalizing the commands could aid in inciting.

At this point, what do I have to lose?

"Raise your gun to your head," I say, my voice coming out hoarse.

"What?"

Jayde starts to lift her arm, then stops. Frowning at me. At the gun.

"Raise it to your head and pull the trigger."

The gun slices upward, turning.

Her eyes widen. "What are you doing?"

"Raise it to your head and pull the trigger."

The barrel is now pointing straight at her own temple.

"*No*," she growls. "What *is* this?"

"Pull the trigger."

My voice doesn't waver. I refuse to die at this woman's hand.

"Pull the trigger," I repeat.

Her face twists in agony as she struggles against my command. I feel her resistance crumbling like a sandcastle against the tide. Breaking apart.

"Pull the trigger, Jayde."

With a sudden, sickening click, Jayde obeys.

CHAPTER 50

The weight of what I've done hits me hard and fast. A crushing sensation on my chest that obstructs my breathing. I can't unsee it. Unhear it.

The hiss of the bullet leaving her silenced weapon. Penetrating her skull.

The fear in her eyes as she pulled the trigger against her will.

The memory plays on a loop in my mind, each detail etched with painful clarity. A torrent of emotions threatens to overwhelm me. Contrition. Shame. Relief. I killed her and it makes me sick to my stomach. I killed her and I'm relieved. She can never tell anyone what I am now. She can't imprison me. Experiment on me. Put me in front of a firing squad.

I've rid myself of an enemy, a dangerous one, yet as I stare at her lifeless body on the floor, guilt claws at my insides. The line between right and wrong blurs into shades of gray, leaving me grappling with my own moral compass.

I told myself I never wanted to interfere with someone's free will. Look at me now.

"I'm here."

When his deep voice fills my head, I almost keel over in relief. I yank him into the room, then close and lock the door behind him.

"Watch the blood," I warn.

Cross glances at our feet, taking it all in. The gun in Jayde's hand. The hole in her temple. The small crimson puddle forming around her blond head.

"What happened?" he says grimly.

"I told you, she had a vision of me. She figured out who I am. What I am."

I bite my lip in disbelief. Everything was going so smoothly before that. Of all the things that could throw a wrench into the mission, this was the last one I expected.

"You shot her?"

I shake my head.

Then I nod.

"Which is it?"

"I don't know." I drag both hands through my hair. I want to tear it out by the roots. "I incited her."

He briefly closes his eyes.

"Cross."

He doesn't speak. Without a word, he examines our surroundings, scanning the room. His cheeks hollow as he sucks them in. Thinking.

Finally, he says, "Okay. I got this."

"What do you mean you got this?"

He's already pulling out his source. "Xavier," he tells the screen, then brings the comm to his ear. There's a pause. "I need you. I'll send the grids." Another pause. "Sanitation."

As he slides the source into his pocket, I fix him with a stern look. "No. I'm not going to let you risk your life for something that I did."

"My life is already at risk." He stares at me. "She's in my father's inner circle. She's a lieutenant colonel. She's on the fucking Tribunal."

"Cross—"

"I'll take care of the cameras. Just go."

"I'm not leaving you."

"Go," he growls. "I mean it, Wren. Go back to your quarters. Get ready for the party."

I gape at him. "We're not going to the party!"

"Yes. We are. You're going to walk into that ballroom wearing your new dress, and you're going to smile at all your superiors. You're going to shake the General's hand and tell him how much you love Silver Block. You're going to congratulate him on twenty-five years of valiant, impeccable rule. Do you understand me?"

I clench my teeth.

"Do you understand me?"

"Yes."

"Good. Now get the fuck out of here."

As much as I don't appreciate his tone, I know there's no way I could've done this . . . sanitation . . . on my own.

I grab my pack from the floor. "Should I use my jammer?"

"Yes. Keep it activated until you're back in your quarters. I don't want a single camera picking you up. Go."

With a weak nod, I leave him to clean up my mess.

———

My anxiety levels don't wane in the slightest. If anything, they only skyrocket when I burst into my quarters, because now I have the privacy to let every turbulent emotion I've been feeling since I killed Jayde bubble to the surface.

How is Cross going to explain why Jayde Valence dropped off the face of the Continent? How? Cross has a brilliant mind when it comes to military maneuvers. But this is . . .

Suicide.

The word lingers in my mind, spurring me to link with him. I'm a little surprised when he lets me.

"Cross, she shot herself. This could be staged as a suicide."

"Go to your quarters, Dove."

He severs the link.

Fuck!

Frustration burns a path through my veins. This isn't fair to him. It isn't fair to Xavier, as annoying as I find him. They shouldn't be fixing something that I broke.

I force myself to follow his orders. I strip out of my uniform and step into the bathroom. I crank on the shower and then stand under the warm spray, trying not to cry.

I like to think I've grown since I got here. I've learned to be more patient. I've learned to trust someone other than myself. I've even started to rein in my impulses. Sort of. Sometimes.

But it feels like all that progress was erased the second I incited a woman to kill herself.

I rest my forearm against the tiled wall and press my face into it. My body feels weak as I'm struck with a bleak, depressing truth.

I think I might be a monster.

I made a woman kill herself.

How are those not the actions of a monster?

With a choked sob, I force myself to get out of the shower and wrap a towel around myself. In my bedroom, I put on a bra and then slip into a pair of boy-cut underwear. As I'm brushing my hair, I find an alert on my source. Lyddie, saying she's on her way to get ready with me.

I forgot we planned to do that. But there might still be time to head her off. Her quarters aren't in this building, but near the admin wings all the way across the base, which is quite a trek if she's not driving.

I'm about to send a comm telling her not to come when the door swings open.

In our earlier exchanges, I told her to let herself in.

Shit.

Lyddie saunters in wearing a sweet white dress with a scoop neck and pleated skirt. Her bright smile lights up the room. "Hi!"

I've never been more grateful for a pair of underwear. They cover my bloodmark in its entirety.

Panic lodges in my throat when I realize how close I came to having her walk in on me naked. Cross was right. It was a careless decision to let Ellis heal me.

Lyddie notes my expression and giggles. "Someone looks frazzled."

Someone is about to have a nervous breakdown.

I manage to paste on a smile. "Sorry, it's been a chaotic day."

"Aw, well, don't worry. Soon you can forget all about it. Tonight is going to be so much fun," she chirps. "I love parties."

"Can't wait." I force another smile, trying to suppress the worry gnawing at me. "My dress is hanging in the bathroom. Let me put it on and then we can do our hair—"

"Wren! Your scars!"

Her gaze falls on my bare legs, eliciting a loud gasp. When I try to keep walking, she hurries over and tugs on my arm.

"They're gone!"

Discomfort prickles my spine. "Yeah. They brought in this healer . . ." I trail off.

"You let an Aberrant healer touch you?" She narrows her eyes.

"We had no choice. Our unit has to do these wellness checks." I start backing toward the bathroom. "He said he could get rid of the scars, so I said sure, why not?"

"Let me see it," she says.

"Oh. It's nothing fancy. Just plain skin now."

She's already in front of me, reaching for my leg. She touches the skin of my thigh, still smiling, but when the bottom of my underwear slides up slightly, I shove the fabric back down and jerk away from her.

Her cheerful expression falters. "What was that?"

"Nothing. I told you, it's just skin now."

"What was that red mark?" She stares at me in confusion. "Was that a bruise?" she asks, but the growing horror in her eyes tells me she knows exactly what she saw. "Wren, what was that?"

"It's just a birthmark."

"A birthmark."

"Yeah. Let me get dressed so we can—"

In a very uncharacteristic Lyddie move, she lunges forward and pushes the fabric up.

I freeze, watching the awareness dawn on her face as she examines the bloodmark. The mark that betrays what I really am.

All the color drains from her cheeks. Her hand flies to her mouth.

"Oh my . . . *gosh*," she gasps, taking a step back. "That's a blood-mark."

"Lyddie," I start, reaching for her, but she flinches as if my touch is going to burn her.

"Oh my gosh. What is happening?"

Gosh. Even in a state of sheer terror, Lyddie can't not be Lyddie, refusing to utter the word *God* even when it's not technically illegal. The General doesn't want people practicing religion or worshipping a higher being, but he doesn't give a shit if you say the word. He's not threatened by a word.

But Lyddie is all about the rules.

"You're Aberrant?" Her voice trembles with disbelief. "How could you lie to me all this time? Oh my . . . *God*!" All her rule-clinging propriety flies out the window as her breathing gets shallow. "How could this . . . Why . . ."

My mind scrambles to find a way to make her see I'm not a threat.

"They know," I blurt out.

She blinks in confusion. "What?"

"They know that I'm Aberrant. Cross and the General."

"W-what?"

And just like that, an entire story comes flowing out of my mouth like water from a tap. This is the reason Uncle Jim liked having me talk to the soldiers in Hamlett: my ability to improvise. It serves me well now.

"I don't have the black bands," I hold out my wrists, "because I'm undercover. They recruited me when I was still in lower school."

"I don't understand what you're saying. You're . . . You're Aber-rant . . ."

"I am. But I've been loyal to the Company my whole life. My parents still serve the General in Ward Z. Our cattle feeds the Command."

"Your parents," she echoes. "I thought your parents were dead."

"No, it's all part of my cover. They gave me a fake Aberrant uncle so no one would suspect what I was."

She stares at me. I can see her vacillating between wanting to trust her best friend Wren and wanting to recoil in terror from the girl with the bloodmark on her thigh.

"What's your ability?" she asks in a weak voice.

"Telepathy, but I don't have anyone to use it with. I'm not a double agent, so I don't really need to interact with others like me. I can read minds, too, but I don't because I respect everyone's privacy. And I can heal."

Her eyes go wider than saucers. "You're a healer?"

"Yes. That's why they wanted me in Elite, because I can heal members of the unit on the field."

Careful.

I'm starting to provide too many details. The best lies are simple. Ordinary. I pull back, relying only on what I've already said.

"They know exactly what I am," I reiterate. "They've always known."

"Why are your burns gone?"

"The General decided it would encourage unity in Elite. It's supposed to be a show of trust, so that my fellows know they can rely on me to always tell them the truth. Look. Lyds. There is so much more I want to tell you," I say, imploring her with my gaze, "and I promise you can ask me a thousand more questions, but right now I need you to promise me you'll keep my cover intact. You can't tell anyone else about this."

"Did Kaine know?"

"No. He died before the General instructed me to reveal myself to the captain. Cross hasn't told the unit yet."

"Told them what?"

I jerk in surprise at the sound of Ivy's voice.

She's standing at my door. The door that Lyddie failed to fully shut.

Holy hellfuck, could this night get any worse?

Jayde Valence's dead body is lying in a supply room. Cross and Xavier are trying to handle it. Lyddie is gawking at me like she's never seen me in her life. And now Ivy is here. Cross's ex-girlfriend who never liked me. We might be friendly now, but we're still not friends.

Before I can answer, Lyddie does the one thing I just asked her not to do.

"Wren is an Aberrant operative."

Ivy is so stunned, she has to brace her hand against the doorway for a second. "What?"

I want to slap Lyddie in the face, but I can't do that when I need her on my side.

"Is that true?" Ivy demands.

I dip my head in a nod. "Only the General and his inner circle know. Cross is briefing the rest of Elite tomorrow. The General decided it would promote cohesion if they knew my real identity." I bite my lip. "I'm a loyalist. I always have been. I promise you, both of you, I'm not a threat. Tonight I'm going to put on a dress, shake the General's hand, and thank him profusely for everything he's done for us, for trusting us to be on the right side of history. Lieutenant Colonel Valence. Ellis. Me. We're not like the others."

Lyddie is softening. I can tell.

"We all know the destruction their powers can cause," I continue. "But I don't destroy. I heal."

And make women kill themselves.

But that's neither here nor there.

I take a step toward Lyddie. Instantly, she shies away in fear.

"Lyds. Come on. If I wanted to hurt you, I had ample opportunities to do it. I don't want anything to happen to you. All I'm asking is, can you please keep this to yourself? Tomorrow Cross will call a briefing and everything will be out in the open. I'll tell him I want you there." I glance at Ivy. "Both of you. You can go through my file page by page if you want."

"Let's see it now," Ivy says coldly.

"I don't have clearance." A laugh sputters out. "Nobody in Elite is even in the system. Not officially. Only the captain can access our files. Please. I'm no threat to either one of you tonight. We're going to a party. That's all. Everything else can wait until tomorrow."

I focus on Lyddie, searching her expression for any sign of trust. Even a tiny trace of it.

"You know me, Lyds. You *know* I'm a good person. Please."

She hesitates.

"All right," she finally says.

A gust of relief blasts through me. "We'll get everything sorted tomorrow," I assure her. "Just promise you won't say anything until then."

She bites her trembling bottom lip. "I won't."

When I glance back at the doorway, I find it empty. Ivy is gone.

She left without making the same promise.

CHAPTER 51

The lilting melody of the orchestra greets me as I walk through the arched doorway of the ballroom. The instruments are set up on one of two stages in the elegant space. The second stage sits empty at the other end of the room, adorned with navy-blue curtains and a backdrop of rich blue hues. I linger near the entrance, watching the crowd and wishing I were anywhere but here.

I arrived alone because Lyddie was meeting her parents outside. My instincts had screamed for me not to let her out of my sight, but short of handcuffing her to me, I can't exactly tell her not to be with her parents. Still, I'll feel better once I have both her and Ivy in my sights again.

That damn Ivy. Where did she run off to? Who has she spoken to? I don't trust her as far as I can throw her, but at the same time, she never told anybody she saw Cross leaving my quarters that day.

I perk up. And . . . maybe I can use that to my advantage now. Convince Ivy that Cross was only there to discuss my undercover identity.

If I can track the damn woman down.

There's a dance floor, but only a handful of couples make use of it.

They twirl and sway across the polished floor, their laughter mingling with conversations filling the room. All around me, uniformed officers mingle with civilians in their finest attire, creating a striking juxtaposition of military formality and Sanctum Point glamour.

Sadly, I'm too shaken from killing a woman today to admire the silk gowns. But I do note that there's more color and life in this room than I've ever seen from the General. Even his broadcasts feature a gray background, and when he delivers them outdoors, it's almost as if the weather knows there's a broadcast scheduled for that day, because it's always overcast.

Cross isn't linking with me, and it's starting to piss me off. I know he's busy cleaning up my mess, but I'm worried about him, and I'm worried he might be pissed at *me*.

It's not like I set out to kill Jayde today. She was a precog. She had a vision. That's completely beyond my control, something I never could have foreseen because, well, *I'm* not a fucking precog.

A waiter hands me a glass of champagne. This party is nice enough that I'm hoping it's real, but when I take a sip, the synthetic flavor slides down my throat. Noted. The General will splurge, but not that much.

Finally, I feel Cross in my mind.

"On my way, Dove."

"You should probably hurry. Things have gone from bad to worse over here. Lyddie and Ivy saw my bloodmark."

"Fuck's sake. You never should have removed that fucking scar."

"I was trying to prove my love to you, asshole. And I did a stupid, impulsive thing. In my defense, I didn't think many people would be seeing my bare thighs. I'm usually wearing clothes unless I'm with you."

"Please don't tell me you killed Lyddie and Ivy."

"Lyddie, no. But I did get rid of your ex-girlfriend."

"Daisy."

"Joking. I fed them a story about how I'm undercover in Elite. I'm your secret weapon and you're going to hold a briefing tomorrow to tell everyone in our unit."

"Fucking hell."

"I know. I honestly don't know how we're going to get out of this, but we need to come up with a plan." I hesitate. "I might need to leave."

"I'm not letting you out of my sight."

"Lyddie loves me. She's not going to do anything that will put me in danger. Ivy... I don't know."

I still don't see either one of them, and my frustration intensifies. I give the ballroom another scan, blinking when a familiar face catches my eye.

Either I imagined it, or that was Adrienne.

I only got a quick flash of her, but I swear that was her face. The wide, sensual mouth. The delicate nose. The features that don't quite blow you away separately, but together make for a striking face.

I search the room, but I don't see her anymore.

"This is probably not the time to say this, but... you look beautiful."

I lift my head to find Cross weaving through the crowd toward me. I melt at the sight of him. He's in his dress blues, the jacket and trousers tailored to his broad body. I suppose as the General's son, he has to keep up appearances. He's clean-shaven, and his dimple peeks out at me as he smiles.

Our relationship isn't public, so he doesn't greet me with a kiss or even a hug. He simply stands beside me, the back of my neck tickling as he asks to link.

"Soldier Darlington," he says formally.

"Captain."

"You look incredible in green. Makes your witchy eyes look even yellower."

I can't stop a smile, but it fades when his expression sobers, as does his tone.

"The list of damage control keeps getting longer and longer."

"I know. I'm sorry. I—"

I lose focus when I suddenly spot Ivy several yards away. She's a vision in blue. Holding a champagne flute, watching me and Cross. Suspicious.

I don't want to be seen standing together in total silence, so I speak out loud. "Ivy's going to report me."

"She might not. Also, that secret weapon story? It might not be so bad. We'd have to get you the black band—"

"I'm not giving myself a loyalist tattoo," I growl into his mind.

"Sorry, you're right. I know. I just can't see a way out of this right now."

We don't have time to dwell on it, because the orchestra stops playing and a hush falls over the room as the General enters the ballroom.

He exudes power. Authority. His posture is pristine, but that's only part of it. It's in the way his gaze slices through you, assessing, as if on the spot he can decide if you're worthy of his presence, of your own existence. His talent for split-second calculations has served him well all these years.

General Redden moves through the crowd, nodding at people. When he passes his son, his gaze doesn't even register me. He simply nods at Cross, who steps away from me.

"It's time," he murmurs in my mind.

"For what?"

"The speech."

He's visibly unenthused as he follows his father. They share the same height. And when Travis joins them, they make for an imposing trio in their dress uniforms. Roe is the last to climb onto the stage. He's rubbing his nose, and I know he just did a stim or two. His eyes have that manic look.

I notice Cross frown at him as if to say, *You couldn't keep it out of your nose for one evening?* Roe gives his brother an insolent smile.

The room falls silent as the General ascends the steps to the stage. He waits for his sons to dutifully stand behind him, their dark uniforms a contrast with the light-blue backdrop. Only when they're lined up like obedient ducklings does he approach the podium.

General Redden clears his throat. When he begins to speak, his voice rings with authority.

"Twenty-five years ago, I cut off the head of the snake."

Lovely. He's not speaking metaphorically, either. Everyone saw the beheading of President Tack Severn, broadcast directly into their homes.

"Violence is necessary in war. Necessary for freedom. And after twenty-five years, a quarter of a century, it's only fitting that we reflect on the sacrifices and the triumphs that have brought us to this moment. Twenty-five years ago, the Primes of the Continent languished under the unjust grip of a corrupt and inept regime. Our society was fractured, and the will of the people was silenced by tyranny. The Aberrant wrestled society out of our ancestors' hands and made us second-class citizens. President Severn tore the very fabric of morality by inciting the minds of both his Prime enemies and his Aberrant allies. But together, the Primes stood united in our resolve to forge a new path—a path of liberation and order. Under my guidance, we liberated ourselves from the aberrations that tried to destroy us. We cleansed the Continent, rooting out traitors and restoring honor to our institutions."

He pauses for dramatic effect.

"But our journey is far from over. As we look to the future, let us remain vigilant in the face of adversity, steadfast in our commitment to preserving the peace and stability that we have fought so hard to achieve. I wasn't asked to lead—I was called to it."

I try not to roll my eyes. Isn't that what all great tyrants say? *Oh, I didn't want this. Please take all my burdensome power away.*

"I was a simple man. I led a unit of men. I served Severn dutifully, and my wife was in the garden, but—"

I blink. And his wife was in the garden? Okay. Strange digression.

From the corner of my eye, I notice Ivy creeping toward me. My shoulders tense, snapping back, but she's only moving closer to the stage to listen.

"—and right before he died, Severn spoke the phrase with which he ended all his broadcasts. *Audaces fortuna iuvat.* Fortune favors the bold. Which is perhaps the only true thing he ever said."

Redden is purposely omitting the rest of President Severn's cry.

Et potentia fluit ad fortes.

Fortune favors the bold, and power flows to the strong.

In his dying moments, Severn was still trying to stick it to those inferior "piss-veins" he so despised.

"We were bold in the Coup, and fortune did indeed favor us. But the world he described is not possible, and we took the train there when my son was five and—"

He stops for a second. An uneasy feeling tickles at my gut.

"It was the kind of day that makes you want to stay at home with your family."

What the hell is he talking about now?

"Severn wasn't the sort of man who would, and before that, I knew. Before that, he knew."

I notice several guests exchanging glances. Obviously, I'm not the only one baffled by this speech.

Redden clears his throat. Glances at his sons. "These three young men behind me will carry that mantle when I'm gone. Which I hope won't be for at least another hundred years if the research grant I've approved for the regeneration ward at the hospital pans out."

His attempt at humor falls flat. Mostly because everyone is still perplexed by everything that preceded it.

He chuckles awkwardly when the crowd doesn't respond. "I've raised my sons to believe that we can be everything that's ever tried to do was not good."

Murmurs of confusion travel through the room.

His features grow strained, as if he's starting to feel it, too. The same bewilderment we feel. He shakes his head. Clears this throat again.

"Twenty-five years and look at all we've accomplished. Our society is a well-oiled machine, and when she was in the garden, she told me—" He halts and blinks. Rubs his face.

I search the crowd for answers. And that's when I see her again.

Adrienne.

It *is* her.

She wears a simple dark-blue dress with long sleeves and a high neck, her red hair secured in a neat bun at her nape. She stands near the far edge of the stage, focused intently on the General.

My stomach twists. She's doing something to him. But what?

Redden continues to fall apart on the stage. Blinking, clearing his throat, getting a sentence in, stopping, blinking, shaking his head, getting another sentence in, a word, rubbing his face.

Nobody is quite sure how to react to the spectacle unfolding before them. His triumphant speech has devolved into a distorted jumble of words.

"And so, my fellow comrades, esteemed guests, and honored friends," he says, then falters again. "Where did Vinessa go?"

Apprehension sweeps through the room like a dark shadow. I hear the people around me speaking in hushed tones, exchanging whispers as they watch Merrick Redden unravel before their eyes.

"Where is Vin?"

Travis steps forward, but the General holds up his hands as if to ward him off. A frown mars Travis's lips.

"Where is she? What did you do with my wife?"

"Sir," Travis hedges. His voice is steady as he reaches for the General. "Maybe we should go get you a glass of water. Your throat sounds dry."

Redden eyes him incredulously. He shoves him aside. "I'm giving a speech, boy."

Travis glances at Cross, who approaches with slow, measured steps. Roe stays put, but he doesn't look so entertained anymore, only fearful.

Tension fills the room as the General insists on finishing his speech. A speech that is now nonsensical.

"And so, I want you to raise your glasses to another twenty-five years. Cross is not, but everybody is. And I saw her there and thought, yes. Or was it no?"

His voice grows increasingly erratic. His gestures wild. Then he scrunches his face and begins thumping his fist against his temple.

When Travis grabs his arm, he loses it, lashing out violently. I search for Adrienne again, but the agitated crowd keeps moving and swaying, obscuring her from view.

The General stops hitting himself. Then he stops talking altogether. He mumbles gibberish under his breath while everyone stands in wide-eyed shock.

He transforms into a pitiful figure up on that stage, and a chill goes through me as I watch his mind slipping away. Seeing him now, without knowing what came before, I would assume he was a fragmented

Mod. But I *do* know what came before. I literally saw it happen, right now, right here. In warp speed. I watched his mind fragmenting in front of me, as if someone was—

Corrupting it.

Jayde Valence's voice reverberates through my brain.

They're unnatural. They're corrupting minds.

The sick notion knocks the wind out of me, just as I spot Adrienne again. I try to catch her eye, but she's pushing away from the stage.

Travis, meanwhile, is attempting to calm the crowd, leaning toward the podium. "Everything is all right, ladies and gentlemen. I think we might have a little blood pressure medication problem on our hands."

Nobody's buying it.

Cross tries to help Travis subdue the General, whose expression has gone completely vacant. The man walked into this ballroom with authority and he's leaving it like a broken child, alternating between batting his sons away and slapping his own face.

"It's okay," Travis says into the microphone. "We'll get to the bottom of this. He'll be fine and—"

The rest of his words are drowned out by the explosion.

CHAPTER 52

Chaos erupts. The soldiers on site snap to action, officers barking orders and shoving their way through the crowd. Civilians shouting that a bomb went off, racing toward the exits in a panic. I'm not concerned. I know where the explosion originated. I know I'm in no danger of more charges igniting. I'm too busy tracking Adrienne's movements.

"The supply room!" someone shouts. "I see smoke coming from there."

I reach the archway and glimpse another flash of red. Adrienne. Stumbling toward the exit. She's hunched over and moving slower than I expect.

I'm on her within seconds, pulling her backward. When she tries to resist, I drag her toward a shadowy alleyway between the venue and loading area.

"What did you do to him?" I demand.

She looks sick. Physically ill. In fact, she can hardly walk, her knees noticeably wobbling.

"What's wrong with you?" I blurt out.

When she keels over, I instinctively steady her, shocked by how cold her skin feels. Yet her face drips with sweat.

"This is normal. N-normal response." She can barely speak.

I suddenly remember the physical sensations I felt at Jim's execution, when I had those eight minds in my psychic grasp. The dizziness. Fatigue. Sweat beading on my forehead. I remember the toll it took on me, using my mind to incite their will. It happened with Jayde, but to a lesser extent.

I search Adrienne's face. "What did you do to his mind?"

Last time we met, her eyes were sharp as daggers. Now they're dull and hazy.

"Not . . . the time, Darlington." Her hand quivers as she touches her ear. "Sara. Where are you?"

At the response, she pushes away from me, only to stumble again. She holds on to the wall to stabilize herself, swaying like she's about to faint.

"What did you do to his mind? You corrupted it?"

Her gaze slides toward me. "Where did you hear that term?"

"Is that it? Is that what you did?"

"Darlington." It's a pained whisper. "I need to get to the rendezvous."

"You're not making it anywhere in this state." I release a heavy sigh. "Let me help. Where do you need to go?"

I see the moment she recognizes her own weakness and admits defeat. Sagging against the wall, she nods toward the transport gate.

"Come on," I urge, guiding her forward.

She leans heavily on me for support, every step a struggle for her. We link arms as if we're just two civilian women trying to leave the scary party where the scary bomb blew up.

With potential eyes on us now, I switch to telepathy, but to no avail. I feel her energy signature, but it's faint. Flimsy.

"Won't work yet," she mumbles. "I expended too much energy."

"How did you do that to his brain?"

Her breaths escape in shallow gasps. I notice the pallor of her skin, the drops of sweat glistening on her forehead.

"How?" I tighten my grip on her arm.

"I don't know. It happens naturally. It's a matter of . . . rewiring."

"Rewiring." I feel like throwing up again. "You turned him into a vegetable right in front of us. I've never even heard of an ability like that before."

"It's rare," she admits. "Rarer than incitement."

We trudge toward the gate, where a line of cars waits to be permitted to exit. Behind us, people continue to stream out of the venue. But the chaos seems less . . . chaotic. The Command soldiers marching by appear to be in full control of the situation.

"I can brief you on all this later," she whispers. "Just let me get back to the base."

"How did you even get here in the first place?"

Although I'm starting to realize the Uprising is far more powerful than Command Intelligence can even imagine.

No sooner does that thought surface than another explosion shatters the air.

It's nowhere near our vicinity, somewhere off in the distance, but I feel the shock wave ripple through the ground beneath my shoes. The same force I felt from the bomb at the weapons depot. It ignites the sky, orange flames licking a black canvas, as the air thickens with smoke and a sickly-sweet odor.

I glance at Adrienne, only to see her disappear into the back of a car that speeds away like a bat bursting out of a cave.

I open a path to Cross, but he's not responding. I need to find him. Figure out what the hell is going on. But I don't make it back into the building. I'm running toward it when someone intercepts my path.

Roe.

I freeze, hoping my panic doesn't show on my face.

"Where are you hurrying off to?" His tone is laced with a cruel amusement.

Recovering from the surprise of seeing him, I flash an irritated look. "Roe. Get out of my way."

Rather than yield, he steps closer. "Why the rush? Afraid of a little fire?"

I clench my fists and try to brush past him, but he gets in my face again.

"I don't have time for this," I spit out.

I dart to the left, hoping to slip past him. But he's faster. His arm snaps out, catching me by the shoulder and shoving me back. Shocked, I stumble, nearly losing my footing.

"You really think I'm going to let you escape? After you tried to blow up a Command installation?"

My stomach sinks like a stone. Fuck. *Fuck!*

Fueled by pure desperation, I spring to action, swinging my fist at his jaw. He blocks it easily, countering with a swift kick to my midsection.

Pain explodes in my ribs at the unexpected blow. I gasp, doubling over. For a moment, I'm stunned into inaction. Roe was always decent in Combat class, but clearly he's been practicing since his total ass-kicking by Cross in the pit.

"Is that the best you've got?" he sneers, circling me like a predator.

I straighten, drawing a ragged breath into my lungs. "You don't want to do this, Roe."

"Oh, but I do. I want nothing more than to bash your Aberrant brains into the concrete."

Ivy.

Hellfucking Ivy.

Fear rips through me. I feint left, then spin right, hoping to outrun him. But he grabs me again and shoves me into the wall behind us. I take him with me, and we crash to the ground, wrestling for control. I manage to land a knee to his stomach. He punishes me with a jab to the chin that brings black dots to my vision.

"You 'fects make me sick," he hisses, then launches himself on top of me.

I land on my back, my skull smacking the ground hard. Roe pins me beneath him, his dark eyes sizzling down at me. Dripping with unadulterated hatred.

I writhe to free myself, but his weight is too much. My pulse grows thin, weak, as Roe slowly bends his head. His mouth brushes my cheek as he drags it toward my ear.

"I want to kill you with my bare hands," he whispers. "However . . ."

He's suddenly on his feet. The sound of hurried footsteps reaches us, and I glance up to see a swarm of soldiers appear, raising their weapons at me.

Nobody stops me as I scramble to my feet. I don't try to run, though. Not when I find myself facing down half a dozen rifle barrels.

With his lazy, impudent stride, Roe moves to stand in the center of the pack. He tilts his head, examining me from head to toe.

"Show us where it is," Roe says.

My forehead wrinkles. "What—"

But he's not speaking to me. He's dragging someone forward, jerking her arm to force her beside him.

Lyddie.

"I promise you, I saw it," she tells him.

I stare at her in horror. "Lyds . . ."

She ignores me. "It's on her left thigh."

"Lyddie," I plead.

But I don't know what I'm pleading for. It's too late. She already turned me in.

Not Ivy, but Lyddie.

She *promised*.

I bite my lip to stop it from shaking, but there's no stopping the sharp, hot sting of tears behind my eyelids.

Roe nods at one of the soldiers, who steps forward.

"Don't touch me," I warn.

The bastard doesn't listen. An outraged growl leaves my throat as he yanks the hem of my dress up to reveal my thigh.

My bloodmark.

Desperation courses through me as I try to link with Cross again. Why isn't he letting me in? I *need* him.

Heart pounding, I focus on Lyddie, willing her to look at me. When she finally does, it's with such bone-deep, spine-chilling hatred that I have to wrench my gaze away.

I turn back to Roe, bitterness twisting my lips. "Are you going to shoot me in the head now?"

"Sadly, I've been asked to show restraint." Roe glances at the soldier to his left. "Take her to the stockade."

———

I'm right back where I started.

In the stockade.

At least I was finally able to link with Cross. Although when I told him where I was, all he said was, "I'll be there as soon as I can."

That was hours ago.

Hours.

I've had time to sit and think. To obsess. To try to make sense of everything that happened tonight. The Uprising is destroying people's minds. Adrienne confirmed that tonight. But on what scale? Does her ability to corrupt have something to do with the fragmented hospital ward I stumbled upon? Were some of those people corrupted rather than fragmented? Were some of them actually Primes? Most of them, from the look of their veins, were Modified. And I can't envision Adrienne being okay with experimenting on our own.

But I also wouldn't have believed she could stand there and fry a man's brain if I hadn't seen it firsthand.

Another thought occurs to me. Had Cross's mother been corrupted? Is he right and she's not Modified? Is Vinessa Redden another casualty in the century-and-a-half-long war between Primes and Mods?

I have so many questions, none of which can be answered unless Adrienne decides to grace me with her psychic presence. But she's not linking, either.

As much as I hate bothering Cross when I know he's dealing with a mountain of shit right now, my impatience spills over.

"Where are you, damn it?"

"Briefings," is the terse response. "They destroyed the entire northern quadrant of the base, including a hangar full of fighter jets."

Wow. That's a huge hit to the Command. Yes, there are other hangars, other airfields, but losing a chunk of the fleet like that . . . I guess their pilot hit the mark this time.

"Are they giving you any trouble? About me?"

"Not yet. I think they will. Right now, they're too distracted by my father."

"How is he?"

"His mind is completely fried. He's a hollow shell."

It's hard to decipher Cross's tone. His feelings about it.

Hell, I don't know how *I* feel hearing it. The General is—was—a cruel, dangerous man. He killed thousands of people. But there's something very . . . pathetic, I suppose, about how he went out. Not by an assassin's bullet or a strategically planted bomb. He didn't get the heroic end I assume he's always dreamed of.

His brain was simply . . . rewired, as Adrienne called it.

"Travis is taking control. The Tribunal appointed him General."

I consider that. All right. From what I've seen, Travis is a practical man. Logical.

"Can we convince him that I'm on his side?"

"After they just bombed our most valuable installation? I highly doubt it."

My breath comes out in a shaky gust.

"Try not to panic."

Yet is the unspoken implication.

"I'll be there as soon as I can, keen?"

"Keen."

Sighing, I stretch out on the narrow mattress and stare up at the ceiling. My heart clenches as I think about Lyddie. I suppose I shouldn't be surprised by her betrayal. I saw her that day in shielding class—the way she recoiled at the mere thought of Amira touching her. Like Lash, her hatred of the Aberrant is so deeply rooted, I was a fool to ever think she could find the tolerance within her. That she could keep my bloodmark a secret.

She probably feels as betrayed by me as I do her.

Yet when I think about her turning me in, fury burns my throat, because I would never, ever do that to her.

You did it to Tana.

My throat closes up. I didn't, damn it. Not intentionally. I warned Tana and Griff because I wanted them to be careful. To protect themselves. I cut that deal to send them to the labor camps because it was a thousand times better than having to bury their corpses.

Tana hasn't spoken to me in weeks.

I don't know how much time passes, but when I finally hear the keypad buzz, I'm a total basket case. My heart jumps when Cross enters. I stumble to my feet, then falter, unsure if I should go to him.

"We're not being recorded." He gestures to the jammer clipped to his belt.

Then he holds his arms open, and I throw myself into them. He brushes his lips over my hair, his hands warm against my lower back. When we finally break apart, his expression is grim.

"Travis has declared war on all known Mods."

My stomach drops. "What?"

"This attack on our base won't go unpunished, not if Travis has anything to say about it. Every Mod we know of is being rounded up and sent to labor camps for the time being, slave *and* loyalist. He says he'll decide whether to let them live on a case-by-case basis."

"But they've been loyal to you all these years," I protest.

"Doesn't matter. You're either a prisoner or you're dead."

"What about me? Am I a prisoner or am I dead?"

There's a beat of silence.

"Cross."

"You've been scheduled to die. Tribunal just let out."

I nod in resignation. "They didn't even see me."

"They don't need to. Lyddie testified about your bloodmark."

Of course she did.

"Is anyone looking for Jayde?" I ask, though that's probably the least of my concerns right now.

"Her body was found this morning. What a shame that she killed herself right after Travis announced that even the loyalists would be detained."

Despite all the turmoil and uncertainties in the air, I have to laugh.

Cross winks at me. "I'm very good at my job."

"Clearly."

His expression sobers. "And my job right now is to get you out of here. Have you been in contact with the network?"

I shake my head in frustration. "Nobody's linking. Let me try again now."

I open a path to Adrienne, and for the first time since she staggered into the back of that car, she allows me to link. Relief spirals through me, but when I speak, it's with the heat of accusation.

"Where the hell have you been?"

"Waiting for my ability to open a path to return. Where are you?"

"I'm in the stockade. One of my fellows turned me in. You need to get me out of here."

"We can't." She still sounds tired. "The wards are on lockdown. Airspace is being monitored, so we can't risk sending an aircraft. We'll be going dark for a while."

"What is she saying?" Cross pushes.

"That they're going dark for a while. Hold on."

"You're just going to leave me here?"

"We can't come to you." I hear genuine regret. "At least not right now. But when you're able to, you're welcome at the Dagger."

"Where is that?"

"It's our base. Located beyond the Blacklands."

I tense up. I remember my fellows talking about a secret Modified base, a hideout somewhere in the wards, but this is the first confirmation of it that I'm getting. Beyond the Blacklands, though? How is that possible?

"What is it?" Cross asks.

I ignore him as Adrienne keeps talking.

"You were an asset in executing this mission. I've already spoken to the Authority on your behalf."

The unfamiliar term brings a frown to my lips. "What's the Authority?"

"It's the council that governs our base."

"I thought you were in charge."

"I am. But not alone. I told them how integral you were to gaining access to the General. Setting the decoy charges. Your admission has been approved. So if you can just hold tight until it's safe enough to get you out—"

"I'm scheduled to die tomorrow morning."

There's a pause.

"I'm sorry, Wren. We can't risk an aircraft."

"What if I come to you?"

"You can only get here safely by air. No one makes it through the Blacklands alive on foot."

"But what if I did?"

After another pause, she says, "Well, then you would link with me when you made it out, and we'll collect you."

"Damn it, Wren. What is she saying?"

I chew on the inside of my cheek. "She says there's no way they can get me out. They won't rescue me."

Cross curses.

"But . . . I might have a way to rescue myself."

CHAPTER 53

He leaves me again, returning in the wee hours of the morning with a jammer clipped to his belt and armed to the teeth. We don't say much as we creep out of the stockade, navigating the maze of halls until finally we emerge outside. I'm grateful to breathe fresh air, but when I inhale, I find it's not so fresh. The smell of smoke fills my nostrils, along with the leftover sweetness from the sugar bomb that took out a Command hangar.

"Where are we going?" I whisper as he leads me toward a waiting truck.

He gets in the driver's seat while I crouch in the passenger side. "Stay down," he orders.

Even at this hour, the base is alive with activity. I suppose that's what happens when a chunk of it gets blown up by an enemy bomb. I don't know how long we have before someone starts noticing Cross entering rooms and then disappearing from cameras.

He drives to a vehicle pool—not the one where I met Adrienne, but a different site near South Plaza. Another vehicle waits in the tunnel.

We slide into the back seat, and I frown when I spot Xavier behind the wheel. "Darlington," he greets me.

"What are you doing here?"

"It's okay," Cross assures me. "You can trust him."

No, but I can trust Cross. So I nod.

None of us speak as Xavier drives away from base. Or rather, Xavier doesn't speak. I take advantage of the silence by sharing with Cross the thought that's been haunting me all night.

"I think the Uprising corrupted your mother's mind."

"What?"

"I don't believe she's a Mod. But I have no evidence of anything I'm saying right now. We can demand answers from Adrienne when we get to their base."

He goes silent for a moment, his jaw tightening. "So much for not harming civilians."

I understand his anger. I can't stomach the idea that they're destroying civilian minds in their war against the Company. The only saving grace, after what I gleaned from Adrienne, is there aren't too many corrupters on the Continent.

"I think it's a rare ability. The fact that nearly all the Primes in society still have their minds intact tells me it's not something they can readily do."

I take his hand, lacing our fingers.

"Thank you," I tell him.

"For what?"

"Not letting them kill me. Coming with me. Being my best friend since I was six years old."

Our eyes lock.

"I love you." His voice is gruff in my head.

"I love you, too."

———

Halfway there, we ditch the truck. Silver Elite has vehicles stashed in nearly every ward, and we roll two motorcycles out of a cellar in Ward C. They're bullet bikes, too. They'll cut the rest of our travel time in half. Cross checks the solar batteries, then straddles the bike while I get behind him. Xavier takes the other one, and we speed off in the direction of Ward K.

When we finally reach the edge of the Blacklands, both guys are on guard. Their gazes drift toward the ominous black mist rising from the earth and hovering far above the top canopy of the trees, blending into the already black sky.

"It's really not that bad," I assure them.

They both stare at me in disbelief. I can't help but grin.

"I lasted in there for three years, and you two babies are scared to walk inside for three hours?"

To be fair, it'll be a longer trek than that, but I don't share that tidbit. They're rattled enough as it is. From what I recall Jim telling me, it's at least a seven-hour walk from here to the clearing. And then who knows how long it'll take to traverse from the clearing to the Blacklands' end.

Brow creased, Xavier crouches on the ground to run a quick inventory of his heavy pack, checking the supplies.

I frown at him. "Are you coming with us?"

"Us?" His gaze shifts to Cross. "You haven't told her?"

All the breath leaves my body.

As my heart flies to my throat, I spin around to Cross.

"No."

"I have to." His voice is rough. Defeated.

I stalk toward him and grab the front of his shirt in my fist. "You are not staying behind. You said you were coming with me."

"Coming with you *here*. Making sure you made it in one piece. But I can't go with you to the Uprising."

"Cross, please. No."

"Hey." He strokes my face. "I can't. You know I can't. I won't leave the entire Continent in my brother's clutches. Either of them. If you thought my father was ruthless, Travis is even worse. And Roe? He'll kill Mods indiscriminately. You realize that, right?"

I bite my lip so hard I taste blood in my mouth.

"Wren."

I release my lip and sweep my tongue over the puncture I created.

Liquid copper coats my taste buds. "Please don't make me do this alone."

"You won't be alone." He nods toward Xavier.

I don't even turn my head. "He's not you," I say stubbornly.

"Someone needs to keep Travis and Roe in line. I don't know what the wards will look like with them calling the shots."

"What do you mean 'them'? Travis isn't going to put Roe in charge."

"Not officially. But he's never even tried to rein Roe in. He's going to let him run loose and do whatever the hell he wants. I need to be here." His expression grows pained. "My mother is here. I can't leave her, either."

I feel my heart splintering in my chest, the sharp slivers scraping over my ribs. It didn't even occur to me that he might not come with me.

"Fine." I lift my chin. "Then I'm staying."

"No. If you stay, you'll die. I can't protect you here. I'm already on shaky ground with them because I selected you for Elite. Travis thinks you fooled me. He seemed to get great pleasure out of that."

"You'll be punished for it?"

"No. He needs me too much. But he suspects we were romantically involved." Cross curses under his breath. "Someone reported seeing me leave your quarters."

"Ivy," I growl.

That makes him chuckle. "Actually . . . It was Sutler. Guess we weren't careful one night."

Kaine?

Even as my heart squeezes for my fallen friend, my jaw drops in outrage. Kaine snitched on me? He's lucky I don't like to speak ill of the dead, that hellfucker.

"I told Travis I was dropping off some paper maps for an off-the-source op. I think I convinced him. Regardless, he and I have never been on the same page about how to run the Command. It might take a while to earn his trust back, but he won't kill me. And you . . . You'll be safer with the Uprising."

"Will I?" I counter. "Because I have no idea what kind of people are working for the network. These corrupters. For all I know, I'm walking into even more dangerous territory."

Xavier pipes up. "Don't worry, Darlington, you'll be safe. I got you."

I growl at him. "I don't want you to 'got' me. I want *him*."

"Damn, you're bad for a man's ego." He lowers his gaze and continues arranging his pack.

I move closer to Cross. Tears well in my eyes as I lean into him, seeking his embrace. "I don't want to leave you."

"I don't want you to go," he says roughly. "But you have to."

He brushes a stray lock of hair from my face, blown free of my ponytail during our hyper-speed ride.

"Please don't leave me," I whisper, embarrassed that Xavier might hear the crack in my voice.

"I'm not leaving you. I'm just staying behind."

"For how long?"

"Until I figure out what the hell is going on here." He grips my chin with his big, capable hand. "I promise I will see you again." He bends his head as if to whisper in my ear, but really, he's opening a path, his husky voice surrounding my senses.

"I'm still in your head, Daisy. You can talk to me whenever you want, you know that. I love you. I will never leave you. Ever."

I cling to him, the tears flowing as I bury my face in his chest. "I don't want to do this without you."

"You're never truly alone. You know that. I'll be right here, every step of the way."

Behind me, I hear Xavier stashing one of the bikes in the brush. As the sun peeks over the horizon, casting hues of orange and pink across the sky, Cross tips his head toward the faint light.

"The sun will be up soon," he says. "You have to go."

"I don't want to leave you," I repeat.

"We spent our whole lives loving each other from a distance. We can do it for a little while longer."

Gulping, I wipe at my wet eyes.

"You can do it, Dove. You're the strongest person I know."

My heart throbs as he presses a final kiss to my lips. Every ounce of emotion he feels for me ripples through my body. I cling to him, my mouth locked with his. I don't care that Xavier is watching. This man is everything. I don't want to say goodbye, but I have no choice.

"Keep her safe," Cross says to Xavier when we break apart.

"I will."

He touches my face one last time. "Be safe, Daisy."

"You too, Wolf."

With a lump in my throat, I watch as he straddles the bike. As he starts the engine and then takes off like a bullet on the landscape.

He's the only person I've ever been completely, truly, unequivocally myself with, and now he's gone.

I twist my gaze away only when I can no longer see him. I glance at the black mist, then at Xavier. "Are you ready?"

CHAPTER 54

"You seriously grew up here?"

Xavier's voice slices through the darkness.

"Only for three years," I answer. "Stop. Stop, damn it."

"Stop what?"

"You're walking too fast. You need to slow down and be more careful."

"Like I keep telling you, I've been a soldier far longer than you," he grumbles.

I halt. Grabbing his arm by feel, and not because I can see it. I curl my fingers around his biceps, keeping him in place.

"You don't get it. This isn't a Silver Elite operation. One wrong step and you're drowning in a pit of black sand. So please, stay close to me. Follow me and I'll get us where we need to go. And should you continue to be stubborn, I'm going to step aside and let the horned bear eat you."

His breath hitches. "Fuck off. There isn't a horned bear here."

"Don't worry. He doesn't usually come out in the morning."

"This is morning?" he squawks.

"Of course. It's positively bright."

He snorts out a grudging chuckle. "I kind of see why he likes you."

"He more than likes me. He's obsessed."

That gets me another chuckle.

We press forward.

———

The first predator strikes thirty minutes into our trek. Some breed of cat. Too hard to discern in the dark. The loud flapping of wings reverberates around us as my rifle shot rings in the darkness and sends the birds scattering.

Xavier's breathing is heavy. So is mine as I ask, "Are you okay?"

He sounds a bit stunned. "Yeah. What was that?"

"I think it was a mountain lion."

I crouch in the darkness and stroke the dead animal's fur, skimming over the damp spot where the bullet penetrated. The fur is coarser than a mountain lion's, the legs shorter.

"No, it's a red cougar," I say in delight. "They are delicious."

"You're a weird woman, Darlington."

We keep walking. The sound of rushing water, a low, lazy gurgle, soon fills the disconcerting silence. Relief tickles my throat. I can't see the creek, but I can hear it, and that's all that matters.

"We need to follow the sound of the water," I tell Xavier.

After the cougar attack, he stopped complaining about me taking the lead. I feel him behind me. His soft, even breathing. The slow echo of his footsteps. I sense his frustration at our pace, at the stifling blackness. Losing a vital sense, particularly to a soldier, is not an enjoyable experience.

"You really a 'fect?"

"What, you think Cross was lying to you?"

"No, he's never lied to me. It's just you hid it well."

"Thank you."

"I'm sorry I wrote on that report that you weren't cut out for covert ops."

I throw my head back and laugh.

"I'm more surprised that he is," Xavier confesses.

"Who?"

"Cross. He told me last night."

"Yeah? What else did he tell you?"

"Last night? Not much. Just that he has telepathy. But this other time . . . This one night, a couple of years ago . . . He was still with Eversea at the time, but he was thinking of ending it with her."

I'm not sure where he's going with this, but I don't stop him. Curiosity tickles my stomach.

"So we went to a bar in the city. Pounded synth whiskey until we were both good and boozed. When I asked him why he was dropping Ivy, he got this really serious look on his face and then said, *Because she's not the girl of my dreams.* And I laughed and said, *Okay, then who is?*"

"What did he say?"

"He said the girl of his dreams loves daisies."

I smile in the darkness.

"Said he'd loved her his entire life. I thought he was just talking crazy, drunk off his ass, so I laughed and said, *Sure you have, buddy.*"

I feel a poke in my ribs.

"I think he meant you, Darlington."

My smile grows so wide it almost cracks my face in half.

———

We walk on. Slowly. Painfully, vexingly slow. As a sniper, I can remain still as a stone for hours. Here, inside this black nightmare, my body is wired, feet impatient inside my boots, fighting the impulse to speed up. Xavier is feeling it, too, and soon he gives up trying to match my pace. He stalks ahead of me, only to curse in dismay when his foot reaches the edge of the first black pit.

I hear it as the toe is instantly sucked into the quicksand like the slurp of liquid through a straw. I lunge toward him, and it takes considerable effort to help him pull it out. He almost loses the boot.

"Why do you refuse to listen to me? I'm not making this shit up!"

"Noted," he mutters.

"Thank you. Now walk slow, stay behind me, pay attention to your footing, and don't fucking touch anything."

Literally twenty seconds later, he touches something.

I growl in the darkness, so annoyed that I'm willing to risk alerting the predators to our presence. At this point, maybe he deserves to get mauled by a cougar.

"Why are my hand and arm burning?" He releases a string of curses. "What the hell was that?"

"You touched a cluster of black snakeroot leaves." I smelled that snakeroot from ten feet away. It releases an unmistakable sour odor.

"Is that what it was? Isn't that shit poisonous?"

"Yes. But if you don't touch or scratch your arm, the hives will go away in a couple of hours. You need to ingest the leaves for the poison to do any real damage. When it's boiled, it corrodes your insides like acid. And you should never eat an animal you killed with black snakeroot. It taints the meat. Passes the poison to its eater."

"How do you know all this shit?"

"This was my childhood home," I remind him with a wry laugh. "My uncle taught me about every inch of this forest. There are tons of poisonous plant hybrids in here, some of them far deadlier than the animals."

"I hate plants," Xavier grumbles, and I laugh.

———

We reach the clearing seven hours later. Seven hours of painstaking steps, another dead predator, and an itchy, burning arm courtesy of black snakeroot. And then we see it.

Light.

The moment we stumble onto the sun-drenched grass, Xavier exhales in relief and sinks to his knees.

"Holy shit." He shakes his head at me in dismay. "Why was that so awful?"

"Is now a bad time to tell you that I don't know if we're even halfway to the end?"

He glares at me. "Fuck you."

Grinning, I drift toward the small hut that Uncle Jim built for us all those years ago. I can't believe it's still standing. In twelve years, in fact, it's barely changed, except that it looks so much smaller now. It felt enormous when I was a child.

I shift the strap of my rifle to my other shoulder and wander into the wooden structure. I'm . . . overwhelmed. Overcome with memories. I suddenly see Jim's eyes crinkling at the corners as he flashed me a rare smile. I see myself chasing birds in this clearing, while Jim whittled a piece of wood or cooked us a rabbit on a skewer over the pit.

Speaking of fire. "We should get a fire going," I tell Xavier over my shoulder.

He glances warily at the tendrils of mist rolling in at the outskirts of the clearing. "Think I'll be safe grabbing some firewood from there?"

"Yep. Just stay on alert for cats and horned bears."

"Fuck you," he says again.

I venture into the hut, smiling at the pieces of twine nailed along the log wall and hanging from the ceiling. All the stupid, silly knick-knacks I forced Uncle Jim to display when we lived here. Feathers. A white coyote tooth we found in the forest. In the corner of the hut sits our supply chest. I should scavenge it, although it might be prudent to leave most of its contents here in case I ever need to come back. The thought is depressing. But not outside the realm of imagination.

I shuffle through the wooden crate, cataloging the various first-aid supplies, balms, solar batteries. Two handguns and several full clips of ammunition. I frown when my fingers feel something plastic at the bottom of the chest. It's a bag, I realize.

Furrowing my brow, I pry it out and flip it over to study the contents. The plastic bag contains a faded white envelope.

My heart leaps into my throat. I instantly recognize Jim's handwriting.

Wren

Eagerness clamps around my throat. The urge to read the letter is so strong, I'm practically clawing the envelope out of its protective enclosure. Before I can unseal it, Xavier's muffled voice comes from beyond the hut.

"Hey. Let's get this fire going."

Shit. I can't do this now. I have no clue what Uncle Jim would even write in a letter to me, and the last thing I want is for nosy Xavier to be peering over my shoulder while I read Jim's words.

I fold the envelope and tuck it into my pocket, then step out to help Xavier.

———

We decide to break camp, even though it's probably only about two in the afternoon. That's usually when the light starts to leave us. When the shadows start dancing over the clearing as they are now.

"It'll be pitch black soon," I warn Xavier.

"At *two*?" he whines.

"Yep. Suck it up, sweetling."

We just ate dried beef from his pack and a can of soup we heated over the fire. He used a lighter to get the fire going, and he's toying with it now, popping the lid open and closed, absently striking it to release a hiss of orange flame.

"Why does this work here but not in there?" He nods toward the mist that surrounds our small haven from all directions.

"I don't know. It's something about the way the light refracts in this clearing."

"You've really never gone all the way to the end? Gotten out from the other side?"

I shake my head. "I was five years old when we came here, and we left when I was eight. There was no way Jim was letting me gallivant around this nightmare at that age."

"Did *he* ever try? Did he leave you here while he went to investigate?"

"Yes, but the longest he ever left me alone was maybe sixteen hours or so?"

Xavier does the math. "So let's say he managed to make his way to the end of this nightmare . . . That's eight hours there and then eight hours to walk back here." He rubs his forehead, looking unhappy. "You're saying we have at least eight more hours to go tomorrow?"

"At least. We might even have to make camp in there."

"Sounds fun."

"But we get to sleep here tonight," I say, trying to cheer him up.

He looks toward the hut. "I call possession of the adult-sized bed in there."

I glower. "It's my house."

"I'm the guest. And I will not share with you."

"I wouldn't even suggest it," I grumble. But it's fine. My child-sized bed, as he would phrase it, isn't actually that bad. I sleep curled up in a ball, anyway.

"Okay, then I'll head to bed. What do you say? Let's try to get a good seven hours to shore up our energy for the journey?"

"Sounds good. I'm going to stay out here a little while longer."

Wary, he appraises our surroundings. "Are those red cougars going to creep into the clearing at night and try to rip our throats out?"

"They might." I'm not going to sugarcoat this experience for him. "But as long as we keep the fire going, most predators should stay away. They don't like the smoke. And if that fails, that's why you sleep with a rifle."

"Good night, Darlington. We'll regroup in the morning. Or night. I don't have any concept of time in here."

I'm grinning as I watch him disappear into the hut. The moment he's gone, the excitement flutters in my stomach like birds taking flight.

I get to talk to Jim now.

His energy signature is no longer in my head, his voice gone, his body full of bullet holes, but here, right now . . . I get to talk to him again.

I fish the envelope out, smoothing out the creases. With a steadying breath, I break the seal and unfold the letter, my fingertips grazing the delicate paper. For a moment, the words blur before my eyes, a jumble of emotions swirling inside my chest.

I press my lips together to contain the joy. His handwriting alone is enough to trigger a big, silly smile. I feel like a kid again. I draw my knees up and hold the letter out in front of me.

Wren,

If you're reading this, then I'm probably dead. Because if I were alive, I'd be there with you right now and I damn well wouldn't let you read this letter.

A laugh tickles my throat. He's an asshole even in written form.

But if you are reading this, I need you to pay attention, little bird. There are some things you need to know.

My smile fades.

The more I read, the weaker my pulse gets. I draw another deep breath, but the oxygen barely reaches my lungs. My mind stumbles over the words. I'm forced to read it a second time in order to make sure I'm seeing it properly.

Why is he telling me this?

The clearing is quiet save for the crackles of the fire and the soft whisper of the wind. My lips tremble as I glance toward the hut where Xavier sleeps. My fingers tremble. Everything trembles.

Sharp, shaky pants escape my throat as I slowly close my fist around Jim's letter, crushing it into a tight ball.

And then I toss it into the fire.

CHAPTER 55

I t takes two days to reach the other side. Forty-eight hours in which we bicker and hiss at each other. In which we talk about Cross and how much I already miss him. In which we talk about Tyler, and Xavier admits that while he cared about her, he wasn't in love with her. In fact, he reveals he's never been in love before. Not with any of the men or women he's dated in the past. He confesses that when it comes to sex, he rarely, if ever, considers the consequences of his actions.

I learn more about Xavier Ford than I ever wanted to know, and by the time we see it, the light penetrating the mist about a hundred yards away, it feels like we're old friends.

"We did it, Darlington," he crows.

Both of us forget that a horned bear could still burst out of the brush and eat us alive. We take off jogging, our destination in our sights, and when we emerge from the darkness, what we find beyond it is . . . incredible.

The mountain valley unfolds like a tranquil oasis in front of us, bathed in the pale glow of the morning sun. A crystal-clear river winds its way through the landscape. In the distance, jagged peaks loom above us. Only a few of them are snowcapped, but that doesn't make them any less majestic. The grass shouldn't be this lush and green at this time of year, yet it is. The sky is cloudless. It's glorious.

"Let me make contact," I say, and waste no time opening a path to Adrienne.

"I'm here."

Her shock is palpable. "Well. Look at that. You made it through the Blacklands. I'm impressed, Darlington."

"Good. Now where is the network assistance I was promised?"

"Do you know your coordinates?"

"No," I admit.

We had to leave all our tech behind. No source. No comms. We even left our Command weapons in the clearing, swapping them out for the ones in Jim's supply chest.

"Project your location," she says.

I focus on my surroundings and push the images through the path into her mind.

"Got it. I know where you are. We can't land there. You see that hill on your left beyond the river?"

"Yes."

"Climb it. There's space up there for the helo to land."

Excitement tickles my throat. This is actually happening.

"How long will you be?" I ask.

"Not long. We're not far."

I cut the link and address Xavier. "We need to climb that hill. Our pickup will meet us at the top."

His dark eyes narrow. "Do they know I'm with you?"

I falter. "I . . . just realized I didn't actually tell her you were coming with me."

He rakes a hand through his hair, then glances behind us at the mist.

"Seriously?" I grin at him. "You want to go back in there? By yourself? You want to repeat that three-day nightmare hike?"

"I could make it," he says with a shrug.

"Look, I won't stop you if that's what you want to do. I told you from the start that you didn't have to come with me. You don't need to be here."

He curses under his breath. "That's the problem. I do need to be here. I promised him I wouldn't leave your side."

"You promised him to get me to the Uprising. You don't need to stay, Xavier. I have no idea what we're going to find at their base."

"Which is precisely why you need the backup." His jaw clenches with determination. "He'd never forgive me if I let you walk in there by yourself."

"You're a good friend," I tell him, walking over to touch his arm. "But I am officially releasing you from your promise to Cross."

"Nobody but Cross releases me from my promise to Cross." Sighing, he shoulders his pack. "Come on. Let's go climb a stupid hill."

I can tell he's not budging, so I let out a sigh of my own and follow him.

It doesn't take us long to ascend the slope. At the top, we find a flat expanse with more lush grass, a green carpet that stretches out for hundreds of yards.

"Now what?" No sooner does he speak than the distant thrum of rotor blades pierces the stillness of the valley.

We tip our heads toward the sky and the sleek gray helo powering through the air toward us. My heart beats faster the closer it gets. I can't tell who's flying it, but the open side door reveals two shadowy figures sitting inside.

The helo banks on its approach and I catch a glimpse of the co-pilot. Looks to be a woman with auburn hair. A white shirt. Long ponytail.

Xavier and I watch as the helicopter touches down on the grass, its landing gear sinking slightly into the earth as it comes to a graceful halt. The blades slow to a steady rhythm, their whirring gradually fading into the background until eventually becoming silent.

I peer into the body of the metallic frame to try to make out who's in there. I hear a creak, and from the corner of my eye see the copilot's door opening. The woman hops out, her ponytail swinging over her shoulder. The pilot's door is pushed open, too. The two people inside the chopper remain motionless. I think it's two men judging by the short hair, but I could be wrong.

The woman stalks toward us. "Darlington?"

I nod.

Her sharp gaze shifts to Xavier. "Who's he?"

"Xavier. He helped me escape the—"

My voice dies in my throat.

I stagger backward, and for one heart-stopping moment, my entire world spins on its axis. A strangled gasp escapes my lips as my mind struggles to process what I'm seeing.

The pilot's sheepish eyes collide with mine as he strides toward us. His hair looks bright in the morning sun. He rakes a hand through it, then lets his arm drop to his side.

We stare at each other for a moment. The corner of his mouth lifts in a crooked smile.

A thousand thoughts clamor for my attention, but amid the chaos of my mind, one thought rises above the rest.

"You fucking asshole!"

I lunge toward him and, with an angry roar, slam my fist into his jaw.

"What the hell, cowgirl?" Kaine rears back in shock, rubbing his chin.

"What the hell?" I echo. All I can do is gawk at him. "*What the hell? How are you alive?*"

I bat at his chest, my rage in full control of my limbs now. He lets me punch him, but he's grinning as I do it, which only makes me angrier.

"We held a funeral for you! I *cried*!"

That gets me a snort. "You cried at my funeral? That's actually pretty sweet."

The auburn-haired woman gives him a warning look. "Not the time, Gray."

"Who the hell is Gray?" I yell.

I'm so busy being furious with my formerly dead friend that I don't see Xavier move. The lieutenant rushes Kaine, nearly tackling him to the ground before Kaine recovers his footing and sidesteps him.

"You godfucking prick," Xavier spits out, lunging again. "You killed Tyler."

I freeze in shock.

He's right.

Kaine walked into that building with her. Yet *he* walked away alive, while Tyler and Noah are dead.

The two men in the chopper jump out to help Kaine restrain an enraged Xavier. I cry out in protest, but they ignore me and get him on the ground, pinning him down. Horror fills my throat as they thrust his wrists behind his back to slap metal cuffs around them.

"Settle down," one of them barks.

"Fuck you," he snaps back.

"Stop this," I tell Kaine. "Let him go. He *helped* me. He's helping us."

My not-dead friend is unconvinced. "We'll let Adrienne and the Authority decide that."

"He risked his life to get me out of the city," I insist.

"I don't think they'll care." Kaine nods at the other man, and they haul Xavier to his feet.

Xavier's dark eyes are blazing like hot coals, and I find myself glaring at him.

"I told you to go," I say in accusation. "Why didn't you just go?"

He replies through gritted teeth. "I don't break my promises."

I watch in dismay as they drag him toward the chopper. Alone with Kaine and the woman, I squeeze my hands into fists and glower at them both.

Kaine glances at her. "Do you mind giving us a minute?"

She leaves without a word.

"What? You call the shots here?" I say bitterly.

"Sometimes," he admits.

A helpless feeling lodges in my throat. "Did you kill Tyler?" I ask, and my stomach drops when I see the regret flickering in his eyes.

"Struck was collateral damage."

"You let her walk into a building that you knew was about to explode. How could you do that?"

"In war . . . we do a lot of things we don't want to do."

I realize those are the same bleak words he uttered the day I killed Bryce Granger.

I take a breath, trying to slow the thoughts speeding through my head, the emotions coursing through me. I don't know what I'm feeling. I'm furious when I look at him, but I also feel relief. A flicker of joy. My friend is alive.

My mind spins to fill in all the blanks. "You infiltrated the Program for what? Just to steal a new piece of technology? A plane? They placed you there for a *plane*?"

He shrugs. "Well, yeah."

"Why?"

"Because I was the only one who could fly it."

My jaw drops. Although it takes a second, understanding finally strikes. Gray. She called him Gray.

"You're Grayson Blake," I accuse. "Mr. Hotshot Pilot."

He bites his lip as if fighting a grin. One of those mischief-laden grins I've missed so desperately since he died. Or didn't die. Fuck him.

"How could you keep that secret from me?" I demand.

He counters by arching his eyebrow. "Look who's talking, Ms. Bloodmark over here." When I narrow my eyes, he narrows his right back. "Yeah, Ellis told us."

Now we're standing there, glaring at each other. Until Kaine—Grayson. Whatever the hell his name is—releases a heavy breath.

"I know you must have a thousand questions, and I'm sure you want to punch me in the face a bit more—"

"A lot more," I mutter.

"But why don't we save that for when we get to the base? We have more pressing matters to take care of right now."

"Such as?"

He nods toward the helo. "Why the hell would you bring Xavier Ford with you, cowgirl?"

"He helped me."

"I don't care. And neither will the others. Why didn't you at least *tell* Adrienne? Like, hey, Adrienne, I'm bringing a Command lieutenant with me, keen?"

"Honestly? I forgot. I was so relieved to make it through the Blacklands that when I checked in with her, I was still riding the high."

Humor lights his gaze before his expression turns serious. He steps closer.

"We really do need to go now. We're too close to the Blacklands to stand out here all day. But before we go, I need you to ask yourself if you're ready for a war, Wren, because that's what you're signing up for by coming here. The bombing of the Command base was just the beginning. The Uprising is coming for the Company."

I bite my lip. "Even if I didn't want that, you've left me no choice." I gesture to the helicopter. "Xavier helped me. I'm not just going to let him rot in some Uprising prison. Or worse, let him be killed when his only crime was risking his life for me."

"That is not his only crime," says Kaine. Grayson. That'll take some time getting used to. "But you'll find that out soon enough."

At that, he turns toward the helo. My gaze drifts past his broad shoulders to find that the woman is already back in the copilot's seat.

Kaine glances back at me. "Are you coming?"

I hesitate for what feels like an eternity. I see Xavier in the chopper, wrists restrained, expression stony. If he weren't here, I might consider walking right back into the Blacklands and disappearing. Jim's words continue to float through my head like a ghost refusing to leave the place where it died. I don't want to remember them, but I do.

I stare into Kaine's familiar green eyes. He's watching me with an intensity I never saw from him until now. He's different here.

"Just . . . give me a second," I say, digging my teeth into my lower lip.

I open a path to Cross and pray that he links.

"Are you okay?"

Relief floods my body at the sound of his voice.

"Yes. We made it. I can't talk, but I just wanted to say . . . to say I love you."

"I love you, too, Dove. Reach out when you can."

I feel empty when the path closes. Uncertain about my future.

"Wren?" Kaine prompts.

Seconds tick by. One. Three. Four. Until finally I nod.

I straighten my shoulders and follow him to the helicopter.

Wren,

If you're reading this, then I'm probably dead. Because if I were alive, I'd be there with you right now and I damn well wouldn't let you read this letter.

But if you are reading this, I need you to pay attention, little bird. There are some things you need to know.

Your name is Stella Hess.

Your mother's name was Marina Serrano. She was executed for concealing her Modified identity from the Company. I loved her deeply, despite what she was.

Your father's name was Jake Hess. He died in the Sun Post attack, a Modified retaliation to the bombing of Valterra Ridge.

The bombing your parents coordinated.

To the Uprising, your parents are known as the Tin Block Traitors.

They are responsible for the loss of countless Modified lives. Your mother betrayed her people, and your father helped her do it.

I love you as if you were my own daughter.

I will love you even after I'm gone, little bird.

Burn this letter after reading.

—JA

ACKNOWLEDGMENTS

This book was an absolute joy to write. Wren, Cross, and the rest of the *Silver Elite* crew (Uncle Jim!) took me on a wild ride, and I loved every second of it.

With that said, I wouldn't have survived this writing process without the help of some pretty incredible people:

Emily Archbold and Sam Bradbury, my tag-team editing duo who were always happy to hop on a call to talk plot (or to just argue about love triangles and Team Edward versus Team Jacob . . . there's no argument here. Edward. Obviously). You guided this book toward its best version, and I thank you for that.

The teams at Del Rey US and UK, for all the support and enthusiasm for this series, and how hard you've worked to bring it into readers' hands. Special shoutout to Jordan Pace and Aoifke McGuire-France, my US and UK publicists respectively. The entire US marketing team: Ashleigh Heaton, Tori Henson, Sabrina Shen, Maya Fenter, and Kay Popple; and their UK counterparts: Issie Levin and Sophie Shaw.

Amy Musgrave for the incredible cover!

Kimberly, for championing this project from the start and finding it a good home. And Jessica and Kristin from Leo PR for coming on board and getting people excited about this series.

My family, especially my favorite sister (you know which one you are)—for accepting that "five more minutes" actually means "three more hours" of writing and for not calling the cops when I disappeared on my weeklong caffeine-fueled writing binges. Your patience deserves a medal.

My friends who now know more about fictional character drama than real-world events. Thanks for letting me text you about imaginary people at odd hours and for not filing a restraining order.

A massive shout-out to my early readers, and my proofer for pointing out I use the word *heart* way too much.

To *you*, the reader. You took a chance on this book, and for that, I'm endlessly grateful. Thank you for finding these characters worth your time and for letting me share Wren Darlington and this new dystopian world with you.

And finally, to all the storytellers who came before me and inspired me with worlds, words, and characters who dared to feel deeply. Writing is a gift, and sharing this journey with all of you has been the best part.

—DF

ABOUT THE AUTHOR

Dani Francis is an avid reader, a lover of all things breakfast, and a hopeless romantic. When she is not creating high-stakes fantasy worlds and complex characters, you can find her spending time with family or trying to figure out why the printer never works.

danifrancisbooks.com
Instagram: @authordanifrancis
TikTok: @authordanifrancis

ABOUT THE TYPE

This book was set in Caslon, a typeface first designed in 1722 by William Caslon (1692–1766). Its widespread use by most English printers in the early eighteenth century soon supplanted the Dutch typefaces that had formerly prevailed. The roman is considered a "work-horse" typeface due to its pleasant, open appearance, while the italic is exceedingly decorative.